PRAISE FOR
RON FAUST

"Faust writes well, with confidence and flair."

—*The New York Times*

"A writer of rare and uncommon talent . . . resonant, sinewy prose."

—*The Los Angeles Times*

"A wonderful writer with a firm grip on character, setting and pace."

—*The Washington Times*

"Faust writes beautifully . . . reminds you of Hemingway and Peter Matthiessen."

—*Booklist*

ALSO BY RON FAUST

Snowkill

The Wolf in the Clouds

The Burning Sky

The Long Count

Death Fires

Nowhere to Run

JACKSTRAW

RON FAUST

TURNER

Turner Publishing Company
200 4th Avenue North • Suite 950 • Nashville, Tennessee 37219
445 Park Avenue • 9th Floor • New York, New York 10022

www.turnerpublishing.com

JACKSTRAW
Copyright © 2013 by Jim Donovan

Cover design: Glen M. Edelstein
Book design: Glen M. Edelstein

Library of Congress Cataloging-in-Publication Data

Faust, Ron.
 Jackstraw / Ron Faust.
     pages cm
 ISBN 978-1-62045-521-0
 1. Mercenary troops--Fiction. 2. Fugitives from justice--Fiction. 3. Suspense fiction. I. Title.
 PS3556.A98J33 2013
 813'.54--dc23
                              2013000920

Printed in the United States of America
13 14 15 16 17 18 19 0 9 8 7 6 5 4 3 2 1

JACKSTRAW

MUNDIAL

I assembled the rifle and secured the telescope to its mounting. The bolt worked with a smooth metallic *snick*. The rifle smelled of steel and oil and wood polish and, faintly, burnt gunpowder. It was the smell of my past, the smell of my future.

At dawn I moved to an open window. A woman, wrapped and hooded by a ropy shawl, walked diagonally across the paving stones toward the cathedral. She flushed a flock of pigeons which swirled like confetti before settling. A limping yellow dog came out of the shadows and began chasing the birds. He had no chance. He knew it; the pigeons knew it. Finally the dog shamefully limped away down an alley.

I went into the bathroom and washed my face with tap water the color of weak tea. The cracked mirror fractured my image into half a dozen oblique planes, like a Cubist portrait, and gave my eyes a crazed slant.

Sunlight had illuminated the parapet and pediment of the National Palace. People were filtering into the great plaza now: churchgoers, early celebrants, lottery ticket salesmen and shoeshine boys, beggars, men pushing wheeled charcoal braziers and food carts. An old man filled colored balloons from a helium tank. Boys kicked around a soccer ball. Policemen in pairs cruised like sharks among schools of bait fish.

Now and then I heard the voices of people passing by in the corridor. A door slammed, a woman laughed, elevator doors hissed open. This was for many an ordinary workday; they would observe the ceremony from their office windows, witnesses to pseudo history.

Blue smoke uncoiling from charcoal fires hung in the air like spiral nebulae. The cathedral's copper-sheathed dome, green with verdigris, glowed like foxfire in the hazy sunlight. At ten o'clock the church bells again tolled, a loud off-pitch clanging whose vibrations continued—like ghosts of sound—to hum in the air ten seconds after the clangor had ceased. Two cops dragged a rowdy young man into the shade beneath the east side colonnade and began beating him with their clubs.

Members of a band were gathering on the steps of the National Palace. Spiders of sunlight shivered over their brass instruments. They wore royal blue uniforms with big brass buttons and coils of gold braid. There were about forty of them and they all looked like admirals.

There was a great cheer as four Cadillac limousines entered the plaza from the north. They moved at a funeral pace. You could not see anything through the tinted windows. Rockets were launched from the four corners of the square; there were prolonged whistles and parabolas of smoke, and then the rockets exploded into stringy flowers of red and yellow and blue.

The limousines halted in front of the palace. Lackeys rushed forward to open the doors. The American candidates, old Hamilton Keyes and Rachel Leah Valentine, exited from one of the limos; the four missionaries from another; and government big shots, in black silk suits and snappy military uniforms, emerged from the other two cars.

The band started playing the country's national anthem. Three fighter jets in close formation roared low over the square, rattling windows and churning the smoke, and when the noise of the jets faded I could again hear the music and the cheering crowd.

*   *   *

The President of the Republic welcomed the people, welcomed the liberated missionaries, welcomed the distinguished American political candidates, welcomed a new day of national reconciliation and international amity. The crowd applauded. The band played a lively *pasodoble,* "Cielo Andaluz," as if the president had just cut ears and tail from a bull.

The American vice-presidential candidate ended her speech with a series of rhetorical spasms.

"Now!" she cried.

"Ahora!" the dark-haired girl near her repeated in Spanish.

Feedback from the speakers situated around the square resonantly echoed the last syllable of each word.

"And tomorrow!"

"Y mañana!"

I crawled forward and propped the rifle barrel on the window sill.

"Forever!"

"Siempre!"

I placed the intersection of the telescope's crosshairs between Rachel's breasts.

"All of the people!"

"Toda la gente!"

"Everywhere!"

"En todo el mundo!"

The crowd loved her.

Rachel Leah Valentine arched her back, spread her arms wide and—ecstatic, cruciform—gazed up at the incandescent blue sky.

I gently squeezed the trigger.

Now. Let it all come down.

PART ONE
GUERRILLEROS

ONE

Paraje was a sad little town deep in the rain forest, a crosshatch of muddy streets and decrepit frame buildings. Here drunks and swine slept together in the mud. Sometimes you saw woodworms crawl out of the timbers while you drank glasses of toxic *aguardiente* in the Hotel Su Casa's bar. Beetles shaped like crabs clung to the veranda screen. Sparrow-sized moths immolated themselves in the kerosene flames; then ignited with a snap and a spectral flash, and for an instant perfumed the air. Odd, old Crowley said as he downed his umpteenth gin and tonic, how they smelled like incense. Otherwise the place smelled of woodrot and mildew and insecticide. And the bugs . . . The frightful thing, Crowley said, was that you couldn't distinguish between your delirium tremens and real life. Stand me another drink, will you, Jack?

After six weeks at the place—six weeks of long nights at the bar—we came to know Crowley well. He was an engineer hired by the government for a project upriver.

The Hotel Su Casa was two stories high with a corrugated steel roof that reverberated like thunder when it rained. You didn't then hear the yowling of the musicians who billed themselves as Los Tres Supremos—a welcome respite. When it rained, Crowley said, it was like being trapped in a kettle drum during the climax of some Wagnerian opera.

A few days before Crowley died two Americans arrived on a chartered Cessna at the airstrip just outside the town. They appeared to have no business in Paraje. They spent most of each day on the veranda, each man playing solitaire and drinking *gaseosa* and sweating through his summerweight suit. Expensive linen suits, one cream and the other sandy brown, both quickly ruined by sweat and spilled soda pop. They didn't drink alcoholic beverages. They didn't smoke. They ate the hotel meals without protest. They even seemed to appreciate the nightly caterwauling of Los Tres Supremos. The two men were young and apparently healthy, yet they behaved like aged convalescents.

"Missionaries," Crowley said one evening in the bar, as if he were referring to IRS agents. The Supremos were on a break, and a distant cacophony of jungle noise served as background music.

"CIA," Cavenaugh said. "Maybe DEA."

"Not likely, old man. No, they're missionaries. They have about them that distinct odor of blind sanctimony mixed with a whiff of evil."

"Exactly—CIA."

I said, "They're environmentalists, here to save the rain forest."

"CIA environmental missionaries," Cavenaugh said, and we all laughed.

I signaled the waiter to bring another round of drinks.

                    *   *   *

The two strangers were reserved though not hostile. They nodded and said "Good morning" and "Good evening" and "It sure is hot," but rarely spoke otherwise and seldom made eye contact. They were implausibly boring, which was why they interested us so much. There was a low-frequency menace in their very blandness. They had registered as Mr. Smith and Mr. Jones.

Cavenaugh and I were using *noms de guerre*; Cav was known here as Carpenter, I was Jackson. That was all right. But we regarded the Smith and Jones pseudonyms as a sort of insolence.

One night I invited myself to their table during dinner while Cavenaugh went upstairs to search their rooms. He had bribed the desk clerk for the keys. He found no weapons, no documents that indicated their professions or purpose, nothing at all besides clothing and toiletry supplies. They traveled light. I chatted with the two men. They were not impolite, but neither did they welcome my intrusion. Cavenaugh also persuaded the desk clerk to open the safe where the two men had stored their passports. The thinner of the two was named Orson Dedrick and he had been born in Lynchburg, Virginia; the other, Roger Clay, was from Hickory, North Carolina.

"Rats," Cavenaugh said of them later.

"Rodents for sure," I said.

"CIA, DEA, FBI—one of those three-letter outfits."

"I don't think so. They really don't fit the mold."

"Well, they're not missionaries."

"No. They probably have cousins who are missionaries, but they're not."

Cavenaugh was a black man with fine features, not as tall as me but built more powerfully. His skin darkened if he spent much time in the sun, turned caramel except for burnished ochre highlights on his cheekbones and brow. His voice was surprisingly high for a big man and he sang beautifully in an Irish tenor voice. I once told him that he was actually an Irishman with a touch of the tarbrush. He replied that I was the result of a pig mating with a hound bitch.

We had worked as a team for almost two decades. He was a better man than I was.

Now he drummed his fingertips on the table and gazed at me. "Let's turn them over to Betancourt," he said.

"That's drastic. Let's wait a bit."

Orson Dedrick, "Smith," was lean and limber and still boyish-looking in his late thirties. In dim light he looked like a fatigued adolescent. He was very smart, you knew that, in a courteous, soft-spoken way. There was something priestly about Mr. Dedrick. His mind was cold, his motives pure, his actions just—he was an ideologue. You could see it in his eyes.

"Jones," Roger Clay, had similarly good manners and soft drawl, but he was a different type. You knew that deep down he was mean. When he removed his eyeglasses he removed the innocence from his eyes; without them he had a mean look, a malignant squint.

* * *

Old Crowley was a frail piece of human flotsam and one night he hemorrhaged his life away in one of the second-floor cubicles. His liver was rotten. His lungs were rotten. He was a British engineer who had lost his health and spirit in some of the world's nastiest places.

His room adjoined mine. Crowley slept in a hammock stretched from wall to wall, and when I entered his room after hearing his horrible strangling cough the hammock was swinging from the violence of his convulsions. There was nothing I could do except keep him company while his life seeped away. I held his hand. His projectile vomiting had spattered the walls and ceiling with bright lung blood. "Will you stand me a drink, old man," he gasped, and then he died.

"I liked old Crowley," Cavenaugh said at breakfast the next morning.

"So did I," I said.

"But he was a helluva sponge."

"He paid for the drinks."

"With what—his wit? His gentlemanly style?"

"With his humiliation."

"Did he really say, 'Will you stand me a drink, old man?'"

"Yes."

He shook his head admiringly. "Damn. And did you really hold his hand?"

"I did."

"That was decent of you. But, Jack—all that blood. There's nothing filthier than contaminated blood."

"Contaminated by what?"

"Name it. Crowley spent his adult life in all the tropical hellholes of Africa, Asia, and Latin America. Places where they eat diseased monkeys."

"We've spent time in some of the same places."

"Crowley's blood was a primal soup of viral and bacterial evil."

"Do you want that last bread roll?" I asked him.

Cavenaugh sighed and shook his head and said, "Raised by wolves." It was his stock phrase for my sporadic displays of uncouthness.

I took the roll, broke it lengthwise and spread the two halves with butter and mango jelly. There was still some coffee in the insulated pot.

Now we could hear the *whap whap whap* of the helicopter

flying over town. The hotel owner's pet macaw, a psychotic bird named Poco Loco, panicked as he did every morning at this hour and fluttered around the room, losing feathers. Cavenaugh said something that I couldn't hear. I pointed toward the sky.

He waited for the helicopter to move away toward the airport and then he said, in his softest voice, "I was not always as you see me now."

"No?" I said. It was coming now: more and more often lately, Cavenaugh veered off into riffs of self-laceration.

"I attended West Point," he said.

I smiled. "I know you did."

"There weren't many blacks at the Point then."

"I know there weren't."

"I played football there."

"I know you did. One of the best runs from scrimmage I ever saw."

He smiled. "You also attended West Point, Jack."

"I know I did."

"And both of us will probably end up like old Crowley, sick drunks begging drinks in some filthy backwater."

"Not me," I said. "My little ranch will be paid for in a few more years. I'll have it made."

"Run any cattle on that ranch of yours?"

"Run jackrabbits."

Cavenaugh waved his hand, indicating the shabby hotel, the decayed little town outside, the reeking forest beyond, the world, our disreputable lives and—as he foresaw it—our sordid details.

"What happened, Jack?"

I was weary of his moods, of this game, but I said, "We fucked up."

"Yeah, but that was twenty years ago."

"We are flawed. Deeply flawed."

Then he laughed. He laughed as robustly as ever, but lately there was a sour note in his laugh and sadness in his eyes. Cav was a strong man and I had always relied on him. Now I doubted that I could still trust him to the limit.

I said, "It's never too late for redemption. Not too late to find Jesus or lose yourself in politics or race or love."

"I love you like a brother, Jack."

"You're not going to eat that?" I reached across the table with my fork and speared a sausage from his plate.

"But I won't hold your hand while you're dying."

*   *   *

When I came down the stairs half an hour later the cadaverous clerk waved me over to the desk. As usual his manner was conspiratorial. He handed me a sealed envelope and whispered that it had been left for me by Mr. Smith. Or maybe it was Mr. Jones.

Cavenaugh was waiting for me in the back seat of the jeep. "What's in the envelope?"

"I don't know."

"Open it."

"It's from Smith and Jones."

"Huh. You think it might go bang?"

I smelled it, held it up to the light. "Probably not."

Our driver steered down the center of the road, careless of loose pigs and chickens and crippled dogs and half-naked children. Men idled on street corners, smoking and spitting, lying, waiting to win the national lottery. Adolescent girls with bleached hair looked down on the street life from upper whorehouse windows. Paraje was a frontier town: every night there were fatal shootings and knifings, and every morning you saw new graves being dug in the cemetery where we had buried Crowley.

Beyond the town there was a strip-slum of shacks made out of salvaged scraps of wood and rusty sheet metal, and palm-thatch huts that sometimes erupted into flame from cooking fires. Morose burros, half-buried beneath loads of firewood or nets containing ceramic water jugs, plodded along the sulphur-yellow road while their masters beat them with sticks.

"Jack. Open it."

I tore open the envelope. Inside was a brief handwritten note and ten crisp one-hundred dollar bills with the enlarged Franklin portrait. I gave Cavenaugh five of the bills. He tucked them away in his breast pocket. He was wearing stars on the shoulder loops of his camouflage fatigues. Cav was a general today. Yesterday he had been a mere captain. Cavenaugh changed his insignia of rank daily as a sort of satire of himself and our absurd command. His increasing frivolity was alarming.

"What's the money for?" Cav warily asked.

"For ten minutes of my time. Smith and Jones want me to talk to a friend of theirs tonight. To, quote, 'seriously discuss a matter of the utmost significance and profit.' Unquote."

"Okay, but why pay for it?"

"They want us to know that they're connected to big money."

"Well, sure," Cavenaugh said. "We'll listen for a hundred dollars a minute."

"They don't want to talk to you. Just to me."

"All right."

"Don't sulk."

He smiled, then leaned back and started whistling.

TWO

The helicopter flew high above the rainforest canopy. The sky was clear this morning but ambient humidity restricted visibility to half a dozen miles, gently obscuring the distances in a bluish mist. It was like flying in the center of a great frosted globe. Water condensed on the helicopter's windshield; the air reeked of vegetal rot and stagnant water. Sometimes a cool dry wind blew in from the west, clearing away the mist, and then you could see all the way to the *cordillera*—green hills rising into brownish mountains which rose even higher into granite cliffs and finally snowy ridges that were cleanly incised into the enameled blue sky.

We passed over a burned patch of forest and the mangled wreckage of a helicopter that had crashed six weeks ago when a sudden eruption of parrots had disabled the rotor. The pilot had been flying too low. Our pilot, Lopez, had learned from that. We hoped.

Cavenaugh sat next to me on a jump seat in the rear compartment. Humid hot air blew in through the open gun ports. The twin fifty-caliber machine guns pointed down toward the green canopy that stretched out all around us. From the air it looked like a vast uninhabited wilderness, but there were family farms scattered along the river and small settlements and, in the deep interior, Indian villages clustered around mission churches.

Ahead now we saw smoke dispersing laterally above the treetops. The men were not supposed to light cooking fires during the daylight hours, but they did. They did many things that were forbidden, not out of insolence or mutiny, but because they didn't understand the purpose of our regulations or the possible consequences of violating them. Nearly all of the men were Indians one or two generations removed from a free life in the forest. Their fathers and grandfathers had hunted with blow pipes and bows; they, the sons and grandsons, shot monkeys with M-16s and fished the river with explosives.

We entered the smoke haze and below saw a clearing with the camouflaged tents arranged in a large circle and the orange glow of fires burning in the center, the communal area. They had constructed their camp in the same fashion as an Indian village.

Cavenaugh mumbled something.

"What?"

He raised his voice. "Did you see it?"

"See what?"

"The other helicopter. Betancourt's here."

Our helicopter's shadow preceded us, slithering over the canopy.

"That arrogant bastard," Cavenaugh said.

The old road had become overgrown during recent years; we could not see the road itself but could trace its route by the narrow swath of new-growth forest that snaked from Paraje to the river. We were approaching the river now.

"I think he's the bastard who stole my Glock," Cavenaugh said.

Then the road abruptly appeared on the flood plain below, a cracked, upheaved ribbon of pavement that ran across the marshy flats to a rusty steel-frame bridge that only half spanned the river. The road and bridge had been Crowley's project. The old government had intended to open the forest to mining and lumbering and farming. The work had halted with the advent of a new regime.

"Did you ever meet Betancourt's sister?" Cavenaugh asked.

I shook my head.

"Elena. Beautiful, but crazy. Crazier than her brother."

Sawgrass rippled and flattened from the rotor wind as the helicopter descended.

"Hey."

I looked at him.

"Maybe Elena pinched my Glock."

*   *   *

There were thirty-four recruits left in the cadre; half that number had deserted. They all looked like members of the same family, and in a way they were—there hadn't been much genetic diversity in these forests over the centuries. They were short with straight black hair and amber skin and dark eyes. Many had splayed feet which blistered from wearing boots that didn't fit properly; some had eyes infected by the filarial parasite. On the whole they were moody young men, cheerful one moment, sullen and resentful the next. They had no real understanding of their purpose or destiny. They knew that they received food and a little money and were allowed to use rifles and grenades. Somewhere in the future— a word and concept that meant little to them—there would be fighting and maybe death.

Today I had twenty of the men; the rest were with Cavenaugh, out of sight around a bend half a mile downriver. Every now and then we heard the dull *crump* of a mortar shell detonating on the southern end of the long sandbar that divided this section of the Iracundo into two channels. The water was low during the drought, choked with mud the color and nearly the viscosity of custard. The persistent throb and hum of the rapids upriver was carried down to us on a faint breeze.

I spent the morning once again trying to teach the recruits how to care for their weapons. They loved shooting but were indifferent to the maintenance of the rifles. It didn't take long to ruin firearms in this climate, especially the M-16, which was liable to jamming.

At one o'clock I sent the boys off to camp and remained behind with one of the rifles and a few clips. There were human-silhouette targets set at a diagonal on the sandbar at ranges of 100, 150, and 200 yards.

There was only a gentle wind; the light was good; the angle simple. I slipped in a clip and set the rifle on single-fire. The M-16 is a combat weapon, not a marksman's tool, but it is accurate enough if you are good enough.

I lay in the prone position and squeezed off two rounds at the 150-yard target. The rifle threw a little high and to the right. I corrected, and placed the remainder of the clip into the heart-lung area of the silhouette. I inserted a new clip and shot eyes in the silhouette, nostrils, a navel, and then, on automatic fire, I obliterated the head.

Shooting was something I did very well. In a small way it was art, at once tense and relaxed, hot and cold, requiring a near-perfect synthesis of hand and eye and will. I had a gift for it, honed by many years of hunting with my father before his divorce. He had won service championships with his shooting, and he had taught me well—perhaps the only thing he had taught me well.

I walked diagonally up the grassy slope and entered the twisting forest path. The canopy was high overhead and only a few sparks of light filtered all the way down to the ground. There was a steamy greenhouse heat. Flying insects hummed through the aqueous light. Drops of moisture ticked downward from leaf to leaf to leaf. I could hear, a half mile down the path, the tinny noise of pop music played on cheap portable radios.

It was a mockery to call those undisciplined boys soldiers, *guerrilleros*. They were sloppy and disobedient. It did no good to shout at them. Beatings wouldn't accomplish anything beyond increasing their sullen resistance. They might very well improve as soldiers after the unit had taken casualties in battle, though that wasn't a comforting prospect—Cavenaugh and I had signed on not only to train them but to lead them into an as yet unexplained action.

The command helicopter squatted at the north end of the big oval clearing. Cavenaugh, Rafael Betancourt and his pair of bookends, Herrera and Baltazar, stood in the shade of an awning woven of palm fronds. They were arguing.

Some of the recruits had gone inside the tents, others sprawled here and there around the clearing, eating, smoking, dozing, listening to music on their radios and cassette players.

Betancourt and his men noticed me. My appearance had changed the equation.

The air was thick with layers of woodsmoke. You could barely see the tops of the trees. Figures at the far end of the clearing drifted like shadows through the smoke. The humidity and the high green walls of the surrounding forest trapped the smoke in a cylindrical column that obscured the sky.

Cavenaugh and Betancourt sat down at a table beneath the

palm awning; Herrera and Baltazar remained standing. All four men were armed. I angled off to the side so that I would have a clear line of fire.

Cavenaugh swore, said something about money. Betancourt shrugged, raised his palms in a helpless gesture: What can I do about it?

Rafael Betancourt, about thirty-five, was lean and serious. He quoted Neruda and Calderon and Lorca. He carried a pocket notebook in which he worked on translating Rimbaud's *Illuminations*. Rafael was vain about being both an intellectual and a man of action. He and his aides-bodyguards were not true soldiers; no doubt they had fought and killed, but it was clear to me that they weren't professionals. Cavenaugh privately referred to them as the "urban terrorists."

"*Calma, calma,*" Betancourt was saying.

"*Calma,* my ass!" Cavenaugh shouted.

Rafael Betancourt was our boss. Who, we wondered, was his boss? We didn't know for whom we worked. El Puño Rojo, maybe. The Red Fist. We'd heard that the Red Fist, a Marxist guerrilla faction, was preparing for an insurgency against the government. We had also heard rumors that our employers were actually the military arm of a powerful drug cartel. But Cavenaugh, a cynical man, a student of Machiavelli, suspected that the guerrilla units in training were financed by the government itself in preparation for an incursion into a neighboring country. A mineral-rich territory was in dispute. There had been sporadic military action along the frontier for many years, legal briefs presented to the World Court, and an arbitration rejected by both governments involved in the conflict. What could be more cunning, Cavenaugh said, than an infiltration of *guerrilleros*, most of them *indigenes*, fighting to liberate their "native soil" from an oppressive and illegitimate regime?

Betancourt laughed, leaned forward over the table, and playfully punched Cavenaugh's shoulder. Cav's smile was cold. Herrera removed a bottle from his backpack and placed it on the table, then he and Baltazar sat down. They all deferred to Cavenaugh: he drank first and passed the bottle to Betancourt, a ritual of relief. The tension had dissolved. None of them were going to die this afternoon.

I walked to the fringe of the clearing and sat in the shade. The M-16 lay across my thighs.

They drank again, rose from the table and shook hands all around. Apparently some bad feeling remained; there were not the usual hearty *abrazos*.

The three men climbed into the helicopter. The pilot started the engine and immediately lifted off in a storm of dust and smoke. It rose straight up and then, barely visible in the haze, hesitated for an instant before darting off toward the southeast. Cavenaugh emerged from the whirlwind, carrying a half-full bottle in one hand and a manila envelope in the other.

"Well," he said. He sat next to me. "We've just been fired."

"That isn't necessarily a bad thing, Cav."

He passed me the bottle. It was a good brand of dark rum.

"There was a dispute about the payment," he said.

"There always is. How much did you settle for?"

"Five thousand dollars each."

"Could be worse."

"They didn't want to pay anything."

"They never do. They always cheat. It's uncanny."

"Yeah, uncanny," Cavenaugh said. "They know exactly how much they can cheat you out of without dying for it."

I took another drink of the rum and passed him the bottle.

"Unemployed again," Cavenaugh said.

"Did you count the money?"

"No. You know how touchy they are about things like that. Not trusting them. An insult. *Pundonor*, all of that."

"Did you at least peek inside the envelope?"

"They were thinking about killing me and keeping the money, but then they saw you enter the clearing. They didn't much like the change of odds, knowing how you shoot."

"Let's count the money."

"Guess they didn't trust the boys to come to their defense."

"Would you?"

"Betancourt said that this unit was going to be absorbed into the Northern Command."

"The more I consider it," I said, "the happier I am. This was a bad situation."

"It stinks. Ten thousand each up front, and now five more each. Fifteen thousand for three months' work. Take out expenses and what have you got?"

"Cav, for Christ's sake, count the money."

He tore open the envelope and spilled money out onto the ground. There were two thin packets of new $100 bills. He licked his thumb and shuffled through one of the packets.

"What is it?"

He shook his head, tore the rubber band off of the second packet, and one by one examined the bills.

"Counterfeit?" I asked.

"Jack, the serial numbers on the bills are consecutively numbered. They're new and still in the order they came off the printing press."

"Cute," I said.

Cavenaugh reached into his breast pocket and removed the $500 I had given him this morning.

I sighed. "You don't have to tell me."

"Right. The thousand Smith-Jones left for you this morning and the ten thousand Betancourt just gave me are consecutively numbered. Smith-Jones and Betancourt's gang. What's the connection? This money's easy to trace. Jack, we're being seriously fucked with."

I said, "I know a guy in Miami who'll change this crispy stuff for clean old currency. He'll take twenty percent."

"We're straight, aren't we, Jack?"

"For sure."

"We give full value for money earned. We don't cheat, we don't conspire, we don't betray."

"We're the good guys."

"I'm sick of this life. I'm going home. I want to see my kids. I want to get an honest job. I want to learn to sleep without a gun under my pillow."

"Maybe Caprice will take you back."

"I hope so," Cavenaugh said. "Man, I really do hope so."

THREE

There was a gazebo in the jungly back gardens of the Hotel Su Casa. Circular, with a conical roof and tight-meshed screens all around, it looked like a giant birdcage. You followed a path through the untended gardens, past a cracked marble fountain and a faux-classical statuary, and crossed a footbridge that spanned a stagnant creek. The air reeked with the perfumes of night-blooming flowers. Parasitic vines twisted like pythons around tree trunks. Bats flitted overhead as you approached the gazebo. You went up five steps and through a screen door; on the platform inside there was a heavy round table, several chairs, and a pair of bright, hissing gas-pressure lanterns hanging from hooks.

Dedrick, Clay, and a third man who sat back in the shadows waited for me in the gazebo. The new man was introduced as Alex Troxel. I remembered him as Cooper. He was big—big-boned, with a big head and big hands and feet and a bullshit grin. There was a sort of cordial contempt in his eyes and smile as we shook hands.

"Hello, Jack," he said. "Long time, huh?"

"Not long enough," I said.

He was not offended; he had the skin of a rhino. He turned to Dedrick and Clay. "You two run along now. Jack and I will be fine."

The two men were not pleased to be so brusquely dismissed, but they hesitated only a moment before leaving the gazebo. We watched them follow the garden path over the footbridge and on toward the hotel's rear entrance.

"What do you think of those two?" Troxel asked.

"Dedrick thinks he's smart."

"He is smart. He's a math and computer whiz—but socially a moron."

"Clay thinks he's tough."

"Right." He snorted lightly. "Sit down, Jack. You're still a drinking man, aren't you?"

"I am."

"Sure you are."

We sat down on opposite sides of the table. There was a liter-and-a-half jug and a pair of glasses on the table. Alex Cooper, now Troxel, broke the seal, pulled cork, and poured the glasses full to the brim.

"Orson and Roger are all right," he said. "I culled them out of a generally lame herd. Do you ever watch television when you're in the States, Jack?"

"Rarely."

"Don't. God, you can hardly turn to a channel without seeing some guy weeping. All of it, the trembling lips, the stream of tears, whimpering. It's enough to make actual men puke. The American male has turned into weepy pudding while the women get harder and colder. These vulnerable, sensitive men—you want to kick them all in their tiny vestigial balls and say, 'Here! I'll give you something to cry about.'"

Troxel lifted a glass. "Let's drink to—to what, Jack?"

I said, "To stoic men and bawling women."

He laughed; we clicked our glasses together, spilling whiskey, and drank.

The buzz and whirr and ticking of insects in the night all around us sounded like radio static. Moths and beetles beat against the screens. We were sweating.

"I hear you're still partners with that smoke Cavenaugh."

"That's right."

"Okay, but I got just one job to offer. Not two."

"What sort of job?"

"The biggest, richest job you ever heard of."

"What are you in the scheme of things?"

"At the moment, I call myself Chief of Security. Tomorrow? Hell, who knows—maybe Keeper of the Flame."

You could still hear a little of rural West Texas in his voice. I had encountered Troxel a number of times in Africa. He had a bad reputation there. He was known as a rogue, a dangerous and unpredictable man. We got drunk together more than once. You could enjoy the company of men like Troxel even while knowing what they were. He might nurse you back to health on Monday, give you everything he owned on Tuesday, and on Wednesday kill you because he wanted your apartment. He was like a pit bull—you didn't know if he would lick your hand or bite it. But he had balls.

"Drink up, Jack," he said. "I carried this jug of whiskey all the way from Washington to this swampy bunghole. Drink."

We drank. He tilted the bottle again and refilled our glasses.

"Do you follow politics?" he asked.

"Not much."

"Funny, because your life has been very political, if you look at the jobs you've taken."

"No. You won't find a pattern."

We drank. Troxel's beefy, whiskey-flushed face looked swollen in the hard glow of the pressure lanterns. The flush exposed the many scars on his face, glossy crescents and pits and a couple of thin sutured scars.

"You've heard of Francois Mitterand, haven't you? The former Premier of France? Of course you have. But you probably don't know that as a relatively unknown young politician he arranged a fake assassination attempt on his own life. The idea was to get big-time publicity for his candidacy and the sympathy of voters. It worked. Of course it worked."

All at once the night flared brightly; every visible window at the rear of the hotel was illuminated. Globes lining the garden path were ignited and a ceiling bulb in the gazebo glowed with an unnatural radiance before the filament popped and it went dark. A radio blared, a siren wailed somewhere in town, dogs howled. The lights flickered, brightened again for a second, and then darkness returned.

Troxel looked at me as if I might be responsible for the light show.

I said, "They've been trying to repair the municipal generators for two months."

"Jesus," he said. "Don't you just get sick of the Third World?"

"I've learned to appreciate inefficiency."

"Maybe so."

Troxel topped our glasses with whiskey and then, in the overly careful way of a practiced drunk, he tapped a cigarette out of a package, struck a match, and leaned into the flame. He squinted at me through coils of smoke.

"Did you know, Jack," he said, "that Ronald Reagan was really not a popular president until after Hinckley shot him? True. That bullet gained him the affection of the American public. And Jack Kennedy was not greatly loved by the public until Lee

Harvey Oswald put a bullet into his brain. Remember, the voters liked Kennedy only a few thousand votes more than they liked Nixon. And Lincoln—hell, he was reviled until Booth put a bullet into his head. Those men were, what's the word—*sanctified* by assassination. But you know, the hero doesn't have to die for that to happen. Reagan didn't, and now he'd be up on Mount Rushmore if the masses could vote on it. A little blood, a cowardly assassin, an evil conspiracy thwarted. It's about good and evil, heroes and villains. You following me, Jack? It's about death and resurrection. Mithras, Apollo, Dionysus, Jesus. The young god is dead, long live the young god." He leaned back and exhaled smoke. "It can be about a goddess too."

This was not the Troxel I knew, the rough, scarred sociopath from Nowhere, Texas; he knew as much about Mithras as the chair he sat in. Tonight he was trafficking in someone else's fancy ideas. And bullshit.

"Are you following me, Jack?"

"I think so. Are we talking about Rachel Leah Valentine?"

He chuckled. "Sometimes you surprise me, Jack. Dedrick and Clay want her to be wounded. A slight wound, naturally, a harmless flesh wound. A couple of days in the hospital and she emerges with a clean white bandage maybe flecked with blood. The arm in a sling, maybe. Waving to the adoring multitude with the arm that hasn't been destroyed. The idiots. Why not a shoulder wound, they say. We know, you and me, Jack, we know what a bullet does to the shoulder joint, smashing the ball and socket, tearing up the muscle and ligaments, maybe cutting an artery . . . ah, you can't talk to them . . ."

I said, "It would be stupid to try for a minor wounding shot. There are too many variables. The range, the angle, the wind. Does she move, flinch as you squeeze the trigger? But she could wear a Kevlar vest."

"There you are, Jack. Exactly. We know about these things. A mortal wound—if she weren't wearing body armor. Knocked down. My Lord, she's been shot! Confusion, chaos, lamentations. We could put her in a hospital for a day or two, issue worried reports on her condition, and then bring her out for a brave, defiant speech. 'I shall not be intimidated by those cowardly enemies of freedom,' etc."

I could hear thumping bass notes and faint, sour music coming from the hotel: Los Tres Supremos were performing their signature song, "*Mi Corazón Esta Muerto.*" My heart is dead.

"Where does this happen?" I asked Troxel.

"In the capital, Mundial. She'll be coming to this country in two weeks to plead for the release of the hostage missionaries."

We were both drunk. We didn't slur our words; our gestures were controlled; but we were drunk. I hadn't heard anything about missionaries being abducted, but I wasn't surprised. American and European captives were pawns in a vicious game played by both rebels and government.

"But, Troxel," I said, "all of this fake assassination intrigue, and the Party has no chance of winning."

"The latest polls show that the American Patriotic Party has eleven percent of the projected vote right now."

"That much?"

"We figure that a fake assassination attempt during her mission of mercy will bounce the Party up to somewhere between twenty-two and twenty-six percent. If we reach that, it's a free-for-all. Three parties, three tickets, with the vote fairly evenly divided going down the home stretch. Can you see it?"

"It's scary," I said.

He smiled, nodded.

"Just what does the American Patriotic Party believe in?"

"Why, Jack," he said in the sort of voice you might use to soothe a child or lunatic, "Jack, the Party believes in what all true Americans believe. God and America and the family and the sanctity of the free market and capital punishment and love. We aren't fringe nuts, Jack. We are heirs to the great American tradition. We believe in offering a helping hand to the rich and an iron fist to the poor. We're in the mainstream. God bless you for asking what we're all about."

Troxel was drenched with sweat, and his dark eyes glittered. I thought he might be suffering the recurrence of an old malarial fever. But there was an element of passion in his cynical litany; he both believed and disbelieved, hoped and feared. Troxel was intoxicated by the whiskey and the malaria and, most of all, the Game.

"A hundred things could go wrong."

"At least," he said.

"Everything would have to mesh perfectly, like the launching of a rocket into orbit."

"They launch rockets successfully all the time. It's in the planning. The details. I'm a detail man, Jack. So are you."

"Does she have Secret Service protection?"

"Not yet. We probably won't qualify for matching funds and Secret Service protection until the first of the month."

"So she'll have private security people around her."

"My team."

"Plus—what? The capital police, the federal police, the army?"

"Not to worry. You shoot and vanish like smoke."

"Where in the capital does this go down?"

"The Plaza Mejor."

"The shooter will have to be elevated, but not too much. Steep downhill shots are always difficult."

"I've got a fourth-story window, very slight angle. The candidate will be standing on a dais in front of the National Palace."

"Fourth-story window?"

"I've calculated a vertical differential of ninety feet from muzzle to impact."

"The range?"

"One hundred and eighty yards."

"It isn't a cinch."

"Not for me, Jack. Not for most riflemen. But it's easy for you. That's why we're talking."

"This is crazy. Does she understand how dangerous this is? And does she really want it that badly? Has she got the courage to stand up there on the platform, making a rousing speech, while knowing that at any instant a bullet is going to smash into her chest?"

"This lady has the courage of a platoon of Recon Marines. And yes, she wants it that badly."

"Can she remain still at the crucial instant, or is she going to be thinking, 'Maybe the shooter is nervous, maybe there's too much wind, maybe a bullet will take off my head.'"

"Rachel has the guts of a Roman legion. There are worries, but she isn't one of them."

"You'd need the right sort of rifle."

"Of course."

"A crowd?"

"Big crowd. You'll be shooting from a building on the south side of the square, over the crowd, to the dais in front of the National Palace on the north side."

"I don't want a noise suppressor. They screw up the ballistics as often as not. Maybe some fireworks could go off at around the same time."

"Easy. It'll be a festive crowd, a drunken crowd, we'll see to that. The crowd is our ally. They'll panic, impede the cops, confuse everything."

"The escape plan?"

"There are several options."

"You understand that I'm very concerned with the escape plan."

"We'll go over it tomorrow, Jack. I'll show you diagrams of the Plaza Mejor, city maps, all of that. Hell, it might be best just to land a helicopter on the roof of the building, pick you up right after the shot. We'll move you outside the city. We'll take you to a safe house in a safe country on the far side of the planet. And money—you'll be a rich man, Jack, very rich, with more money coming in all the time. We'll take good care of you. You have a problem? Call us— we'll take care of all problems. Whatever you want."

"I have a lot of questions."

"Naturally."

"I haven't said I'll do it."

"You'll do it, Jack. We both know that. This is the adventure of a lifetime for men like us."

"I'm drunk. Exhausted. We'll talk tomorrow."

"I've told you an awful lot," Troxel said.

"I understand."

"Keep your pal Cavenaugh out of this."

"Of course."

"I mean it."

"I know you do."

"Tell no one."

"Do you think I just hatched?"

His lips peeled back in a cannibal smile. "I hope I didn't make a mistake."

"We'll talk," I said.

"Did I make a mistake, Jack?"

"I have to control my part of it," I said. "Totally."

"Goddammit, you're not a lone psycho gunman, you're part of a team and you'll be a team player."

"We'll talk," I said.

He splashed the rest of the whiskey in our glasses. Troxel was relaxed now, confident. He believed that our implicit personal duel tonight had concluded in his victory and that he had established dominance.

He lifted his glass. "A last drink. To what? How about—to a true shot?"

"And true hearts," I said.

FOUR

Cavenaugh had moved into Crowley's old room. I knocked hard on the interior door, waited until I was certain that he was fully awake, and entered. He slept with a pistol, and lately his nerves were raw. He flinched at unexpected noises; he was often rude to waiters and clerks; he had nightmares—some nights I woke and heard him moaning and talking in his sleep, plaintively calling out. And now he slept with a kerosene lantern burning on a table in the center of the room. Cavenaugh had become afraid of the dark.

"Did I wake you?" I asked.

"Hell yes."

"Sorry."

"What time is it?"

"Almost three."

"I'm finished now, I won't get back to sleep."

"I'm sorry, Cav, but this is important."

His figure was indistinct behind a white tent of mosquito netting. The netting appeared phosphorescent in the dim light. I could smell Cavenaugh's sweat, smell his socks and boots that lay on the floor, smell insecticide and mildew and stale cigar smoke.

"You okay?" I asked.

34

"What do you want, Jack?"

"Do you remember a guy named Cooper? He goes by the name of Alex Troxel now. Big, blond hair, lots of pockmarks and scars on his face and neck."

"Texan?"

"Yeah."

"Angola?"

"Mozambique."

"Right. He was the bastard who came over to our group in the last days."

"He was trying to get his loot across the border into the Transvaal."

"Swell guy."

"A humanitarian. Now he's in with Dedrick and Clay. They want me to shoot Rachel Valentine, but not hurt her."

"And she is?"

"The vice-presidential candidate on the American Patriotic Party ticket."

"You're shitting me." He paused. "What party?"

"Don't you ever read the newspapers?"

"No. Never."

"The APP is a third political party that came out of nowhere a year or so ago and is doing fairly well."

"Why not shoot but not wound the presidential candidate?"

"This is serious, Cav."

"You're drunk."

"They think they've got an outside chance of stealing the election in November."

"Jack, you're drunk. Go to bed."

"Humor me. Why did they pick me to be the shooter?"

"You're a mercenary."

"But not an assassin. Or fake assassin."

"You're a damn good marksman with a rifle. Though I don't understand exactly how they expect you to shoot her without hurting her."

"Kevlar vest. It's going to happen down here. Why pick an American shooter instead of hiring some local talent?"

He thought for a while. "It'll play much bigger to the American electorate if an American of dubious ideological background does it."

"They want a Commie?"

"Bingo."

"But I'm not a Communist."

"You are whatever history decides you are."

"It's a set-up, isn't it?"

"Jack, I hope these are rhetorical questions. You do know the answers, don't you?"

"I'm being set up. But by whom exactly? And for what purpose? What is really going to happen?"

He sighed. "No one is going to tell you the plans because you aren't actually a player, you're the designated fall guy."

"Plots go awry."

"In real life, yeah, all the time, but this is fiction. The conspiracy is a fiction, the assassination attempt's a fiction, and most of all, Jack, you are a fiction. You are what they make you on television after you resist capture and die in what they like to call a hail of bullets."

"What if I actually killed the candidate? It could happen. I don't want to be a party to murder."

"That might be in the script. She might not be wearing a vest."

"Tricky business, huh, Cav?"

Cavenaugh sighed. "Jack, you can't be thinking about walking into this cesspool."

"Maybe just knee-deep."

"There is no knee-deep here. You stay out of the sewage altogether or you drown in it."

"Someone has to keep a close eye on these people. They're crazy."

"Write anonymous letters to the FBI and the Secret Service."

"I really should infiltrate them," I said. "It's my patriotic duty, isn't it, Cav?"

"Now you're just trying to piss me off."

"Did I ever tell you that my parents owned a cottage on a lake?"

"Only a thousand times."

He stared up at the ceiling. "When I was a kid I saw a length of twine on the ground. Ordinary bailing twine—it came on big spools. I was nine years old and I decided to follow the twine to the other end. It ran along the lakeshore, cut up through a small wood, crossed a cultivated field, then a prairie, and then went into another, a bigger wood. I followed that twine for three-quarters of a mile at least. The other end led down into a hole, a burrow."

"And you jerked on the string."

"Right, I tugged at the twine and a big, angry badger came rushing out of the hole."

"I'm a city boy. Don't know nothin' 'bout badgers, Huck."

"It's a big member of the weasel family, the size of a small bear relative to a skinny nine-year-old kid. They've got very long, sharp claws, and pointy teeth, and really nasty tempers."

"Right now I feel like one of those badgers."

"He scrambled out of the hole, snuffling and snapping. Went after my leg, tore my pants. I ran like hell. Never looked back. Ran all the way home."

"Did you ever learn what brave idiot tied one end of a three-quarter-mile-long string around a badger's neck?"

"No, and that's always bothered me."

"So the point of your story is that Cooper-Troxel has handed you one end of a string and you're going to follow it."

"Maybe not all the way to the end."

"To the end, Jack. You can't let go, they won't let you. You've got a badger—hell, a dragon—by the neck."

"Yeah, well . . . Sorry to wake you, but I wanted to talk."

"And you know what will happen now. You'll sleep like a baby and I'll be awake all night wondering how to extricate myself from your asshole dilemma."

He stopped me when I reached the door. "Jack?"

I turned.

"Did they offer you a lot of money?"

"Oh, yeah, big money, bushels of dream dollars. But you know I'm not doing it for the money."

"No, you're doing it because you're still a nine-year-old kid."

"They know they can't win the election except by some near-miraculous fluke. I think they hope to get enough votes to get a stalemate in the Electoral College."

"Then what?"

"Then the U.S. House of Representatives arbitrarily decides the issue."

"And?"

"I'm not sure. I guess you'd see a sort of partisan *Götterdämmerung*."

"At least you'd get to hear 'Ride of the Valkyries' . . . Then what?"

"I don't know, Cav. I'm not an informed, responsible citizen. But maybe all the masks would come off and we'd see who is really running America. That could get ugly."

"Jack, you're not inviting me in, are you?"

"No. I'm part of a conspiracy. I'm not supposed to mention this to anyone."

"I don't want any of it. I'm sorry I listened this long. I'm leaving for the States tomorrow. Jack . . ." There was a long silence. "I don't want to hear from you after I've gone. Not even a postcard. You understand? You're a former partner, a former friend." He smiled—I could hear it in his voice. "At least to everyone else."

"Okay."

"Because, you know, when this goes down, everyone who has ever known you is going to be dragged in. People you sat next to on a bus twenty years ago will be investigated. They'll exhume your father, interrogate your dog, they'll trace your life back to that badger. I'm in deep trouble already. When they grill me I've got to tell them that we split, that I had no part in this. They won't believe me. I'll probably go to jail. But I'll survive it, with luck, since I won't be anywhere near you when it happens. Am I being clear?"

"Perfectly."

"Jack . . ." He paused. "You haven't been the same since the accident. Beth's gone. It's been a while, and you need to get over it. We both have plenty of life left to live. You've been acting like you got a death wish lately, like you don't care about anything. Don't think I haven't noticed you out there—walking around all oblivious to gunfire, acting like Benteen on Reno Hill at the Little Bighorn. And this . . . now you're really scaring me. I'll miss you. But if you do this—please don't come near me or my family."

I said nothing. He stirred, a dark figure within the glowing web of mosquito netting. For a moment I had the illusion that I was observing a huge mutant larva writhing inside its bright spun-silk cocoon. It was a terrible image, no doubt brought on by the alcohol. That I could imagine him this way meant that I was at least as responsible as Cav for the end of our long friendship.

FIVE

The next morning Cavenaugh chartered a light plane for the trip to Fortaleza on the Caribbean coast; from there he would catch one of the twice-daily flights to Miami. He refused to keep his share of the money we had received for Dedrick and Betancourt. It was poisoned, he said, and would lay a trail that ultimately led to a cell in some federal penitentiary.

Last night's conversation was not referred to. We both were stiff and awkward until it was time for him to board the airplane, and then he suddenly grinned—the old warm Cavenaugh grin—and we shook hands.

"Go to hell, Jack," he said.

"Go to hell."

"Sure you won't come along?"

"No. I want to see how this thing plays out."

He sighed and shook his head. Neither of us could think of more to say. This was the dissolution of twenty years of friendship. Each of us had changed, veered off in a different direction—Cav taking the sane, adult route. We had been through a lot together, in war and in peace; he had saved my life a couple of times, and I had done the same for him. But we were ex-comrades now.

"*Suerte,*" I said, and embraced him. I held him a second longer than I should have.

"And good luck to you, Jack," he said, and turned to climb aboard the airplane.

I watched it until it disappeared completely out of sight.

*   *   *

The pilot returned to Paraje early that afternoon and brought two packages to the hotel. They were boxes made out of stiff cardboard and fastened with tape. Cavenaugh had sent them back from Fortaleza.

Troxel and I were sitting at a table, drinking gin and tonics and eating salty cashews, when the pilot delivered the boxes. It was very hot; I had rolled some ice in a towel and laid it over the back of my neck.

I said, "I wonder where they get the ice, since there's no electricity."

Troxel looked suspiciously at the boxes. "From Cavenaugh?" he asked.

"Yes."

"You didn't mention the plan to him, did you?"

"No."

"Nothing?"

"Of course not. I don't want him involved."

"Good boy," Troxel said.

"The fewer people who know, the better."

"Aren't you going to open the boxes?"

"Yes," I said.

"Do you know what's inside?"

"I'm pretty sure I do."

"Look, pal, I don't like mysterious packages. Tell me if I should get away from here."

"It's okay," I said. "Though I do wonder why Cav borrowed my alarm clock."

"Always the wiseass."

I cut the tape, pried the lid off one of the boxes, lifted the shrunken head out of the packing material, and placed it on the table. Troxel recoiled.

The fake shrunken head had its mouth and eyelids stitched shut. It was about the size of a small grapefruit, with the skin stretched tautly over the brows and cheekbones. Its hair—actual human hair the same dark brown as my own—was long, and the thing had a full beard. The head smelled faintly of urine-tanned leather.

"What the hell . . ."

"A good likeness of me, don't you think?" I asked.

"Jesus!"

It was a good replica; it looked as I would look if the skin of my head and face had been removed entire, tanned, and shrunken and mummified with repeated infusions of hot sand.

"It's a joke, sort of," I said. "Old Crowley's head is in the other box."

"Keep that stinking thing away from me."

I told Troxel about the heads. One morning, about a month ago, Cavenaugh, Crowley, and I had wandered into a tourist shop during a visit to Fortaleza. They sold forest Indian artifacts, authentic and phony—blowpipes and darts, bows and arrows, fetishes, wood carvings, straw baskets, head and shell necklaces, odds and ends. In a backroom craftsmen fashioned shrunken heads for the tourist trade, bizarre souvenirs to display to the folks back home in St. Louis or Denver. The men stretched goatskin over fiberglass molds and used human hair for the eyebrows and scalp, mustache or beard, patiently sewing in the hairs one by one, then crudely stitching the eyelids and lips closed as was the custom among the Jivaro headhunters in the old days. The result was a scale version of your own death's-head.

Cavenaugh, Crowley, and I had gone into the shop and had our heads measured with tailor's tape, and we were photographed from various angles. They demanded full payment before commencing work.

"You're crazy," Troxel said. "Don't you know that thing is bad luck?"

"Originally," I said, "the Jivaro and some other tribes took the heads of their enemies and shrunk them for obscure religious purposes. But then early in the century anthropologists traded for heads, and museums bought some, and then private collectors— so finally the Jivaro started shrinking heads for profit rather than spiritual improvement."

"You're a boring guy, Jack."

"My hometown museum had the head of a Dutch botanist who happened to wander into headhunter territory. He had fair skin, blond hair and beard, and a couple of moles on his cheek. That Dutchman was an innocent victim of new market forces."

Troxel was disgusted. He got up from the table. "That thing is jinxed."

"Maybe," I said. "But is it bad luck if I keep it or bad luck if I destroy it?"

I put the head back in its box and replaced the lid.

"It's just plain bad luck," he said.

*　　*　　*

Not long after Troxel left, the screen door opened and a woman carrying two pieces of heavy luggage struggled onto the veranda. The door slammed behind her. She dropped the bags, closed her eyes, arched her back, and whimpered like a lonely puppy. She was tall, about thirty, and had been seriously beat up by the heat and the fatigue of travel. She had auburn hair, more red than brown, and with it the classic redhead's freckled complexion.

"Eventually," I said, "someone will be along to take your bags." She pivoted and gave me a challenging stare.

"In the meantime," I said, "you look like you could use a drink."

"You look like you've had a few too many."

"I have gin, tonic, limes, and ice."

"Aren't you the seductive devil?" Her voice was pitched low and her accent sounded mid-Atlantic—sort of British, sort of American, pleasant to the ear.

I smiled. "You remind me of someone I used to know." Then I had to turn away for a moment when I thought of Beth.

The woman's eyes were red-rimmed, her skin blotchy, her lips dry and puffy, her hair lank in the extreme humidity. At the moment she looked like a girl who had been roughed up and had her feelings hurt while playing football with the boys. She had a grievance against us.

I lifted my glass and rattled the ice.

"All right, Mephistopheles," she said, and she walked over and sat at the table.

"I don't want your soul," I said.

"I can guess what you want."

She watched while I filled a tall glass with ice cubes, poured in the gin, the tonic, then squeezed in a quarter lime.

She rolled the cold glass across her forehead, pressed it against one cheek and then the other, tilted the glass, and drank half of it in a few gulps.

"Think you're quite the guy, don't you?"

"Let up," I said. "I'm only an innocent bystander."

"What do you look like under that beard?"

"Like the devil."

"I don't trust men with beards. Beards deceive. They can conceal a petulant mouth, a weak chin."

"Or conceal a determined mouth, a noble chin."

"I'll grant you the chin." She lifted her glass and finished the gin and tonic. "Make me another."

"Maybe you ought to quench your thirst before you quench your thirst," I said. I made another drink and pushed it across the table.

"God, it's hot," she said. "This is hell, all right." She drank half of the new gin and tonic.

"Go slow."

"Go slow yourself, Beelzebub."

"Call me Jack."

"I'm Anna Fontenot, and it's hot, and I've been traveling for about sixteen straight hours, and I'm . . . vexed. I'm vexed off."

"Welcome to Paraje, Anna."

"Paraje—God."

"Paraje grows on you."

"I'm sure it does. Like ringworm. What's in those boxes?"

"Shrunken heads."

"No, really."

"Really."

"You *are* a devil. Show me."

I removed the tape and lid from the other box, lifted out

Crowley's head, and placed it on the table. I was reaching for the other head, my "head," so I didn't see her initial reaction, but when I turned I saw that the blood had drained from her face, leaving her skin a glossy white, like candle wax. Her breathing was rapid and shallow.

"Are you all right?" I asked.

Her pale face was filmed with sweat, and she began to shiver and gasp for air.

"Anna?"

She had gone into shock. Perhaps it was due to the combination of heat and her fatigue and the alcohol, and, finally, the sight of the shrunken head. Or maybe she was suffering a severe allergic reaction, anaphylactic shock. I grabbed a hand. Her skin was clammy, her pulse quick and fluttery.

"Anna, do you need medication? Are you diabetic? Do you have adrenalin or some other medicine in your purse or luggage?"

"My father," she said.

"What?" I looked at the head. Was she saying that Crowley was her father? "God," I said. "The head is fake. It isn't real."

She fainted then. I carried her across the veranda and laid her supine on a wicker couch. Her eyelids fluttered. She licked her lips. She remained unconscious for a minute or two, and then gradually color returned to her face and her breathing smoothed. She looked up at me.

"Did you hear?" I said. "Anna—the head is fake."

"Are you crazy?" she said.

"Did you come down here to see Crowley—your father?"

She nodded.

"We've got to talk."

SIX

Anna Fontenot rested in her room for several hours. At twilight, we took a taxi out to the municipal cemetery. Sleep and a bath had transformed her; she looked cool and immaculate in a white sundress, and her mood was quiet.

The cemetery was a big muddy field scribbled with footpaths that tacked among the stone cairns and rough wooden crosses and gardens of plastic flowers. There weren't many people around at this hour: three men—convicts in vertically striped, pajama-like outfits—who were digging a grave; a family of dejected mourners; peddlers selling religious trinkets; a few beggars.

"Are you lost?" Anna said.

"No," I lied.

I could not remember exactly where Crowley had been interred. Cavenaugh and I had paid for the cemetery plot and coffin and had attended the unceremonious burial, but there was not much difference between one area of the cemetery and another.

"It's over here." I led her to a mound covered by thousands of small, white-painted stones. There was no marker.

"I'm having a monument engraved," I said.

"To what point?" Anna looked down at the absurd stoneheap and slowly shook her head.

I wondered who might actually be buried here: a peasant, maybe; a laborer; a clerk; a whore; a woodcutter; a gambler killed in a saloon fight.

"Your father was a good man," I said.

"He was a tramp."

"I liked him."

"Oh, he was charming, all right. Charm was currency for Dad. But why, for God's sake, did he choose to die in this jungle hellhole?"

"I don't know. He just stayed on after the bridge project was cancelled. And the government—it's not much of one."

"In his rare letters," Anna said, "he talked about my legacy. Fancy talk. 'Don't worry, my girl, I'm going to leave you very well off.' Right."

"Your father was a well-regarded engineer at one time."

"And now he lies here forever, under these stones."

"Yes."

She looked at me. "Did you paint all of those little stones by yourself?"

"I couldn't find the grave. I'm sorry."

"Let's get away from here. I want a drink and a good meal."

"The drink is easy."

I took her to a patio restaurant that specialized in river fish. The fish was always fresh and usually well-prepared, though you couldn't trust the salads and the starch was often a skinned manioc root with a bitter cream sauce. The place smelled of flowers and insecticides.

"This isn't so bad," Anna said. "I was expecting the Cannibal Café."

The candlelight softened the planes of her face, burnished her hair, and gave her sea-green eyes the illusion of a cat-like slant. She didn't look like Beth at all, but there was something about her smile. They both had that same damn unguarded smile.

Anna talked and laughed easily. She was not married; she had simply elected to use her mother's maiden name, Fontenot. She told me that she'd never felt like a Crowley. Her mother was an American from New Hampshire, where she now lived with her second husband. Her mother and father had met in London and quickly—too quickly—married. Anna had spent the first seventeen years of her life in England, the last fourteen in the States. The family had been fairly well off during the early years, even though she did not often see her father—he was usually off somewhere, to India or Africa or Colombia, working on various engineering projects. He visited them once or twice a year on leaves that rarely lasted more than three or four weeks. He was a semi-stranger. Then one day, in 1987, he walked out of the house enroute to someplace— Botswana?—and that was that. When it became clear that he was never coming back, Anna and her mother left England.

I said, "Crowley had a drinking problem."

"No kidding."

"Like I said, I liked him."

"Oh, he was a wonderful man in some ways. Bright, charming, witty, even strong. Yes, strong. But, I don't know, his character gradually eroded, and finally he was bright, charming, witty, and very weak. And now he's buried in a pauper's grave of inexact location."

"I'll find the grave tomorrow."

"Never mind, I was just teasing," she said. "Did he ever mention me?"

"No."

"He wrote me letters, sent me gifts. He wrote often at first, then less and less often, maybe twice a year during the last five years. His letter reached me a month ago."

Anna was a staff writer for a San Diego-based magazine named *Scientific Horizons*. It was a monthly aimed at an audience interested in the "soft" sciences: psychology, archeology, anthropology, the history of ancient civilizations. A typical issue might contain articles about the autopsy of an Egyptian mummy by a famous forensic pathologist; dream legends of the Australian aborigines; the discovery of a two-million-year-old fossil hominid in East Africa; Hopi kachinas; a brief history of the original Olympic games, which commenced in 776 BC.

Most of the articles were lightweight stuff, Anna said, done in a sort of breathless prose, but the magazine was edited for the general reader, not the specialist. Even so, you could occasionally slip in a piece of genuine science reporting.

Anna had planned to visit her father here in Paraje for quite some time—she had intuited that, despite his chirpy letters, his health was poor—but she could never save enough money to make the trip. In his last letter he had written about the Isquito Indians, whose culture and religion, whose survival as a people, was threatened by the combined forces of government hostility and Christian charity. Both Church and State, with contrary intent, were causing the extinction of a culture, a life, a people.

"So, eureka," she said.

The magazine had approved her proposal for a long piece on the vanishing Isquito, and of course agreed to pay all of her expenses. Two birds, one stone: she could visit her father on the expense account and get some work done at the same time.

"So you'll be going upriver to the Christ the Savior Mission?"

"When I can. The Mission radioed the hotel and said they were making repairs on their airplane—they won't be able to pick me up for two or three days."

"Good."

"Good, is it?"

"People have fallen in love in two or three days."

Anna laughed. "Well, show me a good time, sailor, and who knows."

SEVEN

The next morning Anna came to breakfast with her features composed in that frozen female expression that indicates that a grievance will soon be presented. She coolly studied the menu, ordered, toyed with her utensils for a moment, then regarded me with a long, accusing gaze.

"You're a mercenary," she said.

"I'm a soldier."

"They told me you're a mercenary."

"Who are they?"

"Mercenary," she said with disgust.

"Soldier. Mercenaries are soldiers, you know."

"Maybe in the technical sense."

"In any sense."

"But it's an awfully sleazy trade, isn't it?"

"That depends on the individual, as in any trade."

"Depends on the individual and the cause, wouldn't you say?"

"Yes."

"What cause do you serve?"

"Now?"

"Yes, now."

"I'm not certain."

"You don't know?"

"Not yet. But so far no one has been harmed."

"Lovely," she said.

Anna was silent throughout breakfast and then, after coffee, she started again.

"Mercenary soldiers are a nasty modern phenomenon."

"A very old phenomenon. As old as fighting. Have you ever read Xenophon?"

"No."

"Twenty-five hundred years ago he wrote a book called *Anabasis*, which is usually translated as *The March Upcountry*. Xenophon and ten thousand Greek mercenaries fought on the side of Cyros against Cyros's brother, Artaxerxes II, the King of Persia. It's a famous book. So you see, mercenary soldiers are not a nasty modern phenomenon."

"A nasty old phenomenon?"

"Anna, mercenaries fought on both sides of our Revolutionary War. Hessians, mainly, on the British side, and French mercenaries, mostly, on the American side. Don't you suppose there were honorable men—German and French—fighting with both armies?"

"Paid patriots."

"If you wish."

"But I imagine that your Xenophon and your Hessians and French at least knew whom they served, in what cause they'd enlisted."

"It's a small hotel," I said, "and a small town. I'll try to stay out of your way for the next couple days."

"But you promised me a picnic in the rain forest today."

"You still want to go?"

"Yes. Don't you?"

"I do, yes."

"Well, then?"

"Anna, will you sleep with me tonight?"

She laughed. "If *I* were a mercenary, I'd say yes—for a thousand dollars."

"Since you're not a mercenary?"

She smiled. "It's not a likely prospect."

*   *   *

I awakened just after sunrise and saw Anna standing nude in front of the bureau. She silently slid open the top drawer and lifted out one of the boxes. Her face and torso were visible in the mirror fixed to the rear of the bureau. Seen through the mosquito netting, she appeared misty, insubstantial, like an Impressionist nude—a Renoir or Monet. She was stealthy as she removed the box's lid, dipped her two hands inside, and lifted out the Crowley shrunken head. She held it cupped in her palms at eye level.

"Anna?" I said.

She turned and looked at me blankly, as if disturbed while sleepwalking, and then she raised her eyebrows and smiled.

"Did you think I lied?" I said.

"No."

"Did you actually think that maybe I possessed your father's genuine shrunken head?"

"No. I just wanted to see what he looked like. All my photographs of him were taken when he was young."

"He didn't look like that," I said.

"Didn't he?"

"To start with, he didn't have his mouth and eyelids stitched shut."

"I hope not."

But it really did look like Crowley; the head was a fairly accurate portrait of the man during the last months of his life. Even the skin was the same jaundiced color, and the bristly eyebrows and wispy spirals of white hair looked the same.

Anna gazed at the head as if surprised to see it in her hands, and with a wince of revulsion, she gently returned it to the box.

"Come back to bed," I said.

"This is very strange."

She removed the other box from the drawer, lifted out the head and studied it.

"Alas, poor Yorick," I said.

"This head looks a lot like you. Cynical, tough."

"It's my little twin."

"Ah. And is he the good twin?"

"Yes."

"And you the bad one."

"Right."

She paused, carefully selecting her words. "It's morbid to keep these things around, isn't it?"

"It seemed clever at the time, when we commissioned them."

"But you still have them."

"It's hard to throw them in the trash."

She nodded. "You mean, you're superstitious about the heads—especially yours."

"I think so."

"If the head of your little good twin is destroyed, why then maybe something bad will happen to you."

"Something stupid like that."

"It's so ugly. I don't mean the heads, though they aren't pretty. But the idea of the heads. You're strange."

"But not a stranger. Anna, come to bed."

"No."

"Then put on some clothes."

"You're the only man to ever tell me to put *on* my clothes."

"Come here."

"There isn't time. I've got to pack."

"The pilot at the mission will radio the hotel when he's ready to leave. You have plenty of time."

She surprised me by bringing the head close to her face and kissing its thread-twined lips. Then she returned the head to its box, crossed the room, crawled beneath the mosquito netting and lay next to me. She stared up at the network of cracks on the ceiling. "Do you remember?" she said. "You told me that people can fall in love in three days."

"I remember."

"What do you say now?"

"I say, Anna, don't go."

"I have to go."

"Go away, yes, with me."

She took a deep breath and said, "Your name isn't Jackson, is it?"

"No."

"What is it?"

"Jackstraw."

"Jack Straw?"

"Jackstraw. Thomas Jackstraw. People call me Jack. No one calls me Thomas except my family."

"There it is—a man who never even told me his true name asks me to go away with him."

"Anna—"

"A mercenary soldier who doesn't know who he works for or what cause he serves—"

"Listen—"

"—asks me to be his girl. Is that it?"

"I won't beg."

"Of course not. Not a big tough guy like you."

We both smiled at the ceiling.

"Not a tough mercenary who marched upcountry with Anabasis."

"With Xenophon. The name he gave his account was *Anabasis*."

"I thought a Xenophon was a musical instrument."

"That's xylophone."

She grinned. "Honey, I had a great time, really I did, and I'm half in love with you, but *finito*."

*   *   *

We waited on the veranda for a taxi that would carry Anna to the airport. The waiter brought us a pot of coffee, orange juice, crusty breakfast rolls, and a bowl of mango jam.

"You know," I said, "going out to see the Isquito is a waste of time."

"I owe my magazine a piece."

"I'll repay the magazine's expenses. We'll go away together."

"Jack—no."

"Anna, they're mission Indians. Their rites and myths and religious practices are now half evangelical Christian and half forest pagan. They wear plastic tennis shoes and baseball caps and T-shirts with logos on the front."

"Maybe their ways aren't totally lost," she said. "Maybe some of them can still sing the old songs and tell the old stories. Anyway, there are still some wild Isquito out in the forest."

"Sixty or seventy," I said. "Miserable, decadent, hunted creatures trying to run from the army and the missionaries. Soon they'll all be dead of diseases for which they have no immunity, and alcoholism, and the general despair that precedes extinction."

"I know," Anna said. "I know."

"Will your magazine print that story?"

"No."

"Look, I own a little ranch in the Colorado mountains near a town called Whistle. I call it a ranch, but it's just a few hundred acres of scrubland that can't support much beyond grasshoppers, and there's a creek and a log cabin. Do you like horses? I'll buy a couple of horses. The air is clean and cool there, it's right at the base of the mountains, and you can fish up there and ride or hike—or you can just be."

"Jack, please, no."

"Let's go there together. Today."

"Please. Why do you have to make it so hard?"

"All right."

"If I ever heard a bad idea, this is it."

"Okay, let it go."

"Don't you think I want to go with you? But, Christ—who are you? What do I know about your past, your life, you?"

"I'll give you my résumé."

"People like you don't have résumés, you have dossiers."

I laughed.

"Or computer printouts."

"The taxi is here," I said.

"I don't cry easily."

"Neither do I."

I carried her luggage outside. The taxi driver was idly rubbing an oily rag over the windshield of his old car and the glass shimmered with rainbows. He was an old pirate who wore an eyepatch and had three fingers missing from his left hand. Not far away a bony dog circled dizzily, biting the tip of his tail.

I embraced Anna, kissed her.

She said, "It was close, Jack. But you didn't have the right words."

"You didn't have a receptive ear."

"Devil," she said, and smiled that smile, kissed me, turned, and got into the rear of the taxi. She lowered her head and wriggled her fingers at me as the car pulled away. She was the first woman I'd been with since Beth's death. I realized I cared for her, though I would probably never see her again.

The dog continued to circle around and around in the dust, obsessively chewing on his tail.

EIGHT

Anna left behind copies of the three major U.S. news magazines, which contained considerable political coverage and gossip even though the general election was still months away. None of the magazines had anything good to say about the American Patriotic Party and its candidates for national office.

Time wrote that the Party's campaign was the political equivalent of a dog-and-pony show. Hamilton Keyes, the presidential candidate, was described as a cross between Midas and Methuselah, and the writer sneered that he was a man whose speeches stopped clocks and reversed calendars. Was he trying to buy the presidency? It was rumored that he had already invested more than $30 million in the campaign, with more to come. He tried to imitate Ronald Reagan, *Time* said, but came across more like an aged Ronald McDonald.

Newsweek called the vice-presidential candidate, Rachel Leah Valentine, the Eva Peron wannabe of the North, and hinted at a past that, when fully exposed, would receive an X-rating. Unlike Hamilton Keyes, she had at least been elected to public office in the past; she'd served three terms as a California Congresswoman, though her voting record had been a marvel of flip-floppery—

Valentine had managed during her six years in the House to hunt with the conservative hounds and run with the liberal hares. And a *Newsweek* columnist wrote that the American Patriotic Party was trying to hatch thousand-year-old political eggs that would surely stink unendurably by election day.

U.S. News and World Report was less flippant, as usual: they expressed concern because, according to the latest poll, eleven percent of the American electorate asserted that they intended to vote for the APP ticket. They were, of course, protest votes, wasted votes, and that was both frivolous and dangerous; it was disturbing that so many citizens were so easily manipulated by the Party's humbuggery and demagoguery. Too many regarded them as a sort of entertaining joke—but at first weren't the Nazis similarly regarded earlier in the last bloody, tyrannical century?

All three magazines carried photos of the Party's presidential and vice-presidential candidates. None were flattering; the photo editors had apparently selected pictures that would correspond to the mocking texts. The seventy-three-year-old Hamilton Keyes was photographed with his eyes shut and his mouth open, as he stumbled while carrying the flag in a Fourth of July Parade, and smiling while standing next to a race horse that was about to bite him. He was portrayed as a comic old cadaver.

Rachel Valentine was photographically frozen in awkward postures too, looking either exalted or bitchy, but even so she projected an extraordinary vitality. She was a thirty-nine-year-old widow, mother, and quirky activist, but there was something that the camera could not exclude, an erotic power that is usually called "charisma" or "star power"—a deeply rooted sexuality, a sort of primal appeal. Rachel Valentine was not a beautiful woman, at least not in the newsmagazine photographs; you might call her "handsome" or "attractive." But you'd walk past a dozen beautiful young women to meet her.

Of course, the American Patriotic Party had no chance despite Hamilton Keyes's huge fortune. They were outsiders. They were eccentric. And it was clear that they would not receive impartial coverage during the election season. The APP candidates had been declared dangerous clowns and there would be no deviation now. The U.S. mainstream media is like a pack of feral dogs—when one bites they all bite, and the poor dog who refuses to bite is soon a pariah.

It was a relief to again be reminded that I was involved in a mad conspiracy that hadn't a dream of success.

*   *   *

It rained off and on again during the next few days. The river, they told me, was rising. Orson Dedrick returned to the States. Troxel and Roger Clay spent each day at the guerrilla camp. Troxel, Clay, and Rafael Betancourt were now wholly in command of the unit. What they were doing, what they planned, was a mystery to me. Troxel refused to discuss the matter except to say that their "operation" had nothing to do with the imminent fake assassination. He was lying, but I couldn't determine to what degree or what purpose. Men like Troxel lied. They lied to conceal or deceive, they lied for sport and profit, they lied to manipulate, they lied because they were smart and you were stupid. Their lives were a spaghetti of lies and ultimately even they could not disentangle the truthful strands from the bogus. There was always a tiny bit of truth in Troxel's lies and a lie at the heart of each of his rare attempts to tell the truth. I'd found him least plausible when most truthful.

On Thursday he returned to the hotel early, a little after noon, soaked from the rain and irritable. The climate was wearing on him; one of his eyes was infected and a few boils had sprouted on his neck.

"Christ!" he said.

He sat down at my table on the veranda. He smelled of sweat and the river and last night's whiskey.

"Where's the fucking waiter?"

"He's around."

"Goddammit, Jack, it's all fucked up."

"Is it?"

"Those assholes!"

Raindrops snapped on the sheet-steel roof overhead and their echoes seemed to burst in the air around us.

"They got Betancourt," he said.

"Who?"

"It's all fucked now unless we can get him back before he talks."

I nodded. This was preparation. Troxel was preparing me.

The waiter arrived and took Troxel's order, six bottles of Medalla de Oro beer on ice.

"They got Rafael," Troxel said.

"They can keep him as far as I'm concerned."

"They've got Betancourt and Herrera and Baltazar."

"Who's got them?"

"The army detachment at the river patrol outpost."

"What were Rafael and his men doing upriver?"

"Reconnoitering. They were—"

"Reconnoitering what?"

"Jesus, will you shut up for a second. All you need to know at the moment is those fascist swine at the outpost captured them yesterday. And you know how those pigs are—the first thing they do is connect your balls to the electrical system. This could blow the whole enterprise. If Rafael talks . . ."

The waiter arrived with an ice bucket filled with bottles of beer and a snack platter of shrimp and squid.

"Leave us alone," Troxel growled when the waiter asked if he wanted anything else.

"Troxel, are you telling me that Betancourt knows about the assassination business?"

"Don't use that word."

Troxel called it Operation Longshot. He liked to use words like "operation" and "liaison" and "coordinates" and "tactical." He was a natural-born noncom who enjoyed playing general.

"How much does Betancourt know?" I asked.

"Not the actual plan, but peripheral stuff, some arrangements in the capital. Maybe enough to make us abort if they get him to talk."

"Beautiful."

Troxel tried to twist off a non-twist bottle cap and lacerated his right thumb and index finger. He swore and licked his fingers, and when he looked up at me there was blood on his lips.

"So you want to go upriver to free Rafael?" I asked.

"That's it."

"Good luck."

"But," he said.

"But . . . ?"

"But the Indians won't obey me. They don't like me, and they hate Roger Clay. They said they would go only if you or Cavenaugh led them."

"Cavenaugh's gone. That leaves me."

"That's right. You've got to help on this, Jack. Otherwise the whole plan is dead."

"You want to raid the river patrol outpost and free Rafael Betancourt."

"Free him or kill him."

Troxel looked comically insane with his bloody mouth and swollen, bloodshot eye.

"Okay," I said. He was unreliable, and possibly sociopathic, but it was too late to back out now.

He smiled. "Good." Then his eyes narrowed. "You'll really do it?"

"When do we go?"

"Soon. Three or four hours. You really will help me, Jack?"

"If you'll stop licking the blood off your fingers."

He looked at me in an almost affectionate way, with a blood-tinged grin. "You're a wise guy, Jack, a smartass. But I like you."

I went up to my room, got out my camouflage uniform, and packed some necessary things in a rucksack. Now I was going to command an assault on a remote military outpost. Soon, maybe, I would shoot an American vice-presidential candidate. It was lunacy, all darkness and fog, but after all, I had elected to follow the string.

I sat on the edge of the bed and cleaned and oiled my 9mm Beretta. I waxed my boots, honed the blade of my sheath knife, polished my insignia, then stood up and trimmed my beard in front of the flaked yellow mirror. I was a soldier. This was a petty and dishonorable venture, but I was a soldier, and there are forms that must be respected.

My image in the mirror began to flutter. I put down the scissors. The room lights blinked rapidly for a time, then burned steadily, and I heard a sudden clatter from the adjoining room—Crowley's old room—and the alarmed cry of the cleaning woman. The city's electrical generators had finally been repaired. I went through the connecting door into the room first occupied by Crowley, then Cavenaugh. The window air conditioner rattled and clanked. The Indian maid backed away as if the machine might devour her. I pulled the plug and the clattering ceased.

"It's nothing," I told her. "Go get me a screwdriver. *Un destornillador.*"

She nodded, grateful to be sent away.

I waited for a while and then, when she didn't return, I tried a coin on the screws and was able to remove the exterior panel from the air conditioner unit. Inside I found a heavily taped hip pocket-sized pipe tobacco tin. The spinning fan blade had dented the tape and metal, but the can was still intact. I replaced the panel, tightened the screws, and returned to my room.

The tobacco can was stuffed with gemstones wrapped in scraps of felt. There were five big emeralds and twenty-six diamonds. Two of the emeralds and about half of the diamonds had been cut. I spread them all out on the bed and watched as the cut stones gathered light into themselves, fractured the light, and then angled it back toward its source. The stones were cold to the touch but their interiors burned fiercely. I was sure all of the stones were first-rate. I didn't know gems, but old Crowley had, and he wouldn't have collected the second-rate. This was Anna's legacy. I hadn't thought to tell her about it, and regretted that now.

It was strange: the man had been a miser, shamelessly stingy; he'd kept his life savings in a pipe tobacco can while cadging drinks and beating the rent and going to the bathroom when the dinner check was due. But I had liked old Crowley, and I liked him more after he had told me that during his lifetime he had squirreled away a fortune for the daughter he had abandoned. That counted for something.

I wrapped all the stones in the patches of felt and stuffed them back into the tobacco tin, then went down the stairs and out the door and walked through the muddy streets to the bank where I had a safety deposit box. I put the stones in the drawer, along with a stash of currency and my fake passports. I had three passports: one Canadian, one Irish, and the third South African. My photograph innocently stared out from each. The South African passport was virgin, but there were entry and exit stamps in the pages of the other two. I was always prepared to run. Exile was always a possibility.

It had stopped raining and now high winds were ripping long blue gashes in the cloud cover.

PART TWO
THE ASSAULT

NINE

The helicopter delivered us to the beach just as the sun was going down, and the river shuttled the dying light into glowing threads of crimson and gold and violet. It was a textured, shot-silk river from the air, lovely, but the color had bleached away by the time we landed.

Two big open boats of the sort used to move cargo up and down the Iracundo were pulled up on the beach. Powerful Yamaha outboard engines were mounted at the sterns. The boats were like ordinary aluminum skiffs except much bigger; each could carry fourteen or fifteen men and their gear without over-crowding.

The Indians, in full combat gear, were strung out along the fringe of forest. They looked drowsy, bored, like passengers waiting for a long-overdue bus. There weren't many of them.

"Brief the men," Troxel told me.

"Maybe you should brief me first," I said.

"Start pulling your weight," Troxel said, and he and Roger Clay walked down toward the boats. I watched them go. Troxel looked and moved like a soldier; plump Roger Clay, in his new razor-creased camouflage outfit and cocked red beret, looked like the kind of weekend warrior who spent his spare hours stalking through the woods with militant dentists and realtors.

More Indians had deserted during the week. Only nineteen remained now, but they were the best of the sorry lot, potential soldiers. I called an impromptu inspection while we waited on the beach. Their weapons were cleaned and oiled. Each man carried the prescribed amount of ammunition and rations. Nothing had been forgotten. All of the equipment had been properly distributed and packed, and there were no rattles or jingles when they moved.

"Okay," I said. "*Está bien.*"

They relaxed, dispersed.

I had never read a military manual that recommended desertion as a means of culling out the malcontents and drunkards and cowards, but it seemed effective. Encourage desertion, raise morale.

I heard Troxel call my name, and when I turned he gestured irritably, as if summoning a lazy servant. Clay, his thumbs hooked in the pistol belt slung beneath his belly, cocked his head and grinned. He was the boss's lackey; when the boss was rude, he was rude.

I walked down through the deep sand. Troxel had a topographical map spread out over the bows of one of the boats.

"Hey, Jack," he said, "do you think this is a beach picnic? Do you think we're here to drink beer and play volleyball?"

Roger Clay shifted his weight, tilted back his head and, as if releasing the pressure of excess mirth, hissed between his teeth.

"Nervous, are you, Troxel?" I said.

"Don't give me any of that nervous crap, pal."

"It's natural to be nervous, but you shouldn't let the men see it. And you shouldn't show disrespect toward another officer in front of them."

"Don't tell me how to soldier. And don't talk nerves to me—I'm a quarter scar tissue, and all the scars are on the front of my body.

No back or butt scars. I don't need an asshole who got kicked out of the Point telling me how to soldier."

Roger Clay muttered "asshole" and expelled another hiss toward the sky.

"Good luck," I said. "I can find my way back to Paraje."

"All right," Troxel said. "I'm sorry. Okay? It's just that if this doesn't work the whole plan is bitched."

"Prima donna," Clay said with suppressed mirth.

"Is he stoned, Troxel?"

"Roger, are you stoned?"

"A wee bit," Clay said.

"Christ!" Troxel snapped the map taut and jabbed the lower section with a fingertip. "We're here," he said. He slowly ran his finger up the long, looping, blue-lined Iracundo. "The mission is seventy-eight miles downriver, on the south, the left, bank. The army outpost is here, at the juncture of the Iracundo and a tributary called Rio Manso, four miles above the mission, on the north bank. You'll take your boat past the outpost a few hundred yards, to here, beach the boat, and attack from above. Me and my men will come in from below. Got that? We'll work out the timing. You'll take eleven of the men, I'll take the other eight. Roger will go with you."

Dusk deepened toward night as we discussed the details of the assault. We stood immersed in the misty blue light, slapping mosquitoes, and I felt myself slipping into that dreamy state that always precedes life-or-death action.

Finally Troxel folded the map and tucked it into his breast pocket. "All right," he said. "Let's get these boats launched."

I said, "I don't want Clay on my boat."

"You don't, huh?"

"You take him."

"Prima donna," Clay said.

"Roger goes with you," Troxel said. "That's that."

We summoned the men, divided them into two groups, loaded the boats, and pushed off into the current. The sky and forest on each side of the Iracundo were black, but the river still glowed a luminous silver, as if the water had hoarded light all day and was now gradually releasing it. Dense low clouds moving in from the southeast had almost completely obscured the stars.

The fragile silence of the rain forest was annihilated by the throbbing roar of the engines. The noise we made voyaging upriver seemed vaguely sinful. It was possible to believe in spirits in such a place, on such a night. We sat in the center of the noise, at its source, as it radiated outward in what I imagined were concentric rings. There was too much noise to talk, and it was too dark to see well; we were isolated, diminished.

Rain had raised the water level, increased the speed of the current and sweetened the river's odor—it smelled fresher tonight, not so sour. During the first two hours we occasionally saw the dim yellow glow of kerosene and oil lamps off in the blackness, and then there were fewer and fewer sparks of light, and finally nothing at all as we entered the true wilderness.

Sound carries clear and far over open water; we shut off the outboard engines when we were still fifteen miles below the mission. The current carried us along at the pace of an easy walk. Two men with oars kept us aligned in the channel. We passed through swarms of gnats and mosquitoes and dank streamers of mist. The men defended themselves against insects with resinous cigar smoke and a repellent that smelled like turpentine. Our aluminum boats reverberated like drums when hitting a snag or banged by a clumsy oar stroke. "*Silencio,*" I'd say.

Birds, mewing like cats, abruptly lifted from the sandbars as we drifted past, and the crepitation of their wings was audible as they beat low over the water. And once, deep in the forest, an alarmed troop of monkeys—a demonic chorus—erupted in a howling that reverberated through the night like sirens. "*Silencio,*" one of the men said, to muffled laughter from his comrades.

The river was about one hundred yards wide in this season, shallow except for a channel in the center. There were low sandbars, snags angled like spears, tangles of brush left behind when the water receded. It took knowledge of the river to navigate it at night under these conditions. During the rainy season you could float a small freighter most of the Iracundo's length, but tonight a canoe would have a hard time.

Troxel's boat usually followed about a quarter mile behind us, an irregular shape at that distance, a cluster of shadows and glints of light; sometimes it was completely lost to view when it vanished behind a bend in the river. Troxel and I had compact handset radios. They contained buttons which could be used for the tapping of Morse when it became risky to speak aloud.

Toward midnight we were struck by a sudden furious rainsquall that turned the river a seething white and reduced visibility to a few yards. Hailstones the size of peas were mixed with the cold rain pellets. Gusts of wind rocked the boat. In the stronger gusts, the rain and vapor blew in horizontal sheets. The air around us felt compressed. There was no lightning or thunder. The storm lasted only a few minutes and then swirled away downriver. A couple of the men began bailing water and hailstones out of the boat with their helmets. The air remained cool for only a few minutes, then we began to sweat again.

I turned and watched the squall move upriver. Troxel was in the middle of it now.

Long holes had been ripped in the cloud cover and for a while I thought the sky was going to clear, but then the holes closed and the stars and moon were extinguished. It seemed even hotter now than before the storm. The air reeked of vegetal decay and the sour river. The men began talking in low voices, with an occasional louder laugh.

The radio hummed. Troxel.

"Jack," he said.

"Here."

"Son of a bitch!"

"You bet."

"Christ. You're okay then?"

"We're dogs," I said. "Wet, stinking, miserable dogs."

"Tell your dogs to keep it down."

"Right."

"Later."

"Right. Out."

I telescoped the antenna into the radio box.

"*Pues*," I said to the men. "*Silencio, mis bravos, mis valientes— silencio.*"

The man nearest me scooped some hailstones from the bottom of the boat and molded them into a lump the size of a golfball. He put it into his mouth and chewed with a bovine sideways grinding of his jaws. His nickname was Zonzo, Fool, and he was the unit's goat, its wise-fool.

I said, "*Esta noche se mueres, Zonzo.*" Tonight you die.

Zonzo finished chewing ice, wiped his mouth with the back of his hand, and said, "*Si, por mi patria, por mi mama, por Jesús, y por sus doláres.*"

The men laughed.

The army outpost was four miles above the mission, at the confluence of the Iracundo and the Rio Manso. From that point, its small garrison could observe and intercept all river traffic, conduct searches, seize contraband, extort bribes, beat and bully and rape and, without consequence, kill. Sometimes they killed "wild" Indians for sport. Their isolation and the government's indifference protected them from sanction. They were thugs, notoriously brutal and corrupt. Yet most of them were young—and good boys, no doubt, at the time they had been conscripted from their towns and villages. Most, under ordinary circumstances, would have lived decent lives. But they had been snatched from their families and friends and priests, cynically trained, given arms and life-or-death authority, and sent off to rot on the frontier. After a year or so of that life they succumbed to despair and then atrocity.

The river was wider and deeper now, and it moved quietly, murmuring only a little. No rocks or snags pierced the surface; the water was smooth except for a scatter of moon-etched scribbles and dimples of current. We floated slowly, dreamlike, down the main channel. The ragged black walls of forest on each bank looked far off, a pistol shot away. There was no breeze. We were tormented by mosquitoes and clouds of gnats that got into our mouths and noses.

Troxel's boat had fallen far behind. I could not see it when I looked back over the expanse of water. He did not respond to my radio signal. Perhaps they had entered a dead-end channel. It worried me; we should not be so widely separated now. And the moonlight worried me. My eleven green soldiers worried me. Roger Clay, with his private smiles, was a worry. Most of all I was worried by the thought of the outpost's patrol boat with its two mounted fifty-caliber machine guns. If the army group had been alerted, if we had been betrayed, if we were caught out on open water in the moonlight . . .

Later, at twenty minutes after three, we heard dogs barking, and then we drifted into sight of the mission. The first thing we saw was a giant cross in the center of the complex, a hundred-foot-tall standing tree that had been stripped of limbs and bark and then fitted with a forty-foot horizontal timber. The cross had been painted a greenish white with some sort of luminous or reflective paint, and it blazed in the moonlight. No doubt it awed and frightened the forest Indians. Perhaps some, with a naïve logic, assumed that the white man's Jesus was a giant who had been crucified on such a massive structure. Crowley had once mentioned the cross to me, but I hadn't appreciated its size and imposing glow-in-the-dark effect.

There was enough moonlight to define the main features of the landscape. We saw a great sweep of cleared forest, cultivated land and pastures; a village of native huts to the south; the frame church with its steeple and small bell tower; some frame houses where the missionary families lived; pens and fenced corrals; and half a dozen scattered outbuildings. All of it was dominated by the gargantuan glowing cross.

A donkey brayed, dogs barked furiously. I didn't think the dogs would necessarily alert the people. The mission remained dark. Surely the dogs routinely barked at wild animals during the long nights.

I still could not raise Troxel on the radio. I inserted fresh batteries into the handset and tried again: silence.

Our last view of the mission was the phosphorescent cross and ribbed moonlight glinting off the corrugated steel roof of the church.

Fifteen minutes later I fully extended the aerial, adjusted the dials, and said, "Troxel?"

The radio stuttered with rapid Morse.

"Repeat," I said.

I listened carefully to the series of dot-dash combinations. PROCEED.

"Talk," I said. "Whisper if you have to."

The radio was silent for a time and then again crackled with Morse: PROCEED SOLO.

"Bullshit," I said.

TROUBLE.

"Talk to me."

GO SOLO.

"Troxel, what kind of crap is this?"

LUCK.

Roger Clay was watching me with a knowing little smile.

GO TEAM, Troxel signaled, and then he broke radio contact.

TEN

Roger Clay and a couple of the boys were sharing a marijuana cigarette. I was sitting in the bow; Clay was on the seat behind, and I had to twist halfway around to see him. We were not far below the outpost now.

When the cigarette was half smoked, I said, "All right now, that's enough. Get rid of it."

Clay defiantly took a long hissing drag on the cigarette, inhaled deeply, held the smoke in his lungs while looking at me, then flipped the butt overboard and exhaled slowly.

Gradually the water became streaked and mottled by the silty Rio Manso, and gained a dank, swampy reek.

I studied the outpost through binoculars as we slowly drifted past. It was situated on a promontory that separated the two rivers. A floating pier, buoyed by fifty-five-gallon steel drums, extended some thirty yards into the Iracundo, with the patrol boat and a couple of skiffs secured to the posts. A wooden stairway led up to the main building, a squat log structure with a railed deck all around and a steep steel roof. It contained the radio room and officers quarters. Troxel had told me that the usual military complement was three officers and eighteen to twenty men.

Behind the main building, scattered over a path of cleared forest land, were the barracks, cook shed, animal pens, and the jail—a concrete dugout without windows or ventilation and only a roof hatch for entry and exit. I had been told that the forest Indians quickly went mad there; they could perhaps tolerate a physical confinement but not the trapping of the spirit underground.

I lowered the binoculars. All of the men were staring over the river toward the outpost. They were eager to fight. They hated the frontier soldiers.

The men stared at the complex until it vanished from sight behind us and then they turned to look at me. Ahead, directly west, the moon had descended to only a few degrees above the black fringe of forest. The final digit of my watch changed: 4:10 now. We were scheduled to hit the outpost at exactly 4:35, at false dawn.

Roger Clay was watching me. He was not smiling now. "What are you doing?"

"Cruising the scenic Iracundo River," I said.

"Funny."

"Yes. Now shut your goddamned mouth."

The current was faster with the increased flow from the Rio Manso. The men watched me as we drifted away from our objective. Their faces were swollen with insect bites.

The temperatures of the two rivers were different, the Manso warm, the Iracundo cooler, and together they bred mists that rose and drifted with the current.

"I'm taking over," Clay said.

"Are you?" I drew my pistol.

The men behind Clay, those in the line of fire, quickly moved away, and the boat canted almost to the port gunwale.

"What's going on, Roger?" I asked.

He did not reply.

I said, "You are about to be summarily executed."

"Troxel's going to hit the mission."

"When?"

"Four thirty-five."

My heart jumped. Anna. "Why is he going to hit the mission?"

"He's going to take some of the missionaries."

"Take. You mean abduct."

"Yeah."

Clay was still stoned enough to try something brave. I held the gun steady on his chest. The Indians watched.

"And we're supposed to put the outpost out of action so they can't go down to help at the mission," I said.

"Yeah."

"Betancourt and Herrera and Baltazar aren't here, are they? They weren't captured by the army."

"No."

Roger smiled. "They're with Troxel."

"They're coming in by helicopter at the same time Troxel hits the mission."

"Very pretty. They're going to kidnap the missionaries now and release them when the candidate comes down to appeal for their release."

"Yeah."

"Well, hell, why didn't Troxel tell me?"

"Trox was afraid you wouldn't like it."

"Not like it? How could anyone dislike such a lovely piece of duplicity?"

"Trox thought you'd abort."

"It's sad," I said, "that Trox doesn't trust me."

"What are you going to do?"

"You mean am I going to kill you?"

"Yeah."

"Do you know the usual penalty for trying to seize command during a military action?"

"Trox said if you backed out, I should take over."

"Trox thinks more highly of your talent than I do."

"If you shoot me," Clay said, "you'll alert the outpost."

"They're a sorry bunch of puppies if they don't already know we're around."

Clay was still wary, but he had begun to sense that I was not going to kill him; there had been too much talk.

"I was only obeying orders," he said. His voice was steadier now as his arrogance returned. "Colonel Troxel is chief of the combined operations."

So this sneak terrorist assault on a remote undermanned army outpost and an undefended church mission was a "combined operation" commanded by a self-commissioned "colonel."

"Roger? The next time you mutiny, shoot your leader first, and then announce you're taking over."

The men were pleased when I told them that we were returning upriver to assault the outpost as originally planned. They had trained hard for three months and wanted their reward, a chance to employ their weapons and skills.

We rowed quietly upriver through silky tatters of mist and then turned up the Rio Manso. Dogs started barking inland. We beached the boat about one hundred yards above the confluence of the two rivers. The moon hadn't yet dropped behind the western horizon and its light lay a filigree over the water and limned the palm trees. A few small caiman slithered down the beach and into the river.

"*Pues*," I said. "*Todos ustedes saben qué hacer.*" You all know what to do.

As arranged, Clay took his seven men and slipped away into the darkness. They were going to hit the barracks. Roger Clay led because he was a Caucasian and Troxel's pal, though any one of my Indian noncoms was better trained and more reliable.

The other four men followed me up the muddy embankment, through a marshy flat whining with mosquitoes. We climbed a low hill to land cultivated with potatoes and plantain and sugar cane. The dogs barked and howled, and some distance to my left I heard a dry rustling as Clay and his men hurried through the canefield. The buildings ahead remained dark. There were no shouts of alarm. I was absolutely certain that we were advancing into an ambush.

The sky had imperceptibly paled to a fish-belly gray-white. Details of the landscape were emerging out of darkness: several rickety buildings, animal pens, a water tank on stilts, clothes drying on a line, and a contrivance made of iron kettles and ceramic jugs and a cat's cradle of copper tubing. These men distilled their own cane alcohol.

Something warm and moist touched my left hand, and I recoiled, pivoted, and swung my rifle. It was a dog that had crept out of the canefield to lick my hand, and now lay squirming ecstatically on its back. A huge pig rushed squealing out of the cane, and then another pig followed by half a dozen piglets. Zonzo, on my right, bent at the waist and wheezed with suppressed laughter.

We reached the log building and climbed the steps, went through a gate onto the side deck. I signaled three of the men to move around to the rear. They knew what to do. Zonzo and I walked to the front where there was a big veranda and a long flight of wooden steps that led down to the pier and boats. The Iracundo was now mostly obscured by a yard-high layer of mist that looked like drifted snow in the half-light.

I supposed the building was empty. Surely, if there were men in the compound, they would have been alerted by the berserk livestock—braying donkeys and barking dogs and squealing pigs and crowing roosters. No one could sleep through that. Maybe the outpost's soldiers were down at the mission; maybe Troxel and his bunch were about to catch hell. No. They would not have left the patrol boat with its fifty-caliber machine guns.

There was not a prearranged signal. Do what you have to do when you have to do it, I'd told the men. And now I heard a series of deep *crumps* from the barracks. They were using both concussion and fragmentation grenades, judging by the sounds. More *crumps*, long bursts of automatic weapons fire, and then a long whistle and a corkscrew of smoke rising high into the dull sky, followed by a burst of incandescence that temporarily blinded me. Some fool had launched a parachute flare.

I heard glass break at the rear of the building. They were tossing grenades inside.

"Get down," I told Zonzo.

Zonzo kicked in a window, threw in a grenade, then another. He grinned at me. His face, illuminated by the flare, shined with an innocent giddiness.

"Zonzo, get down!" I yelled. But he didn't know English.

The entire building shook on its frame as seven or eight grenades serially detonated. I could feel the concussions in my chest. The door blew off its hinges and cartwheeled downslope toward the river. Window glass exploded outward and sparkled briefly in the light of the flare. Clouds of dust and smoke spewed out the door and window frames and erupted out of the roof ventilators.

When I looked up again, Zonzo's face and torso were bloody. He had been badly cut by flying glass. His face was a red mask. He wiped his face, looked at his bloody palms and then, unbelieving, again wiped his face. The blood faded from crimson to pink to rust as the flare sputtered out.

Now the men in the rear were firing into the building through the window frames. They burned clips, inserted more, burned those too. Splintery holes blossomed on the wall around me.

I flopped face-down on the deck and yelled, *"Alto! Alto! Bastante! Alto!"*

Zonzo, dazed but not seriously injured, stared at his bloody palms. *"Pues,"* he said. *"Pues."*

Then he was hit several times by rounds coming through the wall and he collapsed, almost dissolved, onto the deck.

I pressed my body down into the planks as bullets ripped through the wall and zinged away toward the river. One of the grenades had started a fire inside the building. I could smell smoke and burnt explosives and the familiar cloying stink that thickened your mucus membranes and stung your nostrils—decomposed bodies. We had waged war on corpses.

ELEVEN

After things had settled down I left my subordinates to sort it out and walked down to the river. I pushed the skiff away from the pier, fitted the oars into the locks, and rowed steadily out into the river. The fog was thinning now in the steeply angled sunlight.

The outboard engine was slow to fire. I pulled the starter cord a dozen times, then removed the cover and wiped away condensation and dried the plugs. It still would not start. I cursed the engine, the river, the men, my complicity in all this madness.

The rainforest had come alive at dawn and now echoed with a piercing dissonance; whistling and trumpeting, the howling of monkeys, shrilling insects, birds whose combined calls blended into a continuous ringing noise.

Finally the outboard sputtered, caught. I turned the prow upstream toward the mission. A flock of parrots flew halfway across the river, panicked, swooped around, and returned to the trees.

I looked back toward the outpost. The veiling mist was crimson with firelight and shot through with spiraling orange sparks. The entire outpost was burning: the pier, the barracks and sheds, the headquarters building, and it appeared that the canefield had caught fire too.

Now, round a gentle curve in the river, I could see the great cross and mission complex. The cleared land was sliced into variously sized squares and rectangles that fitted together like the pieces of a puzzle: the church and churchyard, the cluster of missionary cottages, strips of cultivated land, livestock pens, the rows of conical thatched huts in the native section of the compound, and the airfield on a patch of grassy land. A small airplane and Betancourt's helicopter were parked at the west end of the field. And behind it all was the high, dark, green wall of the forest.

I put on my sunglasses, tied a bandana over my lower face, and angled the skiff toward shore. Troxel waited for me on the beach. Colonel Troxel. He had pulled a woman's fine-meshed stocking over his head to make identification difficult. Fold-around sunglasses concealed his eyes. Troxel was a big man and looked even bigger in his combat outfit, but the stocking made his head appear abnormally small. He stalked the beach impatiently.

The giant cross was ten yards behind him; the church another sixty yards beyond that. For an instant I saw a pale face framed in one of the bell tower ports, then it vanished.

Troxel helped me drag the skiff up onto the sand.

"What the fuck happened up there?" he asked. "It sounded like the end of the world as we know it. There wasn't supposed to be that much resistance."

"Long story. How did it go here?"

"Smooth, quick, clean. No shooting, no conflagration. I was afraid you might be a fucking wild psycho cowboy, Jack. Was I right?"

From our position we could look downriver and watch three separate columns of smoke rise and then twine together in a single thick braid. Troxel removed a half-pint silver flask from his hip pocket and gave it to me. The flask contained harsh brandy. He had torn a hole in the stocking so that he could drink and smoke.

"I suppose you deserted your troops, too," he said.

"They'll be along soon."

We heard a pair of explosions, the second louder and deeper than the first, and looked downriver to see a fireball rising up through the mist and smoke. The fuel storage tanks had blown.

"Christ," Troxel said.

Then fifty-caliber ammunition began detonating in a continual stuttering that—even while knowing it was happening four miles away—made both Troxel and me flinch.

Troxel, smiling a little, slowly shook his head. "I don't know, Jack. I think you might just have taken some casualties."

"Took one earlier," I said. "Zonzo."

"Zonzo. The simple-minded kid?"

"It was friendly fire."

"Don't you love that? 'Friendly fire.' And 'collateral damage.' Love it, Jack, always have."

I thought he might be half drunk; drunk on brandy, or triumph.

A hundred or so Indians were being detained in a corral below their thatch village. Troxel's soldiers—some of them perhaps related to the captives—casually guarded the prisoners. They didn't require much guarding; there was no rebellion in them. They were glum, docile Indians, dressed in donated cast-off polyester.

"Where's Anna?" I said. We had run into Troxel in the bar one night before she had left, and I had introduced them.

"The Fontenot woman? Don't know. I've got some people looking for her."

"Looking—why?"

"Jack, come on. She knows us. We'll find her. She might be

hiding in one of the bungalows. Or she might have run off into the forest. Some of the Indians ran away. Old ones, mostly."

"Good for the old ones."

"All right, now—what the fuck happened up there?"

I told him. We had gone into the headquarters building and found the blackened, bloated corpses of the three officers. They had been dead for several days. The stench was overwhelming; grenades and M-16 fire had punctured the corpses and allowed the gases to escape.

It was the same in the barracks except that we found a single survivor among the twenty-three deliquescent bodies. The man was barely alive, blind and paralyzed, unable to move or speak. Roger Clay killed him. That was all right, it had to be done; but I hadn't liked the way Clay eagerly volunteered for the job, nor the glint in his eyes when he did it.

"I ordered the men to burn it all."

"Sure. Christ. But what killed them?"

"A poisonous batch of cane alcohol, I think. They had a still, and there were a lot of bottles and glasses around."

"Not disease?" Troxel looked at me as if I might be the carrier of a lethal new plague.

"Maybe," I said. "But I think it was the booze."

We had found five dead Indian prisoners in the underground jail. They had died of suffocation or dehydration. Naturally, none of the soldiers, sick and dying themselves, had been able to bring them water or open the hatch. It was terribly hot in that concrete bunker-like jail, with little ventilation and not much space.

"Fever, pestilence," Troxel said. "Jesus."

"We found some women, too," I said. "Girls, really. Indian girls. One in the headquarters building, two in the barracks."

"Well, shit."

"I'm going to take a walk," I said.

"Sure, walk it off. But stay close, we should be out of here in ten minutes."

The church was narrow and deep with a corrugated steel roof and rows of rough benches on either side of the central aisle. Four steps led up to a platform which contained a lectern, an old upright piano, and a railed choir stall. A door on the back wall led into the dirt-floored belfry shaft. The vertical ladder ascended thirty feet to an open trapdoor. I climbed the ladder and hauled myself up into the tower.

Anna Fontenot was sitting with her back against the wall beneath the east port. She recognized me immediately despite my uniform and the bandana covering my face.

"Don't hurt me," she whispered. She wore peppermint-striped pajamas and felt slippers. She was wide-eyed, her breathing rapid and shallow, and her face, pale with fear, looked sculpted out of translucent wax in the light.

"Hello, Anna." I pulled down the bandana.

"Please, Jack."

There was a bronze bell dimpled with hammer marks and green with patina. Four open window ports looked out over the cardinal points of the compass: north to the flashing river; west to the missionary cottages; south to the wall of forest; and east to the Indian village and the cultivated land and the airstrip.

"You were right to hide," I said. They would have killed her.

"Please don't hurt me."

"I would never hurt you, Anna."

"Are you going to kill me?"

"Anna, we spent time together, nights together. Don't you know me from that?"

"I won't ever mention you, I swear."

What did Anna see in me that I did not recognize in myself?

Outside now, three armed men—Betancourt, Herrera, and Baltazar—were herding the missionaries and their families down toward the beach. Troxel, hands on his hips, watched them approach.

"Why are you doing this?" Anna asked.

"It's complicated."

"Those poor people. God."

"The hostages won't be harmed."

"Won't be harmed! Jack, you're crazy. You think you can terrorize people, kidnap them, and say they won't be harmed?"

Anna's fear and anger were blending together into a confusion that might end in hysteria.

"Stay calm," I said. "You'll be all right."

"This is lunacy!" she cried.

"Don't attract attention to yourself, Anna. Do you understand?"

The missionary group was forced to sit in a row on the beach. There were eleven of them; four adults, a couple of adolescents, and five small children. Two families, probably.

The rotor of the helicopter started turning and at the same time I heard a low, reverberant buzzing from upriver—my men were on their way down in the aluminum boat.

"We'll be going soon," I said.

Anna closed her eyes and bowed her head over her drawn-up knees.

"You'll be okay."

I looked out the east port. The hundred-plus Indians penned in the corral were docile. The men were tame. The women suckled their babies. None showed interest in the proceedings. They had been coaxed and bribed and coerced out of the forest, turned from hunters and farmers, deprived of their religion and tribal culture, their collective past. They were deracinated. They had become tourists in other people's nightmares.

Troxel, standing near the giant cross, was looking up toward the bell tower. I could not determine the exact trajectory of his stare because of his insect-eye sunglasses.

"Anna," I said. "Did you have time to research your article, talk to the Indians?"

She did not reply.

"Curious, isn't it, that with over seven billion people on the planet, there isn't room for a few hundred stone-age people. Well, hell, they don't produce, they don't buy, they don't sell, they don't have the correct beliefs."

Anna had buried her face in her palms. She was trembling. Now she looked up, and said, "God, Jack, you aren't really taking a moral stance on the plight of Indians, are you?"

Now, down on the beach, Betancourt and his aides were selecting the hostages. They stalked among the frightened people, pointing, gesturing, commanding—little gods.

I said, "You see me as amoral, but—"

"*Im*moral."

"—but I've fought them all my life. The Troxels and Betancourts, and the people who direct them. I've tried to fight on the right side, when there was one."

"And now you've joined the wrong side."

"No. It might look that way, but no."

Now the big aluminum boat, trailing a frothy wake the color of root beer foam, was angling in toward the beach. I counted the passengers: ten men, plus Roger Clay. Zonzo's body had been left behind, either buried or burned. Clay stood erect in the prow, pointing this way and that, issuing irrelevant orders to men who knew no English.

"I'll be going soon," I said.

"Go, then. Please, just go."

Now Betancourt separated four from the missionary group: two men, a woman, and a twelve- or thirteen-year-old girl. The hostages were eager to please. They moved awkwardly in their fear. When Betancourt selected a woman with a small child, Troxel intervened, and the two were allowed to return to their place.

"Anna, I don't have it with me, but I found your legacy. It was concealed in your father's hotel room. You're rich."

"Go. Why can't you just go?"

"I'll see that you get the objects."

Betancourt and his men were herding the four hostages diagonally up the grassy slope toward the helicopter. The captives moved with a queer lack of grace, like exhausted people, or drunks. You can half forget how to walk if you're frightened enough. You can forget your name.

The boat had landed. Clay walked up the beach and stood next to Troxel. They talked for a moment, then both men turned and stared toward the bell tower.

The four hostages and Betancourt and his two men climbed into the helicopter, and a moment later it rose straight up for a hundred feet, tilted, flew over the beach, and rapidly clacked downriver.

Now the men were boarding the two aluminum boats for the return to camp. Troxel and Roger Clay hadn't moved; they stood together near the giant cross, looking up toward the bell tower. I considered how easy it would be to kill them both. Clay drew his pistol and walked a dozen paces toward the church before Troxel called him back.

"Anna," I said. "I'm going to fire off a few rounds. You won't be hurt."

She looked at me in terror.

I lifted my rifle.

She squeezed her eyes shut and turned her head to the side.

I fired a burst into the planks a yard away from her head. Anna cried out, touched her cheek, and looked up at me. Her cheek and hand were bloody. A wooden splinter had penetrated her face below the cheekbone.

"Keep down. Don't move." I leaned down and as gently as possible removed the sliver.

She touched her fingertips to the wound and stared at me. I smeared some of her blood over my shirt. My hands were also bloody. Troxel would see the blood and believe that I had killed her.

"Goodbye, Anna," I said.

TWELVE

The sun was well above the trees when we launched the boats and started upriver. All of the mist had burned away. Troxel and I and eight of the men were in the lead boat; Clay and the others followed a hundred yards behind. We were motoring fast against the current and the bows sheered off glassy sheets of water that left rainbow mists suspended in the air. We were going much too fast; if the helmsman lost the channel we would pile onto the rocks.

"Where is Betancourt taking the hostages?" I asked Troxel.

"To the capital—Mundial. In a roundabout way."

"And Rachel Valentine will plead for their release soon."

"Right."

"I've never heard of anything so cynical."

Troxel grinned. "Slick, isn't it?"

The river narrowed and twisted into a series of tight coils. We held on. Our boat skidded on the sharper turns. Flocks of birds erupted along the shore and circled overhead. The men behind me were grinning at the speed and danger, still high on adrenaline.

Troxel, speaking loudly to be heard above the engine noise, said, "The Fontenot woman was hiding in the bell tower?"

I nodded.

"Maybe you shouldn't have gone looking for her. Just let her be."

"I suppose."

"She recognized you?"

"Yes, when I crawled up into the tower."

"Then you had no choice."

"No." Troxel looked down at my hands, where some of Anna's blood could still be seen. "I spent a night with her at the hotel."

"I know."

"I liked her," I said.

"Roger volunteered to do it. Maybe that would have been better."

"Roger would have enjoyed it," I said.

"It's tough, Jack," Troxel said in a tone that he probably thought sounded sympathetic, "but she had to die. There was no other way, really. We're playing for huge stakes."

"Right."

We passed through the last coil in the series. The river ran straight for a few miles and the channel deepened.

"Look," Troxel said. "I'm sorry about keeping you in the dark. I just wasn't sure I could trust you."

I shook my head. "All those lies."

He grinned.

"Do you trust me now?"

"Sure, Jack. You've proven yourself."

"Implicated myself."

"There's that."

"I nearly called off the raid on the river station."

"That was what I was afraid of. But you didn't call it off. Why should I distrust you now? You led an assault on a government outpost and the entire detachment was killed. They were already dead or dying, but no one will ever know that. You took out the Fontenot woman. That was hard, that was tough, but you did what you had to do. And you're involved in the kidnapping of the missionaries. Of course I trust you now."

The recitation of my crimes said, *We own you.*

"What's next?" I said.

"We're going to Mundial."

"What about the boys?"

"They'll be paid off and told to disperse."

"They'll talk, some of them."

"Sure. There'll be a lot of talk, most of it contradictory, exaggerated—a bunch of babble. Cheer up, pal. Like Thomas Jefferson said, we'll either hang together or hang separately."

"That makes me feel much better. But it was Ben Franklin."

"You Point guys and your history." He laughed and punched my shoulder. "You have entered the machine—the machine of history. Jacko, with lots of guts and lots of luck we can alter the course of events. Hell, we can change the world."

PART THREE
ASSASSINS

THIRTEEN

Two days later Troxel, Roger Clay, and I flew to the capital in a chartered Cessna. I half-slept during the 300-mile flight, vaguely aware of the changing engine pitch and the drone of voices, and fully awakened only when the aircraft entered a circling pattern high above the city. It was a clear day: the air had a liquid sparkle and you could see mountain tops—like islands on a foamy sea—rising above the clouds to the south.

The city below was a symmetrical arrangement of cubes and rectangles set in the grid of streets. From this height you could see the nucleus of the old city, enclosed by crumbling stone walls, and the spread of the modern city, which had escaped the walls and spilled out over the surrounding countryside.

Troxel, sitting across the aisle, buckled his seat belt. He stared straight forward. The boils on the back of his neck had swollen into a large scarlet lump, and he was careful about the way he moved his head.

The plane banked and began to steeply descend toward the airport southwest of the city.

"Got your extra head in your luggage, Jack?" Troxel asked. "Is the head safe?"

"You bet," I said.

"You talk to it at night? Confide in it?"

"We chat. Gossip."

"Keep that goddamn thing away from me."

"No problem. The head doesn't like you."

"Yeah? Maybe it's thinking too much."

"It wonders what comes next."

"Tell it to be patient, be cool."

"I'll do that."

"You're a funny guy," Troxel said. "And weirder since your wife died."

I reached over and grabbed him by the collar and pulled him toward me. "Don't mention her name again. I mean it." He didn't move. I stared into his eyes for a few seconds and then pushed him away. At that moment the plane bumped and skidded over a patch of rough air, then smoothed out, and the angle of descent was reduced. Troxel smoothed out his shirt front but said nothing.

Roger Clay, sitting in the seat ahead of Troxel, awakened and yawned and looked around with his mean little eyes. He began polishing his glasses with a soiled handkerchief. He resembled the kind of heavy, squinty boy who bullies the small kids in grammar school. Every school has one. Roger was that fat boy, grown up, and with his bullying nature well evolved toward sadism. Little Roger had punched small kids, tortured cats, molested girls; big Roger had recently taken pleasure in shooting a dying man.

"We're going to stay real close to you in Mundial," Troxel told me, as if nothing had happened between us.

"You mean I'm a prisoner?"

"Nah. Nothing like that. But we've got to protect you. Keep you clean. This is a very sensitive business."

"I understand," I said.

"You're the wild card."

"The joker in the deck."

"I'm not fucking around, Jack. Discretion is imperative."

"I hope so," I said. "I hope so."

FOURTEEN

People who live and work in the vicinity of an international airport are accustomed to strangers, foreigners, and aren't likely to remember you if you behave normally. Troxel, Roger Clay, and I checked into a big airport hotel on the outskirts of the capital. We wore conservative business suits. We carried expensive luggage. We registered under false names. I signed the register left-handed with a smeary felt-tipped pen. We didn't overtip or complain about the service or bring women into our rooms. We were American businessmen, corporate cyborgs, and very serious because making money is more serious than damnation.

After two days we checked out and registered in a nearby, almost identical hotel, using different names; and again, two days later, we moved to another hotel.

In all three hotels, for all six days, our rooms were aligned on one of the upper floors; Troxel on one side of me, Clay on the other. I was under a sort of house arrest. Troxel was gone much of the time; he usually left early in the morning and returned well after dark. He was arranging things, coordinating, conspiring. It was Clay's task to watch me, but he had help; half a dozen big, impassive men who worked in teams. They waited in pairs outside the hotel, and followed me down to the corner newsstand or to a café. They were local hard men, cops or former cops, I was sure; men with watchful eyes and souls the size of gravelstones.

One night Troxel phoned and told me to join him in his room. The door was unlocked. He had just showered and wore a pair of white shorts printed with a pattern of four-leaf clovers. The welted pits and whorls of scar tissue on his torso were sharply defined against the redness of his skin. His neck now sported several boils. The man had the worst skin I'd ever seen.

"Scotch?" he asked.

"No. I'm not going to drink anything until after the shot."

He sat on the edge of the bed. I took the desk chair.

"Getting impatient, are you, Jack?"

"Get rid of the thugs," I said.

"Can't do that."

"They're just more men who'll have peculiar stories to tell after this thing goes down."

"We've got to shelter you. You're the invisible man, Jack."

"It seems like a very sloppy business."

"But it isn't, you're wrong. The stakes are so high, the details so tricky . . . There's a lot you don't know, have no need to know. It isn't enough to do it, pal, we've got to get away with it. You understand? Concentrate on your job. Leave the big picture to us."

"What's the big picture look like today?"

"There's been a tremendous stink about the kidnappings in this country and in the States. You know that. Tomorrow, our Rachel is going to make an impassioned speech in Tulsa. She'll deplore terrorism in the strongest possible terms, come out in favor of religious freedom, plead for the release of the innocent, noble missionaries. And she'll announce that she's coming here to personally negotiate with the terrorists to free their hostages. Et cetera."

"Maybe I can catch her speech on TV."

"No doubt."

"So she'll arrive here late tomorrow?"

"Early the day after."

"I want to see her."

"I didn't hear that."

"Tell her when she arrives that I want to see her."

"Impossible."

"Tell her."

"It's stupid."

"It can be arranged. It might reassure her, steady her nerves at the right time, if we meet."

"Don't push."

"Fix up a meeting with her, Troxel."

"I may have made a mistake with you," he said. "I hope not. But mistakes can be erased."

"Not always."

"You're reckless, Jack, wild. A psycho. I didn't know that."

"Of course you knew it."

He stood up. "Sure you won't have a drink?'

"I'm sure."

He walked to the drink cart and poured a few ounces of whiskey over a glassful of ice.

"There's something else," I said.

"No, there's nothing else."

"I want some money. I've heard talk of money, big talk, but I haven't seen any."

"We'll take good care of you, Jack."

"A man can starve to death on promises. I want two hundred and fifty thousand dollars in cash."

"Back off now. I mean it."

"Make it in old bills, clean money. None of that crisp, consecutively numbered currency."

"Wake up. I couldn't get hold of that amount in cash in just a few days even if I wanted to—and I don't want to. What is this shit? Get on board, man."

"The candidate can bring the money down in the plane."

"Are you crazy?"

"She isn't a bag lady? Then locate your bagman and get me my money."

"You push much too hard. Pretty soon you're gonna get pushed back."

"Troxel, I didn't agree to do this because I'm a Party loyalist."

He slammed down his glass. "All right, you bastard. I'll see if I can get you some earnest money—say fifty thousand."

I shook my head.

"Jack, you're on the team or off it. I like you, you know that. You piss me off every chance you get, but I still like you. But there are people who don't trust you. I can't protect you if you continue to act like a fucking headcase."

"Two hundred and fifty thousand."

"Now people are looking at me funny. Because I recommended you, because I hired you for this job. You see the position you put me in? I don't want a bullet in my head. Do you want a bullet in your head, Jack?"

"Does Rachel Valentine?" I got up and walked to the door.

"Jack." Troxel stared hard at me for maybe ten seconds, then he exhaled and said, "I'll see what I can do."

I opened the door, paused. "Troxel, what have I ever said or done to make you think I'm an imbecile?"

"Go on, get the hell out of here."

*   *   *

The hotel provided satellite TV reception, so I was able to watch Rachel Valentine's Tulsa speech the next morning. She addressed a large crowd in a park at the center of an impressive complex of buildings that was the headquarters of the Children of God Ministry. They had sponsored the Iracundo river mission.

At first Rachel Valentine spoke in conversational tones. She explained the plight of the kidnapped missionaries—the dedicated fold who had devoted their lives to ministering to the Isquito Indians, those poor, lost souls. Then, speaking louder, she described, as told by "survivors," the dreadful night when cruel renegades had massacred two-score young soldiers (just boys, really) at a nearby army outpost while at the same time other renegades had terrorized the Indian villagers and brutally dragged off four hostages—one a thirteen-year-old girl. She skillfully modulated her tones. She knew when to raise her voice in anger, when to lower it to an effective whisper. Unlike many women orators, her voice did not sound strained or shrill on higher registers. And she was always aware of the positions of the television cameras.

She paused, as if wondering at the enormity of such crimes, and then told the crowd that even the terrorists, even those brute killers, were fellow humans and fellow sons of God, and now she pleaded with them, she begged them to please free those innocent people, and in return she would ensure that their political complaints would be heard. Yes, she wished to speak to them, reason to them, even to help them if she could. And if it were only money, damned money, why then she herself would raise funds to ransom the hostages.

She became calm, reflective, and after a silence, as if the thought had just occurred, she vowed to interrupt her very busy schedule to go to South America and personally negotiate the release of the missionaries. The crowd's mood ranged from indignation to fury to a sort of dreamy passivity depending on the text of Rachel's speech and the emotion evident in her voice and posture.

She was more attractive on television—moving, gesturing, smiling, frowning—than in the still photos published in the news magazines. She was not beautiful. You thought, watching her, that she probably had been beautiful a year ago and might be beautiful next year, but now she looked a little plump, a bit frowzy, tired. I supposed that she deliberately muted her looks and sexuality in order to gain the trust of voters.

The speech was trite, standard political rabble-rousing; but Valentine had talent and style, she turned the clichéd thought and leaden words into oratorical gold, she convinced you of the quality of her passion and the purity of her heart. It was comical in a sour way. Terrorists, hostages. They were *her* terrorists, *her* hostages, and their imminent deliverance was cynical political theater. She was something, this Rachel Leah Valentine.

After her speech, the reporter onsite in Tulsa and two studio analysts agreed that Rachel's emotional appeal to the terrorists and her vow to travel to South America to personally plead for the release of the hostages was further evidence of how far from the mainstream the American Patriotic Party's campaign was. And, to say that she would, if necessary, try to raise ransom money herself, was so naïve, so wacky, that it was safe to say that the APP had committed political suicide this fine afternoon.

A studio talking head summed it up in concise talking-head style: "Rachel Valentine and the American Patriotic Party have only recently emerged from obscurity, and now it seems certain that they'll soon return to the same place."

Just wait, buddy, I thought: wait until she parades those freed missionaries before the cameras; wait until you see her, on the evening news, take an assassin's bullet between those shapely breasts.

So far my name had not been associated with the "massacre" of the soldiers or the seizing of the four hostages. Anna Fontenot had not denounced me to the authorities. She must, I thought, be very frightened of me. Terrified. I was, at least in that respect, a genuine terrorist.

FIFTEEN

I unpacked the rifle while Troxel smoked a cigarette at the creek's edge. Beyond him, Clay trudged downslope toward a grove of poplars. One of the ex-cops, a man named Garza, waited in the car which was parked a couple hundred yards up a dirt road.

It was an old rifle, well cared for; the steel parts were thickly coated with cosmoline, and someone had spent a lot of time rubbing linseed oil into the stock.

We were in a pretty little valley some thirty miles south of the city and ten miles off the main north-south highway. The coarse grass was calf-deep on the valley floor. A fast, clear creek with a pebbly bottom snaked the length of the valley, dividing it into equal, nearly symmetrical halves; wooded hills rose up on both sides, with bigger hills behind them, and at the V-notch at the far end I could see snowy mountains rising steeply out of the foothills.

There was a cleaning kit in the cherrywood case. I wiped away all of the excess grease and then took a rod and ran four gauzy cloths down the barrel. The last patch came out clean. I lifted the barrel section and looked through it toward the sky; the rifling grooves were cleanly incised and there were no rust pits or hot spots. It was a Chinese rifle. I had seen weapons like it in Africa. The Chinese

111

had manufactured many of them during the seventies and provided them to "armies of liberation."

"There's trout in this creek," Troxel called out to me. He pronounced it "crick."

Roger Clay walked toward the grove of poplars. He wore cowboy boots and a cream-colored cowboy hat today. Troxel, forty yards away from me, flipped his cigarette into the creek, yawned and stretched.

There was no serial number or manufacturer's name stamped into the steel, no identifying marks at all. You wouldn't easily trace this rifle. It was a sniper's tool, a bolt action thirty-caliber killing machine cheaply produced and reasonable accurate. It was almost a toy compared to the precision sniper's rifles used by the American military, but it could do the job well enough.

Clay had reached the poplars; he pinned a white square of cardboard to the truck of one tree, then moved crabwise toward another. Troxel, walking along the creek, lifted a hand to touch the mass of boils on his neck.

I assembled the rifle, inserted the bolt. The telescope was encased in a stiff leather tube. Like the rifle, it contained no identifying names or numbers. I secured it to the barrel fittings and removed the front and rear lens caps.

Roger Clay pinned the last of four targets to tree trunks. His eyeglass lenses, when he turned to look back toward me, were silvery disks of light. He waved, then took cover behind a pile of boulders on the left.

The rifle was well balanced, though a couple inches short for my height and build—the Chinese had snipers of small stature in mind, and I was an inch over six feet.

I placed the crosshairs directly on the back of Troxel's neck.

The optics were good at least at this range; there was no peripheral distortion, no lens flares. The mass of crimson boils was pulled right up to the muzzle. I slipped a cartridge into the chamber and closed the bolt with that oiled metallic *snick* that can't be confused with any other sound.

Troxel twisted at the hips and stared back at me. His face filled my field of vision; a meaty, ruddy face pitted by small scars, one eyelid drooping a little, his mouth twisting.

"Hey!" he shouted.

I held the rifle on him for a while longer. Troxel, despite his usual old-comrade routine, seemed to hold me in contempt. That was dangerous for me, and for him. I thought that he ought to fear me at least as much as I feared him and his fellow conspirators.

He swiftly walked toward me. His face was swollen and mottled with rage. "You son of a bitch!" he rasped.

I had never seen a man's face swell up that way. The freckling of tiny scars was a glossy white against his blood-flushed cheeks. Blue veins bulged on his neck and forehead. He stopped a few yards away. The rifle stopped him.

"You cunt!" he said. "You ever do a thing like that again, you're dead."

I said, "If I ever do a thing like that again, Troxel, *you're* dead."

He began pacing about and shaking his hands at the wrists, as if flicking electrical charges of fury from his fingertips. When he had gained control of himself, he said, "Okay, then. Right. Your message received. Now let's see if you can hit one of those fucking targets."

I burned twenty rounds sighting in the rifle. It shot with a flat trajectory at about 200 yards. Troxel had told me that the candidate would be standing 180 yards away during the fake assassination attempt, with a ninety-foot vertical between muzzle and target. The rifle was certainly reliable at that range. I could hit a patch the size of a playing card twenty times out of twenty at that distance. The sighting in was not a complete waste of time. I had gained a little confidence in the rifle. But the telescope would be dismounted now and remounted later for the shot, and any slight error in the calibration or mounting could easily eliminate one candidate from the political campaign. And of course, if it were raining that day, or windy . . .

"What do you think?" Troxel asked while I cleaned the rifle.

"I could do as well with any mass-produced three-hundred-dollar deer rifle."

"So it's an easy shot," he said.

"Then you do it."

"I would, if the object was to kill. That's easy. But it's absolutely essential that Rachel isn't hurt, and that makes it hard. I've got nerve, you know that, but not that particular kind. And," he said grudgingly, "you're a better shot."

"Are you in love with Rachel?" I asked.

"Love? Christ, I hope not." And then, as if surprising himself, he said, "Yeah, I guess I am." A moment later, he said, "Fuck you."

I sat with the driver in the front of the car on the ride back to the city; Troxel and Clay were in back. After a few miles Troxel placed the muzzle of his revolver against the hollow at the base of my skull. I heard multiple clicks as he drew back the hammer. Consciously, I was sure he wouldn't kill me, but my body was without faith; my shirt was almost immediately soaked with sweat and my heart jumped around as if it were trying to jump out of my chest. He held the gun to my head for maybe a minute, then lowered the hammer. Nothing was said by any of us.

*   *   *

Since our flight to the capital was a chartered aircraft, I had been able to bring my 9mm Beretta and three full clips. Now I carried the pistol at all times, and at night I slept with it cocked, safety off, on the bedside table. I had also taken from Paraje two fragmentation grenades. Sometimes, before going to sleep, I amused myself by imagining that I stalked the hallway at 3:00 A.M., kicking in doors and rolling grenades under the beds occupied by Troxel and Clay.

SIXTEEN

On the day before the shoot, Roger Clay followed me down to the hotel coffee shop. He appeared freshly barbered. Roger was the kind of man who could obtain an ugly haircut anywhere in the world, and he had the kind of build that made even an expensive tailored suit look shabby.

He hesitated a moment in the doorway, then walked directly to my booth and sat down.

"Morning," he said.

"Good morning," I said.

"You ready?"

"You bet. As soon as the waitress comes, I'll order breakfast."

"That ain't what I meant."

"What did you mean?"

"You know."

"What?"

"I meant, are you *ready?*"

We both ordered breakfasts of eggs, bacon, juice, and coffee. When the waitress brought the plates, Clay asked for ketchup, and when that arrived he pumped some on his easy-over eggs. He ate with an odd delicacy, like a rough boy who had been taught genteel manners by a spinster aunt.

"I wanted to do it," Clay said.

"Did you?"

"I asked Trox for the job. Before he hired you, I asked to do it."

"And what did Troxel say?"

"He said he didn't think I was quite good enough."

"And you told him . . .?"

"I told him I was plenty good enough."

"Are you?"

"I can shoot," he said.

"Not so loud. A lot of these people know English."

He foxed the English speakers by spelling the word: "I can just plain s-h-o-o-t."

Roger was the weak link in any criminal enterprise.

"Anyway," he said, looking away, "good luck tomorrow."

There was, as always, a duplicity in Clay, a sly air of knowing things that you did not know. He had come to the coffee shop to show me the kinder of his two faces while privately relishing a secret knowledge. It made him feel superior. You were ignorant when he possessed essential information, special orders, and a malice that would soon be rewarded.

"You're going to see her tonight?"

I nodded.

"I asked Trox if I could come with."

"And he said . . .?"

"No."

"Did you ever meet her?"

"Not exactly, but I've stood real close to the lady."

When the waitress brought more coffee to our table, Clay notified her that the ketchup wasn't *American* ketchup. The restaurant would do well to order some real ketchup from the United States of America.

"It's going to rain," Clay told me.

"Is it?"

"Tonight, anyway. Maybe tomorrow too."

"Good news for farmers," I said.

"A hard rain when you pull the . . . lever?" He shook his head. "And maybe a gusty wind with it?" He shook his head again, smirking, enormously pleased that he had given me something to worry about.

I got up to leave, sticking him with the check, but liberally tipped the waitress on my way out. Roger, on moral grounds, did not believe in tipping service personnel.

SEVENTEEN

That evening, with a certain sense of self-mockery, I prepared to practice the assassin's trade. I dressed in black: black shoes and socks, a black summerweight wool suit, and a black tee-shirt. In the black outfit, with my ragged hair and beard, I looked something like the monk Rasputin. He had been a lover, a mystic, and a man very hard to kill. I hoped that at least I might be the latter.

I packed my things in a duffel, wiped all of the room surfaces that might hold a print, then sat down to think. I posed half a dozen problems to myself and in each case failed to arrive at a solution. There was too much I didn't know, too many variables, so much treachery.

Troxel admitted me to his room at eleven-twenty. There was a chemical odor in the air; he was medicating his neck.

"You'd better get those boils attended to," I said. "A staph infection like that can be dangerous."

He pointed to a gym bag that sat on the desk. "There's your money." He waved at a drink cart, and said, "That's forty-year-old cognac. It cost me two hundred bucks. Pour us some, I'll be right back."

"I'm not drinking," I said.

"An ounce won't hurt you. We ought to drink to the occasion."

He went into the bathroom, leaving the door open. I poured two brandies into snifters, a big drink for Troxel, a very small one for me.

"Count the money," Troxel called.

I unzipped the gym bag. It was full of currency wrapped in packets secured by rubber bands. It was mostly old hundreds and fifties, though there were a few packets of twenties as well.

Troxel came into the room. "You aren't going to count it?"

"I trust you," I said.

He smiled, though his eyes didn't. "You're a sweetheart, Jack."

We picked up the glasses. They were good crystal snifters and chimed like fairy bells when we touched them together.

"To a true heart and a true aim," Troxel said.

We drank the brandy.

"All right," Troxel said. "Grab your stuff."

I zipped the gym bag and stuffed it down into my duffel.

"What have you got in there?"

"Tools of the sniper's craft," I said.

Rachel Valentine had arrived in Mundial this afternoon and was staying at a hotel in the modern section of the city, in the center of a dozen square blocks of highrises and luxury shops and cultural institutions. Tomorrow's ceremony, and the fake assassination, would take place in the old city.

Troxel was driving a dented old Volvo. A steady rain was falling. The streets were slick and smoked with vapor and every light was ringed by a hazy corona.

"This is stupid," he said. "You know why things go wrong? Because people are stupid."

"Right," I said.

"The assassin has a secret meeting with the victim the night before the shooting."

"I'll never be identified. Isn't that what you told me?"

Troxel parked in the rear of the hotel, and we ran through the rain to a service elevator. It had padded walls and fluorescent lights protected behind wire screens. A strip of tape covered the lens of a security camera.

Troxel looked at my duffel. "You won't need that," he said. "I'll lock it in the car."

"I'll keep it."

"Goddammit, no one's gonna steal your money."

"I'll keep it," I said.

"You got a gun in there?"

"You bet."

"You can't take a gun with you to see Rachel."

"Why not?"

"Figure it out, dummy."

"Are you afraid I'll shoot her?"

"You're a goddamned pain in the ass," Troxel said.

The elevator halted with a bump and the doors slid open to reveal a big storage room with a firedoor at the far side. Troxel pushed the *No Servicio* button so that no one could summon the elevator to another floor.

"Wait," he said. "I'll make sure no one's around and that the security cameras are taped."

While he was gone I combed my hair and beard with my fingers and arranged my damp clothes. I had an interview—no, an audience—with a candidate for the vice-presidency of the United States.

Troxel returned and led me through the storage room and down a hallway which widened into an alcove that contained a sofa and a couple of chairs. On the right wall was a passenger elevator; on the left, the door to the penthouse suite. I saw three security cameras spaced along the hallway, all with the lenses taped.

"You got twenty minutes," Troxel said, then he pivoted and walked back down the corridor.

I knocked on the door, paused a moment, turned the knob and entered a foyer filled with baskets and vases of plants—a floral tribute to the candidate. Another door, partway open, led into the suite. Rachel Valentine, wearing a bullfighter's outfit, was in the center of the room, passing an imaginary bull. I had interrupted her performing a series of *veronicas*. She ignored me. The magenta and gold cape filled with air, flared, with each pass. Years ago I had spent a few months in Madrid, and attended a few *corridas*: she executed the *veronicas* correctly and with style. She inclined her body forward, twisting at the waist, and led the fantasy bull's horns past her thigh, then finished the series with a flashy *serpentine*.

I said, "*Ole!*"

Directly behind her was a white baby grand piano, and beyond that a tall bank of windows that slanted up to a vaulted ceiling. City lights, white and colored, shone like remote galaxies in the darkness outside.

She turned to appraise me. "So you're the man who's going to shoot me."

"With your consent."

She folded the cape and tossed it onto the piano. "You have it."

Her suit of lights was the real thing, several thousand dollars' worth of materials and craftsmanship: very tight bottle-green pants with heavy gold brocade, a short matching jacket, a ruffled shirt with a thin black tie, white stockings, and ballet-type slippers. She was not wearing a *montera*, the mouse-eared hat. Her hair was sleekly combed back into a chignon.

"I wanted to meet you," I said.

"And I, you." She continued to stare at me.

"There are risks."

"Alex told me it was safe."

"Troxel isn't going to take a bullet on his chest."

"He isn't, is he?"

Few women had the figure to wear such a costume. Rachel Valentine was taller than I supposed, with long legs and a narrow waist, and she was slender. No doubt she deliberately dressed to appear a bit heavy, dowdy, when appearing in public—voters might distrust a female candidate so young-looking and attractive.

"What shall I call you?" I asked.

"Rachel. And you're Jack?"

I walked further into the room. She smiled. She was aware of the effect she had on me, on men.

"Would you like a drink?" she asked.

"No, thanks."

"Alex told me you were a drinking man."

"I am. But not now, not until after the shot."

"That's reassuring."

"I'll have a glass of soda water if you have it."

"Of course. Sit down, Jack."

I watched her cross the room to the wet bar. The television cameras could not record her aura, the life in her eyes and hair and skin, the subtle grace of her movements. She was not quite beautiful, but you could fill a room with beautiful women and she would be the one you looked at, thought about, approached if you had the nerve. Of course, it wasn't just her looks; she was a complex and intelligent woman, and maybe a little crazy. Her schemes were crazy. And that hint of madness, danger, intensified her sexual force.

She returned with a glass of red wine in one hand and a glass of soda in the other. For a moment she stared up into my eyes—not a seductive gaze, but a searching one. Her own eyes were hazel, a gold-flecked green with a gold-brown ring around the irises.

There were matching white leather sofas on an elevated platform near the bank of windows. I sat on one, she on the other. She toed off her slippers. Through the rain-blurred windows, the lights of the city were symmetrically arranged along the grid of streets.

I said, "If you could be any historical figure, who would you choose?"

"I don't know."

"Think of someone."

"The first Queen Elizabeth?"

"The Virgin Queen? I don't think so."

She smiled. "Let me think. All right, then. I guess I would choose to be Cleopatra."

"A suicide?"

"It was not an ignoble death."

"Still, Cleopatra—a famous concubine."

"She was Queen of Egypt. Now it's your turn. Who would you choose to be?"

"Either Caesar or Marc Antony."

"Gallant of you. It this some sort of pop-psychology game?"

"The question just popped into my mind."

"No," she said. "I don't see you as a classical figure. There's something medieval about you."

"Medieval how?"

"I'm not sure."

"Medieval as in backward? Primitive?"

"I've studied your curriculum vitae," she said.

"My dossier."

"Since West Point you've led a roguish life as a modern *condottiere*. Or go back further—a knight errant, the original free lance. One of those desperate medieval characters filled with exalted notions of honor and service, but who really were just opportunistic bandits and killers. Hired swords. Thugs in armor."

"You're awfully judgmental for a demagogue."

She laughed. "What interests me about people is the gap between what they think they are and profess to be, and their actions. The disparity between the ideal and the real."

"The disparity is often large," I said. "Especially among politicians."

"Indeed." She mocked me with her eyes and smile.

"And you, how large is the gap between your ideal and real selves?"

"Almost nonexistent. I am what I am, and no other."

"You believe your public and private selves are identical?"

"I didn't say that. But I know when I'm being hypocritical. It's always a tactical choice. Humans are hypocritical. It's who we are. It's how we make it from Monday through Friday."

"Not always."

"No, there are rare individuals who have no hypocrisy in them. Jeanne d'Arc? There was no guile in her. They burned her at the stake. They burned Giordano Bruno at the stake, too, for believing the same things that Galileo believed, but the Inquisition didn't kill Galileo, because he was a hypocrite. Jesus? Socrates? What happened to them?"

"I think you're missing something here."

She sipped her wine, set the glass down on the coffee table, and leaned toward me. She appeared both amused and combative. She was a politician: she liked to argue, and she was good at it; she had the politician's gift for sophistry, logic-chopping.

"Are you so honest?" she asked. "You were expelled from West Point for cheating on examinations."

"I was expelled for violating the honor code."

She smiled. "Yes?"

"The others were expelled for cheating. Joseph Cavenaugh and I were expelled for not reporting that they cheated when we had knowledge of it."

"Isn't that a rather fine distinction?"

It seemed that I would spend my entire life explaining this one incident. "The distinction," I said, "between cheating and refusing to denounce friends who did cheat."

"You worry me," she said.

"Because of my poor character?"

"No, because of what you regard as your good character. I'm concerned by your vanity and pride—the cadet who chooses to be dishonored and lose his career rather than denounce his friends. His cheating friends. Are you a man who might decide that I'm a threat to the American republic, and put a bullet through my brain?"

"It isn't too late to get someone else. Roger Clay is eager for the job."

"Oh, I think you'll do, Jack."

"And how will the country, the American people, the world, do if you're miraculously elected to office in the fall?"

"Well, first, I wouldn't have the power to do much of anything. I'm only the vice-presidential candidate."

"The presidential candidate is old and apparently *non compos mentis*."

"But he's filthy rich and deeply respected for that. We Americans are fools about money, fools about the people who have accumulated money. The source doesn't matter. Money is seen as a negotiable virtue."

"Say he dies in office. How would you guide the country?"

"What do you expect me to say—a car in every garage and a chicken in every pot? Who knows what's going to occur next week, let alone next year. War, pestilence, famine? Peace, health, prosperity? How much control do you think political leaders have over events? We're all—the whole world—on a runaway train. If I were president I would do fine things, great things, if they'd let me—the people and the Congress and the bankers and the global corporations and various irrational, hostile entities. You're a baby, Jack, if you think politicians have the power to solve problems that actually are inherent in human nature. Greed, envy, hatred. Powerlust, fanaticism, sadism. It's very hard to do good."

"But easy to do harm."

"Yes. Oh yes."

"You haven't got a chance of winning."

"Maybe not. But what a wild, crazy, exhilarating ride this is! We're already, in a small way, shaking the country. I am me, laughing at it all, and at the same time I'm another, a sort of tacky pop-goddess who's being created day by day, who's evolving into God knows what—Superbitch?"

"You don't talk that way to the electorate."

"Have you concluded that I'm an idiot?"

"Not an idiot. Certainly not. But not completely sane, either. Look at it; forming a guerrilla unit to raid an army outpost and mission, taking hostages, arranging a fake assassination."

She regarded me with mock solemnity, her brows furrowed. She was amused. I was a source of mirth for the candidate.

It was raining harder now. The sky outside pulsed with lightning, dimmed and brightened, and the steamy plate glass windows vibrated from the concussions.

Our conversation was mostly sparring, a cool testing of each other, but it had gradually turned into intimacy. I could feel it, and I knew she could also. It was talk conducted on two levels: there were the words, trivial and hostile; and there was a contrary emotional undercurrent. This was a form of courtship. We were flirting in a perverse way.

"My time is up," I said.

"Yes. I must rest."

"I wish I had another twenty minutes."

She half-smiled, and her nostrils flared. "Yes. Too bad. But it would take nearly that long to get me out of these pants."

"It's a pretty costume, but an odd one."

"You don't like it?"

"Well, a bullfighter's outfit, a suit of lights. It does flatter you, but it seems odd."

"I would go crazy if I couldn't be eccentric in my private life. The people and the cameras absorb you, drain away your essence. Your lies empty you. That's why politicians and celebrities are so vapid, robotic—there's a kind of vampirish soul-sucking that takes place in public life. I have my own ways of restoring myself to myself. I practice with the cape, I dance, I read, I fuck."

"I could get those pants off in just a couple of minutes," I said.

"Jack, I'd love to sleep with you tonight. For the usual reasons—you're a big, goodlooking guy with a strong jawline. You do know that's what we respond to, right? And that scar on your cheekbone—well. And maybe for a kinky reason as well. Do you know what that is?"

"Because you think I might possibly kill you."

"Yes. That's very exciting. Why is that, do you suppose?"

"Let me stay."

"I want to fuck you, I really do. But we can't now. Let's save it. We'll have each other soon, I promise."

"A special incentive to shoot well."

"Yes. And I am special, Jack."

Politicians know how to dismiss a visitor without obvious incivility. Rachel finished her wine, set her glass down on the coffee table, stood up, and began drifting toward the door.

Following, I said, "Wear a thick Kevlar vest tomorrow. Wear two, if they're thin ones. A rifle bullet has terrific impact and penetration power, even at one hundred and eighty yards."

When we reached the door, she halted, then backed into the room.

"Jack. Shoot when you see me like this." She placed her feet together, twisted her body a little to the right, and spread her arms.

"Isn't that pose a little obvious?"

"Like this. I'll hold the position for a moment. Shoot then."

She stood in the center of the room, feet together, upper body inclined slightly to the right, arms lifted and spread.

"Remember to move away from the microphones. You don't want the bullet deflected."

"Like this, Jack."

"Bang," I said.

"Yes."

She relaxed and started walking toward me. "Shoot straight and true, lover. If you decide to kill me, do it cleanly, don't allow me to suffer."

She came close, melted into my arms, and kissed me. We tasted each other in a gentle, slow way. Pressed together, kissing, we moved our bodies in a sort of dry coitus. Then, when she started to draw away, I kissed her again, violently, hurting her. I let her go. My passion and anger surprised us both.

"I'm sorry," I said.

Her lips were already beginning to swell. They would be swollen and bruised tomorrow.

"Hold some ice against your mouth," I said. "That will keep down the swelling."

There was no fear or anger in her eyes. Her mouth still open, she breathed heavily.

"Sorry," I said.

"Was that the kiss of death, Jack?" she said.

"I don't know. Maybe—for one of us."

EIGHTEEN

Troxel was sullenly waiting for me in the storage room. We entered the elevator. He pressed the *tierra* button and we began to slowly descend. I could smell the astringent lotion he used to medicate his carbuncles, the alcohol on his breath, and the licorice that was meant to disguise the alcohol.

"Well?" he said.

"We had a nice chat."

"You were in there a long time."

"About thirty minutes."

"Lots of talk."

"We made love most of the time."

"Don't fuck with me tonight, pal."

"Does she have a boyfriend? A lover?"

"Yeah, every male voter is her lover. Unrequited."

"And women voters?"

"Daughters, sisters, mothers, grannies."

"She's a movie star," I said. "A vampire, a *femme fatale*, Cleopatra. And she's delusional."

"Think again," Troxel said.

The elevator reached the ground floor and the door hummed

open. Troxel cocked his head and looked at me for a time. He said, "You really didn't fuck her, did you?"

"No."

"I knew it. The lady's got class."

I believed that Troxel might have killed me then and there if I had said "Yes." He was infatuated with her.

The storm had passed off to the east, and there was only a fine mist in the air now. We drove down a wide boulevard for a few miles and then turned off into the old city. There were few streetlights there, few lights of any kind, and the cobblestone streets were narrow and crooked. We passed a crumbling section of the seventeenth-century wall. Troxel did not speak. The windshield wipers squeegeed away the speckling of mist; the eyes of a cat reflected yellow in the headlight beams. The place smelled of stone and wetted dust and woodsmoke and sewage. The place smelled four hundred years old.

"She wouldn't let a jerk like you touch her," Troxel said.

"You're right. She's saving herself for Julius Caesar."

The street abruptly emerged into the city's Plaza Mejor, a huge square of irregular black paving stones that gleamed wetly in the opalescent night.

Troxel parked the car. I got my duffel and we walked away from the curb. Rain-dimpled puddles reflected the faint light. The plaza was a masonry desert; there were no grass or trees or statuary or fountains, just the expanse of flagstones a couple hundred yards square. It was cool now, and quiet except for distant sounds that were funneled down sidestreets and amplified into a persistent humming. I heard remote traffic, tires hissing on wet concrete, the ticking of falling rain, and threaded through it all a music so faint that it might have been imagined. As we approached the center of the square, a flock of pigeons erupted into flight with a soft, explosive sound, like gasoline igniting.

We stopped and stood quietly in the mist. I dropped my duffel.

"This is the place," Troxel said. "How do you feel, Tarzan?"

"Tarzan feel pretty good," I said.

The cathedral with its twin bell towers and copper-sheathed dome occupied the entire west side of the square. The National Palace was to the north; old colonnaded buildings stretched the length of both the eastern and southern blocks.

"There," Troxel said. "Fourth floor, eleven windows over counting from the left."

"Sash windows?"

"Yeah."

We looked south toward a six-story stone building with Gothic windows on the top floor, overhanging cornices, and a parapet topped with a low railing. It was a single long building with three entrances, one on each corner and another in the center. Lights burned in a few of the windows.

"You all set then, pal?"

"I suppose."

"Any questions?"

"I think you told me all I need to know."

"Just be sure to remember this: the helicopter will land on the roof within two minutes of your shot. Get your ass up there quick, I mean double pronto, because the pilot's not likely to hang around long."

"Right."

"You got that sketch I gave you of the building's layout?"

"Got it."

"You might want to walk your escape route to the roof a couple of times tonight. So when it counts, you'll know exactly where you're going."

"Stop fussing, Troxel."

"Christ," he said. "Look at this." He held up his right hand, and even in the dim light I could see its tremor. "Eight, ten hours to go and I'm already shaking. Buck fever, and I'm not even the shooter."

"I'll get going," I said.

"Don't hurt her."

"Relax."

"I mean it, Jack. You understand? Don't hurt her."

We shook hands, and then Troxel surprised me by impulsively grabbing me in an *abrazo*. He hugged me and thumped my back, then stepped away and regarded me with a smile.

"Luck, buddy," he said.

"You too."

"We fight like cats and dogs, but we're comrades, aren't we?"

"We'd better be," I said.

We separated; he went toward the car, I picked up the duffel and walked through the mist toward the building.

A security guard sitting at a desk in the lobby buzzed me inside. He was a white-haired old man dressed in a khaki uniform with brass buttons and a Sam Browne belt, and there was a nickel-plated pistol in his holster. Troxel had given me a plastic laminated building pass, but the guard didn't ask to see it. He was a lonely old guy who wanted to talk: talk about the weather, the prospects of the national soccer team, tomorrow's visit of the *Señora Presidente* of Los Estados Unidos. He thought Rachel was the president. He asked about my accent: Are you a *norteamericano*? I lied: No, *inglés*. Ah, the *inglés* have some very good soccer players.

I said goodnight to the old guard, rode an elevator to the fourth floor, and then walked down the corridor, reading the numbers on the doors. It was an ancient building with high ceilings and hardwood floors and crumbling plaster walls. I passed the offices of lawyers and accountants and dentists and public scribes. No name or title was printed on the door numbered 422. This might be a famous room someday: Here the cowardly assassin lurked, here he ate a cheese sandwich, here he lifted his rifle and killed an angel.

I took a pair of latex gloves from my pocket, pulled them on, then fitted the key Troxel had given me into the lock. The tumblers smoothly turned.

I entered the room, closed and locked the door behind me, and waited. Was I alone? I stood quietly for a minute, peering into the darkness, listening, sniffing the air, trying to intuit this unfamiliar space. Thin rectangles of light outlined the three window shades. Mice scrambled behind a plaster wall. A clock ticked. And I could hear, from somewhere in the lower levels of the building, water rushing through pipes. The room smelled of stale tobacco. Tobacco, wood polish, sweat, mice.

I located a wall switch, turned on the lights, and found myself in a large room which contained six desks, stacks of metal filing cabinets, a humpbacked sofa, and a trestle table littered with newspapers and magazines and pots of rubber cement. The rifle, in its cherrywood case, lay on one of the desks. This was the main room in a suite of offices. The door to my right, apparently not a part of the suite, was locked from the other side with a couple of deadbolts. The door to my left led into a small office with a single desk, and then into a rectangular room that was empty except for offset camera machinery and a battered old printing press.

I returned to the big office, sat at a desk, and skimmed through a few newspapers. These were the offices of a weekly periodical called *Noticias de la Revolución*. It was a communist tabloid that lamented the plight of the suffering people and deplored the fascist rule of their oppressors. The trinity of Marx, Lenin, and Stalin were reverentially invoked. It was solemn, dreary stuff except for the cartoons, which were incendiary. In one, the Statue of Liberty was portrayed as a blowsy whore, naked and holding a phallus aloft in one hand and clutching a sheaf of dollar bills in the other. Small, rat-faced men identified as Latin America's leading politicians were shown hanging from Liberty's teats or climbing mountaineer-style up her massive thighs—the first climber had half vanished into Liberty's cleft. The cartoon was bitter, obscene, even treasonous by local standards, and it was a wonder that the government hadn't by now shot or jailed the cartoonist and the entire editorial staff. But the paper continued to operate because the government chose to allow it. That would change tomorrow, no doubt. Tomorrow the Reds would be implicated in the attempted assassination of an American vice presidential candidate. God help them.

I removed the gym bag from my duffel and counted the money. It was all there, $250,000 in packets of $10,000 each. All of the currency was old and worn. There were no sequentially numbered new bills, and I saw none that looked counterfeit. I removed all of the rubber bands and poured the loose money into an empty wastebasket.

A phone on the next desk twittered like an electronic bird. There were nine beeps, a period of silence, and then five more. I resisted the temptation to pick up the receiver. It might be Troxel, I thought, calling to change or halt the action. But it could also be someone—maybe Troxel—calling to compromise me. Surely the phones of a radical rag like *Noticias de la Revolución* were tapped, the conversations recorded. I made up a bluesy song and chanted the words under breath: *Don't you ring my phone/don't come knocking at my door/don't come 'round/I don't live here anymore. . .*

I got a *gaseosa*, warm now, from the duffel and snapped the top; then dipped again into the duffel for one of the two ham and cheese sandwiches prepared for me last night by the hotel coffee shop. The dusting of talcum powder on the latex gloves I wore did not improve the taste.

The long muscles in my right thigh began to spasm; I pounded them with my fist until the spasms ceased.

The telephone bleated half a dozen times. I got my shaving kit from the duffel and carried it into the bathroom. Orangy water spouted from the tap. The mirror above the sink was webbed with cracks. I took a scissors and cut my hair short, hacked away at my beard, lathered and shaved, then made sure to find every stray hair in and around the sink and on the floor. I had not seen the bald face for a long time, and it looked unfamiliar, like the face of an old acquaintance whose mouth had turned hard, maybe bitter, after several years.

It was twenty minutes to three. The building was silent. There was no traffic on the streets outside. I found a deck of pornographic playing cards in a desk drawer and sat down to try a hand of clock solitaire. The orgiasts, photographed in garish comic-book colors, were young and athletic; but even while most torturously engaged their expressions were abstracted, as if they had retreated to a mental zone of privacy and were thinking about something else, payday, maybe, or shopping. The last card I turned, the Queen of Hearts, looked a little—just a little—like Rachel Valentine.

Troxel's pencil drawing of the building's layout showed my recommended exit after the shot. The route to the rooftop was marked by arrows: down the hall, around a corner and down a shorter hallway to a stairway, up the stairs past the fifth and sixth floors to a fire door. That door opened onto the roof where, Troxel had promised, the escape helicopter would be waiting. I burned the map in an ashtray and stirred the ashes with a pencil.

I rummaged through the duffel and withdrew my pistol and spare clips, the two grenades, and a transistor radio that I'd bought in a hotel gift shop. It was three o'clock—I turned it on. A male news announcer who rolled his Spanish r's in the grand style stated that the four kidnapped American missionaries had been released by their captors. They had just been dropped off (blindfolded and with their hands still bound) just a few blocks away from headquarters of the Federal Judicial Police. A spokesman reported that the ex-hostages were in good condition despite having endured eight days in captivity, and that they wished to express their heartfelt gratitude to God, Rachel Leah Valentine, the government's negotiating team, and all of the people, all over the world, who had prayed for their safety.

There were three six-foot-high sash windows on the north wall. I lifted the shades. Either of the outside windows would serve well enough for the shot. I opened them part way. A four-bladed fan had been inserted in the frame of the middle window. One switch regulated the speed of the fan's revolution, the other reversed its spin. You could adjust it to suck fresh air inward or expel the stale office air. I studied the fan for a time, thinking, and then removed it from the window. It was heavy, about four feet square, and filthy with grease and caked dust. I detached the front and rear protective grills and reinserted the frame into the window space. Now it was just a frame, electronic motor, and fan blades. You might sever a finger if you weren't careful.

I turned off the lights and stretched out on the broken-spined sofa. My ears buzzed. Fatigue scrambled my thoughts. This entire business was like playing stud poker with an opponent who received his cards face-down while you were forced to play the usual way, with four cards up and one down. I had one hole card; Troxel had five.

Rest was essential now. When action is long delayed your adrenaline burns up and leaves you depleted, slow. Athletes often talk about leaving games in the locker room. Experienced athletes and soldiers learn how to control that spurt of adrenaline, save it for the crucial moments which will determine victory or defeat, life or death.

I dozed then, and dreamed that I was a boy sleeping on a cottage veranda while flies buzzed; the boy dreamed that he was an adult who had gone to far places and done strange things, and who now lay drowsing on a musty-smelling sofa in a cluttered foreign room, dreaming of that small boy sleeping on a cottage veranda in fly-buzzing heat. Dreams within dreams within dreams, circular and absurd, but perhaps conveying a coded message that I could not now penetrate. And perhaps not: I might just be cracking a little under the tension.

NINETEEN

At false dawn I got up and moved to an open window. The air was cool and fragrant with the scents of rain and cedar woodsmoke. A police car with a walleyed headlight slowly cruised down the east side of the square. A woman, wrapped and hooded by a ropy shawl, walked diagonally across the paving stones toward the cathedral. She flushed a flock of pigeons which rose in a swirl and, when she passed, settled like confetti. A limping yellow dog emerged from the shadows and began chasing the birds. He had no chance. He knew it; the pigeons knew it. Finally the dog shamefully limped away down an alley.

At six o'clock the church bells commenced a sour clanging. A crescent of sunlight glowed on the copper-sheathed cathedral dome, but the rest of the plaza was in lavender shadow.

The locked office door to my right worried me; one of Alex Troxel's hole cards might lay behind it. I tried the knob; still locked. I went outside, walked a few yards down the hallway and looked at the door numbered 420. *Nuestro Cabello* was printed on the frosted glass. Our...what? Our horse? No, horse was *caballo* in Spanish. Our onion? That didn't make sense and, anyway, I vaguely recalled that onion was *cebolla*, not *cabello*. *Nuestro Cabello* did not sound very sinister, whatever the meaning. I returned to the more sinister offices of *Noticias de la Revolución*.

There was a crackle of static on the transistor radio, perhaps because the sun was rising, but I found a station that alternated music with news. Hamilton Keyes III, the presidential candidate of the American Patriotic Party, had only a few minutes ago arrived at the national airport and would join Rachel Valentine, his vice-presidential candidate, in the ceremonies scheduled to take place later this morning at the Plaza Mejor. The four liberated missionaries would also be present to express their gratitude to the American candidates as well as the leaders of the Republic, who had been instrumental in securing their release.

It was not surprising that the country's bosses were claiming a big share of the credit for freeing the hostages; they were politicians, after all, and eager for the favorable national and international publicity resulting from this even. The fake assassination would chill their enthusiasm. And it was not surprising that Hamilton Keyes had quickly flown down from the States to hustle a part of the acclaim; he too was a politician and, no doubt, jealous of the attention Rachel was receiving.

Sunlight had illuminated the parapet and pediment of the National Palace. People were filtering into the plaza now; churchgoers, lottery ticket salesmen and shoeshine boys, beggars, men pushing wheeled charcoal braziers and food and drink carts out onto the paving stones. One man filled colored balloons from a helium tank. A few boys kicked around a soccer ball. Then a flatbed truck halted in front of the palace and men began assembling the speaker's platform.

I switched on the radio and listened to a woman sobbing about her broken heart, and after the song a newsreader stated that the government, in recognition of the terrorist's good faith negotiations, were offering conditional amnesty to the individuals responsible for the kidnapping of the missionaries and the brutal assault on the army river outpost. Come forth! Surrender your arms and take the oath of allegiance to the legitimately constituted government!

The cathedral bells clanged: eight o'clock. The huge square was about half-filled now, and more people streamed out of side streets and merged into the carnival. The mood was festive. I could smell cooking foods: roasted corn, tortillas, chicken and pork, *cabrito*. Not many people were eating, but the drink peddlers were busy; their carts contained big glass jugs of colored liquids, lime and lemonade, orange juice, watermelon juice, and a beverage the color of lilacs.

The speaker's platform was completely assembled. It had a steep flight of steps and was encircled by a wooden railing. Workmen were busy carrying things up the stairs: microphones and amplifiers, a lectern, chairs, brightly colored banners which were strung around the railing. Then three big flag standards were brought onstage and erected at the rear: the national tri-color, the American flag, and another which displayed a blue crusader's cross on a white field.

The muscle in my right thigh spasmed again, and I thumped it with my fist, hard enough to leave bruises.

Members of a band were gathering on the steps of the National Palace. Spider of sunlight shivered along their brass instruments. They wore royal-blue uniforms with big brass buttons and slinky coils of gold braid. There were about forty of them and they all looked like admirals.

I moved to the center window, lifted the shade, and switched on the fan. The blades spun counterclockwise, expelling the room's air. Papers were sucked off one of the desks; motes of dust spiraled toward the window. It was quiet except for the whirr of the electric motor and a ticking that seemed to echo the tick of the wall clock. I lifted the sill so that there was an open space of eight inches between it and the top of the frame. Vibrations caused the frame to dance a little, but it looked fairly secure; it wouldn't soon dance its way out the window.

My thigh hurt, my eyes were gritty, and there was a ringing in my ears.

At nine-forty the radio informed me that the motorcade was now enroute to the *Plaza Mejor*.

I went to a window. Undulating layers of charcoal smoke, radiant in the sunlight, writhed above the crowd. Cops in pairs moved in a bullying way through the festive mass of people. The band, arranged on the palace steps behind the speaker's platform, began to play a brassy *pasodoble*.

A radio voice informed me that citizens lining the motorcade route—Boulevard of Martyrs—were cheering and throwing flowers, waving flags and singing their national anthem. They were, he said, delirious with patriotic joy. It sounded greatly exaggerated to me. It sounded like bullshit.

A yellow helium balloon escaped a child's grip and ascended. I watched it carefully. It rose straight up for about forty feet and then, like the smoke, was caught in a swirl of air that lifted it in larger and larger revolutions until it was freed and sailed off above the cathedral. Often, in cities, winds were funneled down narrow side streets, heated, compressed, then gusted erratically when reaching an open place like the plaza. The bullet had to penetrate those winds and remain true.

I checked the *Nuestra Cabello* door again to make sure it was still locked, then went to a desk. The radio voice told me that the motorcade had turned off on el Camino de los Heroes. I checked my pistol to make sure it was cocked, a bullet in the chamber, and the safety off. The muscle in my thigh fluttered. This was crazy, of course. I was crazy. I looked down into the wastebasket filled to the brim with loose money. Why not stuff all that green stuff into my duffel, pick it up, and walk out to the street? Take the money and run? Well, no, you had to follow the string all the way to the badger's—or dragon's—lair. Still, I was tempted to take some of the money; I probably would need it later on. Again, no: to take even a dollar would compromise me in my own eyes.

I reached into the duffel and removed the tobacco tin filled with Crowley's—Anna's—gemstones and placed it in my inside suit jacket pocket. It was heavy. The two grenades, one in each of the jacket's patch pockets, were heavier still.

The band was now playing a Sousa march, "Stars and Stripes Forever." The band members had hit their stride. The music blended into the multitude of crowd noises, which sounded a little like the rumble of an approaching freight train. The music, the crowd noises, and the aromas of smoke and cooking foods were all strangely unified into a single perception, as if my senses had been confused by drugs or fever into a kind of synesthesia.

I removed a white dress shirt from my duffel, scissored off the collar, put the collar around my neck, and stapled the wings together. I'd bought a heavy silver cross and chain at the hotel gift shop yesterday; now I placed it around my neck, got up and went into the bathroom to look into the mirror. Black suit, black tee-shirt, turned around white collar, silver cross. *Ego te absolve.*

A string of firecrackers detonated beneath the window. A voice boomed over the loudspeaker, and the band commenced another march.

I got the telescope from the cherrywood case and kneeled at the window. The square was filled; there were at least ten thousand people milling about, eating, drinking, talking, singing, content with the fiesta itself but waiting for something more, something that might excite them toward a heightened (or lowered) consciousness. They wished to be taken out of themselves. They wished to join a powerful collective. They were benign now, but any crowd can quickly turn into a mob.

I assembled the rifle. The bolt worked with a smooth metallic *snick*. The rifle smelled of steel and oil and wood polish and, faintly, burnt gunpowder. It was the smell of my past, the smell of my future.

I went into the bathroom and washed my face with tapwater the color of weak tea. The cracked mirror fractured my image into half a dozen oblique planes, like a Cubist portrait, and gave my eyes a crazed slant.

The telephone let out a single electronic beep, then went silent.

Now the band was playing the popular movement of "Pomp and Circumstance."

Now and then I heard the voices of people passing by in the corridor. A door slammed; a woman laughed; the old elevator doors rattled open. This was for many an ordinary workday—they would observe the ceremony from their office windows. They would be witnesses to pseudohistory.

I returned to the window. My telescope extracted individuals from the mass: the cherubic face of a boy riding on his father's shoulders; a drunken thug careening through the crowd like a running back; a pretty girl waiting with a bright and expectant smile; an old woman whose face was cracked and furrowed like dry mud.

I scanned the building that extended the length of the east side of the square. People looked down on the crowd from many of the windows, and others were lined along the roof parapet. It was no doubt the same in this building—I was just another face looking out of another window.

Blue smoke uncoiling from charcoal fires revolved in the air like spiral nebulae. The great cube of space beyond my window was smoky, and the cathedral's copper-sheathed dome, green with verdigris, glowed like foxfire in the hazed sunlight. At ten o'clock the church bells again tolled, a loud off-pitch clanging whose vibrations continued, like sonic ghosts, to hum in the air ten seconds after the clangor had ceased. Two policemen dragged a rowdy young man into the shade beneath the east side colonnade and began beating him with their truncheons.

The door to the adjoining office had been unlocked. The knob turned when I cautiously tested it. I stepped back. I could see, through the crack between door and frame, that the security bolts had been withdrawn. I listened for a time, but the band music and crowd noises drowned out any sounds from within. Then it came to me: *Nuestro Cabello* meant "Our Hair" in Spanish. The Our Hair people had opened shop.

Then there was a great cheer, and four black Cadillac limousines entered the plaza from the north. They moved at a funereal pace. You could not see anything through the tinted windows. Rockets were launched from the four corners of the square; there were prolonged whistles and parabolas of smoke and then the rockets exploded into stringy flowers of orange and yellow and blue.

The limousines halted in front of the palace. Lackeys rushed forward to open the doors. The American candidates, Hamilton Keyes and Rachel Leah Valentine, exited from one of the limos; the four missionaries from another; and government big shots, in black silk suits and snappy military uniforms, emerged from the other two cars.

They all mounted the steps and took their places in the semi-circle of chairs at the rear of the platform. Politicians, generals, missionaries, security personnel. It appeared that the American Embassy was snubbing the candidates, boycotting this event.

The band started playing the country's national anthem. Three fighter jets in close formation roared low over the square, rattling windows and churning the smoke, and when the noise of the jets faded you could again hear the music and the roaring crowd.

Then the band played "Hail To The Chief." This was a serious violation of protocol, since Hamilton Keyes was only a candidate, not the President of the United States, but I suspected few in the crowd knew, and even less cared.

I went to the desk and tried a hand of solitaire, but I couldn't concentrate. It was awkward turning the cards while wearing latex gloves. I notice that the girl who had posed for the Queen of Hearts also appeared on some other cards, performing strange acts that are usually described in Latin.

A voice boomed over the loudspeakers situated around the square. This was the secondary introducer, whose job was to introduce the primary introducer.

It was hot in the room. Flies buzzed, the wall clock ticked, the fan turned, the soporific voices droned.

The President of the Republic welcomed his people, welcomed the liberated missionaries, welcomed the distinguished American political candidates, welcomed a new day of national reconciliation and international amity. The crowd cheered. The band played a lively *pasodoble*, "Cielo Andaluz," as if the president had just cut ears and tail from a bull.

A general addressed the terrorists in equivocal tones, in effect saying: Accept our generous offer of conditional amnesty or die like rabid dogs.

The male missionary thanked everyone and everything on behalf of Jesus and his coreligionists.

The telephone twittered. I looked at it while it twittered again. For no good reason, I picked up the receiver.

"Luis?" a woman's voice said.

"*Si.*"

"Maria."

"*Buenos días, Maria.*"

"Luis?"

"*Si.*"

"*Te amo,* Luis."

"*Iqual,*" I said. *I love you too.* I hung up the phone.

TWENTY

The area around the platform swarmed with media personnel, television and radio and print. They moved arrogantly, like members of some elite technological priesthood.

I watched Rachel through the telescope. She wore a blue suit with a ruffled white blouse and a wide-brimmed straw hat with a yellow ribbon tied around the crown. She looked lithe and slender. Perhaps she was not wearing a double-thick Kevlar vest, as I had advised. Perhaps she was more concerned about her figure than her survival.

She freed the microphone and moved away from the lectern so that the crowd could clearly view her. "*Muy buenos días,*" she said in a whispery voice, though of course her amplified whispers could be heard throughout the enormous square. "*Los misioneros están libres.*" She smiled. "*Gracias á Dios.*" She moved sideways along the platform. "*Me llamo Rachel,*" she whispered and then her voice rose and took on a husky, throbbing quality. "*Y sus? –El nombre de sus estan la Gente!*" And your name is the People!

The crowd rewarded her tribute to them and her display of passion, not with applause, but with silence. In just a few seconds, a few banal words, she had established rapport with them. Rather, it was more than rapport; it was a sort of complicity. You sensed that she was unpredictable, obscurely dangerous.

A gust of wind lifted her straw hat. Rachel clutched it and, laughing, sailed it like a frisbee into the crowd. Now they cheered. All around her the air flickered with puffs of light as photographers tried to freeze that careless gesture.

Rachel was something new in politics, and especially to these people: a synthesis part demagogue, part evangelist, and part sexy rock star.

Now she began addressing the crowd in English; her words were then repeated in Spanish by a young woman who closely mimicked Rachel's gestures and throaty, emotional tones. The translator was a beautiful dark-haired girl, maybe seventeen, whose performance doubled every rhetorical effect. They were a team, and there was even a physical resemblance between them aside from the difference in coloring.

There were many security men scattered around, on the platform, the palace steps, and at ground level. The government bodyguards, slim and dapper, looked like dancers, mambo *suaves*; Rachel's men resembled pro wrestlers or bouncers at a tough nightclub. I did not see Troxel.

Now Rachel commended the terrorists for heeding her plea to release the missionaries. That was generous, that was good. Now she asked that they repudiate their program of violence. Liberty does *not* come out of the barrel of a gun. Social justice is not achieved through bombings and kidnappings, anarchy. Don't you know? Democracy is a process, not a result.

She obliquely criticized the government by conceding that the insurgents and the people they claimed to represent had legitimate grievances. There was too great a disparity between rich and poor, the educated and the ignorant, the hope-filled and the hopeless. But the terrorists should lay down their arms. The terrorists should come out of night into the bold light of day. The terrorists should enter honestly into the democratic political processes.

She called upon the government to honor their offer of amnesty to the terrorists who, by their action in freeing the hostages, had perhaps, *perhaps*, signaled their willingness to join the people in building a better life for all.

And now, she said, she wished to speak directly to all the assembled people here today, and all the millions of people in their wretched barrios and remote villages. She spoke of hard lives. Hard lives, short lives, hungry children, despair. Not enough food, ever, no medical care, no education, no hope for the future. Did it have to be this way always? Always? Did God truly ordain that a thousand families should drink water fouled by sewage so that a single family might enjoy French champagne? Must a thousand families go hungry so that a single family might spend its summers in Paris?

The generals and politicians onstage were impassive: they could not be pleased with Rachel's rabble-rousing. Allies talked of progress, of the prosperous future, of law and order. They praised their friends. Was this bitch not a friend, after all?

Rachel gradually turned ten thousand individuals into a collective. She touched the best in some, the worst in others, as she molded them into a single beast. The ideas and words were trite, not very important; the crowd understood her (and the translator, who was like a young dream-Rachel) at a deep, inchoate level. She appealed to a complex of longings and resentments. She was fierce on their behalf. She was sympathetic, maternal, sexual—a counterfeit goddess. The crowd belonged to her; she could make them cheer or weep or riot, as she chose.

The crowd stimulated Rachel, too; they exchanged energy, passion, maybe even love. I did not wholly understand what was happening here today. I remained unaffected. I, like a few others scattered through the crowd, had long ago been inoculated against the psychology of mobs. It seemed to me that Rachel had made a mistake in surrendering to the mob she had created; she would not appear quite so charismatic when viewed on television screens back in the States. The voters there should have been her real audience. Today's message was too radical for home consumption.

I moved away from the window. Rachel was winding up her speech now. She ended each sentence on a rising inflection. There was something orgasmic in her voice now, in the husky throbbing tones, the abandon. I slid back the rifle's bolt and inserted a cartridge. I carefully secured the telescope to its mounting. The calibrations looked all right. Still: unfamiliar rifle, remounted telescope, factory ammunition, smoke, wind, maybe a moving target. And I realized that I had neglected to remove the latex glove, and my touch on the trigger would not be as sensitive as it should be. No time to fumble with the gloves now.

The American vice presidential candidate ended her speech with a series of rhetorical spasms.

"Now!" Rachel cried.

"*Ahora!*" the dark-haired girl repeated in Spanish.

Feedback from the speakers situated around the square resonantly echoed from the last syllable of each word.

"And tomorrow!"

"*Y mañana!*"

I kneel-crawled forward and propped the rifle barrel on the window sill.

"Forever!"

"*Siempre!*"

"All of the people!"

I placed the intersection of the telescope's crosshairs between her breasts.

"*En todo el mundo!*"

Rachel Leah Valentine shifted her weight, arched her back, spread her arms wide, and—ecstatic, cruciform—gazed up at the infinite blue sky.

I gently squeezed the trigger.

TWENTY-ONE

A second later I saw a puff of dust and fibers erupt from Rachel's suit jacket a couple inches to the right of her heart. Her knees buckled, she stumbled back a few paces on her heels, then half-turned and collapsed.

For a moment everyone on the platform remained frozen in place. Two military men reacted first, throwing themselves face-down on the planks, and a black-suited politician dove over the railing and into the street below.

Rachel did not move. She looked crushed, as if she had fallen from a high place.

The cathedral bells began clanging. Noon.

Hamilton Keyes, moving like a sleepy old man, hesitantly walked toward where Rachel lay. He stooped, gallantly offered his hand, and then a rifle cracked in the room next door and Hamilton Keyes's head appeared to dissolve in a cloud of red mist.

At first I did not understand the second shot. Perception was delayed. I vaguely thought it might be the echo of my own shot. For an instant I failed to connect the report with the way Keyes's head exploded.

The shouts and screams of the people on the platform and at

154

the front of the crowd were amplified by the speaker system; it was aural chaos to match the visual chaos across the plaza.

Then I heard three more shots from next door, in the room called *Nuestro Cabello*, pistol shots this time. I acted without thinking. I had done my thinking during the long night. I threw aside the rifle, took a few quick steps toward the door while pulling the pin on a grenade, snatched the door open, tossed in the grenade, then pulled the door closed. I drew my pistol and prepared to enter the room after the blast.

But even before the concussion, I heard sharp cracks from the other, the hallway, door. Wood around the lock turned white, splintery, but the lock held.

Now, in the *Nuestro Cabello* office, the grenade detonated with a concussion that caused ceiling plaster to crack and sift down all around me.

The hallway door shivered on its frame. A boot crashed through one of the panels. A polished boot, a few inches of gray trouser. His foot was stuck in the door panel. I put four rounds into the door, spacing them, and fired a final round into his boot sole.

I felt numb, stupid. I succeeded in acting only because I had long ago been programmed for action. I pulled the pin on the second grenade, snatched open the *Nuestro Cabello* door, lobbed it inside, then again slammed the door shut. It was slow going off. I feared that it might be a dud, but then the door shook violently on its frame and more slabs of plaster fell from the ceiling, and a crack like a lightning bolt streaked across one wall.

Time had become queer, mystical. Time had split into contrary entities. Time was greatly accelerated for me but seemed drastically slowed in the world below. The church bells were still tolling.

I walked through into the room next door and blindly fired off two shots to make them duck their heads. The room was foggy with smoke and sifting plaster and wiry filaments that writhed like worms in the air. The filaments were black and red and blonde, and there were thousands of them.

Herrera was sitting with his back against the wall, his legs splayed, his bloody face in his hands. I shot him twice.

Rafael Betancourt was crawling through the debris. His face and tunic were bloody. He lifted his pistol and aimed at me, but hesitated for just an instant—I had cut off my beard and wore an outfit like a priest's—and I shot him twice, in the chest and the head.

There were dozens of mutilated figures scattered around the room. Glazed flesh, pink lips. Most were female. They smiled blandly at me from every corner.

Roger Clay lay on the floor near an open window. He looked dead. I shot him once to make sure, once again for spite.

It was all going to shit as I expected it might. Crazy with adrenal rage and fear, I ran into the big room, snatched up the waste basket and carried it to the center window. The fan hummed and ticked, chopping the room's air and blowing it outside. The window above the fan's frame had been left open eight inches. I poured half the money out the opening. Some currency fell back into the room, some drifted down to the colonnade roof below, but most was blown out and then lifted by a gusty updraft. The bills dispersed, rising and floating and side-slipping, a windborne flotilla of fifty- and one- hundred-dollar bills. In the milling crowd below, faces were lifted, hands clutched the air.

Sirens whooped out in the city, police vehicles and ambulances, and here in the building the fire alarm began clanging.

I slapped a full thirteen-round clip into my pistol, worked the slide, and returned to the blasted *Nuestro Cabello* office. Betancourt was dead. Herrera was dead. Roger Clay was dead. On the floor, next to Clay's corpse, lay a Chinese-manufactured sniper's rifle identical to the one I had used. Clay had shot Hamilton Keyes, of course, and then he had been killed by Betancourt and Herrera. Fall guy. Fall guys, me and Roger.

Nuestro Cabello was a wig shop; all over the room there were cracked busts and punctured mannequins, male and female, most bald now but with smiles intact. I returned to the big office, dumped the rest of the money out the window and watched as it lifted, swooped and fluttered, above the greed-crazed mob. I looked down at all the distorted faces and claw-fingered hands. An old man succeeded in clutching a falling bill; a young man took it away and knocked the old man down. Sirens wailed in every quarter of the city. A fire alarm bell clanged out in the corridor. I didn't hear a helicopter.

I picked up my duffel and again crossed into the wig shop. The room reeked of blood and dust and burnt gunpowder. Bloody corpses and bald mannequins lay together in a lewd and comic intimacy. Everything was broken, shattered, dead. Filaments of falling hair settled on the wreckage.

Outside, people were running down the hallway. The alarm bell continued ringing. I removed my latex gloves, stuffed them into the duffel, stepped over the bodies, and went through the door into the hall.

Two women with anxious faces ran past me. "*Por Dios!*" I said. A man on crutches skillfully levered himself across the tiles.

To my right, Baltazar lay sprawled on the floor; his right leg was contorted, his foot penetrated the splintered door panel. He, like Betancourt and Herrera, wore an olive uniform with red epaulets and collar tabs and an arm patch embroidered with the P.J.F. insignia—Policía Judicial Federal.

A man and three women, their faces like the Greek masks of tragedy, ran past me toward the elevators.

"*Qué lástima!*" I said. *What a pity!* I followed them.

The old security guard was still on duty in the lobby. He had drawn his nickel-plated pistol and was looking around in a confused way, as if he knew that there was someone he should kill but he was unable to decide exactly whom. When he turned to look at me, I shook my head and said, "*Qué lástima!*"

I paused outside in the shade of the colonnade. The crowd's mood was wild but not yet riotous. Most of the currency had fallen, though some still floated like butterflies in the air above the plaza. The weak grabbed money that was soon after seized by the strong. Policemen, working in teams, swung truncheons and took money from both the weak and the strong, men and women and children.

I turned the corner and walked south down the sidewalk. Sirens howled. An old woman crossed herself as I passed. People jogged past me toward the plaza, the tragedy, the sky that miraculously rained money. A street urchin teased me by raising his hand with the index and little finger extended—horns, the sign of the devil. I piously drew a cross in the air. Bless you, my son.

Three blocks away from the plaza I noticed a bicycle that someone had left in a doorway. A good bike, a Peugeot. I mounted it and peddled rapidly through the clots of vehicle and pedestrian traffic, down a labyrinth of lanes and alleys and sidestreets, up hills and over masonry bridges and across dusty soccer fields, past bronze equestrian statues and grand marble fountains, the wind cool on my face as I peddled into the future.

PART FOUR
LIES

TWENTY-TWO

Florida was nearly as hot and humid as the rain forest. I drove a rental car north from the Miami airport to a condominium complex a dozen miles beyond Fort Lauderdale, where three identical eighteen-story buildings rose out of the palmetto scrubland just west of the ocean. My father had bought his condo twenty years ago, when they were new, just after retiring from the military. Construction had been shoddy, and now the stucco facades were cracked and peeling, the ironwork rusty, the paint smog-stained to a dirty amber, and even the royal palms were dying of some disease. I saw no one around the pool and tennis courts.

When I arrived late in the afternoon, the buildings—the three monoliths—cast long diagonal shadows over the beach. They were like the ruins of an extinct civilization.

My father's widow, his second wife and my stepmother, was not pleased to see me. She hesitated before inviting me into an air-conditioned room that, after the sultry outdoors, felt as cold as a meat locker.

"And where are you coming from?" Sarah asked with fake enthusiasm. "And where are you going?"

I followed her through the foyer and into the big living room.

Ahead, French doors led out onto a balcony cluttered with lawn furniture and potted plants.

"Thomas, I'm sorry, I'm busy with my website. Make yourself a drink, dear, sit down, I'll get back to you in a minute."

She hurried into another room. Sarah was about sixty now, still fussy, heavier than when I'd last seen her, with beauty-parlor gold hair and skin tautened from a recent facelift. She did not look at all like my mother; the Brigadier had gone for an altogether different type the second time around.

I went into the kitchen, took a bottle of beer from the refrigerator, and returned to the big room. It was a three-bedroom condo, polished, vacuumed, dusted, disinfected, laundered, sterilized.

Some of my father's medals and ribbons—Bronze star, Silver star, Purple Heart, others—were displayed against silk in gilt frames above the fireplace. It might have been a touching memorial except that it was not Sarah who had erected the little martial shrine, but my father himself, when he had moved into this place.

I went to the French doors and looked out at the sea, which was a dull gray at this hour and wrinkled with three-foot waves from beach to horizon.

There was a copy of today's *Miami Herald* on the coffee table. On the front page a big photo showed Rachel just after she'd been shot, falling back, on her toes, knees bent, her arms spread wide, looking up toward the sky with a strange serenity. She was captured in another photo as, smiling broadly, she skimmed her straw hat out into the crowd. Another picture, lifted from videotape, showed Hamilton Keyes lying supine on the platform while in the background other men scattered—one was frozen in flight, performing a swan dive over the railing.

Most of the paper's front section was devoted to the assassination and related stores. There was a long, slightly ironic obituary of Hamilton Keyes on the second page.

Rachel had been discharged from the hospital and, just before boarding her flight to the States this morning, vowed that neither she nor the American Patriotic Party would be intimidated by cowards and thugs and murderers; she had picked up the torch first raised by her friend, her mentor, her idol, Hamilton Mayfield Keyes III. She was en route to Chicago to fulfill Party campaign engagements.

A story praised the heroic Federal Judicial policemen (Betancourt, Herrera, and Baltazar) who had been brutally slain while heroically engaging the terrorists in a gun battle. All three men would be buried with honors in the nation's Sacred Pantheon of Patriots.

The assassination and murders had taken place in the offices of a radical leftwing periodical, *Noticias de la Revolución*, whose staff members and associates were being detained by the police. *Noticias* was a political front organization for the notorious terrorist army known as El Puño Rojo—the Red Fist—which was believed responsible (the story claimed) for the kidnapping of the missionaries, the assassination, and the conscienceless slaughter of soldiers at the army's river outpost.

One member of the assassination team had been killed when police stormed the office complex, and government sources close to the investigation suggested that the dead man, a Caucasian male of about thirty-five years, was a North American. Reliable identification was expected soon. Dumb Roger.

There was a piece about the hundreds of thousands of dollars that had blown out into the square, causing a near-riot that seriously impeded efforts to capture the fleeing assassins. The Chief of the Federal Judicial Police was quoted as saying: "This cowardly conspiracy was well financed—by whom, we don't know. But we will find out."

There was a sappy feature about an old, blind lottery ticket salesman who claimed that his sight had been miraculously restored moments before Rachel had been shot: he swore that he had looked at the platform and seen, actually *seen*, not Rachel but the Madonna, and since that instant his vision was so acute that friends now called him *El Aguila*—The Eagle.

The U.S. Government had offered to send highly trained FBI and Secret Service agents to assist in the investigation.

Most of the reporting was, as usual in a big breaking story, compounded of fact, half-fact, inaccuracy, rumor, speculation, misquote, myth, and outright falsehood. The history of that day was already confused beyond recall; the contradictions would never be resolved. Torrents of information would continue flowing. Thousands of voices would be heard, volumes of evidence accumulated. And the investigators and media would weed and prune, patch and fill, until finally they arrived at—not the "truth" they always advertise—but a plausible narrative.

Sarah bustled into the room. "Sorry." She saw me reading the newspaper. "Isn't it dreadful?" she asked.

"Terrible," I said.

"That poor Rachel. Lucky for her she was wearing a bulletproof vest."

"Lucky indeed."

"Keyes refused to, they say. I didn't like the woman at all before, but she was so compassionate about the missionaries, and so brave when this awful thing happened."

"I've never seen anyone braver, man or woman."

Sarah smiled vaguely and then sat in a chair near the balcony doors. She was not going to offer me food or another beer; she would not invite me to smoke.

"I have a business on the Internet," Sarah said. "It keeps me busy."

"What sort of business?"

"A consultancy. I'm a consultant."

I waited for elaboration. It seemed that everyone was a consultant these days; only the particular area of claimed expertise distinguished one from the other.

She looked at her watch. "Did you visit the Brigadier?"

"No." The Brigadier's ashes reposed in a vault at the Elysian Fields Memorial Park.

"It's unfortunate you couldn't attend the ceremony and all."

"Word came late," I said. "Anyway, I was far away at the time."

Her smile was skeptical, sour. She glanced again at her wristwatch.

I had always felt, when with my father or my father's friends, as if I were a parolee who was unlikely to reform, whose parole might be revoked at any moment. It was obscure: there seemed to be no doubt that my crimes were deplorable, though never specified; one simply had "bad blood"—my mother's blood. The Brigadier's friends were usually more judgmental than the Brigadier himself. All my father's friends thought like my father. He wouldn't have friends who thought differently, or wrongly in his view.

"Thomas, I'm sorry, but I do have an engagement this evening."

"I just stopped in for a quick visit," I said, "and to ask a favor."

Her eyebrows raised slightly. A favor in her world usually meant money.

"My father promised me that I would get his service pistol when he died. It belonged to his father, my grandfather, and now it's mine. The Brigadier wanted it to remain in the male family line." My father had made no such promise, but before leaving South

America I had disassembled the Beretta and scattered the parts. I needed a gun.

Sarah looked at me for several moments without comment.

"Sarah?"

She got up and left the room.

The light had changed and now the sea and sky were the same dull gray.

Sarah returned with a marquetry box that my father had carpentered years ago. Inside, wrapped in an oily cloth, was the Colt .45, with a full clip in place ("An unloaded gun is worse than no gun at all," he said more than once) and a stack of spare clips taped together. It was an old pistol: most of the bluing had been worn away and the checked walnut grips were smooth. My grandfather, John Thomas Jackstraw, had worn the pistol in 1916 while, with Pershing, he futilely chased Pancho Villa into Mexico.

"And," I said, "I'd like a few pictures from the family photo albums."

Sarah concentrated her stare a foot or two over my head. "I was married to the Brigadier for eighteen years. They aren't, you know, actually *your* family's photo albums. Exclusively."

"I don't want any pictures of you," I said. "Or of my father. Either of you, individually or together. I just want a few pictures of my mother and one or two of me."

"No, I don't think—"

"Sarah," I said, "It isn't too late to contest my father's will."

"Do your best," she said coldly.

"Or you can give me a few photos that by right and by decency belong to me."

She left and stalked into the hallway.

I understood, of course, that my parolee status was not unjustified:

I had not lived an exemplary life, and now I was involved in the kidnapping of missionaries and the assassination of a presidential candidate. Sarah didn't know that, but she soon would, I was sure.

She came back with an armful of albums and dropped them onto a table. While she watched, arms crossed, I plundered the album of photos—a few of my mother, more of myself, almost all of them taken of me as an adult. Sooner or later the FBI would call on Sarah to inquire about the fugitive, Thomas Jackstraw, and they would naturally ask for some fairly recent photographs which could be shown online and on TV and printed in newspapers and magazines and pinned up in post office lobbies.

I took only one with my father—a black-and-white snapshot of my parents and myself taken when I was about eight, on the dock of a lake. My fondest early memories were of that trip, taken before I was old enough to become fully aware of our family's problems, and though I could bear to leave all the rest, this one I couldn't. As I gently pried it from the album, Sarah took a deep breath but then clamped her mouth shut.

We parted with a minimum of civility.

"Goodbye, Sarah."

"Goodbye, Thomas."

I stood out in the hallway, listening to her work the security locks. I didn't know if I should consider the slamming home of those deadbolts as evidence of Sarah's confinement or prophetic of my own.

TWENTY-THREE

I drove up Highway 1 to West Palm Beach and the Willowdale Special Care Nursing Home. The "Special" indicated that their "guests" suffered from a variety of mental disorders—senile dementia, mostly, but they also cared for patients afflicted by schizophrenia or manic-depressive disorders.

It was dark when I parked the car. I could smell the sea and the perfumes of night-blooming flowers. Palm frond crackled in the wind. A piglike dog in a parked car barked furiously at me as I walked toward the front door.

Two black women wearing starched white uniforms were gossiping in the reception area. They told me that it was well past visiting hours.

I said, "If you could make an exception . . ."

"Sorry, sir," the older woman said.

"I'm flying to Chicago in two hours. I won't be back this way for a long time."

"The guests have eaten—they're resting now. Lights-out is in—" she glanced at her wristwatch—"twenty-five minutes."

"I won't stay long. I promise." I offered my most disarming smile.

She looked at the other woman, silently calculating the probable penalty if they were caught breaking the rules. "The patient's name?"

"Betsy—I mean Elizabeth—Jackstraw. My mother."

"Whyn't you say so." She sighed and stiffly rose from her chair. "Maybe for a few minutes. If Elizabeth isn't having a nervous episode."

She walked down a hallway leading off into the east wing. The younger woman at the desk smiled at me.

"Thank you," I said.

She shrugged. "It's your mother. And she don't have many visitors."

"None?"

"An old man used to come see her once a month, but he ain't been here in a while."

"My father. He died."

"And you—I remember you coming to see her, but that was a long time ago."

The older woman returned. "Down that hall. Just a few minutes now, hear?"

There were several patients in the big lounge, a pair of old men playing checkers, a man and two women slouched in front of a television that flashed with an old sitcom from the sixties.

My mother sat at a low table next to a lighted aquarium that sprinkled rings of light over her face. She wore a floor-length patchwork housecoat, slippers, and a paisley scarf over her shower-wet hair. Disease, more than time, had ravaged her looks.

I sat down on the other side of the table.

"Hello, Tom," she said, with a trace of a smile.

"How are you doing?"

"Oh, well, you know . . ."

She was tranquil, sleepy, and I assumed that she had recently been medicated. My mother was schizophrenic. The drugs that partly controlled her disease also stunned her into a sort of quiet despair.

Neither of us could think of much to say to the other. Too many of our shared memories were painful ones. After a few long minutes I gave her one of the photos I had taken from the album: in it, five years old, I sat on a pony's back while my mother held my arm and fondly gazed at me.

"What was the pony's name?" she asked. "Do you remember, Tom?"

"Hobo," I said.

"That's right. Silly name."

The photograph both pleased and saddened her. She smiled as tears formed, and she said, "Waste. God, so much waste."

"Yes."

"Why, Tom?"

We were silent for a moment, and then she said, "Look at the fish, Tom. Aren't they lovely?"

While I glanced at the fish, she slipped the photograph into her housecoat's pocket. She thought she was stealing the picture, that I might take it away from her.

"I've got to go," I said. "They broke the rules to allow me to see you. But I'll come back to see you soon. Promise." I did not expect to return soon, if ever. My future seemed limited to either sudden death or long imprisonment.

I kissed my mother's wet cheek and returned to the reception area.

The older woman looked at me suspiciously. "You didn't upset her?"

"A little, I think." I removed two fifty-dollar bills from my wallet and placed them on the desk. "I found these blowing across the parking lot. Maybe you can locate the owner."

"Money always blowing around that damn parking lot," the young woman said.

TWENTY-FOUR

Three twelve- or thirteen-year-old boys in baggy pants and high-top Nikes left the sidewalk and angled toward me over the grass. They had a predatory look about them, like kittens stalking a bird. I looked directly at them with my toughest stare and they altered course.

It was hot and humid in Chicago too, even at seven in the morning, even in the deep shade of a great oak. Early risers, joggers and bicyclists and skaters, glided around the park's sidewalks and along the lakefront esplanade. Through the trees I could see Lake Michigan, smooth and amethyst-blue on this still morning. A few yards from my bench some mendicant pigeons bobbed their heads *yes yes yes* over the crumbs I'd thrown them. I had bought two large cartons of coffee and half a dozen donuts and the *Tribune* before coming to the park to meet Cavenaugh's ex-wife.

I had phoned Caprice last night from the airport to ask if she knew where Cav was staying. "Staying in the morgue," she bitterly replied. The brief story was in the Metro section of the *Tribune*: Joseph Cavenaugh, forty-two, a newly hired security guard at the Total Recall Corporation, had last night been killed by gunmen whom he had apparently surprised during a burglary attempt.

172

Mr. Cavenaugh had died of multiple gunshot wounds. Police were investigating.

The details were sketchy: there was no bio of Cav, no mention of his ex-wife and two children, nothing about his unorthodox military career. It was, so far, just another murder during the commission of a felony, the kind that happened every day.

Poor Cav: to survive half a dozen small wars and as many guerrilla actions, to finally repudiate that risky vocation, and then to die while wearing one of those poorly fitted rent-a-cop uniforms with a chrome badge pinned on the shirt and meaningless chevrons on the sleeve and an officer's cap that surely was too big or too small. It was painfully ironic. I told myself that his death might have been coincidental. There were many coincidences in this perilous world. It wasn't certain that he had been murdered by Troxel's people.

The front pages of both newspapers dealt with Rachel Valentine's visit to Chicago. She was here for a couple of fund-raising dinners, a campaign rally at a South Side church, and a visit to the children's ward of the Cook County Hospital.

Rachel had announced that after much thought and consideration she had acceded to the request of her advisors, and she herself would now be the presidential candidate on the American Patriotic Party ticket. A search was being conducted to select a suitable vice-presidential running mate; he must be highly qualified, of course, and, regardless of prior party affiliation, in tune with the political philosophy of the APP.

The assassination of Hamilton Keyes, Rachel's survival of an assassin's bullet, and her successful effort to obtain the release of the missionaries had bounced the APP's poll numbers up to twenty-four percent of the electorate. The Republicans were alarmed; the Democrats were dismayed; and the editorial writers and columnists, after some oily phrases about the tragedy in South America, scolded the public for its lack of serious thought in this most serious duty of electing a president. The events of recent days, despite our grief and sympathy, did not qualify a party, nor an individual—no matter how attractive and courageous—to occupy the Oval Office.

You could sense the first stirrings of panic in what used to be called the Establishment.

I saw Caprice approaching and got up from the bench to greet her. She paused a moment beneath a sycamore, unsteady, and looked around as if trying to recall how she had reached this place, this time. Then she continued toward me. She wore jeans and sandals and a salmon-pink blouse, and was carrying a battered leather satchel. She was still slender and strikingly pretty. Caprice had been a highly paid model and now operated her own agency.

We embraced briefly, then sat together on the bench.

"I can't stay long," she said. She had been weeping; the skin around her eyes was puffy and bruised.

"Caprice . . . I'm so sorry. How are the boys taking it?"

"Hard," she said.

She pushed the satchel down the bench. "This is for you. I don't want it in the house."

"Was Cav staying at your place?"

She nodded. "In the guest room." She shook her head. "Joseph was a guest there much of his life. That's what he was, mostly, guest husband, guest father, guest ex-husband. He was sort of a guest in the world, like you, Jack."

"Hungry?" I asked. "I brought some coffee and donuts."

She shook her head again. "Look, I didn't mean to sound so bitter with that guest speech. But you know how it was. Joseph would be away for six or eight months, then home for six or eight more months, waiting for the phone call—from you, Jack—that would take him away for another six or eight months. This morning the boys said that it wasn't all bad, him being away so much of the time, because when he was here he was *here*. He took them to ballgames, the beach, museums, boating and fishing, concerts, everything. When he was with them he was really with them."

"How old are the boys now?"

"Nicky's fourteen, Michael's ten."

"Well, they had him during the most important years."

"You've got nerve, saying that. If anyone had him then, it was you."

"They're good kids, aren't they?"

"Sure they are."

"I didn't mean it to sound like that . . . Cav lives in them now, for good."

"Jack, don't make me listen to this kind of crap, okay? He didn't come home this morning. And what would you know about raising kids? How long were you and Beth together—five years? Why didn't you ever have any?"

"We planned on it. We were waiting. I wish I knew now what for." We were both silent for a while. I said, "Were you two getting back together?"

"We talked about it. Mostly he talked about it. He said he was finished with all of that bullshit. Said he wasn't going to waste any more of his life. Said he was going to find a good job—the security thing was temporary. I was skeptical. I had heard all of that before."

"It was true. He definitely was out of it."

"I've got to go. The boys are waiting."

"Do you need money, Caprice?"

"No. My business is doing well, and Joseph left a large life insurance policy. We'll be all right."

"Well, if you ever need anything . . ."

"Thanks." She stood up.

"I'll walk you to your car."

"No."

I rose from the bench and faced her. "Caprice, an absolute shitstorm will be coming down soon."

"Involving Joseph?"

"No. I don't think so. But it's just as well for you and the boys if you forget you met me here this morning."

"Is this . . . shitstorm . . . is that why Joseph was killed? It wasn't just a burglary?"

"No," I lied. But I hesitated just a half-second before responding, and she knew.

"God." She started to cry, but then she quickly regained her composure, tried to smile, abruptly pivoted and walked toward Michigan Avenue.

I opened the satchel. Inside, as I'd expected, was Cav's shrunken head—the replica crafted in Fortaleza. I had buried the other two heads, Crowley's and my own, in the garden behind the Hotel Su Casa in Paraje. Now I would have to dispose of this one.

I hefted the head in my palms. Alas, poor Cavenaugh; I knew him, Horatio. It looked like Cav despite the stitched lips and eyelids, the reduction in size, the color a shade too dark. A Joseph Cavenaugh whose expression was more mirthful than grim, more ironic than accusing. Not unlike the way I wanted to remember him, the only true friend I'd had.

TWENTY-FIVE

On the way back to my hotel I passed through Daley Plaza and was startled to see Rachel standing in front of the huge Picasso sculpture. She was addressing a small crowd in conversational tones. More people, singles and groups of two and three, wandered toward her from other quadrants of the square.

"I miss him very much," she was saying. "But it isn't just my loss, it's our loss, America's loss. We all will miss Ham's courage, his conviction, his vision of what this country can be."

Big buildings rose up on all sides: the Daley Center, with its rusty steel façade, lay behind the Picasso; City Hall occupied the block on the west; and on the south the Brunswick Building, with the Chicago Temple, a small church, on its roof. Also to the south, another monumental abstract sculpture, this one by Miró, seemed from my angle to be returning the enigmatic gaze of the Picasso. The works of fellow Spaniards, squared off and engaged in a staring duel across the length of the plaza.

Apparently Rachel had refused Secret Service protection. Of course: she could not permit the men of a federal police agency, outsiders, anywhere near her campaign, her criminal conspiracy. She was guarded by half a dozen of Troxel's thugs. They stood

177

near her, methodically appraising the faces, the movements, of individuals in the crowd. They appeared calm, bored even, though they had to be concerned by the security dangers in this impromptu rally. One man, with a radio bud in his ear, cocked his head in a dreamy way, as if listening to faint, ethereal music.

I stood well back, watching and listening as Rachel eulogized Hamilton Keyes and deplored the madness, the senseless violence, that so often deprived the world of its wisest, its most compassionate leaders.

A member of the crowd told me that Rachel had been briskly walking with her security detail and some media people when she saw the massive Picasso sculpture, halted, and then curiously approached it. Several tourists had greeted her. A few more people had joined the group, and then a few more, and now there were at least a hundred men and women gathered in a semi-circle, and more coming.

"Just what do you want?" a man called.

Rachel had a slight case of laryngitis from all her campaign speeches and media interviews, and in a low husky voice she said, "Why, I want what you want, what we all want, what we most desperately want and need."

Troxel was not present, but I saw "Mr. Smith," Orson Dedrick: he looked like the sort of man who washed his hands thirty times a day.

"Isn't it time?" Rachel was saying. "Really, isn't it time, after more than two hundred years, time that America completely fulfills its noble promise to itself and the world?"

A uniformed Chicago cop wandered among the crowd. He gave me a long, speculative look, and I realized that I was standing forty feet away from a presidential candidate while carrying a concealed pistol and holding a satchel that contained an authentic-looking shrunken head of a man who had been murdered last night. Was there something in my stance, my expression, that had caught the trained eye of a policeman? I did my best to ignore him. Finally his gaze moved on, and so did he.

Rachel was talking about education. She looked a little different each time I saw her, in life or in photographs; this morning she was fresh and pretty, sexy in a subdued suburban mom way, apparently untouched by the events in South America or jet lag or the rigors of her schedule.

"For how many years, how many decades, is our educational system going to remain inferior to those of other nations? Why are we short-changing our children?"

More people joined the crowd. They came out of curiosity, because of the TV cameras and the large gathering, and they stayed because Rachel had become a celebrity, a star. She was different now, not like us, someone special, four-dimensional, a media goddess. The politics hardly mattered. Her distinguished running mate had been assassinated in a far-off land. Rachel herself had been shot and, in a way, resurrected. Her voice and image had infiltrated the public mind. You could not pick up a newspaper or turn on a television without seeing Rachel Valentine smiling, waving, embracing a freed missionary, blowing kisses, falling—falling back from the force of an assassin's bullet. She was the heroine of a self-devised melodrama. She was a superstar.

"The majority of our children are being prepared for a form of economic bondage . . ."

Rachel selected individual members of the crowd and spoke directly to each for a time, making and holding eye contact, then moving on to another person. And she made each one of them feel special. A born politician—she reminded me of Bill Clinton in his prime.

"Every year hundreds of thousands of foreigners are recruited by big American corporations. These outsiders come here to work at jobs that require education and training, the good jobs, while so many of our kids are being prepared for not much more than frying hamburgers or operating a punch press. Can't we properly educate our own?"

Our gazes intersected, and for a moment Rachel spoke to me of our children's needs, our children's future, America's future, and then her glance slid away. But her expression was troubled. She faltered, lost her rhythm. My beard was gone, my hair short; recognition was slow.

I was smiling when she turned back to look at me. Our gazes locked for a second, I nodded, and for an instant she froze and turned chalky white. But Rachel was tough; she swiftly recovered, smiled at me, and resumed speaking. She was afraid, I knew it, but she didn't let it show. She was clearly not wearing body armor.

Orson Dedrick followed me from Daley Plaza. I walked several blocks, stopped, and waited for him in the doorway of a bookstore. He looked like a high school kid at twenty yards, but gained a year with each stride.

"How are you doing, Orson?" I said.

He didn't waste effort in greeting inferiors; he handed me a sheet of paper torn from a notebook. It contained a telephone number and a time: ten o'clock.

"What do you hear from Roger?" I asked.

He watched me as an entomologist might study an unfamiliar species of insect, and then he turned and walked away in his stiff-backed prissy style.

❋   ❋   ❋

Late the previous night I had checked into a pre-World War Two, ten-story residential hotel a long walk from the South Loop, in a neighborhood past due for demolition. Old people dozed among the dusty plastic foliage of the lobby. It was the sort of place you came to stay when your pension was inadequate, your prospects dim, and your children indifferent. There were tarnished brass light fixtures in the hallways. The threadbare carpets were sooty and scarred with cigarette burns, the woodwork flaking, and the wallpaper water- and age-stained to a uniform sepia. In the room I rented there was heavy old furniture upholstered in an itchy maroon fabric and iron floorlamps with greasy parchment shades.

I slept for an hour, and was awakened by the sound of someone trying various keys in the door lock; by the time I reached the hallway he was gone.

TWENTY-SIX

I spent most of the afternoon in the downtown library, piecing together a more or less coherent biography of Rachel. Much had to be inferred, extrapolated. You had to read between the lines. But there was plenty of material; strong personalities left tracks.

Rachel Lee Carter was born in Marin County, California, in January of either 1966 or 1968, depending on whether you believed Rachel or the county's Registry of Births. She was the second child, three years younger than her brother, Hugh. The family lived near Sausalito, on Richmond Bay, and in later years Rachel liked to say that she could see Alcatraz Island from her upstairs bedroom window. The San Quentin State Penitentiary was forty-some miles to the north. Rachel once told an interviewer that as a child she had dreamed of caged men pacing like cats, men strapped to tables in glass-walled chambers, men in striped "pajamas" howling in the night, men convulsing in electric chairs, their skin scorched and their hair smoking. She had while very young become an opponent of capital punishment.

Rachel's father, Preston, was a successful orthopedic surgeon. He belonged to the right clubs, athletic and social, and served in various professional organizations. Her mother, Marian, was an area "cultural leader," chairwoman of a book discussion group, a Sunday painter, head of the local amateur theater, and active in fundraising for the San Francisco Opera and the San Francisco Ballet.

Rachel was from "good family." The Carters wore the right clothes, drove the right cars, lived in the right area, sent their children to the right schools, belonged to the right church (Episcopalian) and the right political party (Republican), and even were descended from the right ancestors if you believed the cynical hired genealogist who had pasted together a glorious coat-of-arms and invented a family tree that stemmed from William the Conqueror.

They were paragons of the upper middle class and it was no wonder that a rebellious spirit like Rachel would eventually repudiate that constricted world. "*Faux* people," she had once called the members of her class.

She attended a very good private girls school that was then known for its high academic standards. That was before the introduction of the curriculum of self-esteem. She studied math, history, Latin, English. She learned a little French, a little German. And she learned to draw, do watercolor landscapes, serve tea, play tennis, make cloddish boys feel at ease during school dances. For years she was a very good student and then, bored, she became a very poor student. No one ever questioned her intelligence or charm; she was a favorite of both teachers and students, and the more she rebelled the more they favored her. She was special. Even the school uniform (pleated gray skirt, blue blazer, narrow-brimmed straw hat with a forked blue ribbon around the crown) could not impose anonymity on Rachel.

And there were lessons outside of school: she learned to sail; she studied ballet; she learned to ride very well, and, with an experienced jumper purchased by her parents, competed all over California.

She was a promising dance student—when she was fifteen she was admitted to a training class of the San Francisco Ballet, with a chance to later join the Corps de Ballet as a full member.

Even so, Rachel drifted. She was rebellious, but what was there to rebel against? You needed leverage, a place to stand, determined opposition. There were no enemies in her life, no injustice, no oppression, only the kind of insidious pressure which vanished when you tried to name it.

Rachel adored her brother. Hugh was her protector, her confidant, her champion. They looked like twins, people said. Hugh was perhaps a version of Rachel without the passion, the spirit of revolt. He was bright, gifted. Years after the incident, Rachel said that Hugh would have either become a fine poet or a superb con man, depending upon how well he defended his idealism against reality. She said that since the age of sixteen, she had never cried except when thinking of Hugh.

Even the great tragedy of Rachel's life had a freakish aspect. Other girls might lose loved ones to disease or accident; Rachel's brother was killed by a shark.

She became famous for a week when she was sixteen. They were at a beach on the Marin Peninsula, Rachel, Hugh, and five or six of Hugh's friends. Rachel was allowed to hang around with the older group because she was mature for her age, smart, very pretty, and amusing in an outrageous way.

Hugh had borrowed a surf board and was sitting far out, waiting for the right wave. The water was cold as usual that far up the California coast. Everything was perfectly normal: a few kids splashing around in the shallow water; people sunbathing; boys throwing a football; surfers sitting on their boards out where the swells began to turn concave.

Rachel remembered the incident as a series of snapshots, with no recollection of the periods between. There was the beach and the sea, sunlight, tranquility; then people were running and shouting "Where is Hugh?" A girl screamed. Friends were trying to restrain Rachel, but she managed to break free. She could not recall swimming those sixty or seventy yards. All at once she was with him in the bloody water. No shark, no fin, just the blood and poor Hugh, white-faced and with a sort of quizzical expression. "Get back," he said. "Get away from me, Rachlee." He called her Rachlee, a combination of her first and middle names, and of course he was not really saying, "Get away from *me*," but away from the shark.

Rachel did not remember much about towing poor Hugh toward shore. A couple of surfers arrived to help, and then a couple of Hugh's friends waded out and carried him up onto the beach. But Hugh was dead by then, or so close to dead that it didn't matter. The bite wounds on Hugh's pale thigh did not look so terrible. Not enough to kill. But the femoral artery had been severed and he bled to death.

Experts determined from the size of the teeth, the bite, that Hugh had been attacked by a great white, though a small one, probably a ten-footer.

The publicity was immediate and overwhelming. Shark attacks were rare, but rarer still the story of a slim teenaged girl swimming out into the "blood slick," swimming virtually into the jaws of a "ravenous maneater," risking everything to rescue her mortally wounded brother. Hugh was merely a victim; Rachel, a heroine, a sexy-looking kid who photographed well.

At first Rachel cooperated with the media. She was in shock. She wanted to talk about her brother, praise him. She wanted to tell the world about Hugh. She hadn't realized, she said later, that there were many who regarded people's lives as commodities. You could make a big name, and big bucks, prying into another's soul.

Rachel scandalized the nation in a small way when, on the third day of the media blitz, she confessed to an unorthodox view of God. A TV reporter asked if she hated the shark that killed her brother. "No," she said. "Since God is in everything, God is in the shark. The shark is God as much as Hugh is God." "Do you believe that your brother is looking down on you with pride and love?" "My brother," she replied, "is in a cemetery, rotting." "Do you attend church?" "Not since the priest molested one of my friends."

Overnight the teenaged heroine became the teenaged bitch. The story was quickly revised: unnamed "credible witnesses" were quoted saying that Rachel had actually run away down the beach during the crisis, and it was another, a "stranger," who had swum out into the blood slick. Hugh's friends protested, and were mostly ignored. Finally a woman came forward with a roll of fuzzy photographs confirming Rachel's part in the incident, but by then the story was dying, and soon dead.

She mourned privately. No one saw Rachel cry. She never mentioned Hugh. Her grief was manifested only by an obsessive dancing regimen; she trained nine or ten hours every day for weeks, until her feet were almost permanently crippled and her mind slipped. Rachel suffered a "nervous breakdown." She was hospitalized for a month, and after her release some said that she had changed. She was different. Remote, inward, silent. Rachel did not return to school that autumn, and she refused to consult the psychiatrist retained by her parents. She rejected therapy, counseling, medication, the consolation of religion. No one understood her awkward attempts to explain her mood. She was thinking, she said. She was thinking hard, reordering her mind, eliminating the false—

sixteen years (sixteen centuries!) of lies. It was a kind of mental surgery. She told them that a large part of the Rachel they knew must be sacrificed to make room for the birth of a newer, truer Rachel. This was not just about Hugh. It was about finding her core nature and then remaining loyal to it. The talk of lies and sacrifice and rebirth frightened all who cared for her. Rachel denied that she was suicidal but was not believed, and so her family and friends imprisoned her in a corral of love and concern.

In December she moved alone to San Francisco. An aunt had left her a little money. She was only sixteen, but her parents were afraid to intervene. And after all, she had not gone far away. She rented an attic apartment, worked part-time at an art gallery, ran around with what her parents considered a disreputable crowd.

When Rachel was seventeen she met a young Vice Consul from the Spanish Embassy, and within a week they had run off to Mexico and gotten married. His name was Rodrigo Valentin, and he came from an aristocratic family who claimed to have traced their roots back to the expulsion of the Moors. They owned a big *estancia* near Jerez de la Frontera, raised cattle and horses, cultivated fields and vineyards, made wine and sherry and brandy. His parents were outraged by the sneak marriage. Who was this girl who did not even bring a dowry to the union? A street waif, a fortune hunter, an American!

Young Valentin was recalled to Spain. He was expected to return alone, but he had guts and he loved Rachel, and so they arrived together. The family allowed them to occupy one of the estate's houses. Rachel was a pariah. Members of the family never addressed her directly; they spoke to her, at her, in the third person. "Does she want more wine?" "Does she not have a more appropriate dress?"

Rachel soon learned that she was smarter than any of them, and better educated even though she had left school at sixteen. She was just as proud, her manners were just as bad, and she could ride a horse as well as any of them. Her riding confused the Valentins. Horsemanship was important to those people, an almost mystical indicator of noble blood. It was understood that no plebeian could learn to ride with grace and style.

Private investigators hired by the family reported that Rachel was not from a low family as feared, not barbarians. Still, she clearly was not suitable to be the wife of Rodrigo Valentin. (But she could ride—you could not deny that she was a fearless rider.) They half accepted her; she half accepted them.

When she was nineteen, Rachel gave birth to a daughter, Rodrigo's daughter (a son would have been better, whispered some), who was named Giselle (strange name for a Spaniard, muttered others). Rachel remained on probation but everyone loved the baby. It was a beautiful child, alert and spirited, with gray eyes and silky dark hair and fair skin. No Moorish or Jewish taint. A Spanish baby. Rachel wryly told her few outside friends that the family seemed to believe that Rodrigo had created the baby all by himself in a sort of Andalucian parthenogenesis.

Repetition made the time pass swiftly. She and Rodrigo spent each spring in Seville, taking in Holy Week and the big *feria*. Rachel rode her favorite horse, Luz, in the daily *paseo*. After Seville, they moved to Paris where they remained until August, when they went to St. Tropez for the month. Each winter they spent three weeks skiing at St. Moritz in Switzerland.

The family complained because after several years there were no more children (though everyone adored Giselle), no son, no heir.

Rodrigo abruptly changed. He drank too much, drove too fast.

Often his temper flared. He gambled and lost, gambled some more. He whored around with his friends. Whored at home, too. He treated Rachel like one of his whores.

And then one night, driving at ninety-odd miles per hour, Rodrigo crashed his Alfa Romeo into a bridge abutment. Rachel was twenty-four and a widow.

An autopsy discovered that Rodrigo had suffered from a malignant brain tumor.

He had not left a will. Rather, the family's lawyers reported that there was no will.

Rachel also learned that the lawyers, with the help of a Spanish bishop and poor Rodrigo's complicity, had months before petitioned the Vatican for an annulment of the marriage. The decision was still pending when her husband entered heaven at ninety miles per hour.

Two days after the funeral Rachel was called into the government's office in Seville and coldly informed that her passport was not in order; that she was illegally residing in Spain; that there was good and sufficient police evidence indicating that she was a woman guilty of the Spanish equivalent of moral turpitude; and that she had twenty-four hours to leave the country or face arraignment on criminal charges. What criminal charges? They will be revealed to you one minute after the deadline for your expulsion. The official finished by stating that the Valentin girl was a Spanish citizen and would remain in the country. Not "your daughter," the "Valentin girl." And then he pronounced Giselle in a Spanish way, "*He-say-yeh.*" Rachel had long before taken to calling her daughter Gigi, but it was the *He-say-yeh* that drove her crazy, and she half wrecked the office before being subdued by security personnel.

Rachel was expelled from Spain. The family would not permit

her to say goodbye to her daughter. The family searched her luggage and removed the jewelry that Rodrigo had given her. They confiscated the jewelry, her credit cards, her checkbook, and most of her cash. They were all there, Rodrigo's mother and father, his sisters, cousins, uncles and aunts, nephews and nieces, all of them.

Rachel arrived in Bayonne, France, with less than one hundred dollars. She rented a hotel room and wired her parents for money: GIGI SEIZED! Her mother and father were generous. Money came, and kept coming. She hired lawyers: Spanish lawyers, French lawyers, American lawyers. They sucked up the money. Nothing happened. She moved to Paris, resumed her dance training, audited classes at the Sorbonne, hung out with a radical, bohemian crowd. Her parents sent her money; the lawyers sent her bills. Nothing happened. The Valentins were too rich, too influential, and the Spanish courts unsympathetic.

Rachel hoped, and feared, and then one day two years after her expulsion from Spain, she concluded that both hope and fear were futile, the tools of weakness. Neither hope nor fear could affect events. You waited, you hoped, you feared, and meanwhile the smart people *acted*.

She hired four mercenaries, former soldiers who had served with the OAS during the Algerian War, hard men who were not paralyzed by bourgeois respect for the law. They had no allegiance to liberal democracy. The word "courts" made them smile. They felt betrayed: for a long time they had been French heroes and then, when the political winds blew from another quarter, they were despised as criminals. Now they were realists. Now, if you could afford their services, they would provide you with a direct sort of justice, circumventing the servile cops and parasitic lawyers and corrupt courts—the apparatus of the ruling class. Of course, they would as well provide you with a satisfactory kind of injustice if you paid for that.

In late June, almost exactly two years after Rachel's expulsion from Spain, a twin-engine Beechcraft was stolen from a private airstrip outside of Limoge and flown to Bordeaux, where it refueled and took on passengers. There were four men and one woman on board when the plane left Bordeaux. It flew directly west, past the coast and out over the Bay of Biscay. Flying only thirty feet above the waves to avoid radar tracking, it continued west for several hundred miles, rounded the northwest corner of Spain, turned south, and cruised the length of the Portuguese coast before angling in toward Gibraltar. Still flying low, the Beechcraft crossed the Spanish border between Cadiz and Sanlucar, proceeded toward Jerez, and twenty minutes later landed on a road leading into the Valentin *estancia*. The plane taxied all the way to the gates of the family compound.

Spanish police later described the raid as well planned and ruthlessly executed. Clearly, the widow of Rodrigo Valentin was familiar with the estate and had carefully briefed her fellow criminals. The pilot remained with his aircraft; Rachel and three masked and armed thugs penetrated the inner compound and separated. Electrical wires were severed. Random gunfire and shock grenades were used to terrorize the noble family and their loyal workers. There was little resistance. No one was critically hurt even though the criminals behaved brutally, and several men were later treated at a hospital. The child, Giselle Valentin, was abducted from her home and dragged to the waiting aircraft. The Spanish authorities, shocked by this barbarous action, complained both to France and to the U.S. State Department.

The wreckage of the stolen airplane was found in a desert south of Infi, in Morocco. It had been burned to destroy any evidence.

The four men were never identified. A week after the abduction, Rachel Valentin and her daughter, Gigi, arrived in New York on a Nigerian Airlines flight. They were briefly detained by customs officials, then released.

Rachel spoke freely to the media—she wanted to get her version of the story out, slant it her way, before the Valentins and the Spanish authorities could affect the coverage. It was an international scandal. She was interviewed on several network and cable TV shows. She told how she had been expelled from Spain just two days after the funeral of her beloved husband, and subsequently cheated of justice by the Spanish courts, forbidden to even visit her daughter. Gigi was photographed and solemnly quoted. Yes, she missed her pony, but she was glad to be back with her mother.

A few commentators and editorial writers deplored Rachel's "lawless abduction" of her daughter, but most Americans, particularly women and feminists, approved of the daring "rescue" and regarded her actions as not only justified but heroic. The story of her brave attempt to rescue her brother from a shark attack was resurrected and elaborated upon. The old snapshot of Rachel and a surfer carrying Hugh out of the water was enlarged, digitally enhanced, and published on the cover of a news magazine.

Rachel and her daughter moved in with Rachel's parents for several months, and then she rented an apartment in a decaying section of San Francisco. Most of her neighbors were what later came to be called the "working poor," people who struggled desperately to avoid slipping into the abyss of breadless and homeless poverty. But Gigi was enrolled in a private girls' school in an affluent part of the city.

Rachel mostly vanished from the public record during the ensuing years. Occasionally she was mentioned in the area's newspapers, usually described as a "social activist" or "radical reformer" or, satirically in a *San Francisco Chronicle* column, "feminist commando." She changed her name in minor ways: an *e* was added to the name Valentin and she altered the spelling of her middle name from Lee to Leah.

In the mid-nineties Rachel announced that she would run as an Independent for a seat in the House of Representatives. No one believed that she had a chance of winning. But a month before the election a network TV docudrama appeared which purported to recreate Rachel's life in Spain, her expulsion and exile, and finally the dramatic paramilitary rescue of Gigi. (A black-and-white slow-motion re-creation dramatized the shark incident.) It was, all the TV critics agreed, a poorly written, badly acted, wholly implausible film biography. One reviewer wrote that the Rachel portrayed seemed a hybrid of St. Joan of Arc and St. Bonnie of Bonnie and Clyde. Rachel herself derided the movie and its pretensions. Even so, she was again a minor celebrity, and Californians are eager to vote celebrities into public office.

Rachel defeated both her Republican and Democratic rivals by a substantial margin. She was elected to two more terms before the voters defeated her by choosing a richer, more celebrated candidate—a local sports hero.

Representative Valentine was disliked by most of her colleagues during her three terms in Congress. Disliked because she refused to play the game; because, as an Independent, she was not subject to Party discipline; because she possessed no coherent ideological stance; because she was a maverick and voted "all over the place." Because she seemed to despise her fellow Members and because, in debate, her wit cut deeply, lacerating outsized egos and puncturing grand pretensions. And most of all she was disliked because, being beautiful and witty, she received an inordinate amount of attention from the national media.

She accomplished very little while in Congress. Her ideas were too radical to please a complacent citizenry in complacent times. Her name appeared on no legislation. She was never invited to the White House. In a cheery election night speech to her campaign workers, while conceding defeat, she said, "I was just trying, in a small way, to fuck up the machinery of the corporate state."

A year later she announced that she was joining the newly formed American Patriotic Party, then being organized by the eccentric billionaire, Hamilton Keyes, and would campaign for the vice-presidential spot on the national ticket. Rachel, a *Washington Post* columnist wrote, was "the evil of two lessers." Keyes and Rachel were the objects of much hilarity until Keyes casually stated that he would inject "one or two or three hundred million dollars into the campaign. Whatever it takes."

There was nothing in the biographical data that might explain Rachel Valentine. No individual can be known. Now and then a series of actions can illuminate, be turned into a neat syllogism: Rodrigo is a good man; a tumor grows in Rodrigo's brain; Rodrigo becomes a violent and irrational man. But a human life can't be charted. A led to B, B to C, C to D, D to a crowded plaza in a South American capital. We can't know ourselves, and so how can we presume to know another?

But I was reminded of what Rachel had long ago said about her brother: Hugh would have become either a fine poet or a superb con man, depending on how well he defended his idealism against realism.

I had to see her. It would be risky, but I settled on a plan.

TWENTY-SEVEN

The American Patriotic Party's B-level campaign fundraising dinner was held in a banquet hall in a large but less-than-elegant downtown hotel. The day's big-money A-category luncheon had taken place earlier, at the Edgewater Beach Hotel on Lakeshore Drive.

I passed through a metal detector manned by members of the private security team, Troxel's people, and strolled down a long corridor. That afternoon I had phoned the Party's Chicago headquarters and made a reservation under the name O'Neill, the name on my counterfeit Irish passport. I had never used it before, so I was fairly sure it would work.

A woman sitting at a low table just inside the banquet hall took my $500 and in return gave me a receipt, two coupons worth "free" cocktails, a pamphlet, and a handwritten card which advised me that I had chair twenty-six at table nineteen. Table nineteen was well below the salt, at the rear of the hall, an arrow shot away from the VIP table and dais.

It was early and the room was only about half full. Few of the people present looked as though they could easily afford the $500 political contribution. Three men and a woman stood together beneath a neon exit sign with the "E" burned out: XIT. Each wore

195

a laminated plastic photo ID card clipped to a pocket. Reporters. They regarded the people wandering around with a sort of genial disdain.

"I wouldn't vote for her, but I'd fuck her," one of the male reporters said.

Another said, "I wouldn't fuck her, but I'd vote for her."

The third man said, "I'd fuck her *and* vote for her."

"I wouldn't fuck her or vote for her," the woman said.

They were cool, jaded, a self-conscious vaudeville team.

More people were entering the hall, couples mostly, middle-aged or older, carefully—though not stylishly—dressed.

"Christ, will you look at these people?" one of the reporters said. "Uncle Jethro and Aunt Mabel."

"Non-voters," the woman said. 'Don't they look like non-voters? God help us all if the non-voters decide to vote."

"Democracy is fragile," a reporter said, "and cannot long survive if non-voters begin voting."

Now Troxel, wearing a tux, came through a curtained doorway at the front of the hall, mounted the steps to the dais, and surveyed the room. He was looking for me; I was expected. As we stared at each other the length of the hall, he raised his eyebrows, grinned, then descended the steps and went back through the curtain.

"What's on the menu?" a reporter asked his friends.

"Guess."

"Stewed chicken with mashed potatoes and gravy. Apple pie."

"*Non.*"

"Salisbury steak."

"*Nyet.*"

"Turkey?"

"*Nein.*"

"Well?"

"Pork chops."

Orson Dedrick, looking like the stiff figure of a groom on a wedding cake, came through the curtains and mounted the dais. He stared directly at me, but without a nod or smile or any sort of acknowledgment.

"One of those salads with shaved carrots and lots of red cabbage," the reporter said. "Apple sauce, peas, and pork chops. Poke chops."

"Washed down, no doubt," the woman said, "by hearty gulps of vintage Dr Pepper."

"Look at that guy," one of the reporters said, speaking of me. "The eavesdropper. A mortician?"

I was wearing my black suit with black shoes and a black tie.

Orson Dedrick descended the dais steps and went through the curtains.

"Sir," the female reporter called to me. "Sir?"

I watched a waitress weave her way through the tables toward the rear of the hall.

"Sir, why do you intend to vote for Rachel Valentine for President of these United States?"

The waitress approached me, halted uncertainly, and then said, "Mr. Tell?"

"Yes," I said. "That's me."

She gave me a folded sheet of paper.

"Thanks," I said.

She performed a sort of curtsy, backed away a few steps, then turned and walked toward the dais.

Jack,

There have been some dreadful mistakes, terrible misunderstandings. Please phone me at ten. *Please.*

Rachel

"Sir," the woman reporter said, "the people really want to
know. Why do you support the candidacy of Rachel Valentine?"

I folded the note and placed it in my pocket.

"Sir?"

"She's going to have my baby," I said, and I walked past them
and down the hallway.

It was raining and car lights and neons were blurrily reflected
on the pavement. The city smelled of wet concrete and automobile
exhausts and wetted dust that stung the nostrils like cordite.

My taxi was waiting. The driver was a chubby Indian named
Ranjit Chatterjee. Earlier I had given him a $100 bill and asked if
he were an honest man. He'd thought about it for a while, then said
that he was discreet, obedient, resourceful, and honest—though
not so honest that any of his six daughters were ever obliged to
miss a meal. I had asked if he could obtain a drug for me. "Oh,
no sar," he'd said. "No drugs." I'd told him that I didn't want a
bad drug; just a sedative, as I often had trouble sleeping. Chatterjee
considered. "It is possible."

Now, when I got into the taxi, he turned and passed me a vial
containing half a dozen white pills.

"What are these, Ranjit?'

"The date-rape drug, sar."

"Date rape?"

"GHB, sar, a powerful sedative they call the date-rape drug."

"Ah," I said. "It just so happens that I have a date tonight."

He gave me a worried look over his shoulder.

"Just kidding, Ranjit. Now please drive me to a good car rental agency."

At ten I called Rachel's number from a public telephone in a Rush Street bar.

She answered after the first ring. "Jack?"

"Hi," I said.

"You bastard. You scare me, Jackstraw."

"You scare me too," I said. "How were the poke chops?"

"Greasy."

"Are you in bed? What are you wearing?"

She laughed.

"Do you love me?" I asked.

"You know I do."

"Miss me?"

"So much."

"I didn't miss you."

"No, you hit me."

"Where is your right index finger at this instant?"

"It's touching the button."

"Clitoral or nuclear?"

"Clitoral. I won't have a nuclear button until after the inauguration. What are you holding in your hand, Jack?"

"Guess."

"Is it big?"

"Yes."

"Is it hard?"

"Yes. It's a telephone."

She laughed.

"In my other hand I'm holding your future, your fate."

"We've got to talk."

"We are talking."

"Face to face."

"And belly to belly?"

"Would you like that?"

"A friend of mine was killed yesterday."

"Yes. Joseph Cavenaugh. I heard."

"I wouldn't like to think . . ."

"Listen," she said, "we must talk. Tonight. Now. Will you meet me?"

"Can you slip away from your babysitters?"

"There are ways. We *must* talk, Jack."

"All right."

"Where shall we meet?"

"Go to the northwest corner of State and Randolph. Wait there."

"Half an hour?"

"Fine. Rachel—no tricks."

"Trust me."

"Sure," I said.

"I trusted you with my life."

"I know you did."

"And I'm again trusting you with my life, now."

"That's true. You are."

"Kill me if I betray you."

"I will."

"I mean it, Jack."

"So do I."

"We'll parley. All right? Maybe I can convince you that there have been misunderstandings, and that our interests actually coincide. Tonight we have a truce. Yes? Tomorrow? Who knows. But tonight we have a truce, don't we, darling, and we'll be friends until the truce expires."

"Half an hour," I said, and hung up the telephone.

TWENTY-EIGHT

I drove past the corner three times before I recognized Rachel: she was the hag in the translucent plastic raincoat, the over-the-hill hooker wearing a platinum blonde wig and a face smeared with makeup—crimson lipstick, cobalt eyeshadow, mascara, and rouge so thickly applied that it had cracked like dried mud.

She got into the car and we pulled away from the light. Her disguise was so convincing that I half expected her to reek of cheap whiskey and cheaper perfume.

"God," she said, relaxing back in the seat, "I feel like a truant schoolgirl."

"You take chances," I said.

"You knew that before tonight."

"You're at least half crazy."

"I don't measure my life out in coffee spoons, if that's what you mean."

"How did you escape Troxel's security team?"

"It wasn't hard. I'm not their captive, you know."

"What if they find out you slipped away?"

"Fuck them. They're just glorified bodyguards. I pay their salaries. I don't fret about the servants, Jack."

202

It was still raining. The city had a smell like burning rubber. I jigged the car up and down some side streets and ran a couple of red lights.

"No one is following us," Rachel said. "I came alone."

"Good."

The shock absorbers were no good, and so the car gently and continually undulated down the rough streets.

"Where are we going?" she asked.

"To a seedy hotel."

"Of course."

"A really seedy hotel."

"Perfect. You have impeccable social instincts."

A pair of headlights remained in my rear view mirror for several blocks, then turned off.

"Were you surprised to see me in Daley Plaza today?" I asked.

"It took me a while to recognize you. Your hair is short now, and you cut your beard. But you're still six-two, square-shouldered, and ramrod straight. But it worried me—who is this hard guy?"

"Were you scared?"

"When I finally recognized you? You bet I was scared."

"You thought I was going to kill you?"

"What would you think?"

"I did have a gun."

"I was wearing a vest," she said.

"No you weren't. Anyway, a head shot. What your associate Roger Clay did to your friend Hamilton Keyes."

"Did you go to the plaza to kill me, Jack?"

"No. Believe it or not, I was just passing by."

"It was your opportunity, though."

"I didn't think about killing you this morning. I thought about doing something else to you."

"Let me imagine what this is."

"Didn't you promise me a carnal night when we talked in your hotel room in Mundial?"

"I believe I did, yes."

"Well, now I'm going to collect."

"You don't make it sound very romantic."

"I know, but my itch ain't love, cupcake."

"Lust works almost as well," she said. "Better, really, in bed."

"We'll see."

"Do I get under your skin, Jack?"

"Like a tick."

I saw two smiles: the old whore's painted grimace and, beneath that, the cool smile of Rachel Valentine.

I said, "You think: So what, it's only a little tick—but then after a few days you start burning with viral fevers."

I pulled up onto the Kennedy Expressway, drove a few miles, then turned down an exit ramp.

"It was cute," I said. "the way you set me up in Mundial."

"That wasn't me, Jack."

"You and Troxel."

"It wasn't me and it wasn't Alex. Rafael Betancourt and his gang betrayed all of us."

"You lie."

"Rafael and his section of the Federal Judicial Police had their own scheme. They double-crossed me, Hamilton, Roger, Troxel, and you, Jack—all of us."

"Sure."

"But they underestimated you, didn't they?" She was silent for a time, looking out the side window, and then she said, "Should I be frightened now? Should I be desperately scared at this moment?"

"Rachel, I'm not as eager to kill you as you like to believe."

"I dream about it. I've had dreams for years where someone is coming to kill me. It's night, and I'm alone, and a man is going to kill me. There's nothing I can do to prevent it, no escape. I can only wait to be murdered. Lately, that man has your face. Do you believe that dreams can be prophetic?"

"Sure, dreams can be prophetic," I said. "Like, say, a stickup man might have dreams about the penitentiary, a killer might dream of being killed."

It was Saturday night and the streets were busy with vehicular and pedestrian traffic. I parked the car on a side street five blocks from the hotel, and we started walking. Loud salsa music issued from the open doors and windows of a dancehall. Groups of young men, indifferent to the drizzle, were gathered on street corners and in front of bars. Rain dimpled the puddles and ticked softly on Rachel's raincoat. The men looked at her with mirth and at me with derision. "*La puta primera,*" one said, and the others laughed. The first whore. Rachel ignored the male scrutiny and the jibes.

"Is this an attempt to humiliate me?" she asked.

"I couldn't find a closer parking space. Anyway, you chose the disguise. Are you humiliated?"

"No." She smiled. "But I'm not flattered, either. Baby, I came out tonight, I'm here, because I intend to persuade you to join me."

"As your vice-president?"

"My gray eminence."

"The man behind the throne?"

We turned a corner. "My life, my heart, my soul," a young man crooned at Rachel.

"I need you, Jack," she said. "I knew all along that something has been missing—it was you or someone like you. Alex Troxel is a man of action, but he isn't very smart. He's a loose cannon. Orson Dedrick is smart, but he isn't a man of action. You're both. You proved that. What you did in Mundial was incredible. I need you. I can't do it alone."

We went up the hotel steps through the door. The lobby lizards and the Pakistani desk clerk looked at us in astonishment: why, with so many pretty young women out dancing and strolling the streets tonight, had the man selected that jaded old tart?

We rode the slow elevator up to the fourth floor and walked down the dim, shabby hallway to my room. There were cigarette burn holes in the carpet; you could smell urine and disinfectant and mold. We went into the room, and I switched on a couple of lights.

"The bridal suite," I said.

Beneath her cheap plastic raincoat I could see patches of color; an aqua-blue blouse, a midnight blue skirt. Rachel kicked off her shoes, removed the platinum-blonde wig and, smiling faintly, looked around the room.

A boxed picture of a wilderness cabin hung on the wall opposite the bed. A light behind the picture came on when I plugged it in, and the cabin's windows and a big full moon—tinted cellophane patches—glowed an egg-yolk yellow. In the foreground a fox with his bushy tail lifted looked yearningly toward the cabin's light and warmth.

"Want a drink?" I asked.

"What do you have?"

"Wine. Piper Heidsieck."

"Lovely. What's the occasion?"

"Sex."

"Not sex and violence?"

"Marx said that religion was the opium of the people. But that was in an age of belief. Now sex is the opium of the people."

"I'm going to clean off this paint," she said.

She went into the bathroom, and I heard the ventilation fan go off, followed by the hissing of the shower.

I dumped the contents of her purse onto the bed: a compact cell phone; a makeup kit; a wallet containing only credit cards and thirty dollars in cash; a deck of Tarot cards; a .25 Astra pistol with a full clip; and a small leather notebook with a gold pen attached. The pages were blank. I removed the batteries from the cell phone, and hid them and the pistol in the closet.

Rachel was wearing the plastic raincoat when she came out of the bathroom, but she was naked beneath it now, and through the translucence I could see peach flesh tones, a glimpse of breast and thigh when she moved, a shadow of pubic hair. Her wet hair was sleekly combed back. She had gone into the bathroom disguised as an old whore and five minutes later emerged youthful, cleansed, and powerfully erotic in a ten-dollar raincoat.

I got one of the wine bottles from the refrigerator, popped the cork, and filled two glasses.

"Is Jackstraw really your name? It sounds made up."

"It was my grandfather's name, and my father's, so I guess it's mine too."

"Do you know of the game, jackstraw?"

"You throw a bunch of straws or thin sticks out in a pile and take turns trying to remove them one by one without disturbing the others."

"Kids call the game pick-up-sticks. It's also known as spilikins. Did you know that?"

"I did."

"I'll think of you as Mr. Spilikins."

Rachel set her glass on a bedside table, unsnapped her raincoat, and tossed it over a chair. She half turned so that I could see the lumpy bruise on her rib cage to the left of, and a little below, her heart.

"The bullet?" I asked.

She nodded.

"Hurt?"

"A little. Some rib cartilage was torn."

"A pretty good shot," I said. I removed my shoes and socks.

"An excellent shot."

She had an extraordinary figure for a woman near forty; she might have been thirty, or even younger. No doubt that was due in part to the luck of her genes, but I supposed too that she exercised daily with the rigor of a professional athlete or dancer, which she had been in her youth, and hers was a dancer's body, lithe and taut, with small breasts and long legs and neck, and she moved with a trained grace. I could not imagine her ever losing her poise, becoming awkward.

I removed my shirt, my trousers. "You're beautiful."

She watched me.

"Though you have the mind of a Borgia." I removed my shorts.

She waited, smiling.

"And the heart of a reptile."

"And you have a fine, hard body, Jack. Though you have the mind of a delinquent Boy Scout and no heart at all."

TWENTY-NINE

At first the sex was a kind of combat, a quick and brutal fusion of bodies. We copulated like angry beasts. I was cruel; she was defiant. There was a mutual hatred in it. But there was no victory for either of us: Rachel refused to be humiliated, and I would not be placated. We spasmed, as barnyard animals spasm. But then, surprising us both, something happened. We were altered in some way. A contrary truth emerged. We kissed, we gently touched, our hearts as well as our bodies engaged, and we made love. And it was love now, no matter how incidental or temporary—it was that rare merging of two solitary selves, and it lasted for hours. It lasted a long time and then, of course, it ended.

We lay there, spent, quiet, for a while. She had awakened emotions I hadn't felt in years—since Beth's accident. Or was it an accident? A drunk driving almost a hundred miles an hour down the wrong way on Interstate 25 who smashed straight into Beth's car, killing both of them instantly and leaving an accident scene in which it was impossible to tell which part belonged to which car. Grown men, veterans of hundreds of wrecks, cried, undone by the sheer unparalleled violence and destruction. And the two bodies that were barely recognizable as human. They had both died instantly. So had a third.

Beth had called me the night before to tell me the news. She was pregnant. She was going to drive to her parents' house to tell them in person—she wanted it to be a surprise. They would be the next to know, after me. No one else knew. And no one else ever did.

Rachel Valentine had stirred feelings I didn't think I still had. But she couldn't be trusted. I had to take precautions.

I showered, and when I returned Rachel was sitting on the edge of the bed, combing her hair with her fingers. She paused to look up at me. She started to speak, halted, smiled, got up and walked past me to the bathroom.

While she showered, I opened the other bottle of wine and poured our glasses full. The directions on the label of the bottle of GHB advised caution. I dropped two of the pills into Rachel's glass and watched them dissolve in the rising bubbles.

We sat naked on the bed with our backs against the headboard, sipping our wine and looking at the painting on the opposite wall where the moon and cabin windows still glowed an egg-yolk yellow and the fox still crouched in the snow with a foxy yearning.

I said, "You told me that Betancourt betrayed all of us in Mundial. How?"

"Jack, it's late. I can't stay."

"Tell me."

"Rafael was a crucial part of our plans. He was one of the top men in the Policía Judicial Federal. He could control things down there. He was a power in the government but working for us. Troxel knew him from years ago and trusted him. A mistake, obviously."

I said, "Betancourt hired me and Cavenaugh and put together the guerrilla unit three months before the kidnapping of the missionaries. You were thinking that far ahead?"

"Yes."

"Why me?"

"Troxel knew about you, knew you from the past. He was sure you'd accept the job of training our little group of soldiers. He told Betancourt to hire you."

"Which he did. But I never agreed to the snatching of missionaries."

"And Alex thought that there was a good chance you'd agree to take part in the fake assassination. You were an excellent marksman, he said, and"—she smiled—"generally a rogue son of a bitch."

"And if I refused to shoot you?"

"Well, then someone else would have to do it. Roger Clay, probably."

"Yeah, but Roger was occupied shooting Hamilton Keyes in the head."

"No, Jack. No, no, no, you've got that wrong. Roger was in the wig shop only as a backup, in the event you double-crossed us. Troxel was afraid you'd run off with the $250,000, so he sent Roger into the building just in case. Betancourt or one of the others, Herrera or Baltazar, shot Hamilton, then they killed Roger. They were going to kill you, too. Kill you, take the money, and pose as the national heroes who had killed the terrorist kidnappers and assassins in a gunfight. They would have it both ways, you see. The money we had already paid them, plus the money they would take from you, and all the glory. Rafael was ambitious. He wanted to be president of his country."

"As do you. But why murder Keyes? You had something to gain from that. Betancourt didn't."

"But he did have something to gain: a reputation, fame, international gratitude and respect as the man who had bravely fought and killed the assassins."

"Help," I said. "I'm falling down a rabbit hole."

"I'm not lying, Jack."

The drug had not affected her. I took our glasses into the little kitchen area, dropped another pill into her glass, and filled both with champagne.

"I want you with me," she said when I had returned to the bed. "Not just like this—though tonight was magical, and there'll be more magical nights for us. I need your mind and your toughness. You will join me, won't you?"

"No."

"Oh, but you will join me, Jack, you've already joined me. The fact that you're here in bed with me now instead of spilling your guts in some FBI office tells me that we're together."

I said, "I'm not in an FBI office now because I'm implicated in half a dozen serious felonies."

"No. We're soulmates. I've been looking for you my whole life, and without knowing it, you've been looking for me. Well, we've found each other at last. It's a true thing. Don't you feel the truth of it?"

"Rachel, if I thought you had anything to do with the murder of Cavenaugh you wouldn't leave this hotel room alive."

"I had nothing to do with it. Believe it or not. Kill me or not."

"Maybe Troxel killed Cav on his own."

"I've got to go now, really. We'll meet again, we'll be together, but not for a while. We've got to get you to a safe place. Out of this country. Troxel is working on it. How does Turkey sound? We have friends there, so you'll have friends there, and plenty of money. Speaking of money—damn you for throwing a quarter million dollars out the window."

Her speech was slurred now, but not much, and she had drunk a lot of wine.

"Why do I have to leave the country?" I asked.

"Think, lover. With Betancourt and his people dead we haven't any control over the investigation. The FBI and the Secret Service are down there now, working with the government, and they won't tell us anything. We're in the dark. They're in Paraje, they're in Mundial, they're everywhere, it's out of our control, and it's certain that your name will come up sooner or later."

"Sooner, probably."

"Even if they do identify you, it will be in connection with El Puño Rojo, leftwing terrorist gangs, all of that."

"Very pretty."

"And now I *must* go."

"Okay. We'll finish the wine."

Rachel had drunk nearly a bottle of wine. She seemed more drunk than sedated; her eyes shone, and she was talkative and very confident.

I said, "When you're in the White House, will I have to address you as Madame President?"

"You may address me—and undress me—as you please."

"Let's drink to the latter."

We sipped our wine.

"You can't win," I said.

"Have you seen the poll numbers?"

"Yeah, but you can't free hostage missionaries and stage an assassination every week."

She passed a hand slowly across her face, as if removing cobwebs. "The voters know me now."

"No they don't. No one knows you."

"They think they do. I have a face, a voice, a style, an image now. Some hate me, some love me, some are indifferent, but I exist in their minds . . ." She trailed off. Rachel usually spoke crisply, she hit all of her consonants, but her speech was slurred now.

"You can't win," I said.

"This—this is a three-party race. I don't need fifty-one percent of the vote. It's possible to win the popular vote with—with just . . . thirty-four percent."

"But then there's the Electoral College."

"That, yes, and maybe the House, but—" she lost her thought. "Jack?"

"Your party will receive seven or eight percent of the vote automatically. That's the protest vote, from people who despise both major parties, who want to register their contempt, who'd vote for Cesar Borgia if he were on the ballot."

Her smile was slack, her eyelids at half-mast. "Or Lucrezia Borgia."

"You might get a few more points from women. When the curtain closes behind them in the booth, when they're alone, some will vote APP, vote female, vote Rachel. Haven't men fucked up the world for ten thousand years?"

"Jack . . ." The glass fell from her hand, spilling the wine. "Oh," she said. "Shit."

"The protest vote, some women, the cranks and malcontents, extremists—not enough votes, Rachel."

She was stunned by the alcohol and sedative, half paralyzed now. She spoke, but I could not understand the words. Her head lolled. Her heavy-lidded eyes were without life or light, and her skin was clammy-cool to the touch.

I said, "I don't claim that you *can't* win. The election is still weeks away. Strange, unpredictable things could happen between now and then. Your election isn't impossible just because all the jackass prophets say it's impossible. After all, the people decide, don't they?"

Very slowly and with great effort, she slid down the mattress until she was lying on her side, facing away from me. Her breathing was irregular; she panted for a few seconds, hardly breathed at all for a time, then again panted.

"But on election day, the people will spit you out like a bite of rotten egg."

Her pulse, like her breathing, lagged for a time and then accelerated. I wondered if her erratic inhalations and exhalations were what doctors called agonal breathing. There surely was a muted sort of agony in it. Maybe I had used too many of the GHB pills—sedatives in combination with alcohol were very dangerous.

I turned Rachel on her back. Her skin was damp; there was a crackling in her exhalations; the fingers of her right hand twitched. I dragged over the kitchen table, balanced and angled the camera on top, set the time, and got into the bed. Ten seconds later there was a click and a flash, and then a whirr as the film advanced. I repeated that shot twice.

Next I removed the shrunken head from my duffel and placed it on the pillow. Even with its eyes and mouth shut it appeared to be leering. Cav leered at me, at the camera, at life and death. I took half a dozen shots from various angles.

I got dressed then, and packed my things, and Rachel's small pistol, in the duffel.

Rachel, though unconscious, turned away from the shrunken head as if in revulsion. You had to listen carefully to determine that she still breathed. Her lips were dry, parted, with flecks of foam at the corners. The bullet bruise on her ribs was purplish against the whiteness of skin. Maybe she would be all right. Rachel was tough.

There she was: about five foot nine, one hundred and thirty-five pounds, an attractive and intelligent woman from a good background. She would draw your eye on the street or in a crowded room. You would understand that, in some indefinable way, she was special. You might fall halfway in love with her.

But the woman had cynically arranged the kidnapping of four missionaries only so that she might receive credit for their release; she had been complicit in the raid on the army river outpost, insuring that other soldiers there could not respond to the kidnappings; she had perhaps ordered the killing of Hamilton Keyes and Joseph Cavenaugh; and all of this with the blithe spirits of a child knocking over a row of toy soldiers. Rachel was as bright and hard as a diamond.

I made five quick telephone calls: the *Chicago Tribune*, the *Sun-Times*, and three local television stations, telling all of them that presidential candidate Rachel Leah Valentine could be found in a very sordid situation in Room 486 of the Hotel Adams. Then I phoned 911 and informed the dispatcher that screams and gunshots had been heard coming from Room 486, in the Adams Hotel.

"And your name, sir?" the dispatcher asked.

"Troxel," I said.

When I paused at the door, Rachel half-opened her eyes and stared at me long and blindly, and then her eyelids slowly closed.

"Goodbye, Rachel," I said. "Adios, Cav."

THIRTY

Two men were waiting for the elevator down in the lobby. Their eyes had that dead look, and they exuded that physical arrogance that only men accustomed to violence can. Cops, maybe, or a pair of Troxel's hard guys.

The desk clerk gave me a half-smile as I slapped the key down on his counter. The clock on the wall behind him read 12:52. "And the lady?" he asked. "Checking out?"

"It looked that way," I said.

Eight or ten old people, some in pajamas and bathrobes, were clustered around the lobby's big-screen television. The picture was of Rachel this morning at Daley Plaza, with the huge Picasso sculpture rising above and behind her. As I walked by, the picture switched to a panning shot of the crowd and for an instant I saw myself in the background, smiling at the candidate.

The rain had slowed to a fine mist. My breath vaporized in the cool air. Many people still roamed the neighborhood and gathered on street corners, and the dancehall band still loudly played salsa. A few belligerent drunks challenged me in both English and Spanish as I walked by. The air had a scorched smell. I could hear wailing police and ambulance sirens, some close, some far away, and behind me the jittery beat of the music.

The rental car was gone. I stared stupidly at the vacant space alongside the curb. It was a year-old Ford Focus, not something to interest a professional car thief, though it might appeal to Saturday night joyriders.

I resumed walking east. There was a fairly busy through street a few blocks ahead where I could catch a taxi to the airport.

The scorched smell became stronger as I went on; burnt steel, gasoline and oil, smoking tires. The intersection ahead flashed with spinning lights, and I heard more sirens. Shadowy figures moved spectrally through a pinkish glow.

There were four police cars, roof lights spinning and radios crackling, a firetruck, and two ambulances. A cop at the center of the intersection directed traffic. Firemen had extinguished the blaze except for smoking pieces of debris scattered over the street. Plate-glass shop windows had been shattered by the concussion or by flying bits of metal. A few yards down the sidewalk a woman, her face bloody, was being attended by paramedics. She might have been hit by a piece of shrapnel. Other paramedics were loading a body bag onto a collapsible gurney. The policemen blew his whistle and gestured for a few more cars to proceed across the intersection. An uncontrollable shiver ran down my back. I forced myself to look.

What remained of the car squatted low in the road, little more than a twisted, sooty heap of scrap metal. The entire roof had been blown off. The flat tires continued to smolder. Now, along with the scorched odor, I could smell the chemical foam used by the firemen to extinguish the blaze. You could not guess at the car's color; all of the paint had been burned off and its license plate was gone.

Nearby, two teenaged boys were disputing a fact.

"It was a Toyota," one said.

"No, man," the other said.

"A black Toyota."

"No, man, I seen it. It was a blue Ford Focus."

PART FIVE
ANGLES

THIRTY-ONE

Early in the morning I took the long taxi ride from the Denver airport to a storage facility on the southern edge of the city. My five-year-old Chevy pickup needed a battery charge before it would start. I got some things from my locker—household possessions, a few books, my guitar, my Winchester carbine—and then caught Interstate 25 south toward Colorado Springs.

It was a cool, clear morning, and I drove with the side windows down, inhaling the wind. After spending months in the tropics, breathing mountain air was like drinking a rare elixir that promised the restoration of energy and hope.

A bland radio voice informed me that the American Patriotic Party candidate, Rachel Valentine, had been taken ill last night and would stay over in Chicago for an extra day or two. A spokesman, Orson Dedrick, stated that Ms. Valentine had suffered a fainting spell. It was nothing serious, a viral infection, but the candidate would rest in her hotel suite before resuming the campaign.

It was easy to figure. The two men waiting for the elevator in the hotel had been members of Troxel's security team, not cops. They had somehow succeeded in getting Rachel away before the police and reporters arrived. It must have been a considerable task to get

223

the unconscious Rachel out of that room, across town, and back into her own hotel quarters without being discovered. No doubt the car explosion and fire had diverted the police and media people for a crucial few minutes. Still, Alex Troxel and his men had performed very well. They were good, and of course, Rachel was lucky. The woman took terrible chances, crazy risks, but she had luck.

Obviously Troxel had found out where I was staying and learned the license number and description of the rental car. Troxel himself had rigged the explosive device in the Ford. He was vain about his demolition skills. The charge had been detonated either by remote electronic command or a time-delay switch. A professional job, but then a car thief had blundered onto the scene, incidentally saving my life and, by delaying the arrival of the cops and reporters, saved Rachel's campaign for the presidency. Good luck and bad luck, distributed as if by a perverse deity.

I stopped at a newsstand in Colorado Springs and bought three newspapers: the *New York Times*, the *Chicago Tribune*, and the *Denver Post*. Apparently the announcement about Rachel's illness had come too late to make the early editions of the papers, but each had a brief story about the destruction of an automobile last night. Authorities said that it was likely that a car bomb was involved. The victim had not yet been identified. Chicago police and the Bureau of Alcohol, Tobacco and Firearms were investigating the explosion.

At noon I stopped at a shopping center in Pueblo to buy groceries, went on a couple more miles, and then turned off the Interstate onto a two-lane road that led directly west across ranch country. I was still on the plains, but ahead now I could see the rocky peaks of the Sangre de Cristo range cleanly etched against a cerulean sky. Snow had collected in the high ravines. I drove west for almost twenty miles, jogged south once more, coasting through the little town of

Whistle. It had been named Whistle supposedly because you could stand at one end of town and hear a man whistling at the other end.

Nine miles out of Whistle I turned off the paved road and onto a rutted track that tacked up a steep hill and then leveled out near my cabin. Home.

I stepped out into the hot sunlight. Off in the brush locusts buzzed like rattlesnakes. A hawk carved diminishing circles in the sky, creating—if you could imagine it—a perfect pinwheel design. The land had a spicy scent.

Everything looked okay at a glance: the place hadn't been visited by squatters or vandals during my absence; the spring hadn't dried up; the cottonwood trees looked healthy.

Cavenaugh had always smiled whenever I talked about my ranch. He had visited me here a couple of times. "Rancho Poco," he called it. It was eight hundred acres of mostly scrubland that lay at the base of the foothills. There was a one-room log cabin with an outhouse fifty yards up the track and a dilapidated springhouse another fifty yards past that. The spring's runoff provided enough moisture so that some big cottonwoods grew around the cabin. Elsewhere there was sage and chamiso, some twisted junipers, and higher up, scrub oak and piñon. "El Rancho Pobre," Cavenaugh called it. "Prairie Dog Estates."

The land was not much good for raising cattle; even worse for growing crops; but it had a million-dollar view of the eastern flank of the Sangre de Cristos and allowed the kind of solitude that was beyond price nowadays. My land was bordered on the east by the road; on the north and west by lands administered by the U.S. Forest Service; and the south by a huge cattle company. Only the coyotes came calling.

Beth and I had been happy here, intermittently, whenever I was not working. We could have been happy a long, long time.

THIRTY-TWO

At a little after ten o'clock the next morning I heard a car engine. I picked up my thirty-thirty carbine, levered a cartridge into the chamber, then went to the east window and lifted the sash. The vehicle was climbing the long incline from the road in one of the lower gears. My isolation had not lasted long.

A black Ford Explorer topped the rise, moved slowly—rocking in the ruts—along level ground, and stopped beneath a cottonwood. The engine was switched off and in the renewed silence I heard cicadas and the pretty song of a meadowlark.

Sunlight silvered the car's windows, and the driver was only a shadow hunched over the steering wheel. The air was powdered with dust that gleamed like gold flakes in the sunlight.

Finally the car door opened and Anna Fontenot stepped down. She took a few awkward steps toward the cabin, then halted. She was scared; you could see it in her stride and, when she stopped, the way she stood with her hands clenched and her eyes round, waiting for something bad to happen.

I put the rifle aside and went out onto the porch. Anna turned awkwardly. She gazed at me with a victim's wounded appeal.

"Hello, Anna," I said.

"Hello." A nervous smile.

Twice I had seen her frightened; once in the bell tower at the Mission, and again now, and both times I had been the source of her fear.

"Want some coffee?" I asked her.

"Coffee would be nice."

"I've got a few stale Danish rolls, too."

"I'm hungry."

"Well, come on then."

She smiled and walked toward me. It was a beautiful smile; her eyes were changed, her grace restored, and the angled morning sunlight ignited her hair as she moved from the shadows. There was a small crescent-shaped scar on her left cheek. The wood splinter.

Anna curiously explored the cabin while I set a pot of coffee on the camp stove, sorted through drawers and cabinets for cups and utensils, got out canned milk and sugar and the bag of raspberry Danishes.

"How did you find me, Anna?"

"You told me in Paraje that you lived in Southern Colorado, near a town called Whistle. Remember?"

"Yeah, but this place is pretty remote. Nine miles from Whistle."

"Finding your turnoff was tricky."

"Did you ask about me in town?"

"No. I didn't think you'd like that."

"You thought right. So how did you find me?"

"Public records," she said. "Deeds, titles, tax rolls, information about water and mineral rights."

"Impressive."

"I spent most of yesterday afternoon at the county seat, doing research."

"Then it was easy to find me."

"Relatively easy."

"Dumb me. I thought I was invisible."

She smiled. "No one can hide anymore."

"And you—you're an effective snoop."

"I'm a reporter, Jack."

"For a popular science magazine."

"I worked for years on newspapers before I got that job. I'm a reporter."

I turned off the stove's burner and set the aluminum pot aside so that the grounds might settle.

I said, "If you were able to locate me so easily, then others can do the same."

"Yes."

"Well. Now I have to get away from here sooner than I planned."

"You're in serious trouble, aren't you?"

I smiled. "Serious ain't the word. I suppose you've been questioned about the kidnappings."

"Oh, yes. At the Mission afterward, in Paraje, here in the States—the FBI visited me in San Diego."

"You didn't tell them about me?"

"No."

"Why not?"

"Because you said you'd kill me if I identified you."

"No, Anna, I never said that."

"You did."

"I said nothing like that."

She was quiet a moment, frowning, and then she touched the crescent scar on her cheek and said, "It was implied."

"No. I told you in the tower that I'd never hurt you."

"That in itself was an implied threat."

"I think this is called a double-bind."

"You said you'd never hurt me, and then you shot a bullet three inches from my face."

"More like two feet."

"And isn't that an implied threat?"

"That was to make others think I'd killed you."

I poured coffee through a strainer into the two mugs. We sat on opposite sides of the table. Anna would not look at me.

"You're still afraid of me, aren't you?"

"No."

"You are."

"A little."

"That's two. Two women who are frightened of me."

"The other?"

"Rachel Valentine. Though her fear is justified."

"You know Rachel Valentine?"

"Intimately, but not well."

"What does that mean? You're lovers?" She looked at me challengingly.

"Why," I asked, "did you come here if you're afraid of me?"

"I want the story."

"The story of what really happened?"

"Yes."

"You want the story more than you fear occupying a shallow grave behind this cabin."

She lifted her coffee cup, drank, lowered the cup and smiled. "I quit my job. I'm free-lance now. I can take this story anywhere—the *New York Times*, CBS, anywhere in the world."

"Anna Fontenot, star reporter, celebrity journalist, hot on the trail of the scoop of the new century."

She picked up a knife and cut her Danish roll into quarters.

"It's very complicated," I said.

"Jack . . . Did you assassinate Hamilton Keyes?"

"Complicated, and dangerous for you."

"Hamilton Keyes. Did you kill him?"

"No."

She slowly exhaled. "Then you weren't involved in that part of it."

"I shot Rachel Valentine, though."

"God. I didn't want to hear that."

"Eat something. Drink your coffee."

"I've lost my appetite."

"Eat, and then we'll go for a walk."

"Are you going to make me dig my own shallow grave?"

I smiled. "I'm going to tell you the whole story, all of it. It will make you dizzy. It'll make you famous."

"A conspiracy."

"You bet."

"Good. Everyone loves a conspiracy." She played with her coffee cup for a moment. "You've got a good smile. I trust you."

"You may regret that."

After breakfast we strolled west toward the mountains. It was warm now and the air smelled bittersweet with the medicinal odors of chamiso and sage and juniper. Off to our left a meadowlark whistled its intricate scale, and then, farther up the track, another repeated the exact melody.

I said, "Each meadowlark has his own patch of territory. You can walk for miles out here and hear male meadowlarks all the way."

"Lovely."

"And one spring I saw hundreds of bluebirds gathered together. They had migrated from the south, Mexico probably, and remained flocked for a day or two. Hundreds of bluebirds strung out on an electrical wire like turquoise beads on a string."

"Who would have guessed that you are a birdie sort of guy," she said.

"You can see hawks around here too," I said. "Redtails, peregrines, kestrels. Golden eagles in the high country."

"That's more like it. Eagles, hawks—tough birds. Not sissy birds like meadowlarks and bluebirds. I bet you like flowers, too."

"God, no."

"Don't lie."

"Women's stuff, flowers. Hate 'em."

"What are those lavender flowers in the field?"

"Don't know. Hate flowers."

"If you were to guess . . . ?"

"I'd guess chicory."

She smiled.

We paused at the old corral, folding our arms over the top rail and looking in at the barren hoof-trampled dirt, the axe-carved wooden trough and the rusty water tank.

"This is fine country for riding," I said. "I've always wanted to buy a couple of saddle horses."

"Why didn't you?"

"I'm away from here most of the time."

"You could always board out your horses while you're gone, couldn't you?"

"Yeah."

We resumed walking. You could see three 14,000-foot mountains from there; rocky monoliths linked together by a ridge system, steep, snow-streaked, thrusting up into the luminous blue sky.

"Beautiful," Anna said.

"Yes, and this is the less interesting side. The western slope is spectacular—great rock faces, rock towers, spires, all of that."

The spring was enclosed by a wooden building like a garden shed.

"Thirsty?" I asked.

"Yes."

I unlocked the door, stepped inside, and filled two tin cups from the pool.

Anna sipped the water. "It's icy cold. It makes my teeth ache."

"Tastes good, doesn't it?"

"It doesn't have any taste at all."

"That's good, for water."

"Is it safe?"

"Sure. It bubbles up out of the ground here."

"This is nice," she said. "I like your place."

"Rancho Poco, Rancho Pobre. Come on."

We carried our cups a few more yards up the track and sat with our backs against the trunk of a big cottonwood. There was enough of a breeze to spin the leaves and they flashed green and silver overhead, green and silver, whispering like old querulous wood spirits.

"All right," I said. "Ready?"

Anna said, "Start, as they say, at the beginning, and end at the end."

"As yet, we're only in the middle," I told her.

THIRTY-THREE

At three o'clock Anna crawled into the cabin's upper bunk for a nap. She had driven straight through from San Diego yesterday, arriving in the afternoon; worked several hours at the county courthouse, locating my place; and then spent a sleepless night in a motel room while drunken men pounded on her door and incoherently begged for love.

I got two towels, one blue and the other white, carried them outside and spread them over the picnic table. A surprise for Anna: her fortune. I removed the gemstones from the dented tobacco tin, unwrapped them one by one, and displayed them on the cloths. Each diamond seemed to gain a carat when viewed against the dark blue; the emeralds were clarified by the white background and cast focused green blurs. All of the cut and polished stones contained fire at their centers, microcosmic suns.

I sat in the pickup for a while, trying to tune in a news station, but radio reception was often poor here in the shadow of the mountains. Reception would improve after sunset.

Late in the afternoon the sun descended behind a high mountain ridge to the west, releasing a shadow that slowly crawled down the slopes, down the foothills to the plain. The air would cool soon. There might be a hard frost tonight.

I built a pyramid of charcoal in the brazier, poured a coffee can full of kerosene over it, and struck a match. After a time the oily smoke vanished and the fire burned clean. I walked up to the springhouse, listening to meadowlarks all the way, and got two chilled steaks and two bottles of wine.

Anna was awake when I entered the cabin. She sat on the edge of the upper bunk, her bare legs dangling, while sleepily brushing her hair.

"Hi," she said.

"I was going to kiss you awake."

"Oh, too bad."

"Hungry?"

"Maybe. What's the chow?"

"Steak, salad, asparagus, potato chips. An anonymous red wine, eight dollars a bottle."

"Wine snob," she said.

"Get out of bed, you lazy strumpet."

I helped her down from the bunk, took her hand and led her outside and around the cabin to the picnic table. She sleepily gazed down at the stones.

"What?" Anna said.

"The legacy from your father."

"Oh?"

"Don't you remember me telling you in the bell tower that I had found your inheritance?"

She looked at me for a moment, then returned her gaze to the display of stones. "Are they real?"

"Diamonds and emeralds, Anna. You're rich."

"Should I be excited?"

"Your father collected these stones over many years. The diamonds in Africa, the emeralds in Colombia. He invested everything in these stones. He sacrificed for them."

She had carried the brush outside and now she again began to brush her hair in long strokes.

"My father was a miser?"

"You told me that he wrote you, mentioned a legacy. Well, here it is."

"He was a miser, wasn't he?"

"I suppose so. Yes."

"He sacrificed everything to collect those cold, hard things— minerals, stones."

"Yes."

"Are they really valuable?" She ceased brushing and looked at me.

"Haven't you been listening?"

"If they're valuable, why didn't you keep them? I would never know."

"They belong to you."

"Are you so honest?"

"I'm not a thief."

"They're marvelous, beautiful things, these stones. You tell me that and I believe you. You know their value. My father knew their value. But I just don't care much about things that don't have life in them. I love your meadowlarks and chicory flowers, but these things . . . To me they're like coprolites."

"Like what?"

"Petrified feces."

I laughed.

"I'm sorry. I'm just not interested in them at the moment."

"Well, take good care of them. You may someday lose your romantic contempt for money."

"Look who's talking. You're the one who threw a quarter million dollars out of a window."

I said, "Give the stones to the Little Sisters of the Poor."

"Make fun of me if you like."

"Trade them in for a generation of meadowlarks."

"I'd trade them all for a kiss."

I moved close and kissed the corner of her mouth. She accepted it but didn't respond.

"I meant . . . I was talking about the past. I meant a kiss from my father, a touch, a gentle word, an hour of his company during the last twenty years. While he was collecting rocks."

I felt sorry for Anna and at the same time I was irritated by her morose father-daughter lamentations. "Anyway, they're yours," I said. "Do what you want with them."

"All right," she said. "Take one. Take two, three, four, whatever."

"No."

"Really. You deserve a share."

"No, Anna."

"Please. I mean it. It's rude to refuse a gift."

I sighed. "Then you pick one out for me."

She looked over the array of stones, touched one, then another, and finally selected the largest of the emeralds and gave it to me.

"Thank you, Anna."

"I'm awfully grateful to you," she said. "And I apologize for being so silly."

"This emerald will always be known as the Anna Fontenot Memorial Coprolite. Like the Hope Diamond."

She smiled, and then surprised me and herself by breaking out in tears.

"You're such a bastard," she said. "And you're doomed."

The charcoals had a dusty white look now, and so I spread them evenly over the bottom of the brazier pan. I uncorked a bottle of wine.

"We need glasses," I said. "Plates, utensils, condiments. If you'll get them from the cabin, I'll put the steaks on the grill."

Anna wiped the tears away with her fingertips. "Did you really sleep with that Rachel Valentine pig?"

"Indeed I did."

"And then you left her for dead."

"Tough love."

"You might have killed the bitch."

"No. You'd need a silver bullet or a wooden stake for that task."

"Listen, all that you told me this afternoon? I want to go over it with you later. I have questions."

"Fine."

"I'll get the things," she said, "but I'm not hungry."

Ann ate her own steak and part of mine, and finished the salad and asparagus. We sat in the twilight while stars appeared one by one above the darker, the eastern, horizon. It was chilly now. I smoked a cigar while we started on the second bottle of wine.

"Jackstraw, why don't you dig a well here? Install a pump, pipes. You know, actual plumbing, running water. Burn down that ghastly latrine. String up electrical wiring."

"And I'll buy lace curtains, adopt a yappy lapdog."

"Stop living in squalor. Get a woman."

"Are you applying?"

"God, no. Try your Valentine vampire."

THIRTY-FOUR

Inside the cabin I lit four kerosene lanterns, hung two from wall hooks and placed the other two on the trestle table. Anna changed into jeans and a bulky knit sweater. When I sat down across from her she switched on a tape recorder.

"No taping," I said.

"Why not?"

"No tape."

"But it's so much easier and more accurate than taking notes."

I reached out and switched off the recorder. "Easy to play to a jury, too."

"Come on. You can read notes to a jury, you know."

"That's not the same. Notes can be challenged and quotes can be denied. There's no wiggle room with a recording."

Exasperated, she got up from the table and returned a moment later with a steno pad and a ballpoint pen.

"Okay?" she asked.

"Go."

"Now, you told me this afternoon that this Rafael Betancourt was the man who hired you for the job of training the Indian soldiers. How did that come about exactly?"

238

"Betancourt flew to Chicago and talked to Cavenaugh, and then—wait. Write your notes in longhand."

"What?"

"Longhand."

"What, for God's sake, is the difference if I take my notes in cursive or shorthand?"

"The difference is, I can't read shorthand. I'll want to review your notes."

"What if I say you can't review my notes?"

"I'll say the interview is over."

"Damn!" she said. Then she flipped to a new page. "Okay, crank it up again, Jackstraw."

"Rafael Betancourt showed up in Chicago last May, contacted Cavenaugh and offered him the job. Offered Cav and me the job—he was specific about that, I had to be a part of the deal. Cav got in touch with me, I flew to Chicago, we met with Betancourt and negotiated the deal. Three months, starting in June; forty thousand dollars total, ten thousand to each of us in advance, with the remaining twenty thousand to be paid when we fulfilled the contract."

"You didn't actually sign a contract, did you?"

"A figure of speech," I said. "In the end, Rafael cheated us out of ten thousand dollars, five grand each."

"Did you know at that time that Betancourt was a colonel in the Federal Judicial Police down there?"

"No. We thought he was an authentic revolutionary, but on the political side. Rafael didn't seem the type to spend years mucking around in the jungle. He was a tough guy, no doubt about that, but in a certain stylish Latino way. Upper-class, well-educated, fancied himself an intellectual, had polished manners when he chose to use them."

I paused, waiting for Anna to catch up with her notes, then continued. "Rafael talked a lot of Marxist-Leninist clichés, but not very convincingly. Cav and I didn't buy it. He implied that he was representing El Puño Rojo, but we didn't buy that either—we figured him for the extreme right. He just didn't have the look, or the feel."

"And he was hired by Alex Troxel to recruit you and Joseph Cavenaugh?"

"Not hired. Betancourt was in no way subordinate to Troxel. Rafael allied himself with Troxel and Rachel for his own purpose and profit. He remained independent."

"But they were friends, Troxel and Betancourt."

"I doubt it. Betancourt wasn't likely to regard a man like Troxel as a friend. But they were acquainted, according to Rachel."

"When did they meet? Where?"

"I don't know."

"So Betancourt and Troxel used each other. Of what use was Troxel and Rachel Valentine and their crazy plot to Betancourt?"

"You can figure he stood to gain money and power, lots of both, and glory—Rafael was infatuated with the notion of himself as patriotic hero. He wanted to become the leader of his country."

"All right. Then what use was Betancourt to Troxel and Rachel Valentine?"

"You have to understand the peculiar nature of the Policía Judicial Federal. It's a dragon with three heads. If you're PJF, you're a federal cop with almost unlimited police powers, and you have an equivalency of rank in the military—a colonel in the PJF is recognized as a colonel in the army. You can also serve in the national legislature. Rafael himself held a leadership position in the ruling party. You see? With the cooperation of a man in Betancourt's position you can do virtually anything down there."

"So then the government was involved in all of it? The raid on the river outpost, the kidnapping of the missionaries, the assassination of Hamilton Keyes? My God. All of that?"

"I didn't say that. Some members of the government were complicit, obviously. Betancourt, Herrera, Baltazar, and no doubt some others. But not the national government, and not the army."

"How do you know that?"

"Easy. None of those hotshot politicians and generals would have been sitting on the platform that day if they knew bullets were going to be flying."

"All right. So you and Cavenaugh were hired to train the guerrilla unit, half of whom—three months later—were to attack the river outpost while the other half helped to kidnap the missionaries."

"Yeah, but Cav and I didn't know our purpose then. Cav later went home; I was kept in the dark until the last moment, when we started upriver in the boats."

"You said the soldiers at the river outpost were dead when you arrived there and shot up the place. Dead for a few days, maybe—of alcohol poisoning?"

"Maybe of alcohol poisoning, maybe of some other poison like botulism, maybe of disease. But the Indian prisoners died of dehydration, suffocation."

"The government says they were massacred."

"Well, they would say that, wouldn't they? Commie atrocity."

"You burned the place down, all the bodies, everything. Why?"

"It was the right thing to do."

"Why?"

"One of the buildings caught fire incidentally. We burned the others down on my orders."

"Why?"

"Decomposed corpses in the tropics, men possibly dead from some communicable disease."

"Sounds weak."

"Plus. Plus that outpost was a source of misery and oppression to the Indians of that area."

"Better. The government says they autopsied the charred remains and found numerous bullets and grenade fragments. They concluded that there was a massacre, and that the place was torched to conceal the evidence."

"I don't care what they concluded. We shot up corpses, not living men."

"Who will believe that?"

"Do you believe it?"

"Jack, who will believe *any* of this stuff?"

"Are you playing reporter or prosecutor?"

"Don't get touchy. I need details, elaboration, explanation. I've got to get this crazy stuff straight in my mind. This whole conspiracy—it's like something out of the Dark Ages, when you had devious popes and scheming princes and mysterious poisonings and vicious throne politics and assassinations and fake assassinations and betrayals and counter-betrayals and, Lord, I don't know, I just can't pin it down. I think: Okay, now it's clear, but then the perspective changes and it all seems delusional. I try to enter the paranoidal state of mind so that I can understand Betancourt and Troxel and Rachel Valentine and you, Jack, but I can't, not quite, I'm too healthy."

"Everything I've told you is true."

"Sure, true in its way. It all fits together precisely and there appears to be a scrupulous logic to all of this, A, B, and C, but my God, it's a dark, inverted logic, paranoid logic."

"Do you think I'm paranoid, Anna?"

"Well, of course you are, at least in part. You'd have to be or you could never survive in that milieu. You *like* playing this dangerous paranoid chess—one bad move and you're carrion."

"Maybe we should take a break."

"Yes."

"As a paranoid," I said, "I detest glib pop psychology."

"I know." She smiled tiredly. "I'm sorry."

I built a fire out of deadwood I'd picked up around the place, chunks of scrub oak and cottonwood and juniper, while Anna brewed a pot of coffee on the camp stove. It was only a little after ten o'clock, though it seemed much later. When we returned to the table the room was warm and smelled of coffee and woodsmoke. Firelight glistened in her hair.

"Okay," Anna said. She quickly reviewed her notes. "You ordered the outpost burned, then took a skiff down to the mission, where the other half of your commando bunch had—what's the word, secured?—secured the mission complex. You say Troxel was running the operation, but I didn't notice him."

"His face was covered."

"The hostages were separated out and taken away in one of the helicopters. Taken to . . . ?"

"To a safe house in Mundial, where they were kept captive for about a week."

"Kept until the witch arrived in town to liberate them."

"Rachel, yes."

"Who operated this safe house?"

"Some of Betancourt's stooges."

"And who selected the site for the assassination? The suite of offices on the fourth floor."

"Betancourt again. I assume that he had the staff of the newspaper arrested a day or two before the ceremony, to get them out of the way. He wanted the radicals blamed. The wig shop? I don't know, but it wouldn't surprise me if it hadn't been a part of a Betancourt operation for a long time, a way of keeping the newspaper radicals under close observation."

"Troxel had you in mind from the beginning as the one who would shoot Rachel Valentine?"

"Yes."

"Troxel had met you in Africa, knew about you, had sized you up. He knew that you were an excellent marksman. He knew you wouldn't choke when it came time to pull the trigger. He figured that you would be tempted by the prospect of bushels of money. He guessed that you were the kind of fool who might regard this lunacy as a sporting enterprise."

I smiled at her.

"And he was right on all counts, especially the fool part. God, Jackstraw, how could you be so dumb!"

"Let's move on."

"And the other fool—Roger Clay. You tell me that he killed Hamilton Keyes. Why? I mean, for God's sake, why did the Valentine witch want Keyes dead?"

"First, for the record, Rachel denies that she had any knowledge of the Hamilton Keyes assassination. She blames it on Betancourt. Betancourt, with maybe some sinister behind-the-scenes treachery by Troxel. Let's assume she's lying. That's always a safe assumption. So: Keyes was used up. Rachel already had a great deal of money, as much as she was likely to get. He had given the Party and campaign a certain respectability at the beginning, as well as money, but people were starting to laugh at him—he was acquiring that goofy old man image. And he was the presidential candidate. Rachel wants to be president. And the murder of Keyes may have been crazy, but it was also a fantastic public relations coup to have poor old Hamilton assassinated while Rachel herself—Saint Joan—was shot at the same time, though miraculously saved from death. You're the one who mentioned paranoid logic. Assassinating Hamilton Keyes wasn't *nice*, but it was sure brilliant."

"And then Betancourt and his chums immediately killed Roger Clay."

"Right. They had to kill him."

"You didn't know that Clay was going to shoot Hamilton Keyes that morning?"

"No. Hell no."

"You didn't suspect it?"

"I would have been a hundred miles away with a suitcase full of cash if I had even dreamed they were going to assassinate Keyes. I suspected something else was going down, but I didn't think it would be that." I sighed. "Maybe I should have. Another reason I needed to get out of that business. Losing my edge."

"So they had to kill Roger, and kill you."

"Yes."

"And even so, you went to that office that morning."

"Wait. I told you that I didn't know that Keyes was going to be killed. I went to the office knowing only that I was going to shoot—but not hurt—Rachel Valentine. I didn't trust Troxel, obviously. I was prepared. But I didn't believe that they would kill me. Why should they? I was deeply implicated in the assault on the river outpost and kidnapping. I was compromised. I had become an integral part of the conspiracy, and Troxel could be sure I wouldn't talk. So why take me out? But all that was irrelevant when they decided to kill Keyes. They didn't want me to leave that building alive. I was then just another fall guy, like Roger Clay."

"But, as you said, you were ready for trouble."

"Certainly."

"You had guns, hand grenades, your paranoia."

"And I had a vacant room next door that troubled me. The wig shop."

"And so you killed Betancourt and his men before they could kill you."

"That's right."

"Four men; Betancourt, Herrera, Baltazar, and Clay."

"I didn't kill Roger."

"You thought you might be forced to kill when you went into those offices, you planned for it, and yet you went ahead with part of the conspiracy."

"Yes."

"And you believe that Troxel killed your friend Cavenaugh."

"I think he did."

"And Troxel was responsible for the death of that poor car thief."

"Yes."

"And Troxel has already tried to kill you twice, in Mundial, probably, and in Chicago, and he'll surely keep trying until he succeeds."

"He'll keep trying."

"Jack, this afternoon and again tonight, I've listened very carefully, hoping that I might hear a word, or even a certain tone of voice, a nuance, that would tell me that at some point you were aware of moral considerations."

"Do you want me to say it? I wish to hell I had never got involved in this business."

"I wasn't talking about regret."

"As for moral considerations—they may be important *before* you've acted. But five seconds of moral consideration in that office down in Mundial and I'd probably now be floating in a tank of formaldehyde or hanging from a hook in a meat locker. Unclaimed bodies in Mundial go to the University. A few seconds of moral consideration and med students would be learning anatomy by dissecting my cadaver."

"*You* chose to go into that office, no one else."

"There are times, Anna, when moral considerations are a bourgeois luxury."

"I refuse to believe that."

"Then you must immediately return to San Diego and ask for your job back at the magazine. Go home, Anna, because if you continue investigating this story you'll be entering the dark nihilistic swamplands, and you may encounter reptiles there who'll eat you up without an instant's moral consideration."

She pushed aside her steno pad. "I'm tired."

"So am I."

"Which bunk is mine?"

"Your choice."

"I don't want to sleep with you, Jack."

"I understand."

I did understand. All day Anna's mood had swung back and forth between good cheer and a sort of brooding hostility. The two Jackstraws were the source of her conflicting emotions. There was the Jackstraw whose company she now shared, the man she knew, had slept with, liked; and then there was the other Jackstraw, the evil twin, devious conspirator and mercenary killer. She could not reconcile the two.

During the night I was awakened by the whining yammer of coyotes near the cabin. They had found the steak bones and food scraps out on the picnic table.

THIRTY-FIVE

The next day I showed Anna some of the surrounding countryside. I drove a meandering route that took us through part of the San Isabel National Forest, across the bridge over the thousand-foot Royal Gorge, and then down into Cañon City where we had a late lunch. Cañon City was a pretty town situated on the banks of the Arkansas River. After eating we strolled along the river walk, past the great stone walls of the Colorado State Penitentiary. Our mood changed. "I couldn't live in this town," Anna said, meaning, I gathered, that the existence of the prison would oppress the spirit of even those who lived outside the walls. The prison was huge, an actual and metaphorical weight, a man-made hell.

"I couldn't live here, either," I said, though we both knew that I might spend the rest of my life in one of the country's similar hells.

We arrived back at my place in the late afternoon. Half an hour after returning, toward dusk, a dented old pickup truck labored up the track and halted fifty feet away from the cabin. Anna was sitting outside at the picnic table, shuffling her notes; I watched the truck from a cabin window.

The engine was switched off. A man got out, limped to an open area and stood quietly, his arms folded. He was giving me a chance to look him over. He was not armed.

We met halfway between the cabin and his truck.

"Hello, Tim," I said.

"Jack."

"Come in and have a beer."

"I can't stay." He looked past me toward Anna and then, reflexively, removed his sweat-stained hat. Tim Bailey was about sixty, thin except for a melon belly, with a bony sun-creased face and jug ears.

"I heard you was back," he said.

"For a while. I'll be leaving soon."

"Sooner than you think."

"Are you sure you won't sit down and drink a beer with me?"

"You don't have time to socialize, Jack. I just came out to tell you there's a pack of Feds sneaking around. Feds for sure, eight, ten of them, plus a bunch of sheriff's deputies. Word is, they're interested in you."

Bailey and I weren't exactly friends. We had drunk a few beers together and shot pool at a bar in Whistle, and had once fished for trout in the upper Arkansas. He was here because he hated the federal government, which for him was personified by the Forest Service supervisor who had refused to renew his grazing lease; the agent from the U.S. Department of Agriculture who had ordered all of his cattle because a few, bought in Mexico, were infected with rinderpest; and the federal tax man who had auctioned off his house, land, livestock, and farm equipment.

"They'll be coming for you after dark, I expect," he said.

"Did you see anyone watching the place on your way in?"

He shook his head. "Well, thought I'd stop by. You don't want to be here when they try the SWAT team bullshit."

"Wait just a second, Tim."

I went into the cabin, levered all of the cartridges out of my carbine, and went back outside. I carried the rifle by the end of the barrel so Tim wouldn't be alarmed. I gave it to him.

"It's yours," I said.

"You sure?"

"It will be confiscated by the FBI if you don't take it."

"Sure, the bastards will take everything. All right, then. Thanks. Good luck."

After he left I walked over to the picnic bench. Anna tilted her reading glasses up on her forehead.

"That's it, then," I said.

"What did he want?"

"Anna, you've got to leave immediately. The FBI and Sheriff's Department people and maybe the ATF will be raiding this place soon. Maybe in ten minutes, but more likely after dark. They prefer to go in after an armed man at night, preferably when he's sleeping."

"My God, it really has come to this."

"Pack up quick. Go."

"They probably know I'm here."

"They'll be coming in with guns, in the dark. Nervous armed men, in the dark. I said go, and God damn it, I mean go. Now."

I followed her into the cabin and watched while she packed.

"Maybe," she said, "you should surrender to them."

"Maybe I should. Maybe I will, in a few days, when I have some control over the circumstances. Not this way. Do you have the stones?"

"They're around here somewhere."

"Find them."

"I don't know if I want them. I really don't. Why don't you hide them somewhere on the property for now?"

"Anna, they'll be bringing in bulldozers and backhoes tomorrow. They'll dig up every square inch of this place. They'll pump all the years of shit out of the latrine and run it through a sieve. They won't miss a thing. And even if they do miss your stones—who will know where they're hidden if I'm dead?"

She got the tobacco can of gemstones from beneath the blankets on the upper bunk, slipped them into her bag, and zipped the bag closed.

"It's been great," she said bitterly.

"How can I get in touch with you?"

"Who knows? Through a fucking medium during a fucking séance."

We walked out to her car. I opened the door and threw her bag inside; she got in behind the wheel.

"Anna Fontenot, girl reporter," I said. "I've given you a hell of a story. And a roll of fine porno snapshots."

"You've given me a hell of a lot of trouble."

I closed the door. She lowered the window, brushed her wet cheeks, and tried to smile. It was one of those smiles that start out fine but then suddenly wrinkle.

"Bye-bye," she said.

"Goodbye, Anna."

She drove off. I was even more sure this time that I would never see her again.

PART SIX
RUNNING

THIRTY-SIX

I packed my rucksack during the last of the daylight. Anna's fragrance—her skin, hair, the lilac scent she wore—lingered in the room. I had never before felt so acutely alone. But there it was: if you live on the edge long enough you'll eventually fall into the abyss.

Nights were cold in the high country and there could be severe storms even in early October, but I really didn't need a tent or tarp. Too much weight and bulk for too little benefit; it was simpler to bivouac. No tent, tent stakes, no five-pound sleeping bag. No hatchet, rope, compact camp stove and fuel, no gadgets, no extra this and compact that.

I needed half an hour to pack. It was more a matter of elimination of items than inclusion. If they came for me now, earlier than I expected, fine, but I did not intend to rush off in an abject panic, in street clothes, street shoes, unequipped, certain to suffer hunger and cold and demoralization. This was not going to be a three-day manhunt.

My father's—and grandfather's—.45 pistol was too heavy to take. And who was I going to shoot? An FBI man, sheriff's deputy, citizen on a hike? But I would carry along the little Astra .25 pistol I had taken from Rachel. You could hunt with it, bluff with it.

255

A knife, of course, my Solingen carbon steel folding knife with the five-inch blade. Candles, matches, a flashlight the size of a cigar, binoculars not much bigger than opera glasses, a few fishhooks and a spool of line, a topographical map of the country, a large aluminum cup that could also serve as a cook pot, three one-pint water bottles, a vial of water purification tablets, compass, can opener, my slingshot with steel balls packed in the plastic handle, the transistor radio I'd bought in Mundial, odds and ends, all the money I had concealed in the cabin—all the money I had in the world—$8,000 in hundreds. I had known that someday I would regret throwing all of the money out of that window in Mundial; this was the day.

It was dark now. I lit a kerosene lantern.

Not much food: a bag of rice, salt and pepper, some cooking oil, coffee, tea, sugar, two tins of corned beef and three of tuna, flour, a bag of dried apricots and another of dried dates, a few candy bars. I could live off the country to a certain extent. The thing was to travel light and move fast, get away from the immediate search zone.

As I packed, I half-expected a dozen armed men to crash through the door. They would probably first break a window and toss in a tear gas or concussion grenade.

Clothing: best to dress lightly for now, so that I didn't sweat too much in the early going. Boots, wool socks, jeans, a wool shirt. Everything else went into the pack: another wool shirt, wool sweater, sweat pants, my beat-up down jacket, a waterproof anorak, rain poncho, stocking cap, mittens, and three clean pairs of wool socks. Extra socks were a necessity when mobility depended on the health of your feet. Even Xenophon knew that.

I hoisted the rucksack on my shoulders, turned off the kerosene lanterns after considering and rejecting the notion of burning down the cabin, and went outside. I stood on the porch for a few minutes to allow my eyes to adjust to darkness. The moon would not rise for another few hours, but I could see fairly well by starlight. You forget how many stars are visible in a dry climate, at high altitude. Above me the Milky Way was so densely packed with stars that it appeared as a luminous haze, a diffused glow bright enough to cast shadows. Individual stars burned bright and cold, without distortion, without twinkling. Those stars made my troubles seem mean and transitory.

It was quiet. There were no intruders out there in the night. They would probably wait until after midnight before storming the cabin. If I were in charge, I would wait until three or four o'clock, come in at the time when a man's morale was lowest and his thoughts confused, even if he were awake.

I started up the rutted tire tracks toward the mountain. The pack felt heavy, poorly balanced. I walked past the outhouse, the rickety old corral, the rusty iron windmill tower, the spring. My depression began to lift. What the hell. I had brought this on myself. Did I now have to endure a lot of interior whining? I could be wretched and regard what was happening to me as a profound misery, or I might elect to view it as a rare, a wild adventure—perhaps my last. Surely there was going to be a worldwide audience for the manhunt: my escape, capture, or death. It was not a form of theater. So then, I thought, never mind the denouement. The details of my life and death had been reduced to a matter of style.

It was hard going at first. I could not seem to gulp enough oxygen. The altitude here was 7,500 feet above sea level—more than 14,000 feet where I was going—and it would take time to acclimatize.

The cool night air carried sharp herbal scents. Isolated sage bushes glowed phosphorescently in the starlight, like balls of St.

Elmo's Fire. There was sage and chamiso and gnarled junipers and clumps of coarse yellow grass. The country changed as I passed from the high desert to the sub-alpine zone. There were piñon pines, scrub oak, and then a lone spruce, another spruce, some white pine trees. The blue spruce, like the sage lower down, gave off a sort of silvery aura in the darkness. Now the air was richly scented with resins. I heard an owl whose call was similar to the cooing of a mourning dove.

Within half an hour I found my hiking rhythm. You had a tendency to walk too fast at the beginning, at your low-altitude pace, but by the time I reached the fence that separated my property from Forest Service land I was moving and breathing well enough.

I angled cross country two miles to a forested notch between big foothills. There was a creek here, low and narrow now in the autumn, but still a creek, with riffles and pools and miniature falls. The water hissed and buzzed as it poured down its steep, pebbly bed. There were trout in these waters, small ones mostly; and you saw hummingbirds and hummingbird moths and dippers—small birds that "flew" underwater. One summer a family of ospreys had nested high in a tree farther up the canyon. I had spent an entire day watching the four young birds practice flying. The next day they were gone.

The path, an old game trail, crossed and recrossed the creek as it ascended. Usually I could jump across, but in places it was necessary to step from bank to boulder to bank, or tightrope my way over a fallen tree trunk. The creek was a flashing swath of light that wound down through the darkness, boiling in places, hissing, the air thrumming with its music.

At about 9,500 feet I reached a narrow, flat meadow of yellow grass and briar and alder and, in season, wild strawberries. The creek widened into a slow-moving pool. You sometimes saw wild turkey and blue grouse here. A hen grouse might try to lure you away from her chicks with the broken wing ruse. Black bears came to feed on the berries, too. They heard you coming and ran off into the forest but their odor, their musky stink, remained behind.

I removed my rucksack and sprawled out on the grass. There was a smell of pine and spruce resins, sweet-sour, and the dank odor of woodrot. The creek exhaled an icy chill. I was sweaty and a bit winded, though not tired.

How much lead time did I have? Maybe at this instant the police, federal and county, were surrounding the cabin. Whenever they arrived, they would notice the tire tracks from Anna's Explorer and Tim's pickup, and perhaps assume that I had escaped by vehicle. They might just as easily conclude that I had gone into the wilderness. But they couldn't easily track me at night, unless they had dogs. Unless they had very good dogs and my scent was fresh.

The path steepened at the upper end of the clearing. Now there were aspens scattered among the pines and spruce, their white bark and the silver undersides of the leaves shining in the darkness. The creek was fast and straight here, and there was a series of falls. In the spring, during snowmelt, you could hear rocks rolling along this section of the stream bed with a sound like the clacking of billiard balls.

Anna worried me. I should have discouraged her involvement. She was idealistic and ambitious and too trusting—unfit for the treacherous netherworld that she was now entering. Troxel would know from press reports that she had survived the raid on the mission, I had not killed her. Eventually he would learn the entire conspiracy. Then, if he got the chance, he would murder her as coldly as he had murdered Cavenaugh. Or Anna might spend the next five years of her life consulting lawyers and being deposed and serving as a witness in trial after trial. She would be sued by bullying cops and prosecutors, and humiliated by the broadcast media savages. It did not ease my conscience to recall that Anna had come to me for her own purposes and benefit; she hadn't been conscripted, she'd enlisted.

After another half hour of strenuous walking, the incline became gentle, then the terrain flattened out into a marshy bowl. The earth was spongy here, saturated with water. Dozens of meandering rivulets combined to form the headwaters of the creek. I passed the last few stunted trees and then I was above timberline. Ahead, a steep slope led upward toward a ridge that was clearly silhouetted against a cloud-free sky. The moon was rising.

I sat on a flat-topped boulder and ate a candy bar. My watch read 11:50. The air was thin and dry and cool. I estimated the altitude at around 11,500 feet. I had made good time considering my lack of conditioning and the difficulties of a night walk.

Where was Anna at this moment? Sleeping, probably, in some boxy motel room, dreaming of her journalistic coup.

Rachel Valentine? I imagined her dressed in her bullfighter's outfit and flourishing a cape, obsessively dancing alone in her hotel suite.

And Troxel? Hunting me. He had little time for rest while I lived. He and his own little pack would join the chase.

I felt good—stronger now than when I had started. Something like exhilaration fizzed in my chest. Surely the hunted might enjoy the chase as much as the hunters, the fox as well as the hounds.

THIRTY-SEVEN

A series of switchbacks led up the final slope to the ridge. I ascended at a measured pace, careful to avoid the many patches of granular old snow. I must not leave footprints. The first third of the incline was grassy; then it steepened and there was a scatter of fractured black rocks; the last third was a talus slope composed of great rectangular boulders which were so symmetrical and close in size that they appeared quarried rather than natural. You could build a fair-sized pyramid out of that jumble of black stone blocks.

I plodded on, my face down, breathing hard, and then I suddenly felt a cool breeze as I reached the ridge. An enormous valley opened out far below: there was a rocky descent to the forest, and then a further descent to the treeless flatlands that extended west for many miles before rising again into another chain of mountains. The moon and stars saturated the vast plain with a milky radiance. It was mostly ranch country down there, although to the south I saw a sprinkle of lights, a town, and far out a set of car lights moving along the straight ribbon of road which bisected the valley.

I turned right, north, and began my long trek into an uncertain future. There were three peaks of more than 14,000 feet along the way, linked together by a ridge that dipped to saddles between each one. I had walked this route several times, but never at night, never with this sense of dangerous buoyancy. The empty space on both sides gave me a touch of vertigo. But it really wasn't dangerous if you kept your nerve—if you could walk a sidewalk or climb a flight of stairs without falling, you ought to be able to traverse most of the ridge, day or night, without too much difficulty.

After a couple hundred yards I adjusted to the exposure, gained confidence, and proceeded at a steady pace. Ahead, the first of the peaks, the Bighorn, defined itself by the tall patch of sky it obscured. It wasn't as difficult a climb as it looked. Anyway, you did not have to climb the peak; you could circle it by a series of broad ledges or, easier yet, by a scree slope lower down.

The northwesterly breeze was cool, the light faint but pure, immaculate. I felt euphoric, partly because of the beauty of the night and the excitement of escape, and maybe too because of oxygen deprivation. I had gone from 7,500 feet to 13,500 feet in less than six hours, and for months I had lived at sea level. My oxygen-hungry brain was in some ways dulled, in other ways stimulated. I had a feeling of second sight: this had already happened before and now I was re-experiencing it. The future was almost visible. This place, this time, this action, were like the fulfillment of prophecy.

Wind had scoured the narrow ridgetop clean of snow and would sweep away my scent in the same way. Dogs were of no use up here.

I circled the Bighorn well below its summit, climbed back to the ridge, which now commenced a several-hundred-foot dip downward before leveling out and then again rising toward Pyramid Peak. The mountain appeared pyramidal only from the west. Its triangular granite face loomed above the valley, suggesting the view of a pyramid greater than that of Cheops. There was a 2,000-foot vertical from the apex of the triangle to its base: a stone dropped from the top would strike the wall only once or twice before ricocheting off the talus far below. I had never attempted to climb that wall; it was beyond my skill and experience. But I had traversed this ridge a few times, and climbed Pyramid Peak from the south. It was moderately difficult, perhaps a grade-four. If you were climbing with someone you'd rope up for the final 200 feet. The ridge thinned as you ascended from the saddle, then broadened into a steep granite wall. There were plenty of good holds. I knew the route. It was not terribly dangerous even if climbing by moonlight, if you kept your nerve, if you didn't do something stupid.

I paused to rest on a level stretch of ridge. My ears buzzed, my legs were weak, and I was very thirsty. Dehydration was always a concern in the mountains. I sipped a pint of water, rested, looked around. The black rock face rising above me was finely etched by moonlight. Stars formed a speckled halo around the summit wedge. Far below in the valley I saw the headlights of a car moving north, then the red taillights, and then it vanished into the pooled shadow beyond a hill.

I got the transistor radio from my pack and switched it on. Reception was good on both the AM and FM frequencies; the batteries were fresh, and at this altitude there were few obstructions between me and the broadcast sources. I spun the dial past snatches of music, rock and pop and country, past talk shows and religious programs, until I found an all-news station out of Phoenix. Four illegal Mexican aliens had perished of heat and thirst in the desert of Ajo, Arizona; a film actor, whose name I didn't recognize, had entered a drug rehabilitation clinic; the Republican presidential candidate had deplored moral laxity in America during a speech in Memphis; some lucky soul had won $40 million in a lottery, and vowed to keep his job as a telephone company lineman. No mention of Thomas Jackstraw, assassin.

After twenty minutes, I got up, hoisted my rucksack, and resumed walking. Now there was a stretch where the ridge thinned to less than a yard in width. For millennia the rock here had been polished by ice and wind. It had a glassy look, like obsidian. The incline was about thirty degrees. It was important not to tighten up. You kept moving—no halts, no hesitation, no internal debates about whether to place your foot here or there. Just walk. It was only the exposure, the abyss on either side, that made what was really a simple forty-yard uphill walk appear so difficult. Fear made you stiff and clumsy.

The ridge gradually widened as the incline increased. Soon I was using my hands to climb; soon afterward, the rock became nearly vertical. Here the ridge had been transformed into a narrow 200-foot rock face. I remembered the route. The granite appeared impossibly smooth at a glance, but then you noticed how moonlight and shadow defined the surface, revealed every crack and bulge, each wrinkle.

I concentrated on moving fluidly. It was possible to maintain three-point contact with the rock throughout most of the climb. About halfway up the wall I traversed several yards to the left, rested a moment, then resumed climbing. The rock was cool and abrasive to the touch.

The last moves—surmounting the right angle between the wall and summit ledge—was awkward, but then I was up on top, immersed in moonlight and wrapped around with stars. A cool breeze evaporated my sweat. The summit itself, highest point in the massif, was a jumble of fractured granite blocks. The larger crevices were stuffed with dirty snow.

I experienced a queer sort of disassociation: fatigue and this magical night and, again, oxygen deprivation, gave me a sense of living in a dream not my own.

A steel cylinder was jammed in the crack between two blocks. Inside were a couple of pencil stubs and a notebook which contained the names of climbers, the routes, dates, and times of ascent, with here and there a few lines of commentary.

I considered signing my name to the register, with a taunt for my pursuers, but quickly decided against it. That was the kind of cocky gesture that would provide more trouble than satisfaction. Did I think I was the Scarlet Pimpernel? Zorro? I put the cylinder back where I had found it.

The descent to the ridge was by a long fracture in the granite, a rock-choked chute that led down to a scree slope and further down to the rocky saddle between Pyramid Peak and North Peak. Two peaks behind me now, one ahead, and then I had a fairly easy ridge walk for the rest of the night.

THIRTY-EIGHT

Just before sunrise I descended 2,000 feet to a dank forest of spruce and aspen and ferns. Here and there enormous rock structures thrust up out of the earth, stone slabs and gothic towers and squarish monoliths the size of apartment buildings. In the gray pre-dawn light it looked like the ruins of a lost city. Water running downslope had carved a declivity at the base of one huge boulder; the erosion had hollowed out a cave some thirty feet long and ten feet deep. I crawled inside, wrapped myself in the poncho, and watched as details of the forest gradually emerged. My little cave was dry, it was shelter, and I was too tired to care about the discomfort of my stone bed.

In the early afternoon I was awakened by the distant clatter of an approaching helicopter. It was far to the south but flying rapidly along the ridge in my direction. It was big, a military-type machine judging by the engine noise and thumping of the rotor. And it was fast—the noise increased to a roar and then, as it passed overhead, changed pitch, softened to a diminuendo, and finally passed out of my hearing. Yellow aspen leaves spun wildly in the downwash. Panicky birds flitted from branch to branch. A few minutes after that helicopter passed I heard another, this one flying over the valley

266

to the east, and not long afterward there came the remote buzzing of a small airplane.

They were searching for me. I had expected that and yet was a little surprised. The roar of the machines was intimidating. They were hunting me, the men and the machines. I was an enemy of the United States of America, and there was no limit to the number of men and resources now directed against me. I had become a pariah, a mad dog. No, I was a louse hiding in a crack.

The helicopters and light aircraft searched the valleys on either side of the ridge for nearly three hours, went away for an hour, and returned in the late afternoon. If there were police groups searching on foot, with or without dogs, I didn't hear them. Sound doesn't carry well in the high mountains. But surely there were police swarming through these forests. And I supposed there were men, deputized or not, who roamed the area with the hope of shooting down the fugitive. It was open season on Jackstraw. There are men who dream of legally killing another man. And there would be more men and machines arriving, and checkpoints on all the roads, and every citizen would be alerted to the beast who prowled among them.

Radio reception was poor in the cave. I dozed at intervals, thought about my predicament, shared a frugal cold meal with a camp robber jay.

At ten o'clock I made my way through the dark forest to timberline, rested a few minutes, and then climbed directly up a steep, stony slope to the ridge. There was not a breath of wind. It was warmer than it ought to be at this height, in this season. A filmy veil of vapor stretched over the vault of sky, dimming the stars and ringing the rising moon with a double corona. Parallel streamers of cirrus clouds were moving in from the northwest. Bad weather suited me. Let it come.

A storm would ground the helicopters. They didn't worry me during the daylight hours when I could easily remain concealed, but at night I was exposed on the ridge, where there was no refuge from infrared or thermal imaging devices.

I walked in the direction of the incoming clouds. The width of the ridge-top varied from a few feet to a few yards. Rock-studded grassy slopes fell steeply away on either side before entering the shadowed forests far below. And ahead, vaguely defined in the faint light, the ridge rose and dipped and twisted until it too vanished into shadow.

The double-ringed moon lifted higher; its light flowed down over the mountains and illuminated the ridge path with a kind of silvery filigree, isolating each stone and blade of grass. I increased my pace. After a while the ache left my muscles. I sweated, I found my wind and rhythm, and hurried on.

At midnight I paused to rest. The parallel bands of cirrus now stretched from horizon to horizon. Pinpoint stars shined out of the long, clear strips of sky, and the moon alternately brightened and dimmed.

I got out the radio and tried several stations. The manhunt was the lead story in each news broadcast. Thomas Jackstraw, accused assassin of an American Patriotic Party presidential candidate, had escaped from his remote, primitive cabin a few hours before the arrival of FBI and local law enforcement agencies. He is believed to have fled into the mountain wilderness of south-central Colorado, where a search for the former West Point cadet and mercenary soldier is now being conducted. Police advise all campers and hikers to leave the search area and warn motorists not to pick up hitchhikers. Jackstraw is known to be armed and dangerous. The governor of the State of Colorado is considering calling up the

National Guard to assist in the massive manhunt. The governor vowed that Jackstraw would not escape the tightening gauntlet.

I got out the topographical map and, in the intervals of moonlight, traced my route. The ridge continued on for another thirty-five or forty miles before descending to a 9,000-foot pass. Some fifteen miles north of the pass, the north-south and east-west two-lane highways intersected at a town called Troy. That, I assumed, would be the northernmost end of their "noose." The place would be swarming with police of half a dozen jurisdictions, federal, state, and local, along with plenty of well-armed volunteers. But that was some forty miles and two or three days away from my present position, and any decision made now would probably be negated by future events. I had to live moment to moment, like any hunted animal.

I could not understand why there were no helicopters in the air tonight. It might be days before they again had good weather. Maybe those in charge didn't want to risk men and machines flying at these altitudes at night.

At three o'clock I stopped to rest on a high, thin blade of ridge. The weather was deteriorating. It was cooler now, and a gusty wind swirled up out of the valley. Static, prophetic of the coming storm, interfered with good radio reception, but I managed to tune in a moderately clear station out of Salt Lake City.

Thomas Jackstraw, alleged assassin of Hamilton Keyes and stalker of current APP presidential candidate Rachel Leah Valentine had in 1983 been expelled from the U.S. Military Academy for cheating on examinations. Both his grandfather and father were graduates of West Point and had served with distinction in the United States Army. Jackstraw, since his expulsion from the Academy, had fought as a mercenary in a number of bloody Third World conflicts in Africa and Latin America. A source close to the investigation affirms that Jackstraw was known to the State Department, the FBI, and the CIA as a professional revolutionary who most recently served the South American Marxist-Leninist guerrilla army known as the "Red Fist," a group believed responsible for the murder of Hamilton Keyes and the attempted assassination of then vice-presidential candidate Rachel Valentine. Ms. Valentine, contacted in Detroit during a campaign stop, issued a statement in which she urged Jackstraw to immediately surrender to the authorities, warning him that neither she nor the American people would rest until he was brought to justice.

I resumed walking. The cloud cover gradually thickened, the stars vanished, the moon blurred and then went out like an exhausted candle. The wind shifted, blowing from different directions and at different velocities. There were lulls. There were moments when I feared that I might be blown off the ridge.

At five o'clock I descended through the dark to the forested slopes. I found shelter in a circular tent-like space formed by the lower boughs of a big spruce, wrapped myself in the poncho, and went to sleep.

I dreamed that I was an insect trapped in a sticky, trembling spider web. The harder I fought, the more securely I was bound. Then the spider—a hairy stalk-legged thing whose many eyes glowed like rubies—rushed toward me. And, in the cheating way of dreams, I leaped free of the web and fell slowly through a vast darkness.

THIRTY-NINE

They came quietly in the late morning, moving with stealth and purpose, careful not to snap a twig or dislodge a rock. Men who knew the forest. Experienced hunters, probably, killers of deer and elk, bear, wild turkeys, but hunting a different and more dangerous game today. Alarmed jays told me they were coming—intruders penetrating into their territory. The men moved silently enough, but the birds gave them away.

I lay in the shallow circular depression beneath a great spruce. The drooping lower boughs formed a partial screen around me. Damp fog drifted through the woods, billowing gently as it conformed to the contours of the land, parting to embrace a tree, a boulder, a man. Mist like lace, like ragged shawls, hung in the high branches of the spruce and aspen trees.

My rucksack and poncho were olive green, my clothes—except for the stocking cap—were dull. A spark of red or yellow in this terrain would immediately attract the eye. I tucked the cap beneath my chest and clawed down through the layers of dead spruce needles and rubbed dirt over my face and hands. I quietly slid the Astra's safety lever back. A .25 pistol was virtually useless now, but it was all that I had. Then I realized there was no clip in it, and it was too late to insert one.

271

One by one they materialized out of the fog. There were three of them, spaced about twenty feet apart, coming up the creekside trail at a steady pace. All were dressed in camouflage outfits with holstered sidearms. One wore a dented old German helmet, and handcuffs were looped over his belt. Another man had a black beard tied into a dozen three-inch braids. Those two carried hunting rifles; the third, the "point" man, had an AR-15, the civilian version of the M-16. It was rigged with a banana clip and, I was sure, had been modified for automatic fire.

The little boulder-strewn clearing where I lay was a natural stopping place. The three men gathered in the center, cautiously looked around, then relaxed. They had been hiking for hours, tensely alert, scared, and now they were tired. Tired, a little bored, their adrenaline burned away. Two of the men sat side by side on a rocky slab; the man with the Armalite remained standing.

"Jesus," the man with the German helmet said. "I'm getting too old for this."

"Too fat," the bearded man said.

"Too slow, or maybe too peaceable."

"Keep it down," the man with the AR-15 said.

"He ain't in this valley, Tom."

"You never know."

"Thinking about it, I'm starting to feel glad he ain't in this valley. They say the guy can shoot. A sniper. One of those guerrilla bozos. Give him a rifle with a scope—"

"Too much fog for a scope to do any good," the man with the AR-15 said.

"Maybe *he's* stalking *us*. Knife in his teeth, a length of piano wire . . . He can kill with his hands and feet, kill with his teeth. Kill you with kindness."

They laughed.

"The only thing he done I don't like, is he didn't kill that Valentine woman when he had a clean shot. Can't forgive that."

They were close: I estimated twenty feet. I smelled whiskey when the man wearing the German helmet unscrewed the cap of a silver hip flask. The predator's eye—and these men were predators today, though relaxed for the moment—was extremely sensitive to movement. And to pattern. They would see me if I moved or if their eyes and brains assembled the amorphous shape beneath the tree into the figure of a man. I could only hope that the parts of my body that weren't hidden by leaves or dirt resembled the dark, lichen-covered rock outcroppings in the area.

They passed around the flask. You could tell by their postures that they were tired. They were in their late thirties or early forties, overweight, not in condition for a long mountain hike at altitude. I was sure they weren't members of any law enforcement agency. They were citizens, husbands, fathers, sportsmen. No doubt similar men searched through the many small valleys that extended east and west of the ridge system. They were a freelance posse, thrill-seekers, manhunters.

"What do you think?" the man with the AR-15 asked.

"Enough," the bearded man said. "Let's go down."

"It's still early."

"You can't see anything in this cloud."

"Maybe if we walk up as far as the scree . . ."

"He ain't around here. We'll go to my place, barbecue some chicken, drink beer. Fuck it."

The man wearing the German helmet abruptly stood up and began walking toward me. He left his rifle behind at the rock slab. The handcuffs looped over his pistol belt tinkled. I could not determine the exact angle of his gaze, but it appeared that he was staring directly at me. I couldn't surrender. They would be proud to capture me, snap on the handcuffs, lead me down the mountain and deliver me to the authorities. Heroes. But I didn't believe that they could control their nerves if I spoke now or stood up. I remained motionless, and stopped breathing.

He passed close by, brushing the lower spruce boughs with his leg, passed on a few more feet before halting. He was behind me. Then I smelled urine, sharp and acrid, and heard a steady stream splashing on the ground.

"Ah," he said softly. "Too long denied." Then he called to his friends. "Too goddamned long denied."

There was a whisper as his zipper was closed, a sigh, and then he walked past my tree, again brushing the lower branches, moving stiffly as he returned to the center of the clearing. He leaned over to pick up his rifle. This is it, I thought; he'd seen me, and now he would murmur to the other men and together they would wheel and empty their weapons into the bough-screened hollow at the base of the spruce. *Fugitive resists capture and is slain.*

"I pissed on some mushrooms," the man with the German helmet said. "Weird-looking fuckers with red gills."

"Mushroom from outer space," the bearded man said.

"Think so?"

"Sure. Alien mushrooms. You did right."

"Killed them. I could hear little voices screaming for quarter. I gave 'em none."

"Fucking aliens had it coming."

"Soaked them mushrooms with highly toxic piss. Maybe I saved the life of a fag gourmet."

They laughed.

"Well, shit, who's going to carry me down off this mountain?"

They finished the whiskey, collected their weapons and, moving stiffly after their rest, walked single file across the clearing and vanished into fog in the same ghostly way they had arrived. They were no longer hunting: I heard their voices for a few minutes as they descended the trail, and then again the forest was quiet except for the bell-like chiming of the creek.

I crawled out from beneath the tree, dragging my gear along. My knees buckled when I stood up. My shirt was soaked with sweat and my hands, normally deft, were clumsy as I fumbled with the straps and buckles of my rucksack. It was the sort of episode that was a horror at the time but gradually evolved into a good story if enhanced by a lie or two. *There he was, a yard away, pissing on my boots . . .*

Helicopters would not fly for as long as this low cloud ceiling remained. I listened to the transistor radio through the ear button while packing my rucksack.

". . . fugitive is also being sought in connection with the murder of Joseph Cavenaugh, of Chicago, a man believed to have been deeply involved in the abduction of four American missionaries and the assassination of Hamilton Keyes. Sources close to the investigation state that Cavenaugh is suspected of being the 'Third Man' of the Mundial assassination team, along with Jackstraw and a man recently identified as Roger Clay, of Hickory, North Carolina. Clay, killed execution-style according to police, was found in a room overlooking Mundial's central plaza, along with the bodies of three Federal Judicial Police officers who were killed while attempting to prevent the assassination. Investigators theorize that Jackstraw killed Cavenaugh, his longtime friend and mercenary comrade, because he suspected that Cavenaugh was prepared to betray the conspirators . . ."

FORTY

Visibility was reduced to thirty or forty feet, and I blundered up through the forest for half an hour before reaching timberline. I needed another half hour to climb to the crest of the ridge. There, a cold wind blew the mist into streamers. I turned right, northwest, and, nearly blinded by the fog, I leaned into the chill, cutting wind and started along the ridge.

It started raining in mid-afternoon; a hard rain, cold and wind-driven. The temperature dropped. Shells of ice formed on the rock and stiffened the dry tufts of grass.

The rain turned to sleet twenty minutes later, and the sleet to snow, big wet flakes at first, and then hard granular snow like tiny hailstones. An inch of snow accumulated, two inches. Slippery snow, slippery ice beneath it, wind gusts that struck my chest like fist blows. Even so, it was safer to remain on the ridge than to attempt a descent of the steep slope down to the forest. I would very soon turn into a human toboggan trying that. The ridge, at least, was relatively level along this stretch, with inclines of no more than fifteen or twenty percent.

But it was narrow, only two or three feet wide. I advanced slowly, taking short steps, keeping my weight centered over my boots. The blowing snow had further reduced visibility; my world was reduced to a narrow, slippery strip which extended a few yards ahead and a few yards behind. My boots weren't made for this terrain, and I slipped a few times, once so badly I fell on my face and held onto the sides of the ridge for dear life. I considered remaining there, but the storm might get worse. I slowly reached my feet and began moving forward again, trying to anticipate the sudden gusts of wind and lean into them. At moments I thought it was me, rather than the blowing snow and fog, that was in violent motion, and each time I halted until the illusion passed.

For some time I had been aware of a remote rumbling in the north. Now thunder avalanched across the sky. Bright, flickering balls of light illuminated the fog. It seemed absurd to continue walking toward the storm, equally absurd to retreat, and stupid to try to descend the ridge. I went on, staggering along the stone tightrope.

Soon I could see snakes of lightning writhe through the glowing balls of light, and the thunder was terrifying, with first a ripping noise like silk being torn, followed by a series of detonations which reverberated along the ridge and through the valley below. The wind added a high, howling note to the crashing din.

I stopped, removed my rucksack, and sat on it. The clouds all around brightened and dimmed, and webs of lightning ripped and cracked, and thunder exploded with a concussion I could feel in my abdomen. The air stank of ozone. My hair bristled with static electricity, and my entire body felt oddly sensitized, as if the skin had been flayed. The lightning and thunder came simultaneously now; there was no delay between flash and explosion. Each sizzling blast was closer than the last. It seemed personal, as if the lightning bolts were adjusting the range, zeroing in on me—it was like being the sole target of a mortar barrage. I had a sense of imminent doom.

Then there was a blinding flash, and I found myself standing erect and shouting. The air had a burnt stink. My guts ached. I had no idea how I came to be standing; it was as if the electrical charge itself had contracted my muscles. So I stood there, afraid that I had been hit by lightning, certain that I would be hit again and again. Nature, not some government agency, would electrocute me.

But there were no close strikes after that. The storm moved away down the ridge. The noise was muted, as if my ears were stuffed with cotton. The last detonation had affected my hearing. Snow continued falling, though not as heavily now, and the wind dropped off.

I lifted the rucksack, adjusted the straps, turned, and resumed walking along the ridge. A few minutes later I reached the end of the ridge, dropped below it, and crawled under the overhang of a large boulder. I burrowed back about six feet to a small space that was fairly dry and sheltered from the wind; an animal smell pervaded the space, though its former inhabitants were thankfully absent. In time the snow turned back to sleet, then again to rain. Let it rain—it would melt the snow and erase my footprints. I could not hear well. My hearing had been affected by the lightning strike, and there was a prickly numbness in my hands and feet. I was still cold and wet, and disoriented, but not miserable. Surviving the electrical storm had raised my mood. I was alive, I was mobile, I was still free. Fuck them. I sat up and got out the radio and extended the antenna: Let's see what they were saying about me now.

I finally found the only station in the area, a country music station. After a few songs, some local chatter, and the weather, they turned to the big news. FBI and ATF spokesmen, in a rare dual news conference, today announced that the victim of a fatal car bombing last Saturday night in Chicago had been identified as Julio Rodriguez Vega, twenty-eight, originally of Baranquilla, Colombia. Vega immigrated to this country eighteen months ago. The car, rented to a man fitting the description of Thomas Jackstraw, was totally destroyed. Jackstraw, an experienced mercenary soldier, is known to be an expert in demolitions. The FBI spokesman refused to speculate on what part Vega may have played in the assassination of Hamilton Keyes, though he did note that associates of Jackstraw, like Roger Clay and Joseph Cavenaugh, and now Vega, tended to die violently when Jackstraw arrived in the vicinity.

After a few hours the rain let up, and the wind died down. I crawled out from my burrow, got to my feet and continued walking, still wet and cold, all through the night, until four o'clock—sixteen hours in all. Toward the end, my muscles were dead, all coordination gone, and I staggered along like a gutter drunk. But I had covered a lot of ground, and tonight, maybe, I might slip out of their zone.

FORTY-ONE

The next day was clear, and you could hear the buzzing of the aircraft from sunrise to sunset. They searched the entire ridge system and all of the surrounding valleys in a grid pattern. I saw only one helicopter, but judging by the sound there must have been several of them, and some light aircraft as well. Most of the activity was concentrated in the south. Most of my hearing had returned, and in the rare silences I could hear distant vehicular traffic, mostly trucks, laboring up the pass's switchbacks in the lower gears, with now and then the blast of an airhorn. The pass was not far, perhaps just over the next hill. Crown Pass was at an elevation of 9,200 feet, and I was probably not more than a thousand feet above it and a mile to the east. I was in a country of rolling hills, grassy on lower slopes, wooded above with scattered patches of melting snow.

I had awakened at the sound of the first helicopter and scrambled through the woods until I found an overhanging wedge of rock that would protect me from the thermal imaging devices. I lay there all day except for one dash out into the woods to pack some snowballs. My water bottles were empty. I had no appetite, but I was thirsty, dehydrated, and I ate the snowballs like apples, one after the other. Every joint, bone, and muscle in my body ached, I was low on energy, and there was still a residual numbness in my feet. I felt ninety years old.

I turned on the radio, found the only station again, and waited until a news break. Things had changed in the big story.

The Colorado governor had decided to mobilize the National Guard to aid in the search for the fugitive killer, Thomas Jackstraw; they were being rushed to the search area. FBI, state, and county police were presently active in the manhunt. Reports indicate that FBI agents had discovered incriminating evidence in the fugitive's abandoned cabin, including materials that could be used for the manufacture of explosive devices, and a .45 caliber pistol. Ballistic tests are expected to determine if it was the gun used in the murder of Joseph Cavenaugh . . .

I slept at intervals throughout the day, usually awakening in time to listen to the hourly newscast, then dozing off again.

In South America, a high government official announced that papers would soon be filed to demand the prompt extradition of Thomas Jackstraw. Since his monstrous crimes—the massacre of a detachment of soldiers, the abduction of four missionaries, the assassination of Hamilton Keyes, and the cold-blooded murder of three brave officers of the Federal Judicial Police—had all occurred in Mundial, it was essential that the trial take place in the aggrieved country. These crimes against humanity and crimes against God must be severely punished . . .

By lying still, and moving slowly when I did move, some of the animals of the forest lost their fear of me. Ground squirrels approached and chittered insults. A covey of grouse strutted and pecked their way past the overhang.

The radio: Duane Huebner, thirty-seven, of Indianapolis, Indiana, had accidentally been killed by an unofficial posse of nine men near the

Utah-Colorado border. Huebner, whom the volunteer posse leader, Everett Porter, said looked very much like the fugitive Thomas Jackstraw, had brandished what posse members though was a rifle, but which turned out to be a walking stick. Porter's wife, Muriel, and their two children had remained behind in the couple's motel room while Porter was out collecting rocks. Mrs. Porter told police that her husband was an avid rock hound.

A doe and her two fawns delicately picked their way through the little clearing. Their eyes were wide, ears erect, moist nostrils flexing, and they drifted past and vanished into the trees like dream creatures.

The radio: Mrs. Sarah Jackstraw, second wife of the late Brigadier General Jackstraw and stepmother of the fugitive, Thomas Jackstraw, has informed police that Jackstraw, while visiting her last week, stole valuable jewelry and jade figurines, as well as her late husband's service pistol. That pistol was found in Jackstraw's abandoned Colorado cabin by FBI investigators, and is now undergoing ballistic tests to determine if it was the weapon used in the murder of Joseph Cavenaugh. Mrs. Jackstraw, responding to a reporter's question, stated that she was not concerned about the stolen jewelry and art objects, which were insured, but she prayed that Jackstraw would be apprehended before he harmed others. "In a way," she said, "It's good that the Brigadier is dead. He could not have endured the shame."

At sunset the rounded hills above and around me blazed scarlet, then salmon pink, gold, peach, and finally indigo shadows crawled up out of the lowlands and extinguished the fires. I packed my rucksack, made a few snowballs, and chewed them while waiting for full night.

The radio: During a campaign stop in Atlanta, Rachel Leah Valentine introduced her vice-presidential running mate to the public:

he is forty-four-year-old Joshua Benoit, an African-American lawyer, civil rights activist, lay preacher, and a politician who had spent eight years in the Georgia State Legislature. It is rumored that he is under investigation by the Justice Department for several unspecified crimes, but the FBI and federal prosecutors refused to comment. (Rachel Valentine called the charges "politically motivated slander.") Both the Democratic and Republican campaign staffs criticized Mr. Benoit as unqualified to hold high national office, and accused Ms. Valentine of shamelessly playing the race card.

I climbed a grassy slope to a hilltop and looked around. The ridge was not clearly defined here; there were just big hills rising all around, dull yellow in the starlight, with a chain of big mountains curving away to the west. I waited there for fifteen minutes, until I heard a truck grinding its way up the pass, and headed toward the noise. I reached another hilltop and there, not far below, I saw the winding ribbon of highway and the lights of a truck. After that truck, there was another, and then a pair of cars which topped the pass and began descending the other side.

The top of the pass was a narrow plateau about one hundred yards long and fifty wide. There was a gravel shoulder on both sides where vehicles could pull off while the engine cooled or snow chains adjusted. An eighteen-wheeler was parked almost directly below me, engine running, its array of red and white and amber lights glowing. Another truck, judging by the sound, was laboring up the southern side of the pass; the headlights swept back and forth across the sky as it navigated the switchbacks.

The highway hooked down the north side of the pass and continued on some dozen miles to the north-south east-west highway intersection and the town of Troy. A roadblock with a concentration of police and journalists, plenty of guns.

If you drove west from Troy for ten miles you would come to a narrow branch road that turned north, tacking through a forest to a basin cupped below a crescent of big mountains. Sited there, alongside a creek, was the Powder Mountain Ski Area. It was not a major resort, nothing like Vail or Aspen, but the skiing was good and the ambience pleasant. I thought it likely that I could break into one of the vacant chalets and wait out the most intense phase of the manhunt.

A truck, followed by a chain of four cars, reached the summit of the pass, changed gears, and proceeded down the other side.

Across the road lay a series of grassy hills which rose step by step to timberline, then rose again to a high, bare ridge, and rose still higher to a series of 13,000-foot peaks. The snow-dusted mountains were clearly visible from my position. They were not so distant as they appeared at night. I believed that if I could quickly find my way through the jumble of hills and locate the true ridge, I might be able to reach the ski resort by late morning.

The cold night air was fouled by diesel fumes. The eighteen-wheeler pulled forward a few yards, then halted. The driver got out of the cab.

I tried the radio: Today the FBI, in coordination with the U.S. Treasury Department and the Cayman Islands' bank officers, announced that pseudonymous accounts in the CIFI Bank Corporation, Cayman Islands, have been traced to three members of the Hamilton Keyes assassination conspiracy. Large sums of money were deposited to numbered accounts now known to have been opened in July of last year by Thomas Jackstraw, Joseph Cavenaugh, and Roger Clay.

Rachel and Troxel had set that up nicely. There would be more connections, more revelations. But I was alive—they had never considered that possibility.

Finally the truck pulled away and drove down the pass. I quickly descended the grassy slope, digging in my heels, then jogged across the road and into the shadows.

FORTY-TWO

The crescent of big mountains ran roughly east-west; two lower forested ridges extended south from the flanks of the central peak, forming a narrow valley divided by a creek that exhaled mist into the morning chill. On the last few miles of the road were scattered chalets and condos, shops and restaurants. More buildings were clustered around the lift terminals and the huge cedar lodge. Sunlight had illuminated the peaks hours ago, but the valley still lay submerged in shadow. Braids of smoke twisted up from stone chimneys.

I stretched prone on the spongy, pine-needled ground, scanning the upper valley with my binoculars. There was not much activity at this hour, this season. A boy fished the creek from an arched masonry bridge; two men, wearing yellow safety helmets, were cutting wood high on a ski trail; four women played doubles on a tennis court near the lodge. The silence was periodically violated by the buzz of chainsaws. At moments I could hear the *pock* of a tennis ball being hit; the sound floated up to me a second or so after I'd watched the stroke that had caused it.

I studied chalets that were more or less isolated from their neighbors. There were five in the upper valley that appeared to be vacant. No smoke emerged from those chimneys. No children played in those yards or on the sundecks, no chained dogs barked at the occasional passing car. The windows, seen close-up through my binoculars, were dirty. Today was the ninth of October: late for a summer holiday and much too early for the ski season.

One house particularly interested me. It was the most isolated, set well back from the road on a level space bulldozed out of the hill. It was two stories high with a steep shake roof, dormer windows, and redwood sundecks front and back. If I failed to break into that one, I would try a big A-frame some distance down the road.

I retreated deeper into the woods and made my bed in a grove of aspens. I was cold, hungry, thirsty, and exhausted. My joints ached, and the long muscles in my thighs were taut, ready to cramp. Helicopters were in the air again today, but far to the south—I had slipped through their "noose."

The radio: Alcohol, Tobacco, and Firearms officials have disclosed that the Chinese-manufactured rifles used in the assassination of Hamilton Keyes, and in the attempted assassination of Rachel Valentine, have been traced to a provincial city in Cuba. They report that the rifles were stolen from an armory located in the city of Cienfuegos in February of last year. Evidence gathered by Cuban police indicates that the suspected assassin, Thomas Jackstraw, spent several days in Cienfuegos during that month.

A hunted man's perceptions are sharpened: a part of my mind remained alert as I slept, as aware of sound as a sleeping dog is aware of scent. I heard the search aircraft, still far to the southeast. I heard the ratchety buzzing of chainsaws and the hammering of roofers down in the valley. I heard the hissing whisper of a breeze in the aspens.

In late afternoon I awakened, took my slingshot, and went hunting. I saw no grouse, but did locate a patch of frost-damaged strawberries, each no bigger than a pea.

The radio's batteries were fading, but I managed to tune in a report out of Denver: U.S. Treasury Department officials conceded that they have so far been unable to trace any of the money recovered following the assassination of Hamilton Keyes. Authorities speculate that several hundred thousand dollars were deliberately blown out of a fourth-story window in a ruse that aided at least one assassination team member in his escape. Most of the money was seized by the riotous crowd, and has not yet been surrendered. It is believed that the head of the assassination team, Thomas Jackstraw, escaped during the confusion in the garb of a priest.

By dusk I was back in my position overlooking the upper valley. The workers had quit for the day. A volleyball game broke up and the players scattered. Lights came on in some of the buildings; one, a green neon in the shape of a shamrock, advertised Murphy's Pub. It was quiet now except for the throbbing rush of the creek far below. Twilight deepened toward night. Then five or six lights, upstairs and down, indoors and out, abruptly and all together glowed behind the windows of the big cedar chalet I had targeted. The lights were obviously operated by an automatic timer. Other lights shined out of the darkness, and I could hear music coming from Murphy's Pub. My breath turned to vapor on the chill air. There was a lull of about forty minutes and then people, some walking, some in cars, began arriving at Murphy's and a nearby pizza place and the lodge's restaurant. Other cars turned down toward the highway.

I waited another twenty minutes, and then slowly made my way down through the dark woods, finally emerging on a hill directly above my targeted chalet. Most of the curtains were open. Light spilled out of the windows and pooled yellow on the ground below.

There were no cars on the road now, no people anywhere in sight. I hurried down the hill and quickly mounted the steps to the rear deck. I found an outside switch for the globed deck light, turned it off, and immediately relaxed. Darkness was my medium.

The door was locked, of course, and the windows securely latched. All of the visible windows, upstairs and down, were stripped by electrical tape. So there was an alarm system, though I saw no sign of outside motion sensors. I looked around, half aware of the faint music and the muted roar of the creek. Floating in the air as well was the aroma of cooking foods, rich and garlicky, delicious. I began to salivate.

I went back down the steps and, skirting the shafts of window light, circled around to the front of the house. Electric alarm systems are usually run off the telephone lines; if I cut those wires . . .

Then I thought, what the hell, you had to have luck too, cunning was not enough. I jogged out of the sheltering darkness and up the stairs to the front redwood deck. There was no outside switch for the wall-mounted flood light. Exposed in the glare, half blinded, I lifted the doormat. No key. I ran my fingers along the ledge above the door, checked all the metallic fixtures for a concealed magnetic keybox, stuck my hand inside the mail slot in the door. So then I must either cut the phone lines or go off and try the A-frame fifty yards to the north.

There was a long woodbox next to the side railing. Inside, beneath a pile of split logs, I found a manila envelope which contained a ring of five keys and a folded sheet of stationery. There was writing on both sides of the paper. I ran down the steps, down the coiled driveway to a wooden bridge flanked by a pair of big fir trees. From there, and from the road a few yards beyond, you could not see much more of the inside of the house than roofbeams and the ceiling. Burning lights and uncurtained windows might discourage burglars, but they wouldn't help the security patrols much. I unfolded the sheet of paper.

Dear Tommy—

Our house is your house! Please enjoy it as you would your own!

Garbage collection is on Wednesdays; put the trash out early—the crew usually arrives before seven. (But don't leave it out overnight—raccoons!)

Don't use the fireplace in the master bedroom as it's not drawing right and smokes up the place. Please activate the alarm system when you leave.

The number is 22139. You then have thirty seconds! Inform Ray or Tony at the security agency (office located next to Post Office substation) that you will be staying in the house—otherwise they might send in a SWAT team. Ha!

London was lovely, Paris even lovelier, and Venice, we expect, will be loveliest of all. Then on to the Eternal City!

Love,
Elaine & Charles

And on the reverse side of the paper:

Dear Elaine & Chas:

I can't thank you enough for your generous loan of this rustic (sort of) palace. My energy has been restored and all of the kinks ironed out of my soul by the solitude, the quiet, the beauty of this place. I even caught a trout from the stream in front of your house! Thank you, thank you, thank you.

Much love,
Tom

P.S. Barb has phoned twice. Maybe there is still a chance of reconciliation.

And I thought: Thank you Elaine, thank you Charles, thank you Tom.

It was easy: two of the five keys on the ring opened the front door locks. I went inside, took a quick look around, located the alarm box and turned off the system.

I was in a big room with hardwood floors, a high vaulted ceiling supported by heavy beams, leather-upholstered chairs and sofas, and a big stone fireplace. A stairway led up to a railed walkway with three doors spaced along the wall. I walked deeper into the room and down a central hallway that had doors opening on both sides—master bedroom, bathroom, laundry room, a woman's dressing room—and at the end, running the width of the house, the kitchen. I dropped my rucksack on the tiled floor. Home.

The kitchen was dark except for a couple of nightlights plugged into sockets at opposite ends of the room. I drank four glasses of water from the tap, washed my face and hands and dried them on a paper towel. You could run a restaurant out of this kitchen. The island chopping block was at least ten feet long and four wide. The refrigerator and a standing freezer were concealed behind sliding oak doors, and I found another freezer, a walk-in, just off the pantry alcove. The cupboards were packed with canned goods, and there was plenty of food in the two freezers—tomorrow, maybe, I would thaw out and broil a couple of steaks or roast a chicken.

The refrigerator had been cleaned out to avert spoilage, but Tom had left behind half a case of German beer and some ham and cheese that were still fresh. I found a loaf of not-quite-stale bread, placed the food and three bottles of beer on a tray, and carried it down the hall to the master bedroom. Big bedroom, a big bathroom with art-deco female silhouettes on the frosted glass of the shower, and a marble jacuzzi.

I took a long hot shower, wrapped myself in a terrycloth towel, and returned to the bedroom. Halfway up the far wall there was a wooden panel that slid open to reveal a large flat-screen TV. The house was rigged with cable.

I made three ham-and-cheese sandwiches, opened three bottles of Paulaner beer, sat on the edge of the bed, and watched a hard bottle-blonde interview a think-tank "intelligence expert" who asserted that Thomas Jackstraw was a longtime Communist, trained by the Russians in the early eighties, and then dispatched to various Third World countries to foment disorder and Red insurrection. Jackstraw had long been known to the State Department, the FBI, and the CIA as a ruthless and dedicated Communist and an effective *agent provocateur.* He was also, the expert said, a KGB-trained assassin. It made you wonder—did the Old Guard in Russia order the Hamilton Keyes assassination and if so, why?

I—rather, the monster who shared my name—was the focus of a helter-skelter media freak-out. Their Thomas Jackstraw had a personal history that in some respects was not too different from my own, but otherwise he was a stranger, and well on his way toward becoming a cartoon villain, a media construct. The media, the experts, law enforcement, were creating a composite Jackstraw out of the materials at hand, in the same way that Victor Frankenstein had created his monster out of diverse body parts. Each day, each hour, there was a greater separation between myself and the evolving monster. I found it darkly comical even while knowing that, if they got the chance, they would execute the man and not the monster they had created.

I lasted until the end of the interview and then fell asleep—the sleep of the dead. I awakened early next morning, made a pot of coffee and carried a mug back to the bedroom. I was just in time to catch "breaking news" on the cable TV channels. The FBI had released information about a diary or journal left behind in the offices of *Noticias de la Revolución* in Mundial; the fugitive, in his haste to escape after the assassination, had failed to retrieve the notebook. In it, Jackstraw had made entries relevant to the massacre of the soldiers at the government river outpost, the kidnapping of four missionaries, and the assassination of Hamilton Keyes. There were quotes from Marx and Lenin, praise of Stalin and Mao. It appeared certain that Jackstraw was high in the outlaw revolutionary organization known as El Puño Rojo.

The FBI provided two incriminating notebook pages to the media. The news-slander cable station screened it at intervals all day and into the night. The handwriting looked familiar; it closely resembled my big, looping script. The forger was good and he had worked hard to fill some thirty pages.

Talking head question: What kind of man confided details of an elaborate criminal conspiracy to a journal? And then forgot it? An egomaniac, clearly, and obviously less intelligent than previously supposed.

Troxel and Rachel had planned well. They were thorough. I knew there would be more "evidence," further revelations, mad connections. They had gone so far as to send a man impersonating me to Cuba in July. Well done.

FORTY-THREE

I stayed in the house for nine days. There was plenty of food, and I found a cache of good wine in the pantry. After a full day's rest, I kept fit by working out with the owner's weight and exercise machines—a stationary bicycle, a rowing device, a treadmill. Days were for sleep; nights for prowling the house, exercise, reading, watching television. There was a small but good library in the upstairs study. I snooped through the desk, files, and letters: Charles and Elaine Nordlund were scheduled to fly Alitalia Airlines from Rome to New York, with connections to Denver, on October twenty-ninth. Charles was a semi-retired stockbroker; Elaine wrote romance novels which failed to interest publishers. Tom, the recent houseguest, was their son-in-law. Tom and Barbara were going through a tough time now, separated and on their way toward divorce. Charles and Elaine hoped that a permanent split could be averted for the sake of the children.

I watched a lot of television, mostly the cable news networks, and kept myself informed, and misinformed, on the status of the investigation and the progress of the manhunt. The "stalled" manhunt. Had Jackstraw escaped the net?

Photographs of me appeared on television dozens of times each

294

day. The one extracted from the Daley Plaza videotape, when I had been "stalking" Rachel, was the most used; in it, I looked just as you'd expect a vicious, smirking mad-dog assassin to look. That picture "chilled the blood" of a female anchor each time she saw it. Another photo, taken by one of the recruits in the forest outside Paraje, showed me bearded and with long hair in a ponytail, in camo fatigues, and apparently preparing to behead a soldier with my machete. Jackstraw the mercenary, the trained killer. There was a photo taken of me as a cadet at West Point, and another, somehow obtained from my mother, when I was a child, dressed in a Union cavalry uniform and sitting astride my pony. I held my saber aloft and stared fiercely at the camera while my mother looked on with fond amusement. It was the photo I had given her during my recent visit. How had that bright, earnest boy, that inheritor of a noble military tradition, turned into a paid killer, the most notorious assassin since Lee Harvey Oswald? Everyone had an opinion. One expert suggested that Jackstraw had a brain tumor. A great many experts were consulted by the television networks.

A former FBI profiler stated that Thomas Jackstraw should properly be classified as a spree killer rather than a serial murderer; they were quite different forms of psychopathology. Jackstraw could be expected to continue on his violent rampage until killed or captured. Suicide, too, was a distinct possibility, if the fugitive were trapped, cornered, without hope of escape.

A forensic psychiatrist asserted that Jackstraw was clearly a paranoid schizophrenic; all of the critical symptoms were present, i.e., delusions of grandeur and of persecution, pathological suspicion, the violent acting out of phantasmal constructions. All of this, he said, is perhaps not terribly surprising when you consider his mother's unfortunate mental history, and the tragic death of his wife at such an early age—the final straw, apparently, in his mental breakdown. They showed a photo of Beth that pierced my heart.

A female psychologist, author of a self-help book titled *Emerging From Darkness,* concluded that, among other problems, Jackstraw suffered from a severe deprivation of self-esteem. This was evident in his sick and futile attempts to gain empowerment through the quasi-magical action of killing the great—or at least well-known . . .

Spectrum Cable News Network disclosed that Virginia Jackstraw, mother of the fugitive, Thomas Jackstraw, had been confined to a Florida mental institution since 1989, when she was accused of murdering her infant son, William, during a violent psychotic episode. A court-appointed psychiatrist in 1989 determined that the defendant was unfit to stand trial on the murder charge.

Other networks picked up the story. The correction came the following day: SCNN acknowledged that they had erroneously reported that Virginia Jackstraw, mother of the fugitive Thomas Jackstraw, had in 1989 been indicted for murdering her infant son. However, it was another patient confined at the same institution, Mrs. Dolores Franken, who was accused of the crime reported. Virginia Jackstraw, as far as was known, had never been accused of any crime. SCNN apologized for the error.

And there was an interview with my mother. I could not imagine how the TV people got through to her, or why the Willowdale Special Care Nursing Home connived with them to mount this public humiliation. The piece was videotaped outdoors on the institution's grounds, at an umbrellaed table beneath a great live oak shrouded with Spanish moss. The interviewer was a young woman with frizzed orangy hair and an oily, insinuating manner. She oozed sympathy, bled compassion.

"Do you sometimes fear that you might have passed on a . . . a troubled nature . . . to your son, Thomas?"

This was one of my mother's crazy days. Perhaps she had neglected to take her medication, or maybe the fuss of cameras and strangers had disturbed her precarious equilibrium.

"Oh, well, you know," my mother said. "Thomas is my son. I am his daughter."

"You mean mother."

"What? Oh, yes. Did I say . . . ?"

"You said you were Thomas's daughter."

"Really? How strange," my mother said, and smiled.

This was a big event in my mother's life: she had visitors, people who were interested in her and seemed to like her, new friends from the outside. She wore far too much makeup—rouge, lipstick, eyeshadow, eyeliner, blush, mascara—and her hair had been curled.

"There are those," the interviewer said softly, "who claim that your Thomas has killed people. Many people, including a presidential candidate."

"Oh, yes, I suppose so," my mother replied. She smiled and vainly lifted her curls with a cupped palm. "His father killed people, too."

"You're talking about Thomas's father, your ex-husband, the now deceased Brigadier Jackstraw?"

"Yes. Oh, he was a killer, my dear. You can't know."

"But that was during wartime, wasn't it?"

"Several wars, I think. I'm not clear on how many."

"But surely there is a difference between killing during war and ordinary murder."

"Have the wars ended?" my mother asked.

At last the interviewer succeeded (you could see her satisfaction) in confusing my mother so much that she wept. The camera close-up lovingly played over my mother's wrinkled face and tear-smeared makeup.

I wept also. I would have killed that interviewer if I could.

And Sarah, calling herself my "stepmother," appeared on a popular interviewer's show. She'd had cosmetic surgery since I'd seen her in Florida, and her hair was now golden blonde. Sarah had become a minor celebrity. She told the interviewer about the villainous Jackstraw's theft of her jewelry and art objects: "He was always a bully and a thief." Sarah elaborated on her earlier story, turning simple theft into armed robbery, saying that I had threatened to kill her; had, in fact, held a knife to her throat. Her entire life has passed before her eyes. "He said, 'I'll kill you, you f'—he used the f-word—'I'll kill you, you f—king bitch.'" Even as a boy, Thomas had seemed, well, not right. Bad, in fact. Sick. It was a family secret until now, but Thomas as a child tortured animals, a pet dog, a kitten, strays. That was before she, Sarah, had married the Brigadier. You may be sure that she had stepped in and stopped *that* kind of behavior.

At that moment I laughed, and shouted to her image on the TV screen, "Now you've gone too far, you evil bitch!" But I was wrong: after her appearance it became common knowledge, endlessly repeated, that as a boy Thomas Jackstraw had tortured animals. Sarah had not been specific, but others, professional truth-seekers—reporters and cops and psychologists—disclosed the hideous details: animals had been blinded, eviscerated, burned alive. He had even tied two cats' tails together and thrown them over a clothesline to watch them claw each other to death.

The lunacy escalated. There were other ghastly "revelations" about me in the more vicious tabloids and on the Internet: whispers of satanic worship, pyromania, pedophilia, necrophilia, ritual child murders, cannibalism. America's sick fringes became obsessed with Thomas Jackstraw. I was now the repository for all the diseased filth that existed in the minds of my craziest accusers. The outrageous accusations made the mainstream media's simple slanders appear credible, even benign. Reasonable voices were drowned out by the mad cacophony. Clearly, it wasn't enough that I was a known kidnapper, a suspected murderer, an alleged assassin: an infectious hysteria was set loose which required that Thomas Jackstraw be inhuman, monstrous. A scapegoat in the classic sense: first you assign all your wickedness to the goat, then you kill it.

Jackstraw was reported seen all over the country and halfway around the world. A pretentious reporter announced that "Jackstraw was everywhere—and nowhere."

A Jackstraw impersonator terrorized the people at a campground in Montana. A Thomas Jackstraw lookalike had been arrested by police in North Platte, Nebraska, detained for several hours, and then released.

A man falsely identified as Jackstraw was severely beaten by citizens in Hutchison, Kansas.

A California State Highway patrolman was killed by a man described by witnesses as closely resembling the fugitive.

Jackstraw was sighted in Portsmouth, England; Torreon, Mexico; Havana, Cuba; St. Petersburg, Russia; Bogota, Colombia; and Teheran, Iraq. Jackstraw was known to be stalking third-party presidential candidate Rachel Valentine. Jackstraw had been seen planting a bomb at an outdoor café in Jerusalem.

A FBI spokesman declared that ballistics testing had determined that the .45 pistol confiscated from Jackstraw's remote mountain cabin had not been the weapon employed in the murder of suspected co-conspirator Joseph Cavenaugh.

I watched television as Caprice Cavenaugh, escorted by her lawyers, emerged from the Federal Court Building in Chicago after having been "interviewed" by the FBI and federal prosecutors. Caprice was immediately surrounded by cameramen and shouting, jostling reporters. She hesitated, looked at them with disdain, and said, "My husband was *not* involved in any assassination plot. And Thomas Jackstraw did *not* kill Joseph." And then she and her escorts plunged through the crowd toward a waiting car. I noticed that Caprice, when she got into the back seat, was bleeding from a cut above her eye. The anchorman said that she had accidentally been struck by a camera.

It was reported that Roger Clay, a key member of the Mundial assassination team, had long been active in various right-wing organizations in the Southeastern United States, including the American Nazi Party and an armed militia group called The Sword of God. Clay had been killed in a shootout with members of the Federal Judicial Police shortly after participating in the assassination of Hamilton Keyes and the attempted assassination of Rachel Valentine. Investigators are said to be puzzled by Clay's inclusion in what was clearly a conspiracy primarily devised and executed by the violent Marxist-Leninist guerrilla faction known as El Puño Rojo.

The Thomas Jackstraw crime drama squeezed the television time available for routine campaign coverage. The candidates hustled around the country, presenting their programs, slandering their opponents, exhorting the American people to follow them into a better future. "We can do better." "Our great founding fathers . . ." "It's time to fish or cut bait." "The new American century." "The greatest people in the greatest country the world has ever seen." Sound bites, waving flags, mediocre high school bands. Rachel, at least, spiced her platitudes with a little irony.

The Republican candidate stated that Jackstraw, by his actions, was an irrefutable argument in favor of the death penalty. The Democratic Party's candidate was deeply saddened by those few nihilistic Americans who recklessly viewed Jackstraw as some sort of political Robin Hood, a rebel against what they falsely believed was an oppressive system. Jackstraw was nothing more than a terrorist thug. Why do we sometimes mythologize sociopaths like Jesse James and Billy the Kid? It was sad.

I prowled the house at odd hours of the night. Charles was not a hunter; there were no rifles or shotguns in the place, no pistols. There was a blue Porsche 911 parked in the garage. I found a set of keys in Charles's desk.

The American Patriotic Party's poll numbers jumped up to 23 percent after Joshua Benoit was named its vice-presidential candidate. Commentators worried that, if the numbers held, the election would ultimately be decided by the House of Representatives. That, everyone agreed, might precipitate a grave constitutional crisis and dangerously upset the balance of the American democracy.

There were rumors concerning an alleged investigation being conducted into the financial affairs of Joshua Benoit; rumors about Rachel's past sexual indiscretions; rumors about APP campaign finance fraud and secret offshore accounts; rumors of deep and pervasive corruption. Rumors about Rachel's chief of security, Alexander Troxel, a man with an obscure background, a shady past, and reputedly a former comrade of the fugitive, Thomas Jackstraw. Rumors about an old German couple somehow involved in campaign security who might or might not be former Nazis, or maybe former Communists, former something. Every day on television there were rumors about rumors: there were ghost news sources, phantom informants, obscure leaks. Psychics were consulted. Some of the rumors were half-true.

Occasionally facts emerged like ships out of a fog. Heirs of Hamilton Keyes filed a lawsuit in federal court against Rachel Valentine and the American Patriotic Party. The suit alleged that Keyes, old and in poor health, addled, had been fraudulently manipulated and coerced into signing a substantial portion of his wealth—$22 million—over to Valentine and the APP. They asked that those funds be frozen by the court pending adjudication of the lawsuit.

I watched a debate between the three vice-presidential candidates. Rachel's running mate, Joshua Benoit, would not allow the others to patronize him. Benoit was bright, tough, and a bit of a showoff—his high oratorical style sounded pompous at times.

And I saw a debate between the three presidential candidates. The Democrat and the Republican used much of their time in attacking Rachel and her party—"outside the American mainstream." The strategy, of course, was to thoroughly discredit the American Patriotic Party, peel away its support, and hope to pick up a majority of those voters who switched allegiance. It was clear to everyone that Rachel's "true believers" were key to the election. That was the strategy in the debate, but Rachel was too quick, and she turned their criticisms against them. She was the outsider, the longshot, and could afford to be spontaneous while the other two were cautious and rehearsed, scared of destroying their chances with an unconsidered remark. Rachel had a freedom denied to her opponents; she did not have to consider the consequences of each word. And so, while the other two candidates appeared slow-witted, she was quick and cheerful and even, at moments, honest. And she was lovely—Rachel, stimulated by her mad adventure, had lost years, become beautiful. And, even more important, likable.

It seemed to me that she had easily won the debate, but to the political reporters she was glib, facile, reckless, uninformed—a "loose cannon."

The media corps seemed to uniformly despise Rachel and the APP, and could scarcely conceal their scorn for her supporters. They deliberately antagonized her. It was a daily game of let's-see-if-we-can-make-the-candidate-lose-it. Rachel fought back in her cool, ironic style, and won over some viewers enraged at how the commentators ganged up on her.

When a male TV journalist asked her if she opposed homosexual relationships, she replied: "For you, no; for me, yes."

Another reporter wondered how she, a single woman for so many years, satisfied her physical urges. Rachel said, "Some physical urges I suppress, like now—I'm not going to slap your face." Then she smiled, which allowed her to get away with such a comment.

"People say you're too sharp-tongued," a female reporter said. "People say you're too pointy-headed," Rachel replied.

A political opponent was quoted as saying that if Rachel Leah Valentine were elected president the country would soon be at war or, "God forbid, in an economic depression." "It sounds," Rachel told reporters, "like he's more afraid of losing his money than losing his life."

But eventually the scandals, the semi-substantiated rumors, the constant attacks by the media and political opponents began to erode her support. The APP's poll numbers dropped— down to 19 percent of the electorate, 17 percent, 14 . . . Rachel, evidently accepting defeat at last, became anarchic and cheerfully vituperative.

She called both print and broadcast journalists "corporate lickspittles." She said she had never met a journalist or news anchor who wasn't an intellectual and social parvenu. As for free speech in America, Rachel asserted that you got what you paid for. She said that the big corporations and the Republicrats were united in opposing anyone or anything that threatened to interfere in their private monopoly game with America's wealth. She said that her political opponents knew that if you lie down with dogs you'll get up with fleas . . . but if you lie down for the Corporate State you'll get up with money. She said that the multi-national corporations— with their media lackeys—and the Republicrat politicians together operated the world's biggest whorehouse, and the citizen had only to ask whether he was going to be screwed fore or aft.

Rachel was daring, funny, and even passionate. She was also a liar, a cynic, a crook; and her hypocrisy, even for a sociopath, was breathtaking. Her poll numbers dropped to 12 percent.

In Seattle, her press secretary announced that henceforth no media personnel would be allowed to ride on the candidate's leased 747. The reporters were furious, and pointed out that their news organizations paid for their passage, and claimed that there was more than sufficient space for them on the airplane. Then Rachel issued a statement saying that she was sick of reporters using foul language and molesting the female campaign workers and drunkenly vomiting all over the seats. The reporters screamed louder: lies, *lies*! But what could they do? Charter an airplane for themselves or drop out of the campaign coverage.

The APP's poll numbers dropped to 8 percent and then, during the week preceding the election, began to rise. No one could understand it. Rachel was politically dead. Every reasonable American, we were told, was shocked and dismayed by this fantastic turnabout. Perhaps, after all, there was a small chance that the election would be sent from the Electoral College to the House of Representatives. The TV talking heads were outraged and puzzled by this dangerous "disconnect," and sternly lectured each other and the voters.

Rachel, naturally, was delighted. She said, "Every day you see more TV pundits and prophets and think-tankers and opportunists who call themselves 'experts'—doesn't anyone flush his toilet anymore?"

A new photograph of me appeared on television. It came to be called "the priest in the window" shot. An American press photographer who had been with Rachel in Mundial had recently found it while developing some misplaced rolls of film. The picture had been taken with a telephoto lens from the south side of the plaza, looking north. The photographer said that he had shot seven or eight rolls of film that day, and could not recall taking that particular picture, though he said that the plaza's colonial architecture had interested him. The photo had been cropped, enlarged, and digitally enhanced, and I could clearly be seen framed in the fourth-story window—the sniper, in the garments of God, coldly observing his prey.

That reminded me that I needed a disguise. I hadn't shaved since leaving my cabin, but I shaved now, leaving a brush mustache, an almost Hitlerian swatch. I thinned my eyebrows, hacked away at my hair with scissors and then, using Charles's electric razor, shaved my scalp, leaving only a short fringe on the sides and in back, a classic male-pattern baldness. In a desk drawer I found a pair of eyeglasses with thick black frames and tried them on. Charles was myopic and I could not see well through the lenses, but they could be worn for brief periods when necessary. I practiced a stooped, shuffling walk. I shaved my head each night and tanned my scalp under a sunlamp. I now looked ten years older. Older and milder, maybe even timid, a man you might notice and then quickly dismiss.

In nine days of watching news I heard no word of Anna or her exposé, the story of the kidnapped missionaries, the fake and real assassinations, the entire conspiracy—nothing at all. I feared that Troxel had killed her.

FORTY-FOUR

On the ninth and final day a uniformed security patrolman came to the house. It was mid-afternoon. It had rained all day but was beginning to clear now. I sat at the escritoire in the big room, talking to the American Patriotic Party's Washington campaign office. A girl who called herself Merilee was eager to thwart my wishes. I told her it was critically important, crucial, that I speak to one of Rachel Valentine's close advisors as soon as possible.

"Ms. Valentine is in San Francisco."

"I know that."

"Tomorrow the candidate will be in Los Angeles, the day after that, in San Diego."

"I know that. I want you to get in touch with Mr. Dedrick or Mr. Troxel and have them phone me back pronto." I gave her the number and the name "Mr. Spilikin."

She was skeptical. "I don't know . . ."

I was wearing Charles's fine silk robe and fleece-lined slippers, and smoking one of his big Macanudo cigars. The door chimes rang throughout the house, upstairs and down, with the first few notes of some popular showtune. I looked up and saw the patrolman, his face framed like an old-style portrait in the oval door window.

307

"This is very important," I told the girl. "Christ, all you have to do is phone or fax San Francisco."

"I don't have time to listen to profanity," she said.

The chimes rang again, and the patrolman breathed vapor on the rain-blurred window.

"Merilee, honey," I said, "this is about a *huge* campaign contribution, about m-o-n-e-y."

The patrolman pressed his forehead against the window glass and tried to peer into the dim room. Had he seen me? The automatic light switch wouldn't trigger for another few hours, and I was deep in shadow. The chimes rang; the face breathed vapor on the window.

"Well, I'll try," Merilee said.

I hung up the phone, crossed the room, unhooked the chain and slid back the bolt, and opened the door.

"Yes?" I asked.

He was a husky kid in his early twenties, with shaggy blond hair and open blue eyes and horsey teeth. His outfit, olive-green with brass buttons and a mysterious insignia, looked like the uniform of a Third World dictator. He wore a Sam Browne belt, with a big nickel-plated pistol in the holster.

"What happened?" I said. "Did I trigger the silent alarm?"

"Someone told me they seen a guy moving around in here."

"Right. That was me moving."

"No one's supposed to be living here now."

"Are you Ray?"

"Yeah."

"I fucked up, Ray. Come on in."

He followed me inside. I turned on a couple of table lamps and made the sort of gesture that can be interpreted as sit down here or over there or just anywhere.

"I've got a pot of coffee on. Want a cup?"

"There was a guy staying here before. He didn't say nothing about anyone else coming."

"You mean Tom? Right. Charles and Elaine let me have the place after Tom left. I was supposed to stop in at your office, see you or Tony, but I forgot."

"How long you been here?"

"Several days."

"I never seen you around."

He was one of those big athletic kids who devote their lives to surfing or skiing or mountaineering or running rivers. He was a skier and this was his summer job. Ray was slow-witted and, like many slow men, he could easily turn suspicious and dumb-stubborn. It is often easier to deceive a smart man, since logic will direct them toward a reasonable conclusion.

"No one said nothin' to me," Ray said.

A smart man might have been calmed by my quickly answering the door and my casual, easy way. Did burglars wear dressing gowns and puff cigars and invite the suspicious security cop inside for coffee? But Ray only knew that nobody had told him nothin'.

"Hang on a minute, will you?" I said, and I walked back into the bedroom and quickly dressed in jeans and a baggy sweater. I slipped the little .25 automatic into a back pocket. There was a cartridge in the chamber. A tall bald man observed my actions from the mirror; when his expression turned amiable, I went into the kitchen, got two bottles of beer from the refrigerator, and returned to the big room.

"Beer tastes better than coffee at this time of day," I said.

He hesitated, then almost reluctantly accepted the bottle. "I don't know. Mr. and Mrs. Nordlund told me about Tom coming to stay. And Tom came to see me when he got here and when he left."

"I understand your concern," I replied. "Charlie and Elaine will be pleased to hear that you're on top of your job. My name is Bill Carter. I'm an old friend of the family."

"Okay," he said with a sullen half-acceptance. He was troubled. I might better have allayed his suspicion with rudeness, a curt dismissal at the door.

"Look," I said. "Charles and Elaine are in Venice. They're staying at the Gritti Palace. It's now"—I glanced at the clock on the fireplace mantle—"about midnight there. Maybe one o'clock. Why don't we give them a call at their hotel."

He frowned, sipped his beer, looked at the clock, looked at his watch, looked at me.

The more plausible I was in bluffing my right to be there, the more pig-headed he became. Indecision was making him morose. By now a man like Troxel would have put a couple of bullets into his head. I had vowed not to hurt any innocent person even if it meant going to prison, but I wasn't sure if I could subdue this kid, put him out of action, while I escaped. He was big and strong and had a robotic sense of duty.

I walked to the telephone and picked up the receiver.

"What time is it over there?" he asked.

"Midnight, maybe one."

"Maybe we shouldn't bother them so late."

I replaced the receiver. "Come by tomorrow morning and we'll give them a ring."

"No. It's all right." He had elected, finally, to believe me. He was no longer troubled. He tilted back the bottle and finished his beer in a few swallows. "It was just, you know."

"Hey, of course. Listen, Ray, I hope the people at my security agency in LA are half as conscientious as you."

I escorted him to the door and followed him out onto the deck. I hadn't been outdoors for nine days and I felt like a turtle suddenly deprived of his shell. The sky was mostly clear, and I saw that the high peaks behind the resort were covered with new snow. A couple of kids were fishing from the bridge at the end of the driveway.

"Say, Ray," I said, "It's Saturday. I thought I'd go into town. Can you recommend a good place?"

"What do you like?"

"I thought dinner, and afterward a few drinks, music, dancing . . . and maybe women." I smiled.

"There's a Western bar in Troy—The Roundup. I usually go there on Saturdays when I get off work. It ain't bad."

"Charles gave me permission to use his Porsche. It doesn't do a car like that any good to sit around for weeks. Why don't we go together into town tonight."

"I don't get off work until ten."

"Well, maybe I'll see you at The Roundup."

"Sure. I'll buy you a beer." He was friendly now that the problem was resolved: Bill Carter was a good guy, not a bad guy. He went down the steps, waved casually, and got into the patrol car.

Back in the house I thawed two strip steaks in the microwave and then put them on the grill. Frozen asparagus went into a saucepan of boiling water. A ten-year old bottle of Bordeaux wine recommended itself.

Would I have killed Ray if that were necessary to preserve my freedom? Maybe. If there was a clear hard choice between committing murder and spending the rest of my life behind stone walls? Probably. I no longer felt in control of my thoughts and impulses; I was beginning to recognize in myself the desperate Jackstraw described by police and media. They were beginning to even convince me.

After eating I took a glass of wine into the living room. The timing device had switched on the lights earlier. Phone Anna? The election was only eight days away now, and yet there was no indication that she was prepared to publish details of the conspiracy. There had been no leaks, no hints, no hype. If she had gone to the FBI her telephone would surely be bugged. Take a chance. I tried her home number: a voice told me that the line had been disconnected, and then recited a new number. I let that number ring ten times before hanging up. Next I called the offices of the magazine, bypassing the voice mail system and talking to a secretary who informed me that Anna had left for the day. Did I wish to leave a message? No.

I telephoned the Valley Security Agency. Neither Ray nor Tony were there, so I left a message: "Ray, this is Bill Carter. I've decided to buzz up to Denver for two or three days to visit friends. I'll activate the alarm. See you when I get back."

I dressed in a cashmere navy-blue blazer that had carved ivory buttons, white oxford cloth shirt, blue tie with thin diagonal red stripes, and cordovan loafers which fit well enough over two pairs of socks. The outfit was a little baggy, but looked all right. I packed some extra shirts, socks, underwear, and two pairs of trousers in a leather valise, and took a last look around.

Several new crimes had been added to my list: illegal entry, burglary, petty theft and grand theft auto—nothing to bother the conscience of a spree killer.

The telephone rang just as I was about to set the alarm. I walked to the rear of the room and picked up the receiver. "Hello."

"Spilikin?" A man's voice.

"Yes."

"Wait, asshole." Troxel.

They'd had four hours to check out this telephone. They knew my general location by the area code and exchange number; they might even have pinpointed my exact position by now—in a comfortable chalet alongside a creek in the upper Powder Mountain Ski Valley.

Five minutes later the phone rang again.

"Mr. Spilikin?" Rachel.

"Yes."

"Hold on."

There was a pause of a few minutes—perhaps they were electronically scanning the line. It had been a surprise to hear her voice; I had forgotten the husky, seductive tone she used when speaking personally.

"Mr. Spilikin?"

"I'm here."

"I'm taking a terrible chance."

"You often do."

"Do the Nordlunds know they have a houseguest?"

"They're in Europe."

"Surely it's too early for skiing."

"Stop showing off."

"How nice to hear from you at last," she said. "Is everything going well with you?"

"Spanking."

"We've been extremely concerned about you during your recent travels."

I said, "I'm sure this phone is clean. Is yours?"

"We have a man who does nothing but try to protect us from alien ears. But one never knows for sure. It's always best to be circumspect."

"Right," I said. "How is your weather?"

"Turbulent. And yours?"

"Hot, very hot."

"Try to stay cool, Mr. Spilikin. We may be able to help."

"I find it hard to trust you."

"I understand exactly what you mean. Trust is reciprocal, isn't it?"

"We should get together."

"Oh, my," she laughed. "Then I'd better make sure my life insurance premiums are paid up."

"Look, about Chicago—I'm sorry."

"I'm sorry too, and I don't remember much about it. What did you put in that lovely wine?"

"GHB."

"Is that what is called a date-rape drug?"

"Yes."

"Darling, all you had to do was ask. How were you?"

"I was good."

"And how was I?"

"Extraordinary."

She laughed.

"Everyone had a jolly time, and then my rental car exploded and killed a thief."

"Do we want to be so explicit?"

"No. Sorry."

"Anyway, I had nothing to do with that. That was the maverick." She meant Troxel. "He did that on his own."

"Of course."

"It's true. He was responsible for the other, too—you remember? South of here."

"Then someone ought to put down the maverick."

"We can discuss that later. But Spilikin, you played a nasty trick on me in Chicago."

"That's so, but my trick didn't send anyone to hell."

"It very nearly did." There was a pause. "You're always running for the moral high ground, Mr. Spilikin. Are we going to cooperate finally?"

"We'd better."

"I'm going to give you a telephone number that you can use night or day. It's not my phone. Someone else will answer. Someone I trust completely. All right?"

"All right."

"It's a cell phone, so you must be very careful."

"Go ahead."

"It's a number you'll find in the book. Do you understand?"

"No."

"Well, it's in the book, and you'll find the book everywhere."

The book. *Biblion*—book. The Bible. Rachel was going to encode the telephone number.

"Go ahead," I said.

"Write this down, Daniel."

"Okay." The Book of Daniel.

"Don't make me repeat it."

"Okay." Repeat: twice. Chapter Two.

"Or we're back to square one."

"Right." The numeral one, squared, was two.

"Indeed, right back to square one."

"I see." The number one again squared. Two and two. Twenty-two. Verse twenty-two. Book of Daniel, Chapter Two, verse twenty-two.

"All right?"

"Got it," I said.

"You're very quick."

"There are only the quick and the dead."

She laughed. "The quick, the dead, and the wounded."

Rachel broke the connection.

It was full night when I left the house. The sky was clear. I tossed my rucksack and the valise into the rear of the Porsche, eased the car out onto the apron, closed the garage door with the remote, coasted down the driveway and over the bridge, turned left and drove down the twisty valley road. Ahead, climbing toward me, I saw the patrol car. I flashed my lights. Ray, grinning at me as we passed, beat out shave-and-a haircut-two-bits on his horn.

There were some CDs in a case on the floor. I picked out a Willie Nelson: *One for the Road.*

PART SEVEN
MELTDOWN

FORTY-FIVE

I smelled the Pacific Ocean before I saw it, at one o'clock, when I was still several miles away. It had a strong, tart, salt-and-iodine odor. I left the freeway at Garnet Avenue and kept driving west until I could drive no farther, until there was nothing but a big pier and some dirt cliffs overlooking the sea. I stood on the cliff top, inhaling the air as a connoisseur inhales the bouquet from a fine wine, and thinking: how pleasant, how wonderful it would be if I were a free untroubled man.

There were men fishing at the end of the pier. Surfers sat on their boards out where the swells were breaking. People walked and jogged along the beach. On the wet sand lay great coils of washed-up kelp, looking like the tentacles of some science fiction undersea monster. Far to the southwest, perhaps in Mexican waters, I saw the bluish, mountainous shape of an island.

That night I went to Anna's house. She lived in Pacific Beach, half a block from the cliffs and sea, in a white stucco place with a ceramic tile roof and big French windows. Light glowed behind the curtains. There were pink and red bougainvillea crawling up the trellised walls, and in the yard a couple small palms and a fig tree.

I went up the walk, up a few steps to a landing enclosed by a wrought-iron railing, and pressed the buzzer. I waited. The breaking surf throbbed through the night like a slow but firmly pumping heart. The outside light went on, the door swung inward, and Anna gazed at me through the screen. She needed a moment to recognize me.

"Oh, God, no," she said.

"Hello, Anna."

"Please go away, Jack. Please."

"Not so loud. Let me in, will you? We need to talk."

She despairingly unlatched the screen door. I followed her into a square room furnished in a hard Mediterranean style. The plaster walls had been freshly whitewashed. There were small Berber rugs scattered over the tile floor. An arch led to the back rooms; a narrow staircase ascended to the second floor. A fat calico cat slept on a chair.

"Do you live alone?" I asked.

She nodded.

"You must pay big rent, this close to the ocean."

"I bought the house."

"Ah."

"It hasn't gone through probate yet, but I took possession right away, furniture and all."

"Nice," I said.

"I sold some of the gemstones."

"Good for you."

"I know I talked like a fool about the stones in Colorado. It was a pose, I guess. I found that I really wanted them, wanted the money."

"Your father would be pleased."

"So thank you. You could have easily kept them. I would never have known. Whatever you've done, Jack, whoever you really are, finding those stones and saving them for me was noble."

"Aw shucks," I said.

She smiled faintly. "Now please go. You can't stay here. My God, you'll ruin my life."

I listened to her quirky accent, like a Brit trying to speak like an American or an American like a Brit.

"I won't stay long, Anna. I promise."

Some of the tension left her, she relaxed a little.

I had hoped to get a good night's sleep here before moving on; I could think of nothing more luxurious than climbing that stairway and getting into a bed, with Anna, maybe, resting at my side.

"I only want to talk to you, rest for an hour or so."

"All right. Thank you, Jack. I'm sorry, I feel like a rat, but—"

"Hush, never mind. I understand. I'm the boogie man."

"You look more like a vacuum cleaner salesman at the moment."

"Do I? Good."

"When I first saw you in Paraje, you were all hair and beard and bad attitude."

"You had a bad attitude yourself," I said.

"Want a drink?"

"Hell yes, and something to eat."

She started toward the arch, then halted, turned. "Jack. I think I'm being watched by some men."

"Police?"

"I don't know. They were big. Not fat, just big, and they seemed like the kind of men who've forgotten how to smile. I saw them three straight days, outside the magazine's offices and the restaurant where I usually eat lunch, and here—last night when I came home from work they were in a car parked across the street."

"You're pretty sure they were watching you?"

"I don't know. I've been so paranoid . . ."

"That's natural, isn't it?"

"But why would the police be following me? You and I aren't linked as far as the police know."

"We were together for a few days in Paraje, where all of this started. And you were at the Mission when we raided it. And you might have left something behind at the cabin that would identify you."

"Of course. I wasn't thinking." She looked as though she might cry, and I wanted to hold her and make her feel better. It had been a long time since I'd been able to do that. "I thought it might be the gemstones I sold. That they might have interested the police or the income tax people or, God, I don't know."

I smiled at her. "And it all might be just paranoia, a justifiable paranoia. I've seen seeing suspicious men for many years."

"They couldn't," Anna said. "They couldn't, really, could they? Think that I was a part of this from the beginning? The hotel in Paraje, the mission, Colorado—and now *here!*"

"Slow down," I said. "Feed me, hydrate me. We'll talk this out."

I followed her through the arch and into the kitchen. Anna started slicing mushrooms while I made two tall gin and tonics. The men she had seen might be cops, or maybe a pair of Troxel's men, which would be worse, or merely a couple of guys who coincidentally appeared in the vicinity of Anna's home and workplace within a few days' time. You could always discover sinister people and events when you were fearful. Everything seemed connected then. The most insignificant meeting or incident acquired a profound significance. Haven't I seen him before? What did that glance mean? I'm sure I locked that door. I know my papers were moved. Why are my friends treating me so coolly? Isn't that the same car that passed my house three times yesterday? After a while you didn't know up from down, and you certainly couldn't tell truth from fiction, or the good guys from the bad.

"How did you locate my house?" Anna asked.

"I called the magazine."

"They aren't supposed to give out our home addresses."

"I was persuasive."

Anna broke four eggs into a bowl, added salt, pepper, and sliced mushrooms, and then started beating the mixture with a whisk.

"I assume," I said, "that you don't believe all of the things they've been saying about me."

"No. How could I? Most of it was ludicrous. I didn't know what to believe, so I believed none of it."

"About twenty percent of what they said is true."

"Don't tell me which twenty percent."

"I don't expect truth from the media. Truth—Jesus. But is it naïve of me to hope for accuracy?"

"Yes. It is. Naïve." She placed an omelet pan on the gas burner, then dipped into the refrigerator for a stick of butter.

"And you're a journalist, Anna. I've slept with the enemy."

"You slept with a science writer." She half turned and looked at me over her shoulder. "Jack, I couldn't do it. I'm sorry. I just couldn't dig into this story and report it, no, become famous, become important. This whole business makes me sick. I'm sorry. I found out that I'm not at all what I thought I was. I'm not ambitious, I'm not tough, I'm not even very smart. I drove away from your place in Colorado, and I told myself, nope, oh no, I want no part of this. I want a gentle, quiet life. I want to be a lady."

"You are a lady."

She sliced a chunk of butter into the pan. "I don't want to know people like you, Jack. Oh, I know you're quite honorable in your own way. I loved you, more than a little, I think, and I'll cry when I hear you died violently, or were executed by the State, or dribbled away the rest of your years in a prison like the one in Cañon City."

"The pan is smoking," I said.

She lifted the bowl and poured the egg mixture into the omelet pan.

"I don't want to ever see you again," Anna said. "This is it. Finito."

"Christ," I said, "give an irritable woman an opportunity to chat . . ."

She showed me a big smile, then began tilting the frying pan this way and that. "You're like a nut. The meat is sweet but a woman will break her teeth on the shell."

"Cook," I said. "No more metaphors."

She turned the omelet. "Do you remember? We drank gin and tonics on the hotel veranda in Paraje. You showed me those ghastly shrunken heads. We flirted."

"You fainted."

Anna dropped two slices of bread into the toaster.

"Your eyes rolled up out of view," I said.

"Ah, nostalgia," Anna said, and she slid the omelet onto a plate. "It's not what it used to be. Here's your chow."

We had coffee and cheesecake in the living room. I could hear the muted thudding of the surf through the walls of the house. The calico cat awakened, yawned and blinked, sleepily clawed the air, and then turned around three times before going back to sleep.

"Jack, the truth now. Why are you here? Is it because of her? Rachel? She'll be in San Diego tomorrow. Do you intend . . ."

"To kill her? No, Anna."

"I wanted to know."

"Listen," I said, "don't be tempted to call the cops when I leave."

"Is that a threat?"

"It's good advice. They'll make your life hell, the police and prosecutors and media."

"Have I heard this before?"

"See a lawyer tomorrow. Hire the best criminal defense lawyer in Southern California. Tell him everything, all of it, and then listen to what he says."

She left the room, and returned a moment later with a nine-by-twelve manila envelope. "Here."

I accepted the envelope. "The photos?"

"They're filthy."

"They're supposed to be. I hoped to kill a political campaign. They weren't commercially developed?"

"No. I processed them myself at the magazine's lab."

"Did you show them around?"

"Go now, Jack. Please."

Anna remained inside the house, behind the screen door, when I stepped out onto the landing. The air was cool and perfumed with jasmine.

"Give yourself up," she said.

"No."

"It's the only way."

I said, "It seems that a while back I entered a funnel. Sort of a metaphorical funnel, a geometrical warp in my life, in reality. It was a large funnel. I thought I could escape it any time I wanted to. I entered the funnel and it began to narrow. There were no exits. It narrowed down to a thin tube. I'm in the tube now, Anna, and all I can do is proceed on to the end."

"What are you going to do?"

"Run. Go to Tijuana, head south into Mexico. Keep going." I smiled at her. "Maybe retire in Paraje, like your old man."

She shook her head. "It's wretched, miserable. How did you get here from Colorado?"

Moths, attracted by the light, were bumping into the screen.

"I hitchhiked, rode a bus, stole a car. I stole a Cadillac in Tucson," I lied.

"It's so awful to see you this way. A hunted animal. Pathetic, enfeebled . . ."

I smiled at her. "I haven't quite reached the enfeebled level."

"Goodbye, Jack."

"Goodbye."

She closed the door.

I had parked the Porsche on the other side of the main north-south road, Mission Boulevard, and I sat behind the wheel and watched the traffic go by. A teenager on a skateboard admired the Porsche with a long sideways gaze as he clattered past. I could hear music—mostly the thumping bass—from a nearby bar.

The first police car turned down Anna's street after a few minutes, then there were three more, and finally an unmarked sedan with two whip antennae. They turned onto her street and cruised swiftly, silently, like hunting sharks.

I started the engine and drove north. My disguise was useless now; the police would be looking for a tall bald man in a blue blazer. And yet—a bald man driving a stolen Cadillac, trying to cross the border into Mexico.

Anna could not be blamed. Her future was at risk. She was a decent woman and she wanted and deserved a decent life. You could not say she betrayed me. She was being faithful to herself. She had rightly decided to ally herself with society. But now society, in pursuit of truth and justice, might very well extract her heart and show it to the world.

FORTY-SIX

I took Interstate 15 north to Escondido, turned off on 78 and drove east through Ramona, over the mountain pass at Santa Ysabel, then down through Julian and across the Anza Borrego Desert State Park to Ocotillo Wells and beyond. It was hot and dry in the desert. There was not much traffic.

I turned on the radio and listened to a phone-in talk show. The host and his guests discussed the rumors of scandal—money and sex and money—surrounding the American Patriotic Party; today's poll numbers; the prospects of the Democratic and Republican candidates; and Thomas Jackstraw. "*Caput gerat lupinum,*" the host said, and then he explained that that phrase had invoked the severest punishment of outlaws in the late medieval Europe. "Let him wear a wolf's head." Meaning that he could be shot on sight, like wolves. Most of his callers agreed that Jackstraw should be shot on sight. One man said that wolves were intelligent social animals that throughout history had been falsely condemned. Jackstraw, instead, should be shot down like a rabid skunk—let him wear a skunk's head.

At the juncture of 78 and 86 I turned and drove north along the shores of the Salton Sea. Municipal police cars cruised the little towns, and I drove carefully through Salton City, Salton Sea Beach, and Desert Shores. Just beyond the town limits of Desert Shores, I stopped at an old thirty-unit motel grandly named Seaside Villas. The parking lot was half-filled with cars and trucks and trailered boats. Behind the horseshoe-shaped building there was a dusty little park with a kid's steel monkey bars and picnic benches and a badminton net stretched between gnarled trees. The lake appeared to have receded in recent years: a ramshackle pier was almost wholly on dry land now, and there was thirty yards of cracked, salt-caked earth between the park and the water's edge.

A wizened old man answered the office bell. He brusquely pushed a pen and registration card across the desk and, while I filled out the card, complained about the hour. It was only 12:30. He had fingernails like a chimp's and quick monkey eyes. I registered as Daniel Spilikin and gave a false address and car license number.

"There's a drive-in restaurant down the road," the old man said as I was leaving. "Don't cook in the room. No overnight guests—that means women. Checkout by eleven or pay twice."

I had room number eighteen. It was a bit shabby though clean enough; there was a double bed, a dresser, a dinette, a desk and chair, a wall-mounted TV, and on the walls the kind of paintings you buy at Starving Artist Sales. One back window held an air conditioning unit, the other looked out on the little park and the glittering saline lake.

The drive-in was still open. I walked along the shoulder of the road. A car passed going north, then another; and then a police car trailing the other two. These little towns were over-policed.

At the drive-in I ordered two cheeseburgers and two orders of fries, and walked back along the road to the motel. There was a feeling of desolation. The dry, bitter air stung my nostrils.

The motel room, like most, had a Gideon bible in the desk drawer. While eating, I looked up the Book of Daniel, Chapter Two, verse twenty-two. Rachel had chosen to comment on my treachery in her selection.

He revealeth the deep and secret things;
he knoweth what is in the darkness . . .

H was the eighth letter of the alphabet; *E* the fifth; *R* the nineteenth. 8519, so far. I went on until I had enough digits for a cell telephone number.

Any calls from the room had to go through the office switchboard, and anyway, it was late. I went outside to the public telephone. A woman answered on the third ring. She sounded young and sleepy.

"Spilikin," I said.

"What? Oh, yes." A pause. "This is a cell phone."

"I know."

"I'll go down to the lobby and use a pay phone there."

"Right. Take your cell phone. I'll call that number again, and then you can give me the number of the pay phone."

"All right. Five minutes."

I waited five minutes and then again dialed her cell phone number. She answered in mid-ring.

"Yes," she said, and she read off the pay phone number.

I dialed an operator, placed the call, and poured several dollars' worth of change into the box.

"Yes," she said.

"Come and get me."

"Where?"

"Drive east out of Los Angeles on Interstate 10 to Indio, turn south on 86 to Desert Shores. Seaside Villas. Don't let the name fool you, it's a dumpy motel. I'm in room eighteen."

"Got it."

"Will you be coming alone?"

"Yes."

"Rachel said you could be trusted completely."

"Mother ought to know," she said.

I watched a nature program on TV while finishing my meal: *!Kung of the Kalahari*. The !Kung had formerly been known as Bushmen. They were a gentle people who scratched a meager living out of the hard desert wastes—maybe a desert not unlike the one beyond the door. Stone Age people, like the wild Isquito Indians in the forests beyond Paraje, and probably destined for an equally dismal fate.

*   *   *

At six-thirty I was awakened by a faint tapping on the door. I got out of bed, went to the window, and peered out through a slit in the curtains. A tall dark-haired woman was standing outside. She was young, with the looks of a top runway model. She wore white shorts, a sleeveless blouse knotted at the waist, sandals, and she carried a white paper bag. A mid-sized RV was parked next to the Porsche.

I pulled on my trousers, unlocked the door, stepped back and let her in. She came into the room like a cat, both curious and cautious, and then stood in the center of the room and gazed at me with what might have been disappointment.

"So you're Jackstraw," she said.

"Yeah."

"You don't look so bad."

"Well, I *am* bad, very bad. I eat girls like you for breakfast."

"That's why I brought food."

She unpacked the bag: a quart of orange juice, two sixteen-ounce cartons of coffee, and four blueberry muffins. She arranged the food on the dinette table, and we sat down.

"You're Giselle," I said.

"Gigi."

"Rachel's precious daughter."

She tore open a sugar packet with her teeth and emptied the contents into her coffee.

"I saw you in Mundial," I said.

"Oh? Is that when you shot Mother?"

"Yes. Your Spanish is very good."

"So is my Italian and French."

"Specialize in the Romance languages, do you?"

"Pass the orange juice, please."

Her hair was a gleaming black and her eyes, set wide apart, regarded me with a private mirth. She did not look much like her mother, but there was about her the same air of confidence— and playfulness.

We ate quietly for a time, then I said, "Why the hell did Rachel send you?"

"She trusts me."

"Isn't there anyone else she can trust?"

"I guess not."

"What about Troxel?"

"That animal." She made a face. "Him least of all."

"I thought he was your mother's right-hand man."

"Troxel has gone psycho."

"Troxel has always been psycho."

"Maybe, but now he's really gone around the bend."

"Rachel shouldn't involve you in this mess. You're just a kid."

"I'm nineteen."

"Rachel involved you in Mundial. She put you on the platform knowing there would be shooting. And now . . ."

The girl shrugged, licked her fingers, and smiled.

"You're in danger."

She hugged herself and feigned a shiver.

"If the police find me, they might start shooting without warning. You'll be in the way."

"We can't let the police find you, can we?"

"They'll charge you with aiding and abetting a fugitive, obstruction of justice."

"I'll say you took me hostage. You snatched me outside the hotel in Los Angles last night."

"I haven't seen you on TV or heard anything about you. Why aren't you campaigning for the Party?"

"Mother wants me with her, but out of sight. Her vanity, I think. She doesn't like to be seen with me in public or have us photographed together. My mother loves me, but sometimes I think she would love me more if I were squat and homely."

"Hmmm."

"Have you slept with my mother?"

I nodded.

"When she was drugged."

"She wasn't drugged at the time. That was after."

Gigi laughed. "A new twist on the old story. First the sex, then the drug."

"I have photographs of her. Want to see them?"

"You *are* a rat, Jackstraw."

"Not a gentleman?"

"A rodent. Have you finished eating? We should go now." She began gathering up our trash.

"Go where?"

"We have to be in Phoenix early this afternoon."

"Phoenix isn't far. Phoenix—and then what?"

"It gets complicated."

"Maybe I can understand if you use short words."

"Later," she said. "Get ready. You'll follow me up to Indio. We'll leave the Porsche there." She turned to me. "Jack—trust me. I promise you my mother wants you safe."

I showered, shaved off my moustache, and then dressed in Levi's and a polo shirt.

When I came out of the bathroom, Gig was lying on the bed, watching the television.

The manhunt for fugitive killer Thomas Jackstraw was now concentrated in the San Diego area, particularly along the Mexican border. Jackstraw was believed to be driving a Cadillac, year, model, and color unknown.

A pencil sketch of me came on the screen: a bald man with a brush moustache and a murderous scowl. It was not an accurate portrayal, but probably close enough for an observant person to make at least a tentative ID.

Gigi said, "Why are police drawings so amateurish?"

"It's one of the great mysteries."

The newsreader came back on-screen and told the world that a woman informant, whose identity had not been disclosed, called police after Jackstraw showed up at her San Diego home Sunday evening. Police have taken the woman into protective custody. A FBI spokesman would not comment on reports alleging that the woman had been complicit with Jackstraw in the missionary abductions and the assassination of Hamilton Keyes.

Gigi thumbed the remote and the TV screen went dark. She sat up on the edge of the bed.

"She burned you."

"Anna burned herself as well."

"Poor woman. Is she the journalist I heard about?"

"What did you hear?"

"Stuff."

"Yeah, she's the journalist."

Gigi stood up. "She'd better start screaming about her First Amendment rights now, don't you think?"

FORTY-SEVEN

We abandoned the Porsche in a Walmart parking lot at Indio. I left the keys in the ignition and the door unlocked; there was a good chance it would be stolen before dark.

While Gigi was in the store I looked around the interior of the RV. It was the standard layout: a double bed above the cab; a compact galley and dinette; a couch at the rear which expanded into another double bed; a bathroom with a shower stall; and plenty of closets and storage lockers. In one closet I found a uniform along with some clothes that belonged to Gigi.

It seemed that nowadays half of the people you saw were wearing uniforms, from cops to motel maids to meter readers to pizza delivery men. Maybe, I thought, there is something in human nature that is irresistibly drawn to uniforms and uniformity. This blue uniform was cut in a military style, with shoulder loops and patch pockets and three gold-braided rings circling each sleeve cuff. Silver wings were pinned above the left breast; thin red piping ran down the outside trouser seams. On the shelf I found three officer's caps, each decorated with silver eagles, and on the closet floor there were three pairs of black lace shoes in different sizes. No doubt one of the hats would fit me, and a pair of the shoes as well.

I returned to the cab and watched Gigi cross the parking lot with long, jaunty strides. She carried several packages. Sunlight flashed silver blurs in her dark hair.

She got in behind the steering wheel, dumping the packages on my lap. "A floppy hat to cover your dome. Sunglasses to conceal your assassin's eyes. Other stuff you can't peek at."

She drove north until we reached Interstate 10, then turned east.

"We have time," Gigi said. "Where would you like to go?"

"Timbuktu."

"No can do Timbuktu. Why don't we just cruise?"

We drove through Blythe and turned north on 95, which ran along the Colorado River for nearly thirty miles before angling northwest across the desert, a parched, stony land with bare furrowed mountains rising into the distant haze.

I said, "What did you mean before when you said that Troxel had gone psycho?"

"He's out of control."

"Troxel was never under control."

"He's a bully and a tyrant. Everyone is expected to obey him, even Mother. Sometimes he's brutal and mocking—his usual self—and other times icy and remote, and then suddenly he explodes into rages. He hits people. He beat up one of his security men—a man named Paul Sintre—for talking back, beat him very badly. Everyone's afraid. Mother tried to get rid of him but he just laughed."

"Right, you can't simply fire Troxel."

"So what can Mother do? Go to the police, the press?"

"Troxel's not too smart, but he's crafty," I said. "A lot of his behavior might be calculated."

"Well, he scares me half to death."

"Your mother told me that she didn't know that Hamilton Keyes was going to be killed in Mundial, that Troxel acted on his own."

"Don't you believe that?"

"Do you?"

"I think I do. Yes."

"Rachel lies all the time. She wants to be President of the United States."

"You don't understand much of this, do you?"

"But she isn't going to become president. And the election won't be thrown into the House of Representatives. Rachel loses votes every time she opens her mouth and lies."

Gigi laughed and glanced over at me. "This is politics—she loses votes every time she *doesn't* lie."

We picked up Interstate 40 at Needles, and crossed the river into Arizona.

"I think Troxel is in love with my mother."

"Poor Alex," I said.

We drove up to Kingman, west for about forty miles, and then turned south on 93. It was harsh desert country with the barren Hululapi mountains on our right and the Aquarius mountains to our left. The bitter air dried the mucous membranes in my nose and sinuses. We slowed to pass through the little town of Wikieup. Phoenix was now about 120 miles to the southeast.

Gigi pulled the RV over onto the shoulder of the road. There were no cars in sight behind or ahead of us.

"This is a good place to change," she said. "You first."

"The pilot's uniform? Why am I going to be disguised as an airline pilot?"

"You want to leave the country, don't you?"

"Not if I have to fly the airplane."

She smiled, a genuine one. "Please—trust me."

I went into the back and put on the airline captain's uniform. One of the hats and one of the three pairs of black shoes fit. I had worn many uniforms during my life, starting with that Union cavalry officer's outfit when I was a boy, but this was the least martial.

Then Gigi went into the rear of the RV. There was no traffic. Heat blurs distorted the horizon. Far down the road a pair of ravens picked over the carcass of a roadkill.

She changed into a belted off-white dress of a clingy fabric that showed off her figure. Her long hair had been pulled back and knotted into a chignon. We examined each other.

"You look all right, I guess," she said.

"You too, I guess."

She smiled and slipped behind the steering wheel. "*Alors,* next stop Phoenix International Airport."

The ravens lifted into the air when we passed, and I saw that the carrion was a flattened coyote. The noon sun had bleached much of the color from sky and landscape.

Why, I wondered, was I going with her—with them? Well, because Rachel and Troxel might actually succeed in getting me out of the country to some remote, semi-safe refuge. I couldn't hope to escape on my own. There was no other choice. This sense of fatalism relaxed me. So then—once more through the looking glass into Rachel's world. I leaned back in the seat and closed my eyes.

Gigi awakened me in the airport parking lot. "Look alive," she said.

"What time is it?"

"Time for our rendezvous."

"There's an old poem—'I Have a Rendezvous With Death.'"

"Don't we all? Get your things, Jack."

I went into the back and got my rucksack from the locker.

"Uh, Captain? Pilots don't walk through airports with rucksacks on their backs. They carry overnight bags, don't they? Take the valise."

Outside it was hot and very bright; the sunlight was both absorbed and reflected by the concrete, and I could feel heat through the soles of my shoes.

Gigi pinned a plastic laminated ID card above her breast; it contained her photograph, a fingerprint, her name, and signature.

"What about the RV?" I asked.

"Someone will pick it up soon. A political campaign has lots of flunkies eager to be of service."

"Like the Mafia," I said.

"*Andale,*" she said, gathering her packages. Walk.

An old couple was standing just inside the door when we entered, and they followed us through the terminal and down a concourse. White hair, ruddy complexions, sun-country clothing—they looked as if they had just come from a round of hacker's golf. Grandma and Grandpa, except that there was a certain no-nonsense look in their faces.

"Who are they?" I asked Gigi.

"Friends of Troxel's. Former Stasi—whatever that is."

"Stasi," I said, "was the East German secret police. You might say the Stasi picked up where the Gestapo left off."

We walked past ticket counters, little shops, lounges filled with red and yellow plastic chairs and bored, waiting passengers. We passed a Phoenix cop, a pair of uniformed airport security men, and then another cop. I was virtually invisible. They all, cops and passengers, men and women, stared at the beautiful Gigi, who now walked with the strut of a fashion model stalking down the runway. I supposed that her look, her walk, were calculated; she had turned up the sexual voltage to draw attention away from me.

She hesitated for a moment in front of a place called Mackey's, took my arm, and guided me through the door. It was a dimly lighted narrow room with a shot bar and five or six tables. A tall man sat at the end of the bar near the entrance. Troxel slouched at the rear table below a red neon exit sign. He grinned at me.

"Hello, Jack," he said. "You son of a bitch."

A plastic ID card like Gigi's was pinned to his lapel. He wore a dark gray suit, a white shirt, and a blue tie with an embroidered gold crest in its center. His big scarred hands were folded on the table.

"Hello, Sexy," he said to Gigi.

Gigi and I sat down. On the table were an ashtray, a bowl of salted peanuts, an empty beer mug, and a sputtering candle stub.

The man sitting at the bar looked familiar. He was big, overweight, with salt-and-pepper hair worn in a brush cut.

The bartender came over to take our orders: a Perrier for me, kir for Gigi, and another beer for Troxel.

"Hey, pal," Troxel said. "Do you remember Anna Fontenot?"

"The name rings a bell," I said.

"Sure. She was the writer you were screwing at the hotel in Paraje. She was the woman you killed up in the bell tower at the mission."

"It's coming back," I said.

Even in the dimness of the bar I could see that Troxel had contracted some kind of skin disease. His boils were cured but the skin of his face was peeling in powdery flakes, exposing the inflamed new skin beneath.

"You dumb bastard," he said.

Gigi watched us. Her eyes flickered from Troxel, to me, to Troxel again. She seemed to be evaluating us in the same focused way you might judge the heft and jaws of a pair of dogs squaring up to fight.

The bartender arrived with our drinks. Troxel paid him with a one-hundred-dollar bill.

"Anyway, the FBI got that Fontenot bitch," Troxel said.

"I know."

"How much does she know?"

"Everything I know and can guess."

The jukebox music abruptly ceased and Troxel's voice was loud in the little room.

"God damn your eyes!" he said.

Gigi smiled at this locution.

The man at the bar got up and put some money in the jukebox. I recognized him now: in Chicago, he had been one of the two men waiting for an elevator in the hotel lobby after I'd left Rachel. And it seemed to me that I had known him before that.

The bartender brought the change on a tray. Troxel tipped him one dollar, waited for the music to start, and then said, "Well, that's it."

"That's what?" Gigi asked.

"It. *It*, you dumb cunt."

Gigi blinked, and looked away from his eyes, his raw peeling face.

The man at the end of the bar got up, placed some money under his glass, and strolled out into the concourse.

"You haven't changed, have you, Troxel?" I said.

The candle sputtered out and a twist of oily smoke rose from the red glass globe.

"Don't count on it, pal." He pushed his chair back. "All right, fuck it. Let's go."

Gigi stood and gathered her packages. I made them both wait, standing, while I finished my drink. Then I picked up the valise and we went outside into the crowded concourse. The old couple was not in sight now, but the man who had been sitting at the bar was nearby, looking up at a screen that provided airline arrival and departure times.

He turned as I approached and said, "How you doing, Jack?"

"I know you from somewhere."

"We met a long time ago in Africa. The Sudan."

"I don't remember."

"I was a diplomat then."

"Diplomat?"

Troxel and Gigi were watching us.

"I was Deputy Chief of Station," he said.

"That's right. Okay. Clifford Blake."

"Blakely."

"And you've sold yourself to Troxel."

"I've sold my services to Troxel," he said, and then, drawling the words, "but not my sacred honor or immaculate soul."

Troxel, Gigi, and I walked down the concourse, rode an escalator to a vast basement-like room, passed a luggage carousel, a fenced storage area, a couple of offices, and passed through a heavy door with a stenciled NO ADMITTANCE sign above it.

"You're Captain Connors," Troxel told me.

His suit was expensive and well-cut, no doubt tailored; but with the absurd crested tie, with his big head and hands and feet, he looked fraudulent—a mean, straw-haired redneck in a stolen suit.

We passed through a door into a square room, its walls lined with metal lockers. Another heavy door led outside. A uniformed security guard in his twenties sat on a tall stool behind a lectern. His name was stitched onto a patch above his right pocket: A. Ramirez.

"This is Miss Valentine," Troxel said. "And Captain Jim Connors. I'm Troxel."

The guard glanced at Troxel's and Gigi's ID cards, consulted a ledger, looked at his watch, and wrote down their names and the time. He looked at me.

"Connors," Troxel said.

The guard wrote down my false name. "Okay." He smiled at Gigi and said, "*Hasta luego, Guapa.*"

We went through another door and into the heat and sunlight.

"What does that mean?" Troxel asked. "*Guapa.*"

"Pretty," Gigi said flatly.

"Airport security," Troxel said. "They pay those guys seven dollars per hour and get less than they paid for."

There were airplanes parked at angles on the stained concrete. A 747, painted red, white, and blue, was about fifty yards away. It was decorated with American flags and, written in Gothic letters, the words "American Patriotic Party."

We walked across the tarmac and ascended the steps into the APP plane. A man in a beige suit was waiting just inside the door, between the flight deck and what, in a standard passenger aircraft, would be business class. Here, though, the section had been arranged into a comfortable lounge, with stuffed sofas and reclining chairs and marquetry tables.

The man was lean and dark, with wavy black hair, hawkish in profile. His lower lip was split and there were purple and violet bruises on his cheekbones and beneath his right eye.

Troxel withdrew a folded sheet of paper from an inside breast pocket. "Here are the names of the people you'll admit on board, Sintre. Only these. No one else. Got that?"

"Right," Sintre said, taking the paper.

"No one else. And—listen to me. Don't look at her. Anyone has a cell or satellite phone, take it away. Computer, take it away. An iPad, take it away. Any means of communicating with the outside—confiscate it. Is that clear?"

"Clear."

You could see that Paul Sintre resented the way Troxel spoke to him, especially in front of Gigi—he flicked a glance at her—but he did not protest.

"Guns," Troxel said. "Am I going too fast? Take away guns. Blakely will be here soon, and the Reicherts. Take their guns, and if they say anything about it, send them to me. Benoit? If he's got a gun, take it. The women? No exceptions. Got it?"

Sintre nodded, shot another look toward Gigi.

Troxel was foolish to treat the man with such contempt. If Sintre was any good at his job—and why would Troxel hire him if he weren't—then he had a past, and he was dangerous.

"Now what?" Troxel said.

Sintre looked at him.

"Sintre? Now what?"

The man removed a Sig Sauer pistol from a shoulder holster and gave it to Troxel.

"There. That wasn't so hard, was it?"

We passed through a curtain and started down the aisle. The seats were bigger and better-spaced than usual on passenger aircraft. We passed the galley alcove, more rows of seats, and some bathroom cubicles. There was a narrow oval private room at the back. Through the open door I could see a bed, a desk and chair, wood lockers and cabinets, and in the rear a hatch that led into the cargo hold. It looked like the saloon of an expensive sail yacht.

It was very hot, stifling, on board. The metal skin of the aircraft had turned the interior into an oven. All three of us were sweating.

I lifted my valise into an overhead compartment, removed my jacket, cap, and tie, and sat down.

Troxel roughly rubbed my shaven head with his right hand. There was no affection in the gesture.

"You got a gun?" he asked. "Give it to me."

"I've got a gun," I said. "But I'm not giving it to you."

Gigi watched us with an expression that seemed partly fearful, partly excited.

Troxel nodded his head while smiling at me. It was his way of saying: *All right, have it your way for the moment.* I knew he was already planning my death.

FORTY-EIGHT

Within the hour people started coming on board. They gazed curiously at me. I returned their stares as they came down the aisle, placed luggage in the overhead compartments, loosened ties, removed suit jackets, selected seats. There was a black family: Joshua Benoit, the vice-presidential candidate, his wife and ten-year-old twin boys. The last I'd heard, Benoit had been campaigning in the East. Then another family: Orson Dedrick, trim and youthful in a seersucker suit, with a plump, mousy woman I assumed was his wife, and a girl of seven or eight. Then the couple, the white-haired Grandma and Grandpa, the Germans from Stasi. Ahead, through the open curtains, I saw two men in uniforms, members of this flight crew.

Finally Rachel, followed by Blakely, walked down the aisle. She paused to kiss her daughter's cheek, spoke briefly to Benoit, and continued down the aisle. She wore a straw hat similar to the one she'd worn in Mundial on the day I shot her. I remembered the way Rachel had sailed the hat out into the crowd and how people had fought over it as if it were a religious or historical relic. Troxel wanted to speak with her, but she pushed on past him while looking at me with narrowed eyes and an artificial smile.

As she passed, she said, "I want to talk to you, Snake."

I followed her into the cabin. Rachel closed and locked the door, wrist-snapped her straw hat into a corner, and kicked off her high-heeled shoes. "You look tanned and fit," she said. She herself had a bruised look, with dark crescents beneath her eyes and puffy lips. Rachel never appeared merely fatigued, but sexually used too, depleted. She turned away from me and said, "Help me with this." I drew down the zipper on her dress and she stepped out of it, then lowered her slip. "The bra, too." I unsnapped the bra. Now she wore only panties and a garter belt that held up dark, finely meshed stockings. She unclipped the stockings and, bending over, removed first the right one, then the left. She removed the garter belt and panties, and moved naked toward a closet, saying, "Fix us a drink, Jack?"

There was a compact refrigerator of the sort you find in hotel rooms: inside I found miniature bottles of various spirits, soft drinks, fruit, and beer. Most of the ice in the freezer trays had melted, but I managed to collect enough slivers to fill two glasses. I poured a miniature vodka into Rachel's glass, scotch into mine.

Rachel had changed into slacks and a blouse. She stepped close to accept the drink, looked up at me in an amused, inquiring way, lifted on her toes and kissed the corner of my mouth.

"What did you think of my Gigi?" she asked.

"I like her."

"Beautiful, isn't she? I was never that beautiful."

"You really shouldn't have permitted her to become involved in this," I said.

"I know. But I seem to have lost my instincts, my rhythm. You understand, I suspect. I've made a lot of mistakes lately."

"So have I," I said.

Rachel moved away and sat on the edge of the bed. I took the little packet of photographs from my pocket and gave it to her.

"What's this?" She withdrew the pictures. There were seven prints and their negatives, all the photographs I had taken that night in Chicago.

Rachel quickly shuffled through the prints, then once again, slower this time. "God damn you, Jackstraw." She held a print up to the light. "What the hell is this grotesque, tiny Negroid head doing on the pillow?"

"Cavenaugh," I said. I explained about the shrunken head replicas, and my conviction that she had been implicated in his murder.

"That's what I'd like to do to you," Rachel said. "Shrink your stubborn head and sew your lips together."

She turned to another print. "This one is like a below-the-waist anatomy illustration. *Labia majora, labia minora* . . . It's more gynecology than pornography. I notice that you're quite respectful of your own modesty."

"You were the star."

She replaced the prints in the envelope and sailed it into the corner where her straw hat lay. "You're corrupt in your own way."

"I wanted to snuff your campaign. I thought these photos would do that."

"Then why haven't they appeared in the tabloids or on the Internet?"

"I gave the film to a reporter. She decided that she didn't want anything to do with it."

"That Fontenot bitch."

"She calls you 'that Valentine bitch.'"

"I could have used these photographs in my campaign flyers."

"Right. Here's your president after being thoroughly debauched by her alleged assassin."

"This Fontenot woman—does she know a lot?"

"All that I know."

"How much, really, do you know?"

"A lot."

"And will she talk?"

"By now she's probably told everything she knows four or five times over."

"Why did you blab to her, anyway?" she said in a weary tone of reproach. "It was stupid. A betrayal."

"Let's not start talking about betrayals. What are you going to do?"

"I don't know. Can you think of anything?"

"I mean—what about me? You said you'd help."

"We'll get you out of the country."

"To where?"

"Fiji? Libya? Oz?"

"Can you be more specific?"

She drained her drink and gazed at me with a sly half-smile. On a child's face it would be a smile of coyness, mischief; with Rachel, though, you knew that you were being enticed into her own bizarre version of reality.

"First," she said, raising a forefinger, "You'll hijack this airplane."

"Ah," I said. "Of course."

"Really, you are about to hijack this airplane, me, everyone aboard, the campaign, the American Patriotic Party, all of it."

I didn't doubt her; it wasn't a jest. The details would gradually emerge, but Rachel had devised a scheme involving the fake hijacking of her campaign airplane. The idea had all the shrewdness, and all the lunacy, one expected of her.

"You brought luggage aboard, didn't you?" she said in a low voice.

"A valise."

"Where is it?"

"In one of the overhead compartments."

"We'll place it in a strategic location. It's filled with explosives."

"No it isn't."

"Darling, I'm really exhausted. You'll have to help me. I can't do the thinking for everyone. The valise is stuffed with powerful explosives. You're a determined, ruthless, terrorist hijacker. Human life means nothing to you."

"Why is the hair on my neck bristling?"

"It will work. You'll see."

"Exactly how did I pull of this brilliant, daring hijack?"

"You took Troxel and Gigi hostage, and you threatened to blow them and half of the airport up unless they contrived to get you aboard the airplane. The explosives were in your valise. *Voilá!* Troxel had no choice but to guide you through the airport security and onto the plane."

"Where did I get the pilot's uniform? The explosives? How did I manage to reach Troxel and Gigi? What about—"

"Let's not fuss about the details now."

"What about the rest of the plan?"

"We'll improvise." She studied me for a time, then said, "You'll probably have to kill Troxel."

"You want me to kill Troxel for you?"

"For all of us, darling. If it weren't for Troxel and Betancourt, no one would have been hurt during this entire adventure. He's ruined everything with his solo actions, his violence and brutality. Do you know what Troxel's problem is?"

"His violence and brutality?"

"No. He lacks a sense of humor."

We looked at each other, grading Troxel's sense of humor, and then we smiled.

Now first one engine, then the other, were ignited, and we had to raise our voices against the noise.

I said, "Are we leaving already?"

"The airports give us a preferred slot."

"When do I officially hijack the plane?"

"We'll wait until we're in the air. If we do it now there will be lots of fuss and delays."

"Am I going to have to stalk up and down the aisle, waving a gun and shouting in a foreign language?"

"Don't be silly. This is going to be a genteel hijacking."

The engines grew louder, and the airplane moved over an expanse of tarmac and down one of the spokes leading to a runway.

"Rachel, do all of the people out there in the cabin and up on the flight deck know they're going to be hijacked?"

"Certainly. I've eliminated all the deadweight, the media swine, advisors, campaign workers, money bigshots. We're down to the inner circle now, the *crème de la crème*."

"The *merde de la merde*. You don't really think that a fake hijacking will invigorate your campaign, do you?"

"The campaign is stone-cold dead. My poll numbers are down to five percent, and—partly thanks to you—there are going to be embarrassing revelations soon."

"Embarrassing. You mean devastating."

"Did you ever read *The Prince*?" Rachel asked.

I nodded.

"Machiavelli wrote something like—I'm paraphrasing: On the side of the conspirators there is nothing but fear, envy, suspicion, and dread of punishment . . ."

I said, "He also wrote—I'm paraphrasing too: A man who wants to be good will inevitably come to grief among so many who are not good. So he must learn to be bad."

We laughed.

"Here's another," Rachel said. "Some things which appear to be virtues would, if followed, lead to one's ruin."

We laughed again.

The airplane had reached the runway and, brakes set, the pilot was increasing the power of the jet engines.

I couldn't guess what Rachel was thinking. I was thinking that the time was perfect for someone to execute a heroic triple play: thwart a hijacking and save the lives of the hostages; end the rampage of a dangerous fugitive; and eliminate a crucial witness to your crimes. And all with a single bullet.

The airplane was now swiftly taxiing down the runway.

Rachel pitched her voice to penetrate the engine noise. "Darling, would you do something for me? Will you massage my sore feet for a few minutes?"

"I'll rub your feet," I said, "if you will be so good as to scratch my back."

"We could do that simultaneously, properly positioned."

"A few other things as well, improperly positioned."

"Indeed."

"I'm beginning to think it was all about money," I said.

"You're a military man, Jack. You've read von Clausewitz, haven't you?"

"A long time ago, at the Point."

"Remember, he said: 'Business is war conducted by other means.'"

"No, Rachel. He said: 'War is diplomacy conducted by other means.'"

She laughed. "How silly of me. I got it all mixed up. Isn't that just like a woman?"

We smiled at each other as the airplane lifted off the runway and climbed steeply into what the military march calls "the wild blue yonder."

FORTY-NINE

When the plane reached cruising altitude, Rachel dressed and led me out into the cabin. We made our way to the flight deck to consult with the pilot for an announcement of the hijacking. On the way we paused while Rachel introduced me to those persons I hadn't met. I think all of us sensed the absurdity of this social nicety in the midst of a "hijacking."

Joshua Benoit was a big, wide-shouldered man with a somber mein and a deep baritone voice. He had an actor's self-awareness: he studied his effects, looked at himself through your eyes. I thought he might make a great Othello: essentially decent but brooding, a victim of his passions. He had done pretty well impersonating a vice-presidential candidate. Benoit and his wife were courteous and discreet, non-judgmental, as if meeting an accused assassin and terrorist were a normal occurrence. Their twin boys had already made friends with the Dedrick girl, and the three of them played at the rear of the airplane.

"Be stout of heart, Mr. Jackstraw," Benoit said, as Rachel and I moved away.

Paul Sintre clearly disliked me. That, perhaps, was because I had been a witness to his humiliation by Troxel. He was a tense, wounded man, seething with resentment.

Orson Dedrick observed me with his lips pursed and his eyes cold as I briefly chatted with his wife. Dedrick, the precise numbers man, could not be expected to understand or approve of someone like me. I supposed that he and his wife must feel very out of place among this group. His wife, Mary Lou, was shy, and silly in a gushing way because of her shyness, but obviously a kind woman. Surely a good mother, a fine cook, a sympathetic friend—how could she have known that her Orson had a criminal twist to his nature? That twist was probably a continual surprise to Orson himself.

Heinz Karl Reichert and his wife, Trudi, the German couple from Stasi, were relaxed and cynical. To them, this was just another con in a lifetime of cons. Treachery was their milieu; duplicity as natural as breathing. They were in their early seventies, with identical Prussian-blue eyes, and white hair—faintly yellow at the temples—that might have been spun from the same batch of raw silk. Both had false teeth, upper and lower dentures, and they often showed them in mirthless smiles. You might mistake them for brother and sister. They made it clear that they considered me stupid, just another violent animal like Troxel. But they appeared to respect Rachel.

Blakely and Gigi were sitting together in the front row of cabin seats, playing cards.

"I guess you know Clifford," Rachel said to me.

"Alas," I said.

Blakely grinned at me.

"Clifford butters his bread on both sides," I said.

He nodded humbly.

"If you don't like the face Clifford shows to you, ask to see the other one."

He said, "Don't start thinking you're as tough as your newspaper clippings say you are."

"Hey," Gigi said, folding then fanning out her hand of cards. "Come on. Clifford?—ten of diamonds."

Rachel and I went through the curtain and found Troxel sitting alone in the lounge. He wore only undershorts and a sleeveless T-shirt even though the plane had cooled since takeoff. His uncombed hair looked like a thatch of dried grass. The skin of his face was flaky, with here and there raw sores the size of nickels and dimes.

"It's done," he said to Rachel. His stare was direct, challenging.

"What do you mean?"

"I mean it's done. We're hijacked."

"Alex . . ."

"Jackdaw here has taken over the airplane. I had Josephson tell the air traffic controller."

I sat on the sofa opposite Troxel. Rachel remained standing, her palm braced against a bulkhead for balance.

"Jackanapes here has a satchel full of C-4 and will blow the airplane and all of us to bits if he isn't obeyed."

First he'd called me Jackdaw, which was a crowlike bird, and then Jackanapes, clown or fool.

I said, "Who says Troxel doesn't have a sense of humor?"

Rachel glanced at me with her eyebrows raised a bit, her head cocked ever so slightly. Her look said: See? You'll *have* to kill him.

She turned back to Troxel. "Don't you ever learn? There were specific points I wanted Josephson to make when he talked to the ground. It was carefully planned. They're listening to us, Alex. Every word, every nuance. If they begin thinking that Jack is *with* us, that this is another fake . . ."

"Is Rach-Rach upset with little Alex?"

"And you were too quick," Rachel said. "You've given them too much time."

"Time for what?"

I said, "Time to organize something. Bring in the Rangers, maybe."

"Delta Force," Troxel said contemptuously. "SEALs. If you were talking about the SAS or the Israelis . . ."

But now there was a hint of doubt in his bluster.

"You are a vain, stupid man," Rachel said matter-of-factly. "Every time you start feeling clever you make a mess that I have to clean up. You're vain and arrogant and stupid and I am sick to death of you."

"Careful," Troxel said.

"You're nothing but a lowlife thug."

Troxel started to rise, but immediately settled back when he saw me reach into my pocket. He lifted his hands palms up and smiled at me, smiled at Rachel, shrugged, and said, "Having Jackass around has made you too bold, Rach. The screwing can't be that good."

"There," Rachel said. "You see? You can't learn. You are incapable of modifying your behavior no matter what the consequence might be."

She abruptly turned away, hissing through her teeth, and walked out the door to the flight deck.

Troxel and I gazed at each other across the aisle. He appeared placid now, amused, but Troxel was a volatile man and I knew that in half a second or half a day he might explode with rage. He was unstable in the same way that old dynamite is unstable. In Paraje, in Mundial, Troxel had exerted a certain amount of self-control and functioned well enough. But he could not maintain discipline—it was not a part of his nature.

"What do you think, Jack?" he said. "Ain't Rach a real formidable fuck? The daughter, too. And the pair of them together . . ."

"Spare me your adolescent fantasies," I said.

He grinned. "Has Rach asked you yet?"

"Asked me what?"

"To kill me."

"Paranoid, are you, Troxel?"

"She tried to get Sintre to kill me. Not directly, but promises—a hint here, a kiss there—both sexual and financial. But Paul doesn't have the balls to try it. You might. But, pal, if you do, you won't last thirty seconds afterward."

He was telling me that he had loyal allies, that if there was a division and we split into two factions, he had the guns and the numbers and the power. He was counting on Blakely; the Reicherts; perhaps Joshua Benoit; maybe Sintre too, despite their conflict.

"Did you kill Cavenaugh?" I said.

"Nah. Why would I kill that mutt? Some nervous punk did that."

"You did rig my rental car with explosives."

He grinned. "Yeah. Exploded real good."

Rachel came through the flight deck's door and sat next to me. She was calm but authoritative.

"All right," she said to me. "We're going to refuel in Atlanta instead of Miami. But Morrison isn't going to announce the change until we're thirty minutes out of Atlanta. They won't have time to prepare any nasty surprises that way."

She confided her remarks to me, deliberately excluding Troxel. Colonel Troxel had been demoted.

"You can talk to the tower, Jack, when we reach Atlanta. They'll have a hostage negotiator there by the time we're on the ground."

"My terms are non-negotiable," I said.

"Oh, I'm not worried about you, Jack."

"They'll try to stall."

"Of course. But you won't let them."

"Jesus," Troxel said.

Rachel got to her feet. She lowered her voice, but it was not so low that Troxel couldn't hear. "We'll go back to my room, darling. We'll have a drink and talk this out. I want to hear your idea."

"Dear baby Jesus!" Troxel said, laughing. "Tell me I'm dreaming."

While we had been forward, someone—maybe Gigi—had cleaned the room and converted the bed into a sofa. Rachel sat down, leaned back, and closed her eyes.

I closed the door. "Do you want a drink?"

"No. Sit down here with me, Jack."

I went to the sofa.

"Put your arm around me. Please."

I placed my arm over her shoulders, and she leaned against me. Her eyes remained closed.

"What are you doing?" she asked.

"Sniffing your hair."

"What does it smell like?"

"Cabbage."

She laughed.

"Like hair, actually."

"Darling, do you remember when I told you that I couldn't do it alone, I needed you with me?"

"I recall something like that."

"I meant it. I can't get you out of my system."

"Rachel, it's so hard to determine what you mean and don't mean."

"That was the night you poisoned me. But you're here now."

"I'm here. Do you want to make love?"

"No, I want you to listen. I'm tired. I am so very tired, baby, and it gets harder and harder to go on. Those people out there. You know

Troxel. Morrison, the pilot, is reliable, but the others—they resist everything. I feel that I'm swimming upstream all the time."

"Just think of what it would be like if you were the president."

"I'm asking—pleading—for your help. Your active participation. We're going into what the media retards call the 'end game,' and I'm not sure I have the resources left to pull it off."

"Exactly what are you trying to pull off?"

"If you'll only take some of the weight."

"Rachel—"

"I can't tell you yet. Not all of the cards have been dealt."

"You appeal for my help, but you won't tell me what we're doing."

"I know. I'm sorry. I have a desperate need for secrecy. I can't help it. Would you rather I lie?"

"Rachel, you do lie. All the time."

I waited a minute for her reply, then realized that she was sleeping. She had gone from full consciousness to deep sleep in an instant. I had known soldiers who could do that, go from waking to sleep and waking without transition. It was a gift possessed by some soldiers and doctors and hunters and psychopaths.

I didn't think they intended to kill me. At least not yet. I was a necessary part of the scheme. No Jackstraw, no hijacking; no hijacking, no . . . what? Rachel was not sure of her future actions. She was reacting. Each choice led to a diminished number of alternative choices. Eventually you had two choices left, then none.

And did she really mean what she said about needing me? Maybe. I couldn't be sure.

By the time she awakened we were only half an hour out of Atlanta. My right arm was numb. Rachel quickly brushed her hair, applied lipstick in two precise strokes, and we went out into the cabin. She went forward to the flight deck. I sat in an aisle seat ten rows behind the curtain.

The children were quiet now, sleeping. Joshua Benoit was reading a book; Orson Dedrick rapidly worked a calculator; Gigi and Blakely still played cards. Troxel, sitting across the aisle, had put on a shirt and slacks, though his feet were bare.

"Hey, Jocko," he said. "What is this? You and Rach diddle while the rest of us burn?"

Rachel came through the curtain and walked down the aisle to talk to Heinz Karl Reichert, who got up and followed her forward. They used the microphone system employed by the flight attendants when they inform you about what measures you should take in the event of a disaster.

"Friends," Rachel said. "Fellow Americans." She smiled briefly. "Just now Captain Morrison informed the air traffic controllers that he was altering course from the Miami airport to Atlanta. Naturally he told them that the change was commanded by the hijacker. He told them that Jackstraw was agitated and making terrible threats, and that they should have a fueling truck waiting for us in Atlanta. There must be no delay."

Rachel paused, holding the microphone easily, casually, like a pop singer waiting for the band to resume playing.

"Now, Heinz Karl has something to say to us." She gave the mic to the ex-Stasi officer.

"*Achtung!*" he said. "You will soon be leaving the American sector." He displayed his big false teeth. "First: as soon as I finish speaking we shall lower all of the shades. Every shade on every window. Yes? There may be snipers in position, waiting for an opportunity to shoot Mr. Jackstraw. At least there will be observers, watching us through high-powered telescopes, astronomical-quality telescopes. Considerable information may be gathered from such observation. An entire mosaic may be inferred from glimpsed fragments. Are the hostages moving freely? Or are they concentrated in one section of the airplane where the terrorist may exert his control? Is this, perhaps, not an authentic hijacking?"

Heinz Karl spoke a careful American English with hardly a trace of accent. His words were weighted with condescension and German whimsy.

"So," he said, "we shall pull every window shade. Two. *Two.* We shall not discuss this event or any other relevant matters among ourselves. Silence! If we must talk, whisper. There are very sophisticated listening devices that may be employed. They can—listen to me—they *can* hear through walls. It is even possible for them to turn this entire airplane into a single speaker system, using the airplane's own wiring. So—silence at all times. If not silence, whispers into the ear. Behave, always, as if this hijacking were real and you are terrorized. Yes? Very well."

He returned the microphone to Rachel.

"We won't be long in Atlanta," she said. "Jack will probably have to deal with the hostage negotiator for a while, and then the plane will be refueled and we'll be off."

Troxel applauded wildly. He stood up and shouted, "Oh yes. Hallelujah, sisters! Hallelujah, brothers. Let us pray."

FIFTY

We encountered turbulence during the last twenty minutes of flight, passing in and out of dark clouds veined by lightning, and it was raining when the airplane dropped beneath the low ceiling and landed in Atlanta. The tower directed Captain Morrison to park the plane on an expanse of tarmac away from the runways. The engines were turned off, and in the ensuing quiet we could hear rain snapping on the aircraft's metal skin.

I raised a window shade an inch and peered out. The tower and terminal were not visible. All you could see was the slanting downpour and rain-dimpled puddles on the concrete. The world was reduced to less than one hundred yards. The feeling was claustrophobic: we were confined in this tubular capsule, further isolated by weather, and ultimately—by our outlawry—severed from normal human society.

Rachel stepped through the curtain at the front of the plane and smiled and nodded. The smile was directed toward me, but actually meant to reassure those who were watching.

I got up and walked the length of the airplane, aware that I was being closely observed, evaluated by the others. Now it was time for the hijacker to do his job.

Blankets covered the windows of the flight deck and it was

dim inside, illuminated only by a few red lights which were reflected off of what seemed like hundreds of dials and gauges. Rachel introduced me to the pilot and co-pilot. They had that easy confidence derived from knowledge and competence. They were fliers; they did a difficult thing very well, and that made them calm and sure. Both men were around sixty years old. Morrison, the pilot, was my size, with salt-and-pepper hair and a bony nose that had obviously been broken a couple of times. Jenkins was shorter, going bald, with a round face. They were close to the mandatory retirement age. I thought that might explain why they had enlisted in this mad venture. Rachel would have promised them money, lots and lots of money, and plenty of excitement. Age hadn't made them timid.

"You know how to work the radio?" Morrison asked.

I looked it over. "I think so."

"You won't be talking to the tower. They had me change to another frequency. You'll probably be talking to some FBI agent."

"Probably so," I said.

They wished me luck and filed out of the cockpit and into the lounge. Rachel sat next to me in the second officer's seat. She smiled and showed her crossed fingers.

I switched on the radio and listened to a hiss of white noise in my headset. I took a deep breath.

"Is you dere?" I said. "Is dat you, feebie?"

"Wise ass." A faint woman's voice.

"Call me Hank," a different voice said.

"Hank."

"That's pretty good," he said, letting me know by his inflections that it wasn't at all good, it was dumb.

"Hank, there's nothing to negotiate. Send out a fuel truck."

"We've got to talk, Jack. Talk seriously and honestly. Truthfully. Pray together, maybe."

I laughed.

"Son, you are lost and alone in the stormy darkness. Lost, solitary, and—we both know this—afraid. I guess right now you're about the scaredest and most miserable man on the planet, stumbling around in the dark, looking for light, looking for your soul."

"Looking for plain talk," I said.

His accent was deep South, his voice whiskey-rough but well modulated. It was an expressive voice, a storyteller's practiced drawl.

"Is everything all right?" he asked.

"So far."

"No one sick, no one hurt?"

"Not yet."

"You don't need medical supplies?"

"Nope."

"Got plenty of food and water?"

Now, I thought, he was trying to seize control by this series of quick questions, establish dominance. He was the giver; I was the receiver. He was the priest, I the penitent.

"Jack? I asked if there was sufficient food and water on board."

"We aren't expecting a long siege," I said.

"Patience. You can't just jump aboard a jet and say, 'Take me to Cuba, take me to Libya.' Those days are long gone, son. There are procedures. Rules of engagement. Criteria must be met. Assurance must be given and guaranteed. All that stuff. You understand."

"No, Hank. I don't understand."

"This is big stuff," he said. "Monstrous big stuff. We got heavy politicians and bureaucrats and media hardasses looking over our shoulders, breathing down our necks."

Rachel gave me an inquiring look.

I said, "I want this airplane refueled pronto. Fill 'er up."

"Jack, you have done it, son, you have reached the crux, the crossroads, and you can continue down the old road, go deeper and deeper into the morass of sin and evil, or you can turn away, turn around, do right, try being a man."

"You come on weird for a hostage negotiator."

"I don't always follow the book. Negotiating with hostage-takers can be creative. Most of them are mopes who want sympathy. Can you imagine? I give the sympathy, I commiserate, I pity them almost as much as they pity themselves. I bullshit the guys who can be bullshitted. I won't try that on you. You're too smart for this."

"Sure I am," I said.

"Now, my friend, it's time for us to get serious about this terrible situation. Let's take it in phases. Let's be clear and orderly and resolve this matter step by step. First, I want you to release the three children and their mothers. I know you won't object to that. I know you aren't the kind of pig who'll hold children hostage, who would willingly harm innocent little kids. You're a good man who has lost his way, gone awry, and is doing something bad. Send out the little children— they have a right to full and complete lives. They have a right to their mothers. Okay? Of course. So, we can expect you to let the three kids and their moms go."

"No."

"Jack, come on. Am I dealing with just another crazy asshole? You want to exchange the children for three pizzas? Am I dealing with that kind of freak? Pizza in exchange for the babies, six-packs for their moms?"

"Hank, you're really starting to irritate me."

"Did I mention that I knew your father?"

"Yes," I said.

This slowed him for only a moment. "We weren't close friends, but we met from time to time, and we played a few rounds of golf. The Brigadier was a fine man, a rock of integrity in all respects but one—he sometimes cheated at golf. A minor and wholly human flaw. He might have been a great man if he'd been born a few years earlier, been old enough, I mean, to have achieved a position of command in World War Two. Eisenhower, Bradley, Patton, Jackstraw. And your grandfather—General Pershing called him 'honor personified.'"

"So I inherited good genes, is that it? Except for my mother. Or maybe you're saying I inherited the dreaded cheat-at-golf gene."

"Jack, come on, man, talk to me honestly. Let's dispense with the semi-witty repartee. Stand up straight. Dig down deep inside yourself and speak straight and true. Dig down and find yourself, the real, the essential Thomas Jackstraw, and we can have this whole mess resolved in a minute."

"I can't tell if you're good at your job," I said, "or a complete fool."

"This isn't a *job* talking to you. We're talking man to man. No, you might say that I'm speaking for the side of you that you've silenced—your conscience. I'm speaking for you, son, for your decent side. Regard this as a dialogue: the lost, destructive side of yourself dueling with the better Jack. But listen to me. I'm saying the things your conscience would say."

Rachel looked at me and silently mouthed the words, "Fuck him." She removed her headset, got up, and left the flight deck.

"Let me tell you, Conscience," I said. "You're losing the argument with my nasty side. My nasty side is getting more and more pissed off with your evangelical fervor, your condescension, and your cheap psychology. Get a fuel truck out here."

There was an extended silence, and when we spoke again his voice was softer, husky with a fake moral weariness.

"And where do you think you're going? What's your destination? There is no refuge in the world for a certain class of criminal—the terrorist, the assassin, the murderer. The planet just ain't big enough for you."

"Then I'll go to hell." I said. "You're very persuasive, Hank. You've more than half-persuaded me to blow up this fucking airplane and everyone on it. What's the point, right?"

A big sigh. "Captain Morrison told us that you've got a satchel of C-4," he said quietly, mournfully. "That plastic stuff is relatively inert. You need reliable detonators, good wire, the right electrical charge. I don't know."

"You push right up to the edge, don't you?" I said.

"I sleep well nights," he said. "I've done things I'm ashamed of, but I've never contemplated killing children."

"Hank, you've got to wake up now. You—*you* are very close to killing all of these people."

"Hey, come on, I thought I was talking to an intelligent—wait. Hold on a second."

There was thirty seconds of dead air, and then he said, "Shit. *Shit!* What's going on? What kind of crap is this, Jack? I thought we had an understanding. I thought we were going to resolve this, you and me, man to man, resolve this dilemma. Honestly, professionally, confidentially. Oh, man . . . for Christ's sake, negotiations are conducted privately. You don't fuck them up by bringing in outsiders, the entire goddamned world. Jack, listen to me. Get her off the telephone. This is not the way things are done."

I switched off the radio, removed the headset, and walked out into the lounge. Both Morrison and Jenkins were sleeping, the pilot on the starboard sofa, Jenkins on the port. Troxel, smoking a cigarette, sat in one of the leather swivel chairs.

"Not going too good?" he asked.

"I'm not sure."

I went through the curtain and walked down the aisle, avoiding looks, questions, and went through the door into the aft cabin.

Rachel was sitting at her desk. She held a telephone with one hand; the other hand was pressed against her forehead as if she were testing for fever.

"Please, he'll kill all of us," Rachel said into the phone. "This is— are they crazy? If the FBI or whoever is playing these games doesn't do what he demands, he'll blow up the airplane."

Rachel was a splendid liar. You could hear the fear in her voice, in the tone and cadence, but it was not overdone. She was capable of subtlety. And you could see fear in her expression and posture, which of course could be heard in her voice. She was feeling the emotion, being true to the terror that would be natural if this situation were real and not contrived. Rachel was a Method liar.

"My God," she said. "Don't they know that there are three little children on board? Don't they care?"

A portable television set was glowing in the corner. The CNN logo glowed in the lower right corner, with the word LIVE above it. The airplane was blurry in the rain and trembling from the distortion of a telephoto lens. I turned up the volume and heard Rachel's whispery, frightened voice.

"He's here with me. He's got a bomb. He'll blow us all to bits, I know he will, if we aren't allowed to leave." Her voice cracked, sobbed. "For God's sake, is this so hard to understand?"

I turned down the volume on the TV, then flashed from channel to channel: all of the major networks, broadcast and cable, were covering the story. Rachel was exerting tremendous pressure on the FBI, the government, by going around the hostage negotiator and appealing directly to the public. She pleaded for the lives of the children, for every one of the innocent people on board, all hostage to a homicidal madman.

Now on the television, there was a picture of a red fuel tanker truck rolling over the rain-wet concrete.

*   *   *

Two F-86 fighter jets picked us up as we passed over the Georgia coast. They didn't establish radio contact. They didn't hotdog, threaten, or harass the airplane, but they stayed close and were visible until dusk, when they turned back.

"Some others will pick us up from the U.S. airbase in Sicily," Blakely said.

"What's the point?" Troxel asked.

"Intimidation."

"Fuck them."

Blakely shrugged. "There'll be an escort all the way."

"All the way to where?" I asked.

Both men grinned at me.

*   *   *

Toward morning four of the men gathered in the forward lounge. Troxel, Blakely, and Heinz Karl Reichert sat on the starboard side of the plane, with Joshua Benoit opposite. Their conversation halted when I came through the curtain. They regarded me suspiciously through coils of smoke, then Benoit offered me a cigar from a nearly full box of Cubans and a glass of twenty-year-old Martell cognac.

I sat on a leather chair. When the cigar was burning, I said, "Fine cigar, great brandy."

"I believe in the best, Mr. Jackstraw," Benoit said. "Only the best, and plenty of same."

"Sound thinking," I said.

"We were just discussing your remarkable escape, wondering how you succeeded in evading capture."

This meant that they had been speculating on the possibility that I had been captured, made a deal with the Feds, and was then released to serve as a sort of undercover operative. It was an implausible notion, paranoid, but one that I might have considered had I been in their shoes.

I told them of my escape through the mountains and my nine-day stay in the vacant chalet.

"Ah," Benoit said. "Very resourceful."

"I was lucky."

"Indeed you were."

"On the other hand, think of how many fugitives remain at liberty for long periods of time—indefinitely in some cases. Abortion clinic bombers, serial killers, terrorists, assassins."

"Yes. That's certainly true." Benoit was an urbane, formal man, but I suspected that inside him there lurked a dirty street fighter.

"A hypothetical," I said. "I am a terrorist hijacker, armed with a bomb and presumably willing to use it if I panic or lose patience. You all are a well-trained and well-equipped military anti-terrorist unit. How do you go about rescuing the hostages? We've landed at an airport, say . . . what airport?"

"The Madrid airport," Benoit said.

"Marrakesh," Heinz Karl said.

Troxel grinned at me. "Algiers."

"Cyprus," Blakely said.

"Cairo?" I asked.

"Not likely."

Blakely, speaking around his cigar, said, "How big is our team?"

"As big as you like."

"I would do it the same way the Israelis did it down in Entebbe. Follow that blueprint."

"You mean, come in late at night, rig charges on all the doors, blow them, and go into the airplane throwing flash grenades and smoke grenades and concussion grenades, tear gas, and quickly blow away the terrorist."

"Sure."

"No," Heinz Karl said. "Entebbe was a long time ago. And it's very risky. I would use modern techniques and materials. Gas, an odorless, invisible chemical that circulates through the airplane the moment the engines are started. A few minutes and everyone is unconscious."

"Is there such a gas?" Benoit asked.

"The Stasi experimented with such a chemical when I was with them."

"But that was fifteen years ago."

"We called it 'Lethe,' after the River of Forgetfulness in the Greek myth."

Blakely, the ex-CIA man, was interested. "How would you insert the gas into the plane's ventilation system?"

Heinz Karl shrugged. "One would have to talk to an aircraft designer or engineer."

"And this gas works?"

"Now? Perhaps yes. But it killed many of the animal subjects during the Stasi tests."

Troxel laughed. "That's more forgetfulness than is required. You're getting old, Heinz Karl."

"Yah, old, feeble, maybe a fool now." The German displayed a sly smile.

"I wouldn't do a thing," Troxel said. "If I'm running this hostage rescue operation, I wouldn't do anything but wait. The airplane is on the ground, right? Parked in the sun in a vacant area of the airport. My team stalls. We stall, then stall some more, and when we're tired of stalling, we delay. And then we procrastinate. It's hot. You're tired, Jacko, dead beat. But. You can't rest for an instant because there are men on board who are perfectly capable of killing you the instant your exhaustion makes you slow or unwary. And that moment will come. I know who's on board, and I know something about them. Troxel. Sintre. Blakely. Heinz Karl Reichert. Joshua Benoit. They aren't your ordinary fat-assed business travelers."

I said, "I've got a valise full of plastic, a couple of detonators, detonator wire, a source of electrical power, and a slick system. I've rigged the charge to blow when a circuit is opened. Maybe I'm using a flashlight wired to the detonators. All I need is a twitch of my thumb to press the flashlight button and everyone is stew meat."

"I'm chief of the anti-terrorist unit. I know you're half dead with exhaustion. You've gone two, three days without any sleep. A moment's inattention . . ." He drew an index finger across his throat.

"No," I said. "I've slept while the plane crossed the Atlantic. I've locked myself in Rachel's cabin or in one of the bathrooms with my valise, and slept like a baby. What can you do? Evacuate the airplane in mid-flight? Scheme against me? So what? I've got my bomb and my thumb and I can blow us all to hell with no more pressure than it takes to ring a doorbell."

"You don't get it," Troxel said. "Alex Troxel is on board. Troxel is waiting. Troxel is watching. Troxel is patient. And when the time comes Troxel will strike like a cobra. Troxel will cut off your thumb and chew it while you watch."

We all stared at him. Benoit started to speak, halted. Troxel grinned at us. He believed that we were looking at him in admiration.

The window ports were glowing with a dull, greasy light.

Details of the lounge emerged from darkness. Now I could see the ocean far below, gunmetal gray and scalloped with foamy crescents. We had been ambushed by the dawn.

The jet engines pulsed, throbbed. Now there were indigo glints in the sea below, pastel blues in the sky around us, puffball clouds that were tinted peach and pink and vermilion. We flew east, out of night and into morning.

"There's one now," Blakely said.

It was like seeing a big shark out of the corner of your eye while diving: sleek, gleaming, sinister, balanced on the air as a shark is balanced in water, the fighter jet eased past our wingtip. I could see the pilot. His face and head were covered by the helmet and oxygen mask, but I knew he was grinning.

And there was a metallic shark on the other side of the airplane and, for all we knew, maybe one above us and another below.

"Cowboys," Blakely said.

My tongue and the mucous membranes of my mouth felt burned by the cigar smoke and cognac, and my eyes were gritty. I realized that I was very tired.

"Fuck them," Troxel said.

"What are they?" Benoit said. "Twenty-two, twenty-three? Rowdy boys. Let them have their sport."

I looked out the window and was at first surprised, then amused, when the pilot—you could throw a stone that far—raised his gloved hand with the middle finger extended. I lifted my hand to the window and returned the gesture. The pilot acknowledged my one-fingered salute by dipping a wing.

FIFTY-ONE

We landed at the Cairo airport in mid-morning. It was a warm, hazy day, the sky brownish from a mixture of pollution and airborne dust. The tower directed Morrison to taxi to a remote section of the airport, off the tarmac and onto a field of cracked, sun-baked clay. The nearest runway was far to the left; on our right was a high chainlink fence, then a road, and beyond the road some shabby red brick buildings that looked like warehouses. There would be men stationed in rooms on the upper floors of some of those buildings, and maybe a couple of snipers on a rooftop. At night, an elite assault squad could scale or cut the fence and be swarming around the airplane in less than a minute.

Heinz Karl Reichert, his German accent noticeable when he was issuing commands, stalked up and down the aisle and shouted that the shades must be drawn on the windows, *all* of the damned windows, and there must be silence.

I walked up the aisle and through the curtain. Jenkins, the co-pilot, was sitting in the lounge, a bottle of beer in one hand, a cigarette in the other.

"We got you here," he said. "Now you've got to get us out."

"No sweat," I said.

"Huh. Plenty of sweat."

Again, all of the windows had been covered by blankets, and it was dim inside the flight deck, even with the red non-operational lights turned up full. Morrison, wearing his radio headset, was writing in a logbook. Rachel sat in the second officer's seat. She too wore a headset. She looked up at me over her shoulder, smiled quickly, formed her lips into a *moue* and touched them with a vertical finger.

"Roger that," Morrison said. He did not pause in his writing.

I removed the pins from Rachel's hair and let it fall freely. She shot me another glance, and again smiled. Rachel relished the sort of extreme tension that made most people sick. I tapped her shoulder and pointed to the side window. She made a face, nodded, then shrugged.

It was not likely that they would gamble at this stage, but a sniper could put a bullet through the side window, the blanket, and—with a little luck—through the head of whoever occupied the second officer's chair. They might assume that I was sitting there now.

"Roger that," Morrison drawled. "He's here. He's listening to us. He's got a bomb. He's got a gun. The gun is cocked and ready to go off. So is he."

Rachel closed her eyes. Her lips moved; she was like an actress who ran the first few lines of dialogue through her mind before going onstage. Her eyes opened wide.

"For God's sake," she said in a strained voice. "Won't you people stop playing games? One of those fighter jets almost crashed into us! There are fifteen innocent people aboard this airplane. Three of them . . . three of them are children." Her voice broke.

Morrison closed his logbook, got up, hooked his thumb in a hitchhiker's gesture, and left the flight deck.

"Think about what you're doing," Rachel said.

I sat down in the captain's seat and put on the radio headset.

"Please do as he says," Rachel said.

Her voice was loud; I adjusted the volume, and spoke into the microphone. "Who is this?"

There was a moment of dead air, then: "Jack? Man, you remind me of one of those dizzy ground squirrels I read about. Their thinking got turned upside down by some sort of chemical contamination, and they believe that they're digging up toward the surface when they're actually going down. They dig all the way down to bedrock, and they still try to dig some more, confused, thinking they're going up toward light and air."

"You're here in Cairo?"

"Yep. We zigged when you zigged, zagged when you zagged."

"Different place," I said, "same demand. I want a fuel truck out here."

"Ms. Valentine? I suggest you leave the flight deck now. Old Jack and I have some serious and private business to discuss."

"Hold on," I said. "Contrary to the point of your metaphor, I'm not a crazed ground squirrel. Hank, *you* don't dismiss *my* hostages. You don't give orders. There's probably something in your manual that advises you to establish psychological dominance over the hostage-taker, but it ain't gonna happen here."

"Oh, Jack, man, if I could only reach the good and decent man who's buried beneath all that hostility."

"You can't. I guess I'm going to have to kill someone to prove that to you."

Rachel half-turned in her seat and smiled at me.

"Jack, if you won't think of your own self and all those folks you're terrorizing, think of your father, Brigadier Jackstraw, think of your grandfather, think about your poor old mother who's right now hurting so bad at what her boy is doing."

I said, "The only thing I hate worse than your push-push technique is your put-on aw-shucks backwoods bullshit. Listen to me. I want a fuel truck out here quick."

"Jack boy, this ain't Atlanta. We're not home now. This is Egypt, an ancient and proud land that is quite rightly jealous of its sovereignty. They're running this show. We can ask, but we can't command, we can't dictate. We're trying to get fuel for you, but they've got their backs up, and I just don't know how long it will take us to persuade them."

Rachel looked at me.

I shook my head. "You're lying."

Rachel drew an index finger across her throat.

I smiled at her. "Don't call me, Hank. I'll call you."

I switched off the radio.

By late afternoon the temperature in the airplane had reached 107 degrees. We breathed and breathed again the same stale air, which reeked of our sweat and exhalations. The children were whiny, and one of the Benoit twins became sick with diarrhea. And both of the old Germans were ill, especially Heinz Karl, whose lips were a cyanotic blue against the ghostly pallor of his skin. He wheezed asthmatically as he slept, or tried to sleep.

Gigi had energy: she inventoried the galley area and compiled a list of supplies. The frozen and refrigerated food had spoiled, and all that remained were things like peanuts and potato chips and melted mint wafers. We were low on water too, although there was beer and soft drinks that might last a couple of days if we rationed them.

Rachel and Orson Dedrick spent all day working together in the small rear cabin. Dedrick, his pale face filmed with sweat, operated a computer; Rachel was busy on a satellite telephone. They were very serious. They were methodical in a resigned way, like gamblers who know the cards have turned against them, the dice have turned, the horse they backed has broken a leg and gone down ten yards from the finish line. It was now simply a matter of calculating the losses. But they were true gamblers, restrained by the gambler's stoicism; they didn't whine or complain, curse, reveal defeat in their expressions or voices. They just—hour after hour—took a severe beating.

Some of the others were losing courage. Sintre and Mary Lou Dedrick wanted me to talk again to the hostage negotiator. Make demands, offer concessions, they pleaded, but I refused. Jackstraw, the terrorist hijacker, could not reveal weakness at this crucial stage of the game. They knew we were suffering. They expected me to contact them, to bluster and threaten and, ultimately perhaps, to beg. Silence was the correct response for now. Let them wait as we were waiting. Let them worry about the condition and fate of the "hostages." The pressure was equal on both sides.

"Tell them my child is sick," Mrs. Benoit said to me.

I shook my head.

"Then let us off this airplane, me and my children."

"No," I said.

Two of the women, Mrs. Benoit and Orson Dedrick's wife, seemed more and more to view our situation as real rather than an improvised drama. Exhausted and confused by the heat, the confinement, their fears, they began to regard me as an actual hijacker and themselves as actual hostages, victims. The enormous stress, the extremity of their emotions, had resulted in a queer, subdued hysteria. Every now and then I looked up and engaged a piteous, desolate, wide-eyed stare, and I turned away while the stare continued. The others could not comfort them. They were beyond logic.

At dusk, Gigi opened the packages she had brought from the

Indio Walmart: Halloween decorations (crepe paper streamers, cardboard cutouts of witches riding brooms, Draculas, a scowling plastic pumpkin) and presents for the children. The kids, hot and sulky a moment before, came alive, began to shriek and wiggle. She gave them Halloween candy, corn kernels and caramels, jelly beans, taffy apples. She gave them paper snakes, and masks—identical Frankenstein masks for the twins, a hook-nosed witch's mask for the little girl. Gigi taped the cutouts to the bulkheads and strung the bright crepe paper in big bows and overhead loops and cleverly fashioned flowers. Her energy stimulated the children and some of the adults, too, but it was very hot and stuffy in the cabin, and after twenty minutes of giddiness, the children tired. The party ended.

A few hours after dark the airplane began to cool, though the air remained foul. Halloween masks and toys and candy wrappers littered the aisle. Streamers of crepe paper—black and orange and yellow—hung like banners of defeat.

After midnight I went into the rear cabin for a can of beer, and saw that Rachel and Dedrick were still working. Row after row of numbers crept up the computer screen. Big numbers, some preceded by the dollar sign, others by the symbol for the British pound or the Swiss franc. Dedrick stared at them, infuriated.

I watched as Rachel hung up the telephone, pressed her fingertips hard against her temples, and slowly exhaled. Her hair was dirty, tangled. She wore no makeup. Fatigue had drawn the skin of her face tautly over her cheek and jawbones.

She looked up and stared blankly at me for a moment; then there was a hint of a smile and she said, "Meltdown."

At around two that morning Troxel, carrying a duffel, went into one of the bathrooms. Twenty minutes later he emerged dressed in combat gear: a starched desert camouflage uniform with the trousers tucked into paratrooper's boots and a colonel's insignia pinned to the shoulder loops; a wide leather belt which supported a holstered pistol, spare clips in leathers pouches, and on his left hip a sheathed combat knife. His boots and leather belt were shined. He wore a red beret cocked at a jaunty angle, and a red silk scarf was loosely tied around his neck. He carried an Uzi machine pistol on a shoulder strap. Troxel, shoulders back and head high, strode through the cabin like a conqueror. You could not look at him without questioning his sanity.

I was sitting at the rear of the airplane. Troxel paused and looked down at me.

"If they're coming," he said, "they'll come just before first light."

"You're going to fight?"

"Yeah. Has all the fight gone out of you?"

"Too many people will get hurt."

"A brave man dies once," he said. "Your type dies a thousand times."

So then, Troxel—like a feudal warlord after defeat or a disgraced samurai—had meticulously prepared for his ritual suicide. He was costumed for glory.

"I'll take out two, three of them before I go down," he said. "I'll take you out, too, Jack. The instant it starts."

"Maybe it won't start."

"Oh, it'll start."

Troxel, I suspected, would be disappointed if there were not an assault.

He nodded to me once, twice, showed me his teeth, and then slowly walked forward down the aisle. Gigi looked at him anxiously as he passed. Troxel sat down next to Sintre, the man who feared and hated him and, maybe, the man who most admired him. Troxel talked. His voice was soft and flat as he told Sintre of his readiness to die.

I got up and walked down the aisle past them and into the lounge. Morrison and Jenkins were sleeping on the two sofas. Did fliers dream of flying? I went into the flight deck, shut the door behind me, and sat down in the pilot's seat. The several red lights were still burning, filling the space with a dim scarlet glow and glinting on the banks of gauges. I closed my eyes.

I had ceased sweating; my head ached. Dehydration. Most of the liquids aboard the plane had to be reserved for the children and the elderly—the cockpit crew and the Stasi pair. You had to wonder how this motley gang had so nearly succeeded in pulling off a coup of this magnitude. Rachel had held it all together, of course; she was the brains and—God save us all—the heart of the whole enterprise. They had siphoned a fortune from the American political campaigns' dirty billions. For a time the crackpot APP had even threatened the two major political parties and come close to collapsing the entire jerry-built electoral process. The power elites had reacted with outrage to this attempted usurpation of money and power and privilege, and jaded whores of media and politics had shrieked like goosed maiden aunties.

I was beginning to half-believe Rachel's claim of relative innocence, of ignorance, anyway. She had been the strategist, Troxel the tactician. She proposed, he arranged. Roger Clay was Troxel's recruit. Betancourt, a man as treacherous and brutal as Troxel himself, had been a partner in the conspiracy within the conspiracy. They had plotted the murder of Hamilton Keyes. Keyes, Roger Clay, Cavenaugh, and maybe even the soldiers at the river outpost, who had been poisoned, though perhaps not by their own toxic distillation of cane alcohol. Still, Rachel had chosen Troxel, unleashed the jackal, and she was fully responsible for the kidnapping of the missionaries. It was crazy, a web of deceit so tangled that you could never hope to separate the individual strands.

I was awakened by shouts, cries, excited voices, a mournful wailing, and I thought: This is it, they've come for me. But there was no *crump* of exploding grenades, none of the brutal shouted commands of an assault team.

I left the flight deck, passed through the now empty lounge, parted the divider curtain, and looked down the aisle. There was a crowd near the center of the airplane. Mrs. Benoit and Mrs. Dedrick were carrying their crying children toward the rear. I stood on one of the seats. It was a confused scene; I needed a moment to separate the figures into a comprehensible tableau. Heinz Karl was lying supine in the aisle, while a man—Captain Morrison—pounded his chest with a fist. Gigi, kneeling on the floor, her back to me, was apparently giving Heinz Karl mouth-to-mouth resuscitation. The others anxiously watched. Trudi tried to reach her husband, but was held back by Clifford Blakely. "*Mein Gott!*" Trudi cried. "*Mein Gott!*"

Troxel, like me, was standing on one of the seats. His camouflage outfit was already wrinkled and sweat-stained. Like all of us, he was exhausted from the heat and tension. He sensed my gaze and looked up. We stared at each other for a time, and then he nodded, climbed over the backs of a couple of seats, stepped down into the aisle, and followed me through the curtain and through the door into the flight deck. I sat in the pilot's chair; Troxel in the other seat.

"Heart?" I asked.

"That or a stroke, probably. The heat was too much for old Heinz Karl.'"

"If he dies . . ."

"He's already dead. They're trying to revive a corpse."

"We can use this."

He smiled wickedly.

I sighed. "Three or four shots in his chest."

"There won't be much blood."

"We won't hang around for the autopsy."

"They'll hear the shots and come at us."

"Maybe not."

Troxel was silent. I could smell sweat, his and mine, and the ointment he smeared over his ravaged face, nauseating in this small space.

He said, "Shoot Heinz Karl at dawn, throw his body out the hatch."

"Right. I'll get on the radio and tell them something like—'That's one hostage dead. Do you want to see another in thirty minutes?'" I didn't like it, but it was too late to turn back now.

"I would storm the plane as soon as I heard shots."

"Maybe they're not as impulsive as you."

"They'll come, sure as hell."

"Fine. Then you can go down like a movie hero, teeth gritted and guns smoking."

"You're first, pal. I meant that."

"Troxel."

"It might work. We've got nothing to lose."

"One thing, though."

"Trudi."

"Will you talk to her?"

"Sure. After she's settled down a bit."

"We've got less than an hour to first light."

"Trudi isn't your ordinary senior citizen," Troxel said. "She'll understand."

"But if she doesn't give her consent?"

"Sure. We'll do it anyway. Fuck Heinz Karl."

At false dawn we lay Heinz Karl's corpse on the floor of the lounge. Two cushions placed beneath his back would absorb the exiting bullets. His dentures had been removed during the resuscitation attempt, and his cheeks were hollow, his mouth agape.

The children, Dedrick, and the women were all together in the cabin at the rear of the plane. They had all been told of the plan, and Trudi had consented. It was all right, she'd told Troxel: that thing wasn't her Heinz Karl. Heinz Karl had vanished like smoke up a chimney and left behind this debris. I felt badly for the children.

We stood around the corpse for a moment, unsure of exactly how to proceed, and maybe from a momentary awe at the mystery of extinction, and then Troxel drew his pistol. He pumped the slide, levering a cartridge into the chamber, and casually aimed. He shot Heinz Karl three times in the chest. The crack of the pistol was loud in the confined space. We clearly saw the muzzle flash and smelled bitter cordite fumes.

There was another brief pause before the men acted: Sintre grasped the corpse's wrists, Blakely the ankles, and they lifted him while Captain Morrison unlocked and slid back the heavy door.

"Do it," Troxel said.

Sintre and Blakely swung the corpse out the open hatchway as you might moon-dive a swimmer into a pool. In motion, falling with arms and legs spread, Heinz Karl suddenly appeared alive, then he dropped out of sight and we heard the body hit the ground thirty feet below with a sickening sound. Morrison closed and locked the hatch.

"Do your stuff," Troxel said to me.

I went into the flight deck, sat in the pilot's chair, and switched on the radio.

"Hank?" I said.

Light was beginning to seep through the blankets that covered the windows.

"Hank?"

"Jesus Christ!" he said. "What's going on? What are you doing, you crazy bastard."

"I told you I'd kill a hostage."

"Oh, man, come on, you didn't have to do that."

"Send out a fuel tanker. They can pick up the body at the same time they refuel the airplane."

"Jack, I *told* you the Egyptians are running things here. They're stubborn. They're trying to prove a point of some kind or other. Be patient, for God's sake."

I said, "I'll kill the next one in thirty minutes."

"Jack—"

"And then another, thirty minutes after that."

Rachel came into the cockpit and stood behind me with her palms lightly resting on my shoulders.

"Slow down," Hank said. "Think. We'll work out a deal with the Egyptians, but it'll take time. Give me—give me six hours. Okay? Six or seven hours."

"I'll kill Rachel Valentine in thirty minutes," I said. Rachel pinched the muscles on either side of my neck. "And I'll kill Joshua Benoit thirty minutes after that."

"For the love of—"

"Hamilton Keyes, Rachel Valentine, Joshua Benoit. Two presidential candidates and a vice-presidential candidate. That's the assassin's hat trick, isn't it?"

"Let me see what I can do."

"I know the people you'll send out with the fuel truck won't be airport workers. If they go for it, I'll blow the fucking airplane."

I switched off the radio.

"You think?" Rachel asked.

"Probably. But if they call my bluff I'll have to shoot you."

She pinched my neck muscles hard. "That's my Jack," she said.

Twenty minutes after we had thrown out Heinz Karl's corpse, Captain Morrison came out into the lounge.

"They're sending out fuel," he said. "Now the negotiator wants to talk to you."

I went into the flight deck, sat down, and put on the radio headset.

"Jack?"

"Yes, Hank."

"A fuel truck and ambulance are on the way."

"You weren't too quick about it."

"I talked to Anna Fontenot on the phone last night."

"Did you give her my regards?"

"Jack, we know this hijacking is a fake."

"Tell that to Heinz Karl Reichert."

"Maybe he was a sacrifice. Maybe he just died of old age. We know this is a fake."

"You know nothing of the sort."

"Let's say we're ninety percent sure."

"That isn't good enough, is it? Ten percent is my bomb."

"Jack, excepting the children, half of the people on board that airplane have been indicted by a D.C. grand jury. The other half are unindicted co-conspirators. The indictments came down a week ago, and remained sealed until now. It was a great scam. I mean that. You could even call it a brilliant criminal enterprise. Never mind how it might have damaged our democracy and turned millions of Americans even more cynical about our system."

"Pure poetry. You ought to put that to music," I said.

"Still, it really was brilliant. But in the end it didn't work. It failed. Just about every penny has either been seized or frozen by the U.S. government in cooperation with a dozen banks and countries. All those offshore accounts—the Bahamas, Panama, the Cayman Islands, Switzerland, the others—defunct. The American Patriotic Party is broke. Maybe it wasn't such a brilliant scam after all. It's pretty funny, though. Isn't it funny, Jack?"

"Hilarious."

"I want you to bring Captain Morrison to the radio. The tower will give him instructions for take-off."

"All right."

"Where do you think you're going?"

"Iran," I said.

"Bullshit."

"Actually, I'm not sure, Hank. Sometimes the hijacker is the last to know."

FIFTY-TWO

We flew southeast from Cairo over a section of the Arabian Desert, a parched, lumpy brown land that was mysteriously scribbled with ancient tracks. It looked like the surface of a dead planet. Later, we passed over the coast, banked, and flew directly down the center of the Red Sea. Some fighter planes with Egyptian insignia escorted us for an hour and then turned back. Now the Sudan was on our right, Saudi Arabia to our left, and below the long narrow stretch of sea that looked—not red, but a yellow-tinged cerulean.

There was a sort of cautious jubilation aboard the plane. We were in the air, we were en route, we had a destination, we were—maybe—free. Joshua Benoit got out his box of cigarettes and bottle of cognac and invited some of the men to join him in the lounge. Mrs. Benoit and Mrs. Dedrick were relaxed, almost cheerful, and the children seemed okay. Their hysteria had dissipated; I was just another passenger to them now. Rachel and Dedrick remained in the rear cabin, reviewing the numbers, the dreadful numbers.

The Red Sea is tightly pinched at the southern end. Captain Morrison flew straight on, crossing the Horn of Africa, Somalia, and a slice of Ethiopia, and then we were above the Indian Ocean. It was all blue beneath us now, no sight of land anywhere, just the blue going on and on, a wrinkled blue thinly etched with white, going on forever.

Gigi was sitting alone in the middle of the airplane. I went forward and sat next to her. She smiled at me. Gigi was generous with her smiles, generous in every way. I had watched her with the children, watched her function under a pressure that had cracked some of us, watched her put her mouth to Heinz Karl's mouth and try to breathe life into his lungs.

"You're my dream girl," I said.

She smiled. "And Mother?"

"My nightmare *femme fatale*."

"And this Anna Fontenot?"

"A daydream, I guess."

"Have you ever been in love, Jackstraw?"

"Yes," I said. "'But that was in another country . . .'"

She completed the Marlowe quote: "'And anyway, the wench is dead.'"

"Gigi, where are we going?"

"Dos Santos."

"Two Saints. I think I know where that is."

I pictured the Indian Ocean: it was a vast body of water, stretching many thousands of miles north-south and east-west, dwarfing the land masses at its margins. On a map it was a huge expanse of blue crisscrossed by latitude and longitude lines, with here and there—like fly specks—archipelagos with names like Maldive and Seychelles and Rodrigues and Diego Garcia and Cocos—barely visible fly specks widely scattered over the uniform blue. I had spent many hours of my life studying maps, military maps and topographical maps and geographical maps, and as I recalled the Dos Santos group was far to the south, near the Tropic of Capricorn at about

80 degrees longitude. They were the tiniest of the fly specks. From there, it was more than two thousand miles west to Africa, two thousand miles east to Australia.

"Why Dos Santos?" I asked.

"It may be the only place that will accept us now."

"Good reason."

"Are you familiar with Dos Santos?"

"No."

"It was a Portuguese penal colony in the nineteenth century," Gigi said. "The Portuguese sent convicts there from Mozambique and Angola. Mostly blacks, but some whites, too. It was a horrible place—Portugal's Devil's Island."

"Don't tell me any more," I said.

"They were given their freedom in nineteen-sixty-two. It's sort of a miniature commonwealth now."

The population, Gigi said, was a racial potpourri: the descendants of African and Portuguese convicts; Portuguese and Creole administrators and guards; Indians who had been indentured to work the sugar cane fields and mill (soon failed); men and women of every race who had, over 150 years, washed up on the beaches with the other flotsam; and Chinese merchants—there was no sandspit in this hemisphere too small to support a few Chinese merchants.

"It sounds like a very limited arena," I said, "for a girl of your age and talents."

She said that she intended to teach school in Dos Santos for three or four years while at the same time she would plank by plank and nail by nail build a small boat and then sail away into either the sunrise or sunset. East, probably, Australia, Samoa, Fiji, Polynesia, the Marquesas.

"Alone?" I asked.

"Well, yes. Who is there?"

"Why is Dos Santos giving us sanctuary?"

"Well, you see, when Orson was opening secret accounts in banks all over the world, he learned about the new bank in Dos Santos. Lenient standards, you might say. He transferred eight million dollars there. I learned what I could about the country. It's very isolated and very poor—Fourth World, you might say. I persuaded Mother to give them a million dollars to use as they thought best."

"And they're grateful. They'll take us in."

"Yes."

I was skeptical. "A million dollars really isn't much money, even to a very small and poor country."

"Well, maybe there's more to it."

Two hours out of Cairo a pair of fighter jets with U.S. markings appeared off our wingtips. Blakely told us that they were undoubtedly from Diego Garcia, a British island group far out in the Indian Ocean. There was an American airbase there.

I said, "Gigi, I want to give you something. But there's a condition."

"A gift?"

"Yes."

"But with strings attached?" She smiled.

"I want you to act against your nature. I want you to be selfish."

I removed the emerald Anna had given me from my pocket, unwrapped the tissue paper, and placed the stone in her palm.

"It's beautiful." She looked at me in a puzzled way, frowning and smiling.

"It's yours, *if* . . ."

"Thank you. But I can't accept this."

"A woman generously gave it to me. Now I'm giving the emerald to you. But you must tell no one, not even your mother. That's the condition."

"Thank you, but really—"

"You're only nineteen. We're all in trouble. The future is uncertain, to say the least. You'll need a start. The emerald is quite valuable. Regard it as your nest egg—nest stone. Use it to ease your way."

"Honestly, Jack, I don't think—"

"Goddammit, just take it, Gigi. You're an angel, but that doesn't mean you have to be a fool."

"Would it please you if I accepted it?"

"Very much."

"All right, then." She closed her hand over the emerald, leaned over and kissed my cheek, and then teasingly said, "I can't wait to show it to my friend Troxel."

I walked back to the rear cabin. The sofa had been converted back into a bed, and Rachel lay supine on it, her hands folded on her abdomen, her eyes closed. She looked as though she were contemplating the concept of eternal rest.

"Jack?"

I got a bottle of beer from the little refrigerator.

"Shut the door."

"It is shut," I said. "I shut it."

She opened her eyes: resurrected. "When is the election?"

"In two days, three. I'm not sure. Have we crossed the International Date Line?"

"Who do you think will win?"

"Not you."

"I scared them, though."

"You scared everybody. You're a scary lady."

She smiled.

"Rachel, was this a money scam all along?"

"For the others, yes. Not for me. I don't care much about money personally, but I needed money, lots and lots of money, just to enter the game. It *is* a game, you know, after you get past the slogans and the sanctimony. Table stakes, no limit. There are really only a few players. I wanted to be a player. And I did win, though there aren't many who will see it that way."

"It was a loss any way you look at it."

"I don't know if you'll understand this: it was all, for me, a kind of theater. Political satire, if you like. I was the author, the director, the star, and the audience was the world."

"What colossal vanity."

She smiled. "Yes. But I put on a grand show, didn't I, Jack?"

"You did that."

"And it was funny, wasn't it?"

"Some of it."

"Very funny."

"Only in retrospect."

"Right. It's only after you walk out of the theater that you can see the play whole, in all of its aspects and moods, and understand it. All the world's a stage and everyone's a player."

"This player got badly burnt."

"No one forced you to join the cast."

"Enough analogy. I suppose now you're going to say that you can't make an omelet without breaking eggs."

"I was trying to do what an artist does, only in life, with real people, on a world stage. It *was* art, wasn't it, in its way. I'm not sorry for you, Jack. You were a fine actor in my satire, you played a crucial role. I'm not sorry for Roger Clay or Betancourt or Herrera and Baltazar—every play needs an antagonist or two. They were vicious men. Their characters were their fates. I'm sorry about Ham Keyes. I'm sorry about the missionaries, for their suffering and the suffering of their families. I'm sorry about your friend Cavenaugh, if he was a victim of my play. I lost control of Troxel. I let things slip out of control. *Mea maxima culpa.* Yet they can imprison me for the rest of my life or strap me to a gurney and inject a cocktail of poisons into my arteries, and I'll never repudiate my play."

"But what was the point?"

"No point, that's the point. No point, no moral, no lesson, no social benefit. Be a big boy, Jack. It was theater. But didn't I make them howl? Didn't I show that the emperor had no clothes? Didn't I, for a few months, draw the curtains and reveal the comic and hideous machinery that rules our lives?"

"And you never thought you might win the election? You never deluded yourself into thinking that you had a chance?"

"Never."

I didn't believe her. Surely there were moments when Rachel thought, hoped, that her "play" would move on to the big stage, the White House.

"How much did you net, before the crash?" I asked her.

"Around one hundred and eighty million dollars."

"Jesus."

"Not a lot, really. Some five billion was spent on the campaigns. We just sort of scooped up the loose change."

"And now the money's gone, frozen, seized?"

She patted the bed with her palm. "Lie down with me."

"Nothing left?"

"Well, there might be a little here and there, hiding in the cracks. But not much."

"This airplane?"

"Leased."

"Gigi said something about eight million in the Dos Santos bank."

"That was the last of the bad news. It turns out that the Dos Santos International Banking Corporation is more an idea than an actual bank. It was a proposed bank, an imagined bank. I mean, there is a bank, sort of, but it exists mostly on the Internet and in the minds of its creators."

"They stole the money?"

"Did Gigi tell you that we made them a million-dollar grant when we wire-deposited the eight million? They maintain that they were confused. They misunderstood: they were not clear about the distinction between grant and deposit, and they've used the money. Beneficially, they say. And they're terribly sorry, and so very grateful. And they're preparing a welcome, a great celebration, when we arrive."

"Yeah. Welcomed by their army—if they have an army."

"We'll be greeted by bayonets. They'll probably march us off to the old prison. It was a penal colony once, you know."

"Dead broke at the world's end. You can work as a prostitute, but what am I going to do?"

"Live off my earnings, no doubt."

"Sure, but how many good years do you have left?"

Rachel laughed. "Baby, we'll be wretchedly poor, but we'll have each other."

That thought raised the hair on the back of my neck.

FIFTY-THREE

I finished my beer and then got into bed alongside her. We embraced. I could feel her warm breath on my cheek, feel the brush of her eyelashes when she blinked. Rachel fell asleep almost instantly, in that eerie way she had.

Intermittent streamers of mist blew past the windows. Mist, blue sky, mist. I was aware of Rachel's pulse and slow respiration. Condensation formed on the windows as the plane moved into thick clouds. Rain ticked on the aircraft's aluminum skin. She'd been wrong about one thing: like it or not, the play continued.

Rachel was gone when I awakened. We were flying well below the cloud ceiling now. The sea, a dull metallic gray beneath the overcast, lumpy with white-tipped swells, reminded me of my earlier view of the Arabian Desert. I did not see any fighter jets; they had probably turned back to Diego Garcia.

The door opened—I thought it was Rachel returning—and Troxel and Sintre entered. Troxel casually held a pistol in his right hand. He still wore his camouflage outfit and beret. Sintre closed and locked the door, then moved deeper into the room

I swung my legs over the side of the bed and sat up.

"Hands behind your head, Jacko."

398

I obeyed.

"Stand. We're going to disarm you."

I got to my feet.

Sintre approached, patted me down, and removed the .25 automatic from my pocket. He was grim, white around the mouth, and he moved with the stiffness of a frightened man.

"You've got the gun," I said. "Now piss off."

Troxel looked even bigger than usual in his uniform, swollen with vanity and power.

"Think you can fly by yourself, Jack?" he asked. "We're going to see if you can fly like a birdie."

I said, "I don't think the cargo hold is pressurized."

"Don't matter."

"It'll matter when you open the hatch, when you try to breathe the air at forty thousand feet."

"Don't kid me, pal. Look out the window. We're flying at about seven thousand feet now."

Sintre was examining the little pistol as if it might be a toy; he removed the magazine, saw that it was full, reinserted it.

"Troxel," I said. "Let's see if I can talk you out of this."

He smiled. "Nah. But look at it this way—you've had a couple extra months of life. You were never supposed to walk out of that room in Mundial."

Sintre pulled the pistol's slide back part way and checked to see if there was a cartridge in the chamber.

"Here's another happy thought for you," Troxel said. "The pilot says we're low on fuel. He isn't sure we can make it to Dos Santos. The rest of us might not live more than an hour or two longer than you. Think about that on your way down."

"Does Rachel know about this?"

"Hey, come on, don't beg. Jesus. Don't appeal to the authority of a woman now. Not your mommy, not Rachel, not the Virgin Mary. Be a man, Jack."

"Sintre," he said.

Sintre unlocked the cabin's rear hatch and slid it open. There was no discernible alteration of the pressure or temperature. Sintre stepped back into the cargo hold. I wondered if he understood that Troxel would kill him as soon as I was gone.

Troxel gestured with his pistol.

"Fuck you," I said. "Just shoot me."

"I will, if that's what you want."

I knew that he would shoot me now, though he'd much rather throw me alive out of the airplane and enjoy my slow-turning descent into the sea. He wished to watch my comic "flight," listen to the diminishing volume of my screams. Troxel regarded the prospect of my 7,000-foot freefall as high comedy. In a flash, I recalled seeing an old documentary film in which a dirigible had unexpectedly, prematurely, ascended. Most members of the ground crew immediately released their grips on the restraining ropes, but a few held on too long and were lifted to a fatal height. The dirigible, with the dangling men, rose swiftly. One by one the men tired, relaxed their grips, and fell. The last man, the strongest, was very high when he finally let go. His legs pumped as if he were peddling a bicycle or running very hard. His body remained erect as he fell, and he continued his frantic running all the way to the ground. It was horrible to see, and yet darkly comic, as that poor man tried to run across the sky.

"Call it," Troxel said.

I crossed the cabin and stepped inside the cargo hold. It was a claustral space, dim, empty, an oval that narrowed toward the tail section. There was no paneling or insulation, just the curved support frames and the dull metal dimples with rivets. The hatch was on the port side.

Troxel followed me. He closed the cabin door. It seemed as if my consciousness were shrinking, retreating to a small, dark, safe place, a mental closet. Sparks arced across my vision, retinal flashes, and I was surprised and puzzled to find that my nose was bleeding. I wiped it with the back of my hand, looked at the blood smear, looked at Troxel.

Sintre unlocked the cargo hatch and cautiously slid it open, exposing a big rectangle of light, admitting humid sea air and a hot blast from the jet engine wash. The open hatch altered the airplane's flight characteristics; a wing dipped, the fuselage half revolved to the left, the plane skewed and started to roll.

I fell down, got up, fell down again. Both Troxel and Sintre were on the deck too.

Captain Morrison quickly compensated for the drag caused by the open hatchway, and the plane lifted, straightened, flew level again.

The hold was filled with swirling particles of dirt and bits of paper, and the noise level from the engines was almost painful.

Troxel was rising now. He had lost his pistol. He looked for it as he struggled to his feet.

Sintre was on his knees next to the open hatch. His left hand was braced against the door frame; his right hand held the Astra .25. He blinked rapidly. His eyes were filled with grit.

I got to my feet. Troxel, his legs widely braced, looked at me.

Sintre, still on his knees, raised the pistol and shot Troxel twice before the gun jammed. One bullet entered Troxel's upper right thigh, the other his right side above the hip. Expanding red spots, like roses blooming in a time-lapse film sequence, appeared on his trousers and shirt. He bellowed with rage. Half crouched, knees bent and arms bowed, he looked huge, apelike, as he roared at us.

Sintre was sitting with his back against the wall. He continued to jerk the trigger of the jammed pistol. He was half blind, dazed, in a kind of fear-shock, and he could not proceed beyond that now futile action.

I started forward. Troxel lifted and curved his arms, as if to embrace me. He lunged, and we wrestled away from the hatch and deeper into the hold. His face was near mine, and I could smell the whiskey stink on his breath. We grappled, each trying to knee the other in the groin, throw the other to the deck. He was very strong. The shock, the bleeding, hadn't yet sickened him. I butted his face with my forehead. I tried again to knee him in the groin, but missed and struck his wounded thigh. He howled, tried to bite my face, lifted his own knee, slipped, fell to the deck. I kicked his head once, twice, but then slipped in a smear of blood and went down. I clubbed him with my fists, left, right, left, right. Sintre was crawling toward us on his hands and knees. I hit Troxel again. He was trying to grab my testicles in both of his hands as I repeatedly hit him. Then Sintre was there, his hand rising and falling as he smashed Troxel's head with the pistol.

"The hatch!" I shouted over the roar of the engines.

Troxel was semi-conscious now. He struggled, but his strength was gone.

Sintre and I each grasped one of Troxel's wrists and, on our knees, dragged him toward the hatchway. He was a big man, a heavy man, and difficult to move even though his resistance was feeble. All three of us were soaked with his blood. Now his head was beyond the doorframe.

"No," Troxel said through his broken teeth, his bloody mouth. "Jack?"

I could feel the edge of the hurricane-force stream of wind outside and feel the heat of the engine blast. The jet noise was a continuous scream.

Sintre and I released Troxel's wrists and, still on our knees, pushed and wrestled him forward. His head was beyond the doorframe, then his shoulders. It seemed that the roar of the jets was issuing from his open mouth.

His strength returned. He was madly strong now, and he possessed a terrible animal vitality. He kicked, thrashed out wildly, clawed at us.

Then he was going, but he had locked a big hand around Sintre's right wrist. Troxel was out of the airplane now, dangling. He did not release his grip.

Sintre slid over the blood-slippery floor. I grabbed his legs. The two men were dragging me out of the airplane. I let go, and they fell into the huge sky.

I looked over the edge and saw that they had clutched each other like drowning men. Face to face, chest to chest, locked in a desperate embrace, Troxel and Sintre slowly twisted and revolved in a ghastly three-dimensional waltz as they hurtled down toward the sea.

I closed and locked the hatch and sat there for a while. I realized I was very glad to be alive. I went into the cabin and, careless of the blood on my skin and clothes, sat on the edge of the bed. My legs trembled from the exertion. Both of my hands ached. Soon, I thought, I'll look into the refrigerator to see if there might be one last bottle of beer. Then I would clean up, change clothes, go forward, and with the others submit to fate.

Jenkins burst in through the cabin door, then abruptly halted. He looked at the blood, the bruises and lacerations on my face and hands.

"What the . . .?"

"It's okay," I said. "I closed the hatch."

"What the hell happened back here? Troxel?"

"With the fishes."

"Good, very good."

"Sintre, too."

Jenkins shook his head. "Christ, what a fucking balls-up this whole thing has been."

"Troxel said we're low on fuel."

"Yeah. We'll probably make it. But the day may come . . ."

I completed his sentence. ". . . when we'll wish we hadn't."

FIFTY-FOUR

Morrison flew low over the larger of the two main islands, Sao Joao do Piani. He had enough fuel remaining to take a careful look before landing. We skimmed in about three hundred feet above the sea. There was a small harbor off the west end of the island, with a stone breakwater, a conical lighthouse, and a dock with a rusty tanker secured alongside. The beaches and soil of the island were a grayish white, the same color and maybe the same consistency as unrefined salt. There were palms, thorny brush, some lemon and lime trees, patches of cultivated land, a single flowering hibiscus in the center of the shabby town square. You would find a few shops there, a café or two, a church, a mosque, an open market.

The landing strip was hardly more than a new two-lane concrete road. It hadn't been completed; there was still some construction underway at the east end, and it looked short. I wondered if they had specially reinforced the concrete. An ordinary road might collapse beneath the weight of a big airplane.

And then, in just a few seconds, we were over the sea, banking, going around for another pass.

The Dos Santos group really wasn't an archipelago. There were just the two main islands, Sao Joao do Piani and Sao Gabriel;

405

the others were islets, scattered high points of the reef, sandy spits of land with a few palms, a couple of shacks, cultivated strips of land. From our altitude I could discern the submarine architecture of the reef, a shadowy Gothic maze—like a buried city—beneath the multi-hued sea. The water's color varied according to the depth and composition of the bottom. There were inky blues, indigo, aquamarine, azure; and greens, lime-green and yellow-green. It was pretty from the air, would be pretty when you dived on the reef, but I thought it likely that the area had long ago been fished out.

We flew over Sao Gabriel, the smaller island, which was oval and mostly filled with the dilapidated stone buildings of the old prison complex. The barracks and administration buildings and residences were arranged around a quadrangle paved with the same rust-colored stones. Ballast stones, probably, carried by the sailing ships that ferried prisoners and supplies to the penal colony in the nineteenth century. The prison buildings—now tenements—were occupied by the descendants of the prisoners and their guards. I saw lines of drying laundry, like the tattered flags of obscure nations, curtains and flower boxes in the still-barred windows, and kids kicking around a soccer ball in the dusty quadrangle.

And then we were out over the sea again and looping back toward Sao Joao do Piani. All of us sat in the forward section of the cabin. Our seat belts were secured. We were silent. It was like the silence of a courtroom when the verdict is about to be announced. The island and islets combined were probably no more than half the size of my place in Colorado. Dos Santos was small, poor, backward, ugly. Purgatory.

No one had commented on my swollen hands and battered face. Troxel and Sintre were not mentioned.

This time, as we passed the length of Sao Joao do Piani, I observed more detail. There was a lot of construction underway. New buildings were being erected among the palm-thatch huts and stone hovels and shacks with sheet metal roofs. Bungalows, cottages, Moorish-style houses with courtyards in the center, and several two- and three-story structures. Some were finished or nearly finished; others were only half-framed. And at the end of the runway I saw a great mob of people, maybe a couple thousand, gathered and waiting.

And then we were over the sea again and steeply banking, looping around above Sao Gabriel, above the mottled reef, angling in, descending. Our speed diminished. We skimmed over the lighthouse, the stone breakwater, the dock and freighter, and then— almost brushing some palms—we settled down on the runway. The tires shrieked as they touched the concrete. The engines were immediately reversed.

Details of the landscape rolled past as we taxied down the runway. Some of the larger buildings under construction displayed big, misspelled banners. VALENTINE HOPITAL, one said. VALENTINE SCOOL.

Morrison managed to halt the airplane just a few yards from the end of the concrete. Stunned, in a kind of shock, we remained in our seats. Gigi was smiling, and the three kids were very happy: they kneeled on the seats and pressed their faces against the glass, cooing at the many children outside—new playmates—and the picture-book palms, a crazed dog, and a tethered burro. This was a child-sized world.

The rest of us were quiet. The faces around me were paralyzed in expressions of dismay and bitterness. Mrs. Dedrick soundlessly wept. Joshua Benoit moved his lips in what might have either been prayer or profanity. No one was more miserable than Rachel; her face was a mask of desolation. She looked as Napoleon must have looked when he first viewed St. Helena, his island of lifetime exile.

Then, like sleepwalkers, we released our seatbelts, stood up, filed through the curtain and into the lounge area. Jenkins slid back the hatch. We crowded together to look outside.

Some men were rolling a boarding scaffold toward the plane. Beyond them, constrained by a rope looped from palm to palm, was the big, howling crowd. They all were shouting and gesturing, delirious with excitement. Those people, with their distorted faces and open mouths, their violent gestures, looked murderous, like a lynch mob or a crowd gathered to witness a public execution. But they were only cheering us, cheering Rachel.

The scaffold was in place now and Rachel gathered herself and stepped out onto the platform. The crowd cheered. Some children slipped beneath the rope and ran toward the airplane. Two men rolled out a "red carpet," a fifty-foot mat of woven palm fronds. Members of the crowd unfurled a banner fastened to poles at each end: when it was fully spread we saw the words:

!WELCOM PRESIDENTE RACHEL!

At first I thought that these isolated people actually believed that Rachel had been elected President of the United States of America, that this was some kind of official visit. No. The islanders, in gratitude for nine million dollars, had elected Rachel president of their impoverished, comic-opera republic.

Rachel, on the platform, half turned to look back at us. Her expression had changed; she was astonished and relieved and, most of all, amused. Her eyes shined, and she smiled. She caught my glance and let me know, with a tilt of her head, that she appreciated the irony of the situation. Rachel, no matter what, remained an ironist, aware of the vast separation between the ideal and the real.

She turned back to the crowd and raised her hands. It reminded me of Mundial, when she had lifted her palms skyward just before I'd shot her. Then slowly, with cool dignity, she descended the stairs to meet the welcoming committee.

The three kids were squirmy, eager to exit the airplane. Gigi remained with the children; Trudi Reichert, looking a hundred years old in her grief, joined the other women.

The mob broke through the rope barrier and engulfed Rachel.

Benoit, Dedrick, Blakely, and the two pilots moved out onto the platform. The crowd cheered them, too. Were they Rachel's presidential cabinet? The queen's loyal courtiers?

Rachel looked up at us. Strangers were embracing her, tugging at her clothes, offering her food and drink and unqualified love. She tossed her hair and laughed.

I thought of Beth, of Cavenaugh, of Anna Fontenot, all the dead and all the living I had cared about, none of whom I would ever see again. I'd made some bad choices, and I'd had some bad luck. Now I was reaping what I'd sown.

And then one by one we followed Rachel Valentine down the steps into exile and, in every way that mattered, long years of penal servitude.